Praise for

Heart Thief

"I loved *Heart Thief!* This is what futuristic romance is all about. Robin D. Owens writes the kind of futuristic romance we've all been waiting to read; certainly the kind that I've been waiting for. She provides a wonderful, gripping mix of passion, exotic futuristic settings, and edgy suspense. If you've been waiting for someone to do futuristic romance right, you're in luck, Robin D. Owens is the author for you."
—*Jayne Castle*

"Returning to the planet Celta, the world of psychically gifted people first introduced in the RITA Award–winning *HeartMate,* Owens spins an entrancing tale ... Although the setting is fresh and totally captivating, it is the well-developed characters, both human and animal, that make this story memorable. Crafty villains, honorable, resourceful protagonists, and sentient pets drive the plot of this fast-paced, often suspenseful romantic adventure. As have others before her (e.g., Anne McCaffrey, Marion Zimmer Bradley), Owens has penned a stunning futuristic tale that reads like fantasy and is sure to have crossover appeal to both SF and fantasy fans."
—*Library Journal*

continued ...

Heart Duel

Robin D. Owens

B
BERKLEY SENSATION, NEW YORK

This is a work of fiction. Names, characters, places, and incidents either are the product of the author's imagination or are used fictitiously, and any resemblance to actual persons, living or dead, business establishments, events, or locales is entirely coincidental.

HEART DUEL

A Berkley Sensation Book / published by arrangement with the author

PRINTING HISTORY
Berkley Sensation edition / April 2004

Copyright © 2004 by Robin D. Owens.
Cover illustration by Tim Barrall.
Cover design by George Long.
Interior text design by Kristin del Rosario.

ISBN: 0-425-19658-5

BERKLEY SENSATION™
Berkley Sensation Books are published by The Berkley Publishing Group, a division of Penguin Group (USA) Inc., 375 Hudson Street, New York, New York 10014.
BERKLEY SENSATION and the "B" design are trademarks belonging to Penguin Group (USA) Inc.

PRINTED IN THE UNITED STATES OF AMERICA

10 9 8 7 6 5 4 3 2

To Mom

With your vignettes and running stories,
you made me a writer

Love, Robin

Acknowledgments

My first-draft readers, critique buddies, and proofreaders: Kay Bergstrom (Cassie Miles), Janet Lane, Liz Roadifer, Sharon Mignerey (www.sharonmignerey.com), Steven Moores, Judy Stringer, Anne Tupler; Leslee Breene (www.lesleebreene.com), Sue Hornick, Alice Kober, Teresa Luthye, Peggy Waide (www.peggywaide.com); Abbey Adams (www.hometown.aol.com/abbeywrite/index.html); Charlotte Ballard, Leslie Dennis (www.leslieanndennis.com), Terry Hennessy, Janet Miller (www.janetlynnmiller.com), Margaret Marr (www.margaret-marr.com), Wendy Onizak, Pam Payne (www.pamelaarden.com), Shelby Reed (www.geocities.com/shelbyreed34/), Delyn Eagling, and Rose Beetem.

Nicole Spencer, who took time to help me with fight scenes even before we knew I'd publish.

Mary O., Red Oak, and Morgan who helped with the Healing scenes.

My Webmistress: Lisa Craig (www.lisacraig.com).

The folks who helped me with Labyrinths at: The Labyrinth Society (www.labyrinthsociety.org/).

Veriditas® The Voice of the Labyrinth Movement (www.gracecathedral.org/labyrinth/index.shtml).

Those who made the labyrinth in the carousel house of the old Elitch Gardens.

And, Mom, when I began writing this, I really didn't anticipate drawing orange tabby Mama cat and seven orange tabby kittens into our lives. But now you have Wilbur the Wonder Cat.

Visit me at www.robindowens.com or www.robinowens.com, where the kittens can be admired.

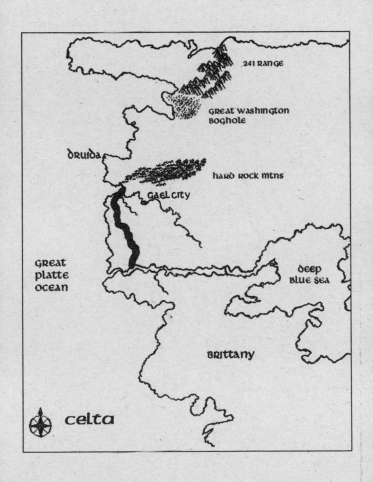

241 RANGE

GREAT WASHINGTON BOGHOLE

dRUIdA

haRd ROCK mtns

GAEL CITY

GREAT PLATTE OCEAN

deep BLUE Sea

BRITTANY

celta

One

The audio page shrieked into Lark's bedroom, wrenching her awake. "Lark, teleport to Primary HealingHall *now!*"

Mayblossom Larkspur Hawthorn Collinson teleported to the HealingHall intake, instinctively channeling her adrenaline rush from being jerked out of sleep into her psi power—Healing Flair. Agony encircled her. Her nose twitched at the smell of blood and other spilled bodily substances.

Lark stumbled into a cleansing tube and croaked her name. A spell whirled around her, whipping her quilted pajamas, sterilizing her. The door opened.

Another Healer grabbed Lark's wrist and hustled her to a body, placing Lark's hands on a trembling, bloody body. "Heal!" she instructed.

Lark focused on her job, her vocation, the reason she'd survived after her husband's death. The present abdominal wound was deep and deadly. Even as she stopped the bleeding, started closing the awful slashes, she knew she felt a broadsword cut. "Blood here!" she ordered.

Her nose quivered again, now noticing the whiff of flesh burnt by blasers. Rage rose with her gorge. She swallowed the reaction and used her fury to pump energy into the dying man.

A duel. A terrible, senseless duel! From the moaning around her and the twelve broken auras she sensed, it had been more than just one-on-one. A melée, a street fight. She mentally listed the four feuds going on. As her eyes adjusted to the light, she looked down at the colors the man wore, dark gray and green—a member of the T'Holly household.

Again she had to swallow. This feud was the worst. The Hollys and the Hawthorns. There'd been hostility between the Hollys and her Family as long as she could remember. She'd hoped the conflict would fade; instead it seemed to intensify.

Both GreatHouses belonged to the colonists' FirstFamilies, powerful in wealth and status and Flair. If the combat continued, it could disrupt the whole city. And as Hawthorn FirstDaughter, she'd be subjected to Family pressure.

When her own caring Healer husband had run to help and died in a Noble skirmish, she'd broken her ties with her Family. Nobles' pride in feuding, nobles' selfishness in wanting their own way at any cost to others, nobles' convoluted affairs had killed her Ethyn. Bitterness had eaten at her for years before she'd regained balance. After a while, she'd managed to reweave a thread with her Family. With this feud, she'd once again have to choose Healing or walk away from her relatives.

A soft-squash container of blood was placed between her hands, on the young man's stomach. "His name's Eryngi Holly; will he live?" asked the other Healer, Myrrh.

Lips compressed, Lark nodded.

Myrrh hesitated. "There are some Hawthorn men here."

Lark fixed her attention on Healing the Holly guard.

"The Hawthorns have fewer injuries. I didn't see your brother or nephew, but your cuz Whitey is here," Myrrh said.

Lark stabilized the man's bloodflow and energy, and Healed the lower intestinal layers. "You can finish Healing his organs and skin. Who's next?"

"Tinne Holly has a blaser burn on his thigh. Holm Holly, his brother, asked for a FirstLevel Healer after Eryngi was seen. A Healer is administering pain relief."

Holm Holly's name plucked Lark from her brooding. "The Heir to the Hollys is here?"

"Yes, with his brother and a Healer in Nobleroom One."

"Of course."

Myrrh raised her brows at Lark's sarcasm. "You'll need to be more diplomatic if you want that appointment as head of Gael City HealingHall."

Lark grimaced. "You're right. Is anyone else injured worse than Holly? Perhaps I should see cuz Whitey." Even though he was her least favorite family member.

"Only this lad bore a life-threatening wound. The others are all being treated. Holm Holly said he'd wait for you." Myrrh slipped her hands under Lark's to take over the Healing, then frowned in deep concentration. Myrrh's complexion paled as she concentrated on chaneling energy from the Universe to use it for complex, delicate Healing.

Lark turned and marched away, re-sterilized herself in the tube, straightened her lavender commoncloth pajamas, then proceeded to Nobleroom One.

As she faced the gold-inlaid door, she inhaled deeply and battled a sense of injustice. Primary HealingHall Noblerooms held all the best furnishings and equipment. Privacy and luxury for the privileged class. Nobleroom One was the best, reserved for FirstFamilies Lords and Ladies.

She shunted aside a contrasting vision of the barren wards of AllClass HealingHall, where she also worked. Noble or common, an injured person needed her Healing skill. This thought came easier now than it had when her husband had died.

As she entered the room, Holm Holly rose from a comfortchair, his expression serious. "How's my kinsman Eryngi?"

"He'll recover."

Holm's eyelids lowered. "Thank the Lord and Lady."

"Yes." She glanced at her patient, Tinne, on the healing bed. He winked at her. ThirdLevel Healer Gelse nodded.

Lark turned back to Holm. She studied him, telling herself she scrutinized him for hurt, nothing else. He looked immaculate, every silver-gilt hair in place, not a smudge on his bloused shirt and trous, not a tear in his elegantly woven cloak thrown over a chair. "You were in the fight, HollyHeir?"

His jaw muscles flexed. "An ambush."

He said nothing about her name or Family, and she appreciated his courtesy. She raised her chin. "You don't appear any worse for wear." There weren't even perspiration marks on his clothes, but then there wouldn't be; the cloth would carry a spell to erase those. With the thought, Lark became aware of his scent, musky and attractive.

"I don't look bedraggled because I'm the best at my skill," Holm said. He dipped his head. "As are you, Mayblossom."

She gritted her teeth. She hated her first name, but hadn't corrected him when they'd had their first real conversation since they'd been youngsters. That was two months ago, after a planning session for the charity ball to fund AllClass HealingHall. He'd escorted his mother, D'Holly.

The way he used Lark's given name reminded her that no matter how she denied her class, she had grown up his equal and he still considered her that, though she was the widow of a common man.

Crossing to the healing bed of layered permamoss covered in silkeen, Lark took Tinne Holly's hand. She nodded to Gelse and smoothly transferred pain relief duties.

"My heartfelt thanks, GraceMistrys Gelse," Holm said, flashing a charming smile.

Gelse looked as if she might melt. Then she shook her head as if to disperse bemusement and left.

Lark stared down at the handsome blond youth of twenty. "GreatSir Holly, it's been a while since I treated you."

"Three years ago, my second Passage, when I fought my death-duels in the slums of Downwind, when I helped T'Ash."

"When T'Ash saved your hide," Holm said.

Tinne grinned, and Lark couldn't suppress her own smile. She lifted the poultice off Tinne's thigh. His trous had been cut from the injury, but the ends of the fabric appeared melted. The burn was bad, a third-degree streak from his knee to the outside of his hip. From the amount of relief she'd been applying, she'd thought it a first-degree burn. He must have a high pain threshold. She wondered if it ran in the family and glanced at Holm, only to meet his intense scrutiny.

His gaze switched to Tinne. "You'll wear a scar from that one," Holm said.

"Really? That makes six," Tinne replied with relish.

Lark set her teeth at the sentiment, but built a layer of Healing energy between her hands and the burn. "So, what have you been doing, GreatSir, besides playing blaser-target?"

"Not my fault. Those fliggering Hawth—"

"Tinne," Holm warned.

"Ah." Tinne pinned his gaze on Lark and smiled winsomely again. She had the unmistakable Hawthorn coloring of blue-black hair and violet eyes. "Sorry, GreatMistrys Hawthorn."

"Call me Lark." Lark carefully repaired the muscle, intertwining lengths of sinew, siphoning more energy faster.

"Yes. I'm grateful for your skill. I don't feel a thing, and it's looking much better—" Tinne started to sit.

Even as Lark jerked her head at Holm, he pushed his brother back to the bedsponge.

"GreatSir Tinne, I'm sure your family has an estate and an occupation for you," Lark said, trying to distract his mind while she Healed his body.

"Yeah. Second sons always get the fighting and fencing salon, The Green Knight." He sounded pleased. "My G'Uncle Tab is teaching me, so I can become a Master and train youngbloods for the duel, street fighting—"

"Exercise and entertainment. Sport. Exhibition bouts," Holm continued easily.

Tinne's gray-blue gaze went to his brother. "Huh?"

Lark used a spurt of anger and disgust to Heal. The muscle glowed with health. The flow of the Universe through her picked up some of her own energy, tiring her. She concentrated harder at sloughing the dead skin away, bringing new skin to the top, transforming the cells to the proper shape and thickness for an outside layer. She quickened her pace, but didn't forfeit an atom of care. In a few seconds she was done. "Finished. Sending record to Primary HealingHall Library and T'Holly Residence."

"Immediate payment authorization of all Holly charges to the HealingHall," Holm commanded.

"Funds transferred," stated both the deep male tones of T'Holly Residence and the comforting feminine voice of Primary HealingHall.

Tinne sat up. With a pretty, rhyming verse, Lark placed a spell on the injury, keeping it clean, but letting the flow of air through to the wound. "The bandage spell will diminish over a week. Have your Healer examine the burn daily."

"Despite the fact that we are the Family that needs one the most, we have no household Healer. Perhaps you would be interested in the position?" Holm asked.

Shock forced Lark to look into Holm's gray eyes. She felt a tiny jolt. Small though it was, it was still a little stronger than the quiver she'd experienced the last time they'd met. The intervals between their meetings were decreasing, just as her reaction increased. She found speech. "Impossible."

"Huh?" Tinne said, no doubt as surprised as she that Holm would invite a Hawthorn into their employ. He glanced at his brother, then his lips curved. He stood and picked up her hand and kissed it. "My thanks—Lark." He glanced at his brother, hesitated, then said, "We would be pleased if you joined Great-House Holly. As you know, ours is a line of fighters, not Healers. We have no Family member who is capable of Healing. You would grace our halls."

Lark smiled at the charming compliment. "Quite impossible."

Tinne put a hand over his chest and sighed. "You have anything for heartbreak?"

Lark laughed and shooed him out. He left with a bounce in his step.

Holm took her hands before she could follow Tinne. A shudder rippled through Holm's body. For an instant Lark imagined fear dawned in his eyes, then the odd expression vanished and he smiled as he cradled her hands.

"Such power and Flair and beauty. T'Holly GreatHouse would honor and respect you, Mayblossom."

She stiffened. His palms were hard but gentle, his warmth and vitality astonishing. She tugged at her hands, but he didn't release them.

"HollyHeir . . ."

"You know it's Holm."

She tugged again.

He waited an instant, kissed one of her hands, then the other. The press of his mouth held an emphasis of tender determination and sent a sensual tingle throughout her body she took as a warning.

Slowly he released her fingers. "Merry meet," he said.

"And merry part," she replied automatically.

"And merry meet again." He shot her a brilliant look. "And we *will* meet again, Mayblossom. Soon."

Her mouth curved in a bitter smile. "I hope not. The feud, the injuries, death." A picture of her slain husband rose to her mind.

Holm's eyes narrowed. He grasped her shoulders and placed a short, hard kiss on her mouth. "We'll meet again."

"I don't associate with fighters," she called as he strode from the room, squelching the intimate memory of those firm lips on hers and the unexpected rush of desire. She buried the new sensations under old bitterness, hurt and anger. "I despise fighting." She yanked a cord for the Flair-technology spell to refresh and sterilize the room. Visualizing her bedroom, she gathered her Flair and teleported home.

*V*oices mumbled, swords swirled and clashed with discordant blows. Holm fought Hawthorns, spinning, using sword and dagger. The flash of a blade thrust at him. He hesitated. Tinne fell. Holm riposted and pierced the Hawthorn's heart.

Screams hit his ears. Words he couldn't distinguish. She drew his glance. Mayblossom Hawthorn, FirstLevel Healer. His Heart-Mate.

He woke on a shuddering groan. Dew coated long grass a centimeter from his nose. He'd curled defensively in his sleep—but only small night animals and birds rustled around him.

Not again! Sleep-teleporting again.

The fourth time in two months.

Holm staggered to his feet, his breathing a rasp. His arm ached all the way to his shoulder from his fierce grip on his dagger.

The night's chill breeze dried the cold sweat on his body. He shivered. He was naked. And alone.

The horizon was eye-level. He looked up, past the branches of a huge ash tree, and found the bright starry skies of Celta dimmed by the light of two waxing twinmoons. Once again he'd 'ported to the crater north of Druida that held the ancient Great Labyrinth—a meditation tool.

He didn't want to meditate or recall being trapped in a blood-colored dream of fighting and death. Or think of the ragged shroud of the previous nightmare where he'd failed his brother.

Tinne had sunk into the black sucking swamp of the Great Washington Boghole—a dream based on reality. Holm had floundered helplessly to save his younger brother, but it was Tinne who rescued them both.

Holm suppressed the groan echoing in his chest, just as he'd suppressed the memory and ignored the dreams since the incident nearly three years ago. He'd hoped he'd banished those forever. He didn't like thinking he'd failed, didn't live up to the standards of a HollyHeir, which was his duty and his identity.

His mouth flattened. No doubt his subconscious thought he needed to ponder some problems. He was at the center of the labyrinth, and it would take a septhour to reach the end where he could 'port out. A person could always teleport to the center, but never out from the center.

He loosened his grip on his dagger and switched hands so he could wipe his sweaty palm on his thigh, wondering what he'd do if this plague continued into the windy autumn and snowy winter. Would he have beaten whatever caused the dreams by then?

Stretching, he worked his muscles and steadied his pulse from the dream's divulgence of his HeartMate.

Holm wasn't surprised. He'd known the minute he'd touched her earlier in the day. The dreams had primed him, her touch that morning had triggered the revelation.

His thoughts unwillingly trailed back to the nightmare. His brother had died. He'd failed again. Holm rubbed his face.

The labyrinth's forcelines pulsed with rainbows of energy. He sighed and started the long walk out. Somehow he was sure that, as always, he'd fail to quiet his busy mind and find the core of serenity inside him that everyone said was there.

*T*he next morning Holm was called into his father's ResidenceDen.

"Please, sit, son," T'Holly, Holm's father, rumbled and gestured to one of the large, comfortable wingchairs stationed in front of his desk.

Holm stared balefully at the chair. It represented all the reprimands of his childhood. When he became T'Holly and succeeded to the title and the estate, that chair would go.

When Holm saw his Mamá perched on the side of his father's

desk, her hand in her husband's, Holm tensed for an emotional blow.

There'd been no "little talks" for long years. He was a man grown with ample responsibilities as the Heir of a GreatHouse. He should not be subject to any further parent-child discussions. He fulfilled every duty.

Except one. There was one outstanding issue.

He grumbled inwardly. He'd known someday this moment would come, but, as usual, they'd surprised him. He'd just run out of time. And he needed time. He wasn't ready to start his wooing. She wasn't ready.

He respected his parents and had sworn a loyalty oath to T'Holly as GreatHouse Lord, but Holm's mind sharpened as he sat. He must play this game of wills smoothly.

His father cleared his throat. "Your mother and I have been talking . . ."

Holm's gut tensed. The worst news always began: "Your mother and I have been talking." Whether it had been problems with manners, duties, his tutor, his psi power—his Flair—he'd always sat in this chair and heard those words. Though his father said the words, Holm knew who prompted the little talks. He stared at his Mamá. She didn't meet his eyes.

His teeth clenched in dread.

His parents exchanged glances, then his father turned his pewter-gray gaze again onto Holm. "You're thirty-seven, and while that isn't the great age here on Celta as it was on Earth, it is time you married."

Holm would have given a great deal of gilt for a stiff drink right then. He sucked in a deep breath, trying to keep his face impassive. "None of my three Passages, the emotional storms that freed my Flair, indicated a HeartMate. I want what you have." Maybe that would earn him a little more time.

His Mamá's turquoise eyes held sorrow. She moved closer to his father. "We know you don't have a HeartMate, dear."

Staying expressionless and meeting her eyes was hard. But the stakes were too important for anyone except himself to know the name of his HeartMate. He hadn't had time to strategize how he'd win Mayblossom Larkspur Hawthorn Collinson.

D'Holly sighed. "Many don't have HeartMates." She nodded with determination. "But it's time you wed. A fine marriage can be had with a good woman. Love can follow, I'm sure." Her voice faltered at the end, since being a HeartMate, she couldn't know personally. She swept her hand wide as if encompassing the city. "The Alders have a perfectly happy marriage, and my sister Nata loves her husband. . . ."

T'Holly continued for his HeartMate. "We need to know the Holly line will continue. We need heirs. At least two sons from you." His father was less than his usual diplomatic self. The fact that T'Holly found the topic distasteful didn't stop Holm from resenting him.

"A few daughters would be nice, too," D'Holly murmured, flashing the charming smile Holm had inherited. "As many as you can engender."

A growl rolled from Holm's lips before he could stop it.

His father raised winged silver brows and looked down his nose. "We expected this reaction."

He tapped a crystal set into the desk. A calendar-moon holo materialized between Holm and his parents.

The ResidenceLibrary spoke. "An appointment with the matchmaker, GreatLady Saille D'Willow, has been made for Holm, HollyHeir. The meeting was expedited for two days from now, on Quert. It is to be a full session, no gilt limit."

Holm winced at the expense. The globe spun faster until it disappeared in a flash of blue-white light.

"We want you to be happy, dear, that's why we're sending you to the foremost matchmaker on Celta. D'Willow won't have any difficulty finding you a suitable wife." His mother sounded troubled but determined.

"But you don't want me to be as happy as yourselves, with a HeartMate marriage," Holm said.

His father snapped into rigidity. "If you had a HeartMate we would do everything in our power to welcome her to the Family."

Holm narrowed his eyes and let a faint smile play on his lips. "Would you?"

"Of course," D'Holly said.

Holm lifted his brows. "By your Words of Honor?"

T'Holly scowled. D'Holly furrowed her forehead. "Yes, by our Words."

"By our Words," T'Holly echoed. "Not that it is applicable.

D'Willow's matchmaking ability is the best. She doesn't personally see very many. If you do a good job courting, we could have
a wedding this month." He cleared his throat and handed Holm a
sheet of papyrus. "Perhaps this will help D'Willow, and you."

Holm didn't have to read the papyrus to know what was on it.
"A list of eligible women from Families with whom it would be
advantageous to form a close alliance?" he mocked.

"Don't take that tone with your father," D'Holly said, in re-
flexive defense of her husband. "I'm sure several of the ladies
listed are women you could come to love. I quite like Hedara of
GreatHouse Ivy and am very fond of Gwylan of D'Sea."

Holm had heard such names before in the form of dropped
hints. He stood. "Speaking of alliances, I trust that this appointment with the matchmaker didn't also include an alliance."

"It's a straight gilt payment," his father gritted.

"Good." Holm went to his mother and lifted her free hand to
his lips. "I will follow your wishes in this." But he didn't smile at
her like he generally did.

He'd go to the matchmaker. Better to keep his parents in the
dark about his mate. A situation they didn't know about, they
couldn't meddle in. He'd have to move quickly now. "I trust you
will be satisfied with my choice of a wife."

They wouldn't.

Two

Matchmaker GreatLady *Saille D'Willow's bright amber* eyes were nearly lost in her fleshy face, but they were shrewder than Holm liked. She was massive. No wonder she never moved from her lavish suite. Great Flair made great emotional and physical demands, and overeating was a way some GreatLords and Ladies compensated.

She sat back in her chair. Her voice, smooth and mellow, tugged at him to relinquish his annoyance at this forced appointment. "Just because you didn't feel a HeartMate when you fought the death duels of your last Passage, doesn't mean that there isn't one for you in this lifetime. Sometimes there are possible mates that require certain circumstances to be met before they become the solid reality of a HeartMate. Souls must grow in compatible ways for a HeartBond to develop."

The GreatLady tapped a finger just below the deep red sticks. They had fallen in a dark and foreboding design when Holm had tossed them earlier. Each stick bore an incised gold symbol, gleaming in the summer light that streamed through large windows. The thin and ancient pieces of wood smelled musky, imbued with centuries of smoky incense.

She continued. "Your Flair and subconscious have spoken. You have a HeartMate. You had to mature to meet her needs.

I congratulate you." Her smile showed small, even teeth, appropriate for the occasion, since every word nipped at him with stinging force.

"HollyHeir, you are a young soul, with just a few lifetimes behind you. Hers is a much older soul, with more experience. You will have to fight hard to keep up with her. You must combat your own nature to fit it to hers. This is the first time you have reached a level where you can meet."

Typical, that he'd have to fight—and this time himself *and* her. Fights didn't bother Holm, but he feared, deep in his heart, that they bothered his HeartMate a great deal.

"In fact," D'Willow said with a penetrating look, "you knew that, didn't you? You know you have a HeartMate."

Holm tired of the way D'Willow spoke in portentous sentences, dissecting his character. He decided not to answer but to wait for another response from her. After all, she was paid five-thousand gilt a septhour to guide him. He lounged back in the chair and coolly met her amber glance.

They sat some moments in silence. Finally D'Willow laughed. "You show promise." This time her smile broadened. "But a few minutes' patience with me will not equal the determination you will need to win your HeartMate." D'Willow gathered the sticks and rolled them between her hands, ready to throw. "Do you want me to ascertain her name and locale?" The matchmaker nodded to the list of eligible brides that his parents had provided "Perhaps it is one of these ladies."

Holm didn't think the daughter of T'Holly's worst enemy would be on the papyrus.

Burning curiosity lit D'Willow's eyes. She wanted to know who his HeartMate was. The GreatLady couldn't reveal the confidential information, but in the shifting alliances of the Noble-Houses, she could act on it for her own benefit while he courted his lady. And it could take a long time to win his HeartMate, D'Willow was right about that.

She shook the sticks between loosened palms. "I can discover your HeartMate for you—"

"No." He wouldn't give D'Willow any advantage to exploit in the FirstFamilies' political games. He surged from his chair and crossed the room to the door, laying a hand on the ornate handle. Focusing his gaze on the sticks, he connected with them and withdrew the energy he'd given them for the Divination. The game of wills he had played with D'Willow—him hiding his HeartMate's name from her, and she wishing to divine it, or see him lose his temper, or both—soured. He opened the door.

She spoke, "I'll inform T'Holly that we've consulted, and of the results—a HeartMate for you. A formal report will be teleported to T'Holly's collection box in the next few days."

Manners won. Holm turned and bowed deeply. "Merry meet."

"And merry part," D'Willow said.

"And merry meet again." Now Holm smiled, showing teeth. "But should you somehow Divine the name of my lady and tell it to my lord and Father, I will remember that you did it against my wishes—for as long as I live, and when I become T'Holly."

Her face solidified until it was like a wax mask, bright eyes piercing him, but he knew she wouldn't dare to mix in his affairs.

Outside D'Willow's gates, he stroked the scabbard of his main gauche strapped to his right thigh, pleased. A game was naught but a mock fight, and he had come out of that skirmish a winner. The matchmaker had looked frustrated that she would gain no knowledge of his affairs. She'd spend some of her expensive time speculating now, about the plans of the HollyHeir and the future of the powerful GreatHouse T'Holly.

And she'd puzzle over who might be his HeartMate. She didn't know the name of his HeartMate. No one did.

Except himself.

What the hell he was going to do?

That night Lark stood in the graceful arch of the floor-to-ceiling window of her apartment and looked out at the large square courtyard. The scene was sketched black, white and gray in the twinmoonslight. Both moons had risen, Eire hovered just above the opposite side of the building, some five hundred meters away. Cymru moon shone brightly, a huge ball high in the sky. Their phases were always the same, and tonight they were both full, indicating that the month of Hazel had begun. The HealingHalls could be busy, and she was the Healer on call for AllClass HealingHall.

She'd been too anxious to sleep. And too responsible to use Flair that might be needed to Heal to indulge in her usual pastime of tinting her walls.

The full moons and fragile summer fragrances reminded her of the evening her husband, Ethyn, had died. A boy from the Downwind slums near the docks, he'd tested high in Healing Flair and labored hard to rise above his birth. He'd done it, studied and received FirstLevel Healer laurels, then been killed in a stupid noble street fight four months later. Tears welled in her eyes as the echoes of grief bruised her heart. Even more tears trailed down her cheeks as she admitted that she could no longer remember his face.

Druida City held too many memories and too many family members who wanted to dictate her life. Even living here, in MidClass Lodge, had been a compromise. She'd wanted to stay in the small house in the common sector in southeast Druida. Both her noble Families wanted her close, so she chose the one middle-class apartment building, near to "Noble Country," where the FirstFamilies kept their castle-like Residences.

It was time to leave Druida. A fresh start was exactly what she needed, which was why she'd applied for the appointment as Head of the Gael City HealingHall, two days away by glider when Ambroz Pass was clear.

She'd miss Maroon Beach and its deep red sand, T'Horehound's Garden, and, most especially, her friend Trif Clover. But Gael City would be good for her. Gael City was more casual than Druida, the capital and oldest city on Celta. Gael City was also less under the thumb of the FirstFamilies and nobles in general. It could use a FirstLevel Healer. There, maybe she could blossom into the woman she sensed she could become, a woman not dragged down by the past or dodging the continual manipulations of her father—but a woman ready to unfurl new wings to fly to the future. A woman more open to people and possibilities.

She bit her lip when she realized the silver shade of the courtyard reminded her of Holm Holly, his gilt hair and his eyes that changed from dark gray to gleaming silver. She wondered if he was fighting and how she'd feel if he got hurt.

Her scrybowl played a lilting melody, announcing an incoming call. She glanced at the timer and frowned. It neared the second morning septhour, 2 A.M. Who would call? Any emergency or Family summons would be announced by starburst-page.

She walked over to the scry bowl. "Here."

A boy's mischievous grin greeted her. A prank?

"Greetyou, GentleLady Collinson." His head bobbed out of sight as he bowed.

He looked a little familiar, more, his general coloring and features tickled her memory—noble features, *GreatHouse* features. Lark frowned. "I know you—"

"Muin T'Vine, Vinni." He puffed out a thin chest. "I'm Great-Lord T'Vine. You delivered me nine years ago. I was your first kid." He stared at her hands. "You have FabFlaired hands, I remember."

Lark repressed a shiver. She didn't doubt it. He *had* been the first babe she'd brought into the world from his mother's womb. He'd been uncanny, with ever-changing eye color. Lark had felt the seed of powerful Flair in him, which was immediately confirmed by the Oracle attending the birth. Old D'Vine, the prophetess, had done the honors of Oracle, and named the newborn as her Heir, bypassing three generations of her descendants. No, Lark didn't need any further reminding of Vinni, the seer.

"I've got your coordinates, you're in MidClass Lodge. I'm there, transnow." His image vanished and his voice lost the tinny scrysound as he spoke again, behind her. "Nice cave. Soft cushions and sweet-smelling potpourri, Phyll will like it. Got any cocoa mousse?" He opened his satchel and an orange kitten hopped out, hissing, with all its hair on end.

Before she bent to pick it up, Lark was in love. "Mine?"

"Zanth, Fam to T'Ash, is the Sire and a feral Downwind queen is the Dam. The kitten was raised by GreatLady D'Ash."

"Good bloodline." She stroked the kitten's head.

Wide emerald eyes gleamed. *Greetyou, FamWoman,* it said.

She held it at eye level, cocked an eyebrow at Vinni, who continued to grin. "Male?"

"Yeah. One tough cookie. One great Fam. He and his brother, Meserv, are really special cats. Make sure they spend a lot of time together."

I'm Phyll. A tiny pink tongue licked her cheek and Lark choked. *You are lonely. I'm here now.*

Vinni looked away and scuffed his feet.

"Phyll. That's not a Collinson name," Lark said.

The boy gave her a sharp, too-adult look. "You're not a Collinson."

"I—"

Vinni cut her off with a commanding gesture. "He was your husband and you had a short time together. He's cycling on the wheel of stars, awaiting rebirth, gone. He wasn't your Heart-Mate."

The word shocked her. She had no HeartMate in this life. She'd never connected with a HeartMate during the turbulent Passages that freed her Flair.

HeartMate, Phyll echoed.

She held her breath.

Vinni continued relentlessly. "Phyll's not your Family name of Hawthorn, either. Phyll's a Heather name, from your mother, Calluna. You carried the name of Larkspur Hawthorn, but don't forget, the skylark is a Heather symbol." His odd-colored eyes went distant, focused again. "Don't think you can run from Druida and your destiny," he whispered.

Lark shivered. He opened his mouth, looked at her, shut it, jerked his head in a nod. "You will do very well." He screwed up his mouth, nodded again. "Think of what Family the name Meserv comes from." Vinni bowed once more. "Merry meet."

Lark resumed breathing; obviously he wasn't going to say anything else about her future right this moment. She chilled as she thought of "destiny." She inclined her head. "And merry part."

"And merry meet again. We *will* meet again." He left with a pop.

Lark shook her head. Far too many noble males were telling her that.

Phyll licked her face with a rough little tongue, his brilliant green gaze fastened on her. *We all have fine fate.* He mewed, his eyes widened more, and he playfully bit at her thumb. *Foood. Mmm-Meserv-vvv. Foood.*

*T*he next morning *Holm sparred with several men at* The Green Knight Fencing and Fighting Salon until his G'Uncle Tab, twelve decades old, overpowered him. Pushing Holm against a wall, Tab braced his gnarly arm across Holm's throat. "I guess I know what's gnawin' at you, boy, but you don' have to take it out on me anymore. I got better things to do than be a beatin' bag for you," Tab panted. He'd gone to sea as a young man, and his accent slipped from time to time into seaspeech.

"I have to marry," Holm said between clenched teeth.

"Yap, you do. Real sorry that ya are between the cauldron and the deep blue sea, but that's an Heir's duty for you. Ya have filled the shoes of a Heir very well." Tab shrugged. "Ya knew this day would come. Make the best of it instead of comin' around to batter my students 'cause ya are antsy."

Holm growled.

Tab swatted Holm's head hard enough to make his ears ring. "And don' try an' take it out on me."

"If *you* can't take it . . ." Holm grinned ferally and whipped his sword out.

Tab promptly twisted the weapon from his grip.

Holm scowled.

"I don' have to take anythin' from ya, boy. And I want ya gone, you're scarin' my students away. This is a respectable place, been in the Family for generations, an' I won' let ya close it down 'cause you're in a snit. If ya wanna fight, go pick on your friend T'Ash."

Holm bared his teeth. "He's no fun since he married. We practice defensive sparring only. Maybe Tinne—" Holm gagged as the muscular arm cut off his air.

"Don' be a-pesterin' that boy. Tinne's my heir. He'll be a-runnin' this place when I retire. An' I want him in good shape to do it. Now sheath your sword, cool your blaser, and master your temper. Ain' nothin' ya can do here that will make your duty any more tasty, an' I'm tired of ya beatin' on me. So, go!" With a strength that belied his many years, Tab marched Holm to the atrium and shoved him out.

Holm winced at Tab's loud binding spell on the door, denying Holm entrance for an eightday. He looked back at the inner doors to the salon, narrowing his eyes. If the place was forbidden to him for a week, he'd go mad. He needed somewhere to work off his restlessness and figure out how he was going to woo and win his HeartMate. The sparring rooms in T'Holly Residence smelled so sour he could barely tolerate them.

He might even find himself looking for fights in Downwind slums—there real danger awaited him.

He jammed his blade into its sheath and stormed from the salon, nearly tripping over a boy of about nine who sat on the steps.

"HollyHeir." Something in the very quietness of the boy's voice stopped Holm. He turned, hand on sword hilt.

The child gave him a cheeky grin.

Holm snorted. "You want me?"

"No, you need *me*," the boy said. "More than that, you need *him*." He pulled something that had made a small bulge in the leather satchel beside him into the summer morning.

Before Holm knew it, the tiny marmalade tom kitten had mewed plaintively and attached all of its small, sharp claws onto his shirt. He sighed—the silkeen shirt was ruined. He scowled at the boy, then froze in recognition.

"You're the new GreatLord T'Vine," Holm said. Muin was the fourth generation son of the old seeress, given the title at so young an age because of his outstanding Flair in prophecy.

"Muin T'Vine, that's me. Call me Vinni." He gave a little bow. Holm would have done better at his age.

Holm scanned the neighborhood. An old established commercial area near CityCenter, it was still no place for a Noble child alone. "You shouldn't be here by yourself."

A dimple flashed in T'Vine's cheek. "Now and then I evade my captors—um, tutors. I'm really just a kid, after all."

Holm doubted it.

"And you need me." Vinni struck a cocky pose, legs wide, hands on hips. "I picked the kitten 'specially for you from one of Zanth's get. Dam was a Downwind feral. His name is Meserv, a Holly name." Vinni's voice became crisp. "I've had a vision." He screwed up his mouth as if thinking how to phrase it.

Holm quashed rising anxiety. He hadn't ever been on the receiving end of a prophecy and he didn't like it.

Vinni jutted his chin. "Think on this and remember when the future comes to pass. You have a hard fight ahead and you also need"—he lifted a finger—"One: to make a HeartGift"—another finger rose—"Two: two protective amulets from T'Ash, and"—a shudder passed through him—"Three: to be reminded of the Null, Captain Ruis Elder of the starship *Nuada's Sword*."

Holm's stomach clenched into a sickening knot. "Not Ruis Elder—" Ruis Elder was a Null, a person who drained a person's Flair, negated their psi powers. No one with great Flair cared to endure Ruis Elder's presence.

"Gotta go. Merry meet."

"And merry part," Holm said through cold lips. He didn't know what Vinni's words meant and wished he could forget them, but didn't dare.

"And merry meet again!" T'Vine skipped a few steps and vanished with a quiet pop and a scent of ozone.

"I won't meet you again, if I can help it," Holm muttered, sure he wasn't alone in the thought. Those Vines were damned uncanny. No wonder people avoided them.

Now the little cat was a source of comfort. Holm cradled it in his hands, enjoying its warmth and rumbling sides.

Fooood. A teeny telepathic voice echoed in his mind.

Holm lifted the kitten to eye level.

It unscrunched its face and opened wide blue eyes.

Fooood.

"I suppose you want cocoa mousse."

A little pink tongue darted out. *Furrabeast bites? First?*

Holm sighed and cuddled the kitten close to his chest. "You're Zanth's son, most definitely."

Meserv settled, sniffed. *Excellent smell. We all have fine fate.*

"*A* HeartMate! Oh, my darling son, I'm so thrilled for you."

Dozing, his mother's voice sounded like it came from a long distance. Though he couldn't see her, Holm knew his mother was dancing. She had a habit of dancing when she was in high spirits. It made for some interesting GreatHouse Rituals.

He grunted and fumbled for his robe. Meserv mewed in reproach at being jostled. Holm lay in the sunlight pouring through the glass dome of the solar on the top level of GreatHouse Holly Residence, drowsing after a strenuous swim.

"You naughty boy, you've been avoiding your father and me."

He had. Unlike most other topics in his life, the interview with the matchmaker D'Willow and its outcome was not something he wanted to discuss with his parents.

"Where are you?" Passiflora D'Holly trilled.

He heard the hasty push of a branch, and the limb snapping back. "Ow! Don't you think this conservatory of yours is getting a teensy bit overgrown, dear? Holm? Holm!"

Reluctantly he sat up from the natural moss bed and pulled the fleecy sorbaroot robe around him, letting delightful wisps of daydreams about Lark Collinson dissolve. He glanced at Meserv, who had rolled over to his back, round belly prominent and forepaws curled over it. The Fam gave a little snuffle of pleasure. He'd gorged on ground furrabeast at lunch.

Holm pushed back wet hair from falling in his face and braced for a conversation with his Mother. It would be hard to avoid all the points he wanted to keep to himself.

"Here, Mamá."

"Holm!" She beamed as she did a dance step and a pirouette. She waved the D'Willow report, which sported four different colored seals. Before he could rise, she came over and gave him a smacking kiss on the cheek. "There's my boy."

D'Holly tickled Meserv's stomach. The kitten burped, slitted its eyes. *Greetyou, D'Holly. Good lunch.*

She laughed. "Lots of lunch, anyway. Go back to sleep."

Meserv's sapphire eyes closed.

His mother glanced at the verdant plant life. "Yes, perhaps we should have the gardeners cut this back a trifle. My, this little alcove is something of a green cave, isn't it? Hmmm."

"I'll speak to them." He'd tell them not to touch a thing.

"Ah, Holm, a HeartMate, I'm so glad for you." She sat down, slipped her arms around him, and buried her face in his shoulder. "You can't know how much that marriage discussion hurt." Her voice was muffled. He swung an arm around her and squeezed her.

"I didn't want to force you to marry, but the demands of the Family . . ." His mother had been a FirstFamily daughter of GrandHouse Apple, taught from infancy about Family demands. It was great luck for T'Holly and GrandMistrys Passiflora Apple that they'd been HeartMates, but just as the Nobles bred for powerful Flair, so, too, did they more often than others find HeartMates. A HeartMate bond for their line was treasured.

"I'm sorry," she said in a small voice against him, "but we would have expected you to marry, HeartMate or no. Just as we expect you to marry quickly now." She rubbed her face on the cloth, then she kissed his cheek once more.

His mother glanced at the report. "But now you don't have to settle for a wife, you have a HeartMate!" Her dimples flashed.

Holm sighed. "I don't think it's going to be as easy as your and T'Holly's courtship."

"No? But a HeartMate bond—it can't be very difficult."

"Tell T'Ash that."

"Ah, T'Ash." D'Holly gave an airy wave. "There were extenuating circumstances, his unfortunate childhood. . . . Nothing like that for you, my dear."

Now was the time for his own dancing—around the subject. He couldn't tell her anything he didn't want his father to know. Holm gave her a final hug, stood, and stretched. His mother rose and nearly matched him in height, a tall, slender woman. The Hawthorns ran to small and curvy. Holm's daughters would be lucky if they got their FatherDam's height.

"Did the report name the lady?" Holm asked.

D'Holly squinted down at it. She said she was too busy to get her eyes Healed back to their youthful acuity. Holm just thought she was too impatient for the eight-day procedure. He came from an impatient family.

"No, D'Willow didn't say who your HeartMate was. Odd. No, ah, but she says *you* know."

He had to tell his mother enough that she'd give him time to woo Lark, yet couldn't reveal his HeartMate was a Hawthorn. That would guarantee that his parents would interfere. The whole situation was messy—and would become even more chaotic if GreatLords T'Holly and T'Hawthorn got involved.

"I've had inklings." Since two months ago when he'd met Lark to plan the charity dance to benefit AllClass HealingHall, and had felt an unexpected pull. Ever since, he'd made it a point to see her at least once an eightday. He fought his own nature to pounce, but also fought a deep, unsettling feeling that if he gave into the desire, his life would change forever.

D'Holly's feet pattered in a little tap dance. "Tell me."

He plucked the report from her fingers and tossed it to the pallet. Meserv opened one eye as if considering a pounce, burped again, and curled onto his side.

Holm took his mother's hands and drew her into a waltz. He

danced her from the small alcove to the cool stones surrounding the deep blue irregular pool.

She laughed and hummed a waltz of her own, one of her first musical compositions. Music continually ran through his mother's mind. She was always accompanied by some mental tune. Music and dancing would distract her.

"My wooing won't be easy. My HeartMate's a Healer."

D'Holly almost missed a step. Her eyes widened, then she winced. "Oh, dear. Healers almost never approve of fighting. And Hollys *are* fighters. Why, you, after your father, are the premier fighter of Celta."

"I know."

"It is the basic nature of the Hollys. Something that we will never breed out of the line."

"I know."

"It is *expected* of the Hollys." She tilted her head. "Perhaps it will take two weeks of courting."

"Yes." He spun her into a sweeping turn. She closed her eyes in pleasure. When she opened them, they focused on the bare triangle of his chest and the dark red scar of a blaser burn.

"Oh, dear," she said again. "Scarred. All of you. My innocent babe that was once so smooth and flawless."

"Not for a long time."

"Who's that dancing with my HeartMate?" T'Holly's voice boomed, then was smothered by plants and the waterfall at the end of the pool. "GreatHouse Residence, music if you please, an Earthen waltz for my GreatLady and me."

Music filled the solar.

"Louder!" T'Holly ordered. The beautiful "Blue Danube" drowned out his voice. He gracefully cut in and took his wife in his arms. "This is a frivolous place, glass and greenery, a pool, and a waterfall. A waterfall! On top of the Residence."

Like many GreatHouse Residences, the Holly home was modeled on an Earth castle. It had no fairy-tale charm but was a real fortress, walls rising five stories before angling outward in battlements—a solid, square building with no turrets and no windows on the outside until the last level. The pool had been in the basement. Holm had hated the dank, moldy place. He'd had to fight for the remodeling, and his father would voice displeasure all of his life. It was worth it.

Meserv mewed and sat on Holm's foot.

T'Holly whirled his HeartMate away. Passiflora threw back her head and laughed.

They made a fine picture, a man and a woman in the prime of their lives: he looking down at her with open adoration, she returning all his love.

Holm fisted his hands and shoved them in his pockets. He wanted that. He wanted that badly. Looking at them, he knew the loneliness of his heart, and the yearning of his soul for that one special person. The longing permeated his being, not only heart and soul, but also his mind and body. Nothing would be right for him until he had his own HeartMate. Lark Collinson. He would get her, and keep her.

We will get her, Meserv said.

Three

❤

Lark blinked at the bright late summer afternoon as she exited Primary HealingHall. She rolled her shoulders. Her four-septhour shift had become grueling when a D'Hazel's noble, greatly-Flaired child had been 'ported to intake. The girl had tried to fly. It had been an exhausting, wrenching case.

Lark's weary, shuffling feet caught on a crack in the pavement and she stumbled. Phyll mewed. She patted the new double bag she carried in reassurance. One side held the accouterments of her profession. The other section, with a meshed end, held Phyll, resting after helping her. Even a tiny spurt of energy from the kitten, when linked with her own, could yield incredible results. When she and her husband had linked, they'd been the most powerful Healing team on Celta.

Two guards wearing Hawthorn colors of purple and gold stepped from the shadows beside the fluted stone columns of the portico. One was her cuz Whitey, completely Healed of the injury he'd suffered the day before. The other man was vaguely familiar. They'd been sent by her father. Her fingers tightened on the bag. Anxiety fluttered through her.

Whitey nodded to her, but glanced at his timer, impatience on his face. The other bowed shortly, "T'Hawthorn requests your presence, GreatMistrys."

It took a moment for Lark to recognize the large, solid man. A harsh white scar that twisted from his jaw to his once-broken nose jogged her memory. Cratag. The slash and the nose hadn't been tended because Cratag had been in the rainforests of Brittany, the southern continent. He was a son of the Maytree branch of the Family who'd emigrated to Brittany several generations ago.

Lark swallowed to ease the tightness of her throat. A summons from her father. For a moment she thought of refusing, but stiffened her spine. No matter how weary, her father had issued a command and would expect obedience. To refuse would be cowardly and postpone the inevitable.

"Greetyou, Whitey," Lark said. Despite the tremor of her nerves, she inclined her head to Cratag, in the manner that had been drummed into her. "Please don't call me 'GreatMistrys,' I'm a GentleLady now." She'd married a common man, flouting her father.

Irony flashed in Cratag's violet eyes. "FirstLevel Healer," he replied, using her professional title.

Her cuz Whitey shifted restlessly. "Listen, Cratag, you wouldn't mind taking Lark to T'Hawthorn by yourself, would you? I'm—ah—late for an appointment." He winked broadly.

With a casualness that belied her tension, Lark said, "I'm sure Cratag and I will be fine without you." She glanced at her wrist timer. "I'm free for the rest of the afternoon."

Whitey clapped Cratag on the shoulder. "Many thanks. You don't need to mention I left to T'Hawthorn, right?"

"No," Cratag said expressionlessly.

Whitey hitched his sword-blaser belt and took off at a lope.

"Shall we go?" Lark wanted to get any interview with her father over with as soon as possible.

Cratag gestured to the side of the portico to the huge, deep metallic purple T'Hawthorn glider hovering above the ground. She walked over, straightening her blandly pastel tunic over wide-legged trous and wishing for an elegant dress as better armor. She pressed her lips together.

At an intoned Word from Cratag, the door lifted open. Lark slid in and onto the padded silkeen bench, carefully placing her bag on her lap.

Cratag started to shut the door and move to the back, but Lark said, "Join me." Company would be welcome.

After a brief hesitation, Cratag took a seat beside her.

"Glider, return to T'Hawthorn Residence," he ordered.

The glider accelerated silently forward on the cushion of air beneath it.

"So, Cratag, how do you like being in Druida instead of Brittany?" Not only was she interested in the man, but she needed distraction from her mounting apprehension.

He narrowed his eyes. "I didn't think you cared much about me."

"Of course I do. You're Family."

He matched her questioning gaze with a serious one of his own. "We've only met a handful of times. As for Family, T'Hawthorn's your father, but you don't visit."

Lark caught her breath at this bluntness. Phyll stirred. Cratag wasn't polite, as every member of a GreatHouse was expected to be. Even Whitey was polite when he deigned to speak to her. It didn't matter, what mattered was the feud. "Tell me, Cratag, do you enjoy fighting?"

He ran his forefinger down his scar. "Not especially. A man does what he must. My Flair's minimal, but my sword skills are useful. They've earned me a place in the GreatHouse, and a room in the Family Residence. I'm grateful."

Lark wetted her lips. "And what do you think of this feud between Hawthorn and Holly?"

He shrugged heavy shoulders. "It's not my place to decide what's worth fighting for, it's T'Hawthorn's. I obey my orders."

"I'm sure you have other skills besides fighting," Lark said softly. "That's not how we are raised on Celta. There's good land and a career for everyone if a person is determined."

"The daughter of a GreatHouse can say that. Someone with exceptional Flair who's powerful herself. Others must use what circumstance gives them." He looked straight ahead. "Land and wealth aren't my goals. I want Family, to belong."

"Yet this feud with the Hollys is dangerous, could very well cause your death. The Hollys are well known as fighters—the Hawthorns are planners and traders. A feud is a horrible thing. It could spiral out of hand, set the entire city against us, against both Families."

He pinned her with sharp scrutiny. "Do you prophesize? Did you have a vision? Is it Flair speaking, Lady?"

She wished she could say yes, anything to stop even one Hawthorn from fighting, but she shook her head. She lifted her hands. "I'm a Healer. I've had no premonitions. I only know that mending bodies shattered by swords and blasers is horrible and unnecessary."

Cratag hesitated, gave a slight nod, then returned his attention to the view outside the glider windows. "Speak to T'Hawthorn."

When they arrived at T'Hawthorn Residence, Cratag ushered Lark into her father's ResidenceDen. She sat in a wingchair of dark blue with dainty golden dragonflies, a Hawthorn symbol. She always chose that chair for any Family discussion. Gently she set down her bag containing Phyll. Just the thought of her Fam comforted her.

"Drink?" asked Cratag, standing in the small alcove that housed the bar.

"No, thank you." After expending so much energy Healing earlier, she knew she'd need all her intelligence to match wits with her father.

"We have cinnamoncaff, caff, tea, cocoa, rootsweet," Cratag offered softly. She wondered how much her nerves showed.

The door opened and her father entered. A stocky man, imposing in spite of his medium height, Lark had inherited her coloring from him. She had the same black hair and dark violet eyes. Time had carved the lines on his face deeper and the silver streaks of hair at his temples wider since the last time she'd seen him a few months ago.

And the moment he walked in, the mantle of GreatHouse FirstDaughter, *his* daughter, dropped over her, and she knew that this time, as always, she would not be able to escape that role. She suppressed an inner, angry sigh at herself, stood, and curtsied to the GreatLord, the Head of the Hawthorns.

"Be seated." T'Hawthorn nodded and settled behind his desk. "Our feud with the Hollys will be escalating."

Lark sank back down into the chair, keeping her face immobile and her hands folded gracefully on her lap. "I noticed the skirmishes increased."

T'Hawthorn glanced at Cratag. "Whiskey. And pour yourself some."

The sounds of clinking glass and gurgling liquid broke the silence. Waiting was something her father did best. Lark sighed inwardly. If this feud was one of sheer patience, T'Hawthorn would easily win. The main traits of the Hollys were impulsiveness and volatility.

But the Hollys were the premier fighters of Celta. Lark didn't see how this situation could end without blood and death.

"Give Mayblossom some brithe brandy. She needs color," T'Hawthorn said.

Cratag handed a short glass of whiskey to her father, kept one for himself, and offered a miniature snifter to Lark, liquid full to the brim. She closed her eyes and inhaled. Just the scent of it restored her a little. When she opened her lashes, she looked at the glass and rubbed her thumb over the etched primroses. The small snifter was one of a set that her mother's mother, MotherDam D'Heather, had crafted for her father and mother's wedding.

"I believe it is time for you to return to live here, your home." His cool gaze measured her as he seemingly changed the topic. To discomfit her?

Lark pulled a quiet breath deep into her body. The issue of her independence hadn't been raised between them for a long time. She wanted to state a blunt "No." But the denial wouldn't be accepted, and her father would comment both on her active disobedience and discourtesy. That would extend this tense meeting. "I am content with my life, and surely you know that I have applied for the position of Head of Gael City Healing-Hall."

His dark brows lowered. "I do not think it appropriate that you move so far away from the Family."

He meant so far away from him and his power.

T'Hawthorn stared at her. "Everyone needs Family. You should have the close presence of Family for comfort. I know you miss my mother, who's been living in the country house."

Lark bit her lip. True. Her father's mother, Eshela, flighty and always bubbling over with good spirits, held a special place in Lark's heart. The vague, rambling conversations she had with Eshela always lightened her mood.

"Eshela is now here," T'Hawthorn said.

He must have ordered her home. Why? So Eshela would be another incentive for Lark to remain in Druida and make

T'Hawthorn Residence home once more? Lark's fingers grew stiff with tension.

T'Hawthorn sipped his whiskey. "I understood when the development of your great Flair demanded in-depth training and you had to live at the Heathers, away from T'Hawthorn Residence. But now you have reached the peak of your profession, with the privileges that such an attainment provides. You may choose your own cases, designate your worktime. And your Residence."

"Yes, I choose my own cases. I choose to work at AllClass HealingHall as well as Primary HealingHall."

He stared at her common tunic and trous, nothing at all like the elegant robes with metallic embroidery that women of her class usually wore, or even well-cut and bespelled silkeen that other FirstLevel Healers wore. He lifted an eyebrow. "The HealingHall at Gael City does not see many Nobles."

"But Head of Gael City is an advancement for me. I doubt I'll ever become Head of Primary HealingHall here in Druida. That position will go to my aunt, T'Heather's heir." Let her father think that ambition caused her to submit a request for the appointment, rather than any nebulous feelings of restlessness or dread of his subtle manipulations. T'Hawthorn understood ambition.

"You belong here in my Residence, doing your duty."

Again she inhaled deeply, and back in her mind she started her well-practiced mantra of calm, and breathe, and serenity, and shield, and breathe, and acceptance.

"My first duty now is to my profession and the HealingHalls. I am content with my life," she repeated, "and I will hear about the appointment in a few eightdays. I anticipate I will be moving to Gael City."

"The Family is seriously feuding. I do not know if I can protect you," he said.

She met his gaze, still something hard for her to do even after all these years. "You do not need to protect me. I am a Healer. That is protection enough. It is rare for a Healer to be deliberately harmed."

He lifted his whiskey and sipped. "But it's not unknown for a Healer to be accidentally hurt—or even killed."

Between them stood the ghost of her husband, who had tried

to help in a stupid Noble fight and had been killed for his compassion. She set her snifter on a nearby table.

Her father had not approved of Ethyn. As a FirstDaughter of T'Hawthorn, one who had never connected with a HeartMate during her Passages, she had been expected to marry well. She had been expected to make an alliance with another FirstFamily, to benefit her House. She had been expected to let T'Hawthorn make the decision of whom she would wed.

She'd disregarded all her Family's expectations and had preferred shy and diffident Ethyn Collinson, who had enough underlying strength to overcome his impoverished upbringing Downwind and win the laurels of a FirstLevel Healer. His strong Flair had attracted her as much as his respect for her as a Healer and a woman. She had bloomed under his gentle care.

"With the additional strife between Holly and Hawthorn, Eshela will worry," T'Hawthorn said. "It would ease her mind were you to reside within these strong walls."

Calm. Breathe. Serenity. Shield. "I am sorry to disappoint her, and you, but my life requires more—flexibility than can be found here, and I may be moving soon. It would be foolish to move twice."

He frowned. "You do too much. You are overextended and do not properly care for yourself. I have spoken with your Mother-Sire, GrandLord T'Heather, about this. He agrees."

Lark's pulse fluttered. T'Heather ruled Primary HealingHall. He could curtail Lark's hours, rearrange her schedule, set limits that Lark would have to accept. Most important, he could deny her the appointment in Gael City. Lark needed to speak to him, soon. Another discussion demanding great effort and diplomacy. Effort she didn't want to spare and diplomacy that she rarely valued anymore.

The shuffling of papyrus brought her from her thoughts. T'Hawthorn had turned over the top page of a report from the stack to the side. He squared the corners of the remaining sheets until they were perfectly alined. When his gaze lifted to hers, Lark was surprised to see real concern for an instant, before it was covered by his usual ruthless self-interest. Or the interest of the Family. Everything her father did was to benefit the Family.

"I have consulted with T'Sea's FirstDaughter, who is foremost in emotional/spiritual insight. You must know of her."

Lark worked often with Shwif Sea, and respected her. "Yes."

"She states that, to her knowledge, no Heather woman has successfully lived more than three years alone."

Shock froze Lark. Where had this come from? How could it be true? But with a quick scan of her memory, she realized she couldn't bring to mind any examples to contradict him.

"The Heather woman's emotional constitution, and we will agree for the moment that your character is more Heather than Hawthorn, is not suited to solitude. You've been on your own for over three years, and after the second, your mental, emotional, and physical health deteriorated."

Slow anger built in Lark. The first two years after her husband had died, a husband her father had never acknowledged, she'd been filled with bitterness and resentment at her own class. As she became more balanced, she'd been better able to work and come to terms with her values.

He continued summarizing the report. "Spiritually, you have not participated in any FirstFamilies, NobleHouse, or even private Family Rituals for nine months. Over the last four years, you have celebrated full twinmoons with us only twice, and new twinmoons not at all. . . ."

"I am no longer a member of the FirstFamilies, GreatHouse, or NobleHouse Councils, so I don't participate in their Rituals. I honor the holidays and Sabbat with close friends," she said steadily, managing to keep her tone neither defensive nor angry.

She was still not so fond of Nobles to let her shields down and bond with them in a circle to carry out Council purposes, or to keep Alban feastdays with them. And to Lark, Family Rituals had never been as uplifting as they might have been.

Now she knew how much of a Hawthorn she was. Steel shot up her spine, steel strong enough to take any verbal and mental abuse and manipulation her father might use. "I do not find your report interesting or convincing. I am not only Heather, but Hawthorn. I am managing my life well and will not return to T'Hawthorn GreatHouse and your rule now, or ever." She found her voice shaking and hated betraying the weakness. At least tears of rage weren't streaming down her cheeks. She stood.

He rose from behind his desk. "Additional shieldspells will

be effected on T'Hawthorn Residence, keyed for those Family members who abide within."

"I understand," she said stiffly. If she left now, she wouldn't be automatically received by T'Hawthorn Residence.

He set relaxed hands on his desktop. "The feud will be financially draining. For the sake of the Family, I must use all funds, including your allowance, to pursue this new goal."

She bent her head in agreement. "Of course." She didn't use his allowance anyway, she'd always banked it and never touched it, living on her noblegilt salary. But gilt was always an issue with T'Hawthorn, and the thought of a feud sent anger spurting through her. "The means to your 'goal' is a feud that will certainly lead to injury and death. I have vows to Heal, never to harm."

He raised a brow at her louder voice. "I have not asked you to betray your vows."

Now she shifted the subject. "May I ask what this very important goal is?"

He studied her a moment, and folded his hands, face impassive. "Land."

"Land!"

His stare remained calm as impulsive words tumbled from her. "Land! Lady and Lord, of all Celta only one quarter of our world has been settled! Humans have not thrived here, not gained population, and you are willing to risk life for more land!" She bit her lip to keep more words back, words questioning his motives and his intelligence, words she'd pay for forever.

His answer came in the same reasonable tone he'd used during the entire exchange. "The Hollys own Hulver Pass to the southwest. The pass leads directly to our richest plantation, Tryskel, in Du Park. I now prefer that the Hollys no longer know who and what goes through that pass. T'Holly doesn't appreciate the land or maximize its potential."

His eyes shuttered a moment and Lark understood there was a use for the land he didn't tell her since she was no longer in the inner circle of Hawthorns who'd be privy to Family secrets.

She didn't miss the stratagems, but did miss being close. She had never been lonely until her husband died and she'd lived all by herself. Sometimes she ached with the loneliness and the silence that pervaded her apartment. But to accept T'Hawthorn's offer would mean a homelife of constant disagreement with him.

Lark tried to copy her father's calm tone, but failed, as usual. "There's a whole world out there without fighting over this little piece."

"There's a whole world," he repeated. "But even with all our Flair and Flair-technology, transport is expensive. Exploration demands a great outlay of Family assets. Tryskel Plantation is close, it's fertile, and it's ours. When we win the feud and we can claim the pass."

"Land." She drained her brandy and placed the glass on the table. She forgot all manners in the anger of old hurt and rancor. "Lives for land. It's a GreatHouse fantasy that a nobleman should get what he wants, no matter what the cost." She shook her head. "I cannot accept that thinking anymore. It's that idea that makes me keep my distance from you. I will not accept this. I will not condone it. I will not participate." She picked up her bag, aware Phyll grumbled in fitful sleep, responding to her high emotion, then crossed to the door.

"Daughter, one moment." Though quiet, his words had an effect like a lash. A GreatLord's command, not to be disobeyed.

She turned and looked at him, unable to hide her anger.

"I heard you treated a Holly last night," he said.

"I treated two. One who would have died, one who would have been crippled."

Her father's face remained impassive, but his eyes burned purple with anger.

She lifted her chin. "Will you ask me to forsake my Healing vows?"

"I am reminding you that you have several loyalties, and the first should be to your Family."

"My Family," she repeated in an agonized whisper. "Who will die? Who will I try with all my might to Heal, and fail? My cuz, Whitey? My brother? Or even young Laev, my only nephew, on the brink of manhood? You?"

He met her gaze without flinching. "We will have guards."

"Guards! You go up against the premier fighting Family of Celta." She stopped. Fury, fear, hatred of bloodshed burned inside her. "Your own pride is involved. You can't negotiate with T'Holly after all these years of insulting each other. This is a dreadful course you have chosen."

His hands were still relaxed on his desk. "It would be better if you rejoined us here in T'Hawthorn Residence."

"You have your priorities. This land comes before your feelings for your daughter, the welfare of the members of the Family." Her eyes went to Cratag, who stared at her with a sad smile, swirling the whiskey in his glass. "You send others to do your dirty work."

A muscle in T'Hawthorn's jaw jumped. "Each member of the Family must do their duty to implement the best course for the Family."

For the first time she dared to openly question him. "Have you consulted anyone besides yourself in this matter?"

"Since your *duty* is with the HealingHalls, it is not your place to ask, FirstLevel Healer Collinson. But to give you the courtesy of an answer, I will say that my heir, your brother, Huathe the younger, agrees with me."

Afraid of words that might spill from her and forever ruin their relationship, she nodded shortly, yanked open the door, and left.

She thought, she hoped, that she heard the sigh of her Father's voice. "Go with the Lady and Lord." But, in the end, she decided she'd imagined it.

Lark willed the tears in her eyes not to fall and her body not to shake until she reached the glider waiting to take her home. She put her bag on the seat, slid inside, and shut the door. As the glider sped away, she gave in to just one sob. Then she straightened and used her last remaining energy to cool her blood, banish all trace of tears, and pretend her life was fine.

It would be fine. Once she lived in Gael City, Family ties could be more pleasant, interaction at a distance could be more frequent. She pulled the satchel containing Phyll onto her lap. She tried not to think about the fact that for the last septhour she had been with members of her Family for the first time in months, and neither Cratag nor her father had touched her.

By the time the glider pulled in front of MidClass Lodge, Lark had regained her composure and exited the vehicle with her head high. She passed through the entryway and down the long corridor to her rooms. Placing her palm against the doorlock, she intoned the entry Word. The scene with her father had drained what little strength she had. Exhaustion clouded her vision, and she was barely able to hold on to the bag with Phyll and her instruments. She dragged herself inside and shut the door.

"Ahem."

She jerked upright.

There, lounging on her brilliant red furrabeast leather sofa, looking outrageously virile, was Holm Holly.

four

♥

At the sight of Lark, Holm's heart stuttered. He'd wondered how the next meeting with her would affect him—now he
knew. His need for her, just to be in her presence, intensified
each time he saw her. He rose from the sofa and moved to where
she drooped in the doorway. The smudges under her eyes, the
sag of her shoulders, sent a pang through him.

"How did you get in?" she whispered, as if even speaking
was beyond her. Slowly she set her bag down.

He shrugged, then placed an arm around her waist, and the
feel of her was sweet, sweet. "The door was open."

It was the truth. A HeartMate could make a key that would
deactivate any security spellshield of their mate. The redgold
charmkey rested in his pocket. Even though he'd thought of her
as his own, his woman, his wife, his HeartMate, he hadn't spoken the word aloud—until he was faced with her locked door.

All he had to do was place the charmkey on the identplate
and say "HeartMate." There had been a whirring as his vibrations in the key meshed with Lark's personal spellshield, and the
door swung open. He'd shuddered at the momentous action.

His whole life had shifted when he'd said that word, acknowledged to himself, Meserv, and an empty corridor that he
had a mate of his own, for the rest of his life, integral to his well

being. And that the time had come to pursue her in earnest.

But he couldn't tell her that. It was forbidden.

"Some GreatHouse Flair got you in, no doubt," she said tonelessly.

Tears welled in her eyes, alarming Holm. He drew her into his arms and stroked her hair, her back. "You're tired. Take comfort from me." He swept her up in his arms, glorying in holding her. Possessive tenderness rolled through him, lodging forever in his bones.

She tensed, then a tremor shivered through her, and he knew that though her mind might want to reject him, her body and inner spirit recognized her mate. Her HeartMate. Him.

She stiffened again. "Shhh," he murmured, setting her next to him in the deeply cushioned couch. "Take comfort from me," he repeated. "It's not so very much. We've been meeting for a while, and now we're no closer than when we worked together in the NobleCircle Rituals as youngsters." In fact, they were less close—then they had loosely linked energy and minds. "I missed you when I graduated to FirstFamilies Circle." He realized as he spoke that it was true.

He'd liked the warm and subtle spirit of the girl, a spirit that never failed to soothe any nervous vitality he'd carried. There it was, he thought. That had been the potential. The link that could become a HeartBond. If he'd grow enough to match her.

He cradled her in his arms. Thank the Lord and Lady he had matured enough to claim such a treasure. He could not face how sterile his life would be if he had to live without her.

"How long has it been since you've been held, Mayblossom?"

"Three and a half very long years," she whispered, as if she couldn't keep the words inside her. "Not since Ethyn died."

Holm shut his mind to her former life, would not let futile jealousy eat at him—more than enough that he had her now. And he would be not simply a husband, but a HeartMate.

He lifted a hand to stroke her tumbled hair, black as the North Iceland Ocean. "You are tired, and lonely. You care for so many, but who takes care of you, Mayblossom?" He wanted her to realize that she needed his care, needed him.

Though he kept his voice quiet, she sat beside him, barely touching shoulder to shoulder. She removed the curve of her hip and thigh from pressing against his body. He didn't like that, but stopped his instinctive reach for her and draped his left arm along the back of the sofa behind her.

"You know I don't like that name." She changed the topic.

He smiled. With his right hand he enfolded her fingers. "I know you didn't like it as a girl. I never knew why."

She huffed. "Mayblossom. All fresh and winsome and pink and blond." She glanced up at him. "Or silver-haired, like yourself. A flower maiden. Not me."

She was so wrong, with her eyes like lavender pansies, rosy lips, a lissome grace. He toyed with her fingers. "Look at these: long, beautiful stems."

Lark sniffed and matched her own with his. "Not as long or elegant as yours."

He stared at their hands. The shape of his hands was acceptable, but the fingers and palms held callouses from blade and blaser grips, and his hands were covered with small scars from the nicks of practice and battle. Her skin was flawless, and would ever be so. As a Healer, her innate Flair would mend all small hurts.

She tilted his hand and frowned at a red welt. He felt a tingle and it vanished. Yet even that small bit of Healing cost her, and she leaned against him once more.

"What makes you so tired, Ma— Lark?" He didn't like that name. Everyone called her Lark. Her husband would have called her Lark. No, he could not call her Lark.

She sighed. "D'Hazel's youngest decided she could fly."

Fear jolted. "The teeney girl? How old is she? Two?"

"Avellana's three."

"Lord and Lady! What happened?"

"Luckily she jumped from a second-story tower window, not the roof."

"She'd be dead if she had. D'Hazel Residence is as tall as T'Holly's."

"As I said, she went from a window. Her nursemaid said she might have flown or teleported or something on the way down; the damage wasn't as bad as it could have been." Lark shuddered. "Brain damage—so hard to mend, nerves so delicate, blood vessels so critical—" She buried her face in her shaking hands. "I gave it everything."

He pulled her close so they were pressed against each other side to side, thigh to thigh, calf to calf.

"She will be well?"

"She Healed. We don't know if we caught all the damage. We do know she will be different."

"Her Flair was great, greater than any other child of her generation."

"Yes, it's still there." She rubbed her eyes. "Whether she'll be able to access her Flair, we don't know. How it might evidence, we don't know. Whether she'll even survive one Passage, let alone three, we don't know. We. Don't. Know." Tears clogged her voice.

Holm placed his palms on either side of her face. With the lightest of touches, he reached for her with his Flair, willed his own strength into her. And they linked.

The bond between them, once forged within the structure of the GreatRituals they had both participated in, now snapped into place, as if only needing awareness. The old connection opened, sending the strength Holm wished to give her to bolster her depleted energy.

"Uhn," she said, shuddering.

He lifted her to sit sideways on his lap. The link spiraled tighter, and he sensed her thoughts, waded into the colorful sea of her emotions. Each step brought him nearer to where he wanted to be. Bound with her forever.

With her eyes closed, she pinched off the connection, as easily and finally as she stopped a blood vessel. "No."

. Stroking her cheekbone with his thumb, he said, "I asked you a question, sweetheart. Who cares for you?"

He jumped as needle teeth sank into his knee and looked down. The twin of his kitten removed its jaw from his trous and sat in front of him, staring up at him with green eyes, even as it delicately licked a forepaw. *I take care of her. I am her Fam, Phyll.*

Meserv, who'd been exploring, trotted up to sit by his brother. Holm frowned. His kitten's belly was noticeably plumper. Meserv also sported a new scratch on his nose, and tooth-indentations on his right ear. Phyll looked immaculate.

I take care of her, Phyll reiterated, jumping onto Lark's lap and circling.

"So you do. But who took care of her before you came?"

Doesn't matter, Phyll said with a cat's disregard for time. *I am here now.*

"That's true. But it's nice to be held." He slipped an arm around Lark. Meserv scrambled up the couch to settle between Lark's legs and the couch.

Holm followed Lark's surprised gaze to the two kittens and cocked an eyebrow. "Let me guess. You had a visit from our young, prophecy-spouting GreatLord."

When she met his eyes, he saw wariness and a touch of fear. "I could tell Vinni knew something of my future, but he didn't say much."

She shivered.

Holm wrapped her tighter in his arms. "My feelings exactly. I shudder with fear," he murmured against her hair, noting that whatever else she had changed, Lark still wore the same scent, the slight musk of white hawthorn flowers.

He liked her bottom on his thighs, the small waist his arm circled, and the fullness of her breast against his chest.

Holm tipped her head to lose himself in her violet eyes.

She licked her lips. It didn't help his control. Still, the shadow of apprehension darkened her gaze.

"I can't imagine you shuddering in fear," she said.

His mouth twisted. "Prophecy can do it."

She turned to grip his shoulder. "He didn't say anything definite to me. Did he say something to you?"

"Nothing I want to repeat." Forbidden, he kept reminding himself—utterly forbidden to announce to a HeartMate that she could be bound to you, physically, mentally, emotionally. To do so was abusive—not allowing choice in the most important of matters. But Holm couldn't remember the punishment for the crime.

"Did he say anything about the feud?" she insisted.

He stiffened. The fighting was nothing important; his wooing all important. "He spoke in riddles."

"Oh." She slumped and he cherished the feel of her.

The kittens became restless, walking back and forth across the couch, over their people, or on the back of the sofa.

Lark looked at Meserv as he tumbled from Holm's shoulder into her lap. "He's fat," she accused.

"Just a little plump. Baby fat," Holm defended.

"I received instructions from D'Ash on my kitten's care and feeding."

Holm sighed. "My mother is enchanted by Meserv. None of the Family hunting cats care for her, but this fellow"—Holm rubbed Meserv between the ears—"loves Mamá as much as he loves me. She slips him furrabeast bites in between meals."

"Mmm-eservvv," Phyll mewed at his twin who sat on Lark's lap while he was on the couch.

"Ph—ph—phhltt," Meserv tried, spitting at Phyll.

Phyll looked disgusted, then attacked. They fell to the floor in a rolling, hissing ball of marmalade fur.

Lark started to intervene, but Holm squeezed her. "Let them be. They're only playing."

She opened her mouth as if to protest.

"You think I don't know a real fight?" Holm asked, amused.

"Absurd. This whole situation is absurd."

"No. It might be complicated, but it certainly isn't absurd. Not funny and not trivial." He couldn't wait. He bent his head to brush her lips with his and claim her mouth.

Just the touch of his mouth on hers sparked something deep inside her. His lips slid against hers, then pressed. She enjoyed the tender kiss—more than enjoyed, delighted in it.

She'd been alone for so long. No one—no man or woman, lover or friend—had treated her as he just had, simply holding her. The huge ache she'd suppressed at the lack of human affection had vanished with the first curve of his arms around her. She trembled that such a basic need had been filled so effortlessly and generously. She hadn't been able to resist him.

For so long, she'd been untouched by any man. And as Holm held her close, trailing kisses over her face—tiny butterfly kisses of infinite gentleness—she let him take her to a new, intimate level.

He enveloped her. The warmth of him—as if he carried the sun itself within his body and shared it to comfort her. The strength of him—as if after all these long and lonely years of coping on her own, she would have someone beside her. The security of him—as if he would always be there to hold her.

She twined her arms around him, this vital man, and pulled him close to feel him, and to feel herself held and sheltered and sustained.

With unintelligible words, he shifted them until they stretched on the wide couch on their sides, legs entangled.

His mouth returned to hers, this time to test her lower lip. Everything changed.

The skim of his teeth, the pressure and pull of them, ignited hot licks of fire within her. She'd wanted this closeness, and now they were too locked together for her to move away, for her to draw back, and all the comforting sensations transformed into something more demanding, something hotter, something wild.

She clamped her arms around his shoulders, grazed her tingling breasts against the hard slab of his chest in a wanton move that she hadn't known before this moment.

She strained toward him, only feeling—the rapid pounding of his heart against her quickly rising and falling breasts, the carnal caress of his lips, rubbing, nibbling at her mouth, her ear, her throat.

With practiced ease he rolled, and she went with him, under him.

Instantly she was enveloped by his heat, his hardness, his weight. How had she missed that he was completely aroused? She could feel the length and thickness of his erection against her. It unnerved her. It thrilled her and swept her mind away.

Hot and strong and vital as the sun was Holm Holly. And she wanted him.

She tunneled her fingers into the rich thickness of his hair, coarser than her kitten's, but equally pleasing against the slide of her palms.

His hands went to her sides and stroked down her, learning her. He stirred and his arousal pressed against her most feminine flesh. A soft cry of yearning pleasure broke from her. Her nipples tightened, moistness dewed lower. Her whole body spiraled into aching, ever-increasing hunger.

She traced the angle of his cheekbones with her fingers, then dipped below his chin. She opened the collar of his shirt and inhaled the essence of masculinity. And she needed, more than she needed anything before in her life, to taste him.

Lark put her lips to the pulse in his throat, drew in a deep breath of Holm Holly. She tasted—arousal, perspiration, musk, man.

He groaned, and his fingers spread wide over her bottom, clenching, kneading.

She panted in desire and passion against his neck, lost in him. He lifted her hips against his shaft.

A flash of pure physical rapture speared her. She bit his throat, savoring the firm flesh between her teeth, and the taste of him.

He groaned again, arched himself against her.

His hands pushed up her tunic until she felt them, calloused but gentle, on her skin. She cried out at the delight of it. A man's hands, Holm's hands, muscular and sinewy hands. And she hungered for his touch.

He inched his hands up her midriff, caressing, until he reached her breastband, curved his fingers over her breasts, plucking at her nipples.

She gasped, but wanted more, wanted his hands on her flesh, not her clothes, but found no words.

The warmth of his hands left her, and she moaned and shook her head in denial, twisted her own hands in his hair and pulled him close, found his throat again. Nipped.

Now his hands plunged downward, slipped into her trous, under her pantlettes, and the feel of those rough palms on her bottom was too much to bear. Passion took her, dragging her into the upward vortex of sexual tension toward ultimate release.

"Mayblossom." His voice came ragged in her ears, low and thick, and added another layer of sensuality to her climb to fulfillment. She was only aware of his voice, his scent, his taste, his touch, and she wanted more. She wanted everything.

"Lark," he whispered, then groaned as she ripped at his shirt tab, peeled it open, and set her nails into his chest. "Bélla."

The cats swirled into the room again, rolling and hissing, bumping up against the couch, right beneath her ear.

Her mind rushed back into thought.

She pushed against him. "No!" How could she have let this happen? How could she have been so wanton?

Willing her fingers not to change the warning into a caress, she set her hands against his shoulders and pushed again, turning her head aside. His hands clenched against her bottom. She bit her lip so pain would stave off overwhelming desire.

"NO!"

His head raised and a molten pewter gaze met her own. "It's right. Can't you tell how right it is?"

She only saw his gilt hair, brighter than the evening sky outside the window. She only felt the strong, hard length of him pressing her into the sofa—the mass of him that told her intimately he was a large, potent male.

"No." She could only get her tongue around the one word.

"I'm your—"

She put her hand over his mouth. "You are an honorable man. Listen to me! I am sorry I lost control and gave into a momentary lust. It was wrong."

He closed his eyes. She wondered if she'd tempted him beyond the point of no return. His lips firmed under her palm in a kiss, and she yanked her hand away.

He lifted himself from her on his arms, face tight. His hair, mussed from her fingers, fell over his forehead.

Holm flung himself off the couch and onto the floor. He put an arm over his eyes.

Lark scrambled to sit. Looking down, she saw his erection bulging against his trous. She jerked her gaze away. Holm's chest heaved. She hopped off the sofa and over him and staggered into the kitchen, wanting something cold. She opened the chillbox and pulled out a cylinder of icyblacktea spiced with cinnamon. Lark unsealed the glass with a word and gulped. The liquid stung her bitten lip.

"I could use some of that," Holm said. He filled the small doorway to the kitchen.

Lark choked on another cold mouthful. She hadn't realized until now that the kitchen doorway was smaller than usual, and that there was only one door. She was trapped.

Holm leaned a shoulder against her doorjamb. His silver-blond hair still drooped over his forehead. "Please?" When he smiled, it was nearly his usual charming one, only a little crooked at one corner.

Watching him, she opened the chillbox and tossed him a cylinder.

"Thank you." He dipped a nod.

She curled both her hands around the glass, grateful for the cold that began taking the edge off her overheated body.

Phyll, she called telepathically.

A few seconds later the kitten barreled into the kitchen.

Holm cocked a brow and looked a little hurt. "You called him, didn't you? There was no need for that." He moved back into the mainspace, but pitched his voice so she could hear. "Whenever you wish anything from me, my Bélla, all you have to do is ask."

Bélla? *Bélla?* Another one of her middle names. He'd called her Bélla when they'd been making love—stop that thought, those images, the revived feelings that quickened her unfulfilled body. Bélla. He'd called her Bélla. First Mayblossom, then Lark, then Bélla, as if tasting each one of her names and choosing the one that suited him.

The intimate note in his voice made her insides shiver, something she decided to blame on the icyblacktea. With a final gulp she finished the drink, then tossed the cylinder in the recycler and used a softleaf to wipe her mouth.

"Phht, Phht, Phlltttt," spit Meserv, peeking around the doorjamb.

Phyll bounded after him.

Lark shrugged to ease tension in her shoulders and strolled from the kitchen. Holm lounged on the sofa, arms outspread on the back, one hand negligently curved around the icyblacktea, and feet crossed at the ankles.

He looked delectable.

She kept to the opposite side of the room, putting its width between them.

Though he lifted the tea for a sip, his gaze followed her.

"I've waited to taste you for a month—eternity," he said.

On the attack. She didn't want to talk about the episode. She didn't want to even think about it.

Still, his words made her catch her breath. "You were interested in me when we met to plan the AllClass HealingHall charity ball?"

He cleared his throat, glanced down his body where his arousal showed. "A little more than 'interested.' "

"But you didn't follow up—"

"I bumbled."

She stared. "Everyone knows you never bumble with women!"

His shoulders lifted and fell a fraction, and his mouth twisted in an ironic smile. "I was afraid." When he gazed at her, she felt as if his eyes alone seared her. "You are—" He shut his mouth, took a deep breath, and began again. "You are infinitely important to me." The cadence of his low voice brushed against her nerve endings, making her tremble.

Who was this man that he should make her quiver with a look in his eyes, a tone in his voice? Who was this man whom she'd known when he was a youth and she a young girl, that she'd known *of* ever since?

She was afraid that she desperately wanted the answers to those questions. She licked her bottom lip and tasted where she'd bitten it. Holm tensed, then stared out the arched windows.

Lark shook her head. She had no time for an affair with Holm Holly, and until this afternoon, no inclination. If it had been last year, perhaps they might have managed an affair. In view of the escalating feud, the whole idea was madness.

And Lark didn't want another husband. General knowledge of the other FirstFamilies was common, so Lark knew that Flair Passages of the Hollys meant death-duels. Holm had never connected with a HeartMate during his Passages. She had experienced great Healing fugues during her Passages but never touched another soul-to-soul as HeartMates were said to do.

There was no reason but basic lust for her and Holm Holly to come together—for a while. The heat of the desire that exploded between them was such that it must burn hot and fast, quickly dying to ashes. She didn't want that. She should focus all her creativity on her Healing career. Lady and Lord knew all her skills would soon be tested to the utmost.

When she looked at Holm again, his expression was stark, jaw set. Since he'd been watching her, he could anticipate her decision.

No. No matter how her body wanted him and what he could give her, it was better that they stop this attraction right now. Being a fighter, he'd only respect bluntness. She squared her shoulders, ready to lay out her decision. There'd be no repeat of the sexual madness.

"I want you out of my life, permanently," she said.

"Then kill me."

She blinked, horror spread through her. *"What did you say?"*

He continued to lounge but raised his brows. "You heard me. I said you'd—"

"I don't think in terms of killing."

His voice came softly. "Of course not. You are a Healer. It is a complication that I am so attracted to you."

"A complication you can quickly eliminate. Just go away and stay away."

"No." His eyes darkened to charcoal gray. "That is quite impossible. You will have to become accustomed to having me in your life."

She lifted her chin. "I have asked to be appointed as the Head of Gael City HealingHall. I hope to be moving there in a couple of weeks."

Stark incredulity lit his eyes. He stilled. She sensed she'd surprised him for the first time that night.

His mouth flattened. "That can't be, Bélla."

She whirled to him. "You call me that Heather name because you don't want to think of me as a Hawthorn, an enemy."

His feet twitched. She realized his languid pose had been false all the time, and wondered at his control, wondered why he bothered to exercise it.

"You aren't my enemy. You will never be my enemy. I will never be your enemy. We both know that. And you are more Heather than Hawthorn."

"Oh, yes?" She speared her fingers into her hair and pulled them through long black locks. She was the image of a Hawthorn.

He smiled faintly. "A Hawthorn in looks only. You have the temperament and the manner of a Heather Healer."

"This is insane." She set her teeth and decided to tell him part of the whole. "My father is determined on this feud."

"I know. I can't believe T'Hawthorn would let you leave Druida."

The feud was more critical than her conflict with her father. Lark waved that distraction aside. "The feud's about—"

"I know what it's about, too," he said. His face softened, and his long elegant hands picked up a small oblong neck pillow that sat in the crease of the couch and stroked it. "Hulver Pass. He's not going to win."

Her heart thumped in her throat. "Stop the fighting. You can stop it."

Five

They stared at each other.

"I can't," he said. "I'm not T'Holly. Even if I were, I don't think I'd stop the feud. Hulver Pass was one of the first pieces of land our Family claimed, in the second generation. It's rugged and deadly. We've cleared the rock, placed great, generational spells on the cliffs to prevent rockslides, built a decent road. And we did that because seven Hollys died in that pass. Their remains are still there, buried under a whole cliff-face of scrag. We have a memorial plinth with their names. It's not only that it is our land, but it is integral to the history of our Family. The T'Holly died there, leaving an infant daughter, and no acknowledged heir. We won't be forgetting that, Bélla."

She covered her face with her hands, a despairing ache settling in the pit of her stomach. No, no Family would give up land soaked with their blood, sharded with their bones. "I can't bear it. A Hawthorn feud. Terrible."

She didn't hear him cross the room, but his fingers curled around her wrists and drew them away. He turned her hands palms up and kissed the hollows.

"Bélla, my Bélla."

"Don't call me that."

"Mayblossom Larkspur Bélla Hawthorn," he chanted softly.

"Bélla is another of your names. A name no one else has ever called you. A name that will be unique to us. What will you call me?"

"Fool. Stup. Idiot." Lark jerked away from him and opened the door to her apartment, waving an arm at the threshold.

"Lover," he whispered.

Heat rushed into her face.

She blinked, then noticed a dark bruise on his throat. "Lady and Lord!" She reached out to Heal it, but Holm captured her hand.

Holm grinned wickedly. "I like it. It's the mark of my lover's passion for me which I'll treasure. The mark will make up—a little—for having to leave you now, Bélla."

He kissed her fingers. Just the touch of his mouth on her hand sent her pulse racing even as her mind noticed how smooth, easy, and accomplished his gesture was.

Holm bowed with exquisite style, then snapped his fingers and teleported Meserv into his hands. "Thank you for letting the kittens play. Play is very important. I think I will have to remind you of that. Often. Expand your horizons." He arched his brows. "Thank you for your company." His gaze swept around the room. "Your home is bright with color, yet very serene, very comfortable. Until we meet again." He blew her a kiss. "Blessed be."

"Go with the Lady and Lord," she mumbled, unable to stay silent.

He smiled and it stunned her. She had never seen him smile like that before, with gentle joy. Lark stood frozen as his footsteps faded.

She was left with questions.

Had Ethyn ever wanted her this much? He certainly hadn't expressed so much passion as Holm, or demanded a response from her. Ethyn had never received such a sexual response from her. Then she shivered. This had just been a kiss. A first kiss.

She'd bitten him, and at the time had liked it, the taste and feel of his taut flesh against her mouth. His touch ignited a wild, primal desire that made her forget everything. Even that she was a Healer, sworn never to inflict pain.

He liked his lover's mark of passion? The way his eyes gleamed, she thought he might want her to bite him again, or more. More? How could she live with the woman she might become with him? She didn't know that woman.

She'd never experienced the sensuality with Ethyn that she had for Holm, the blood-sizzling, thigh-loosening, deep-pooling erotic sensations that Holm had created.

Stop! Don't think of this. Don't dwell on it. The situation is impossible. Impossible!

Surely the man would see that.

Phyll wobbled to her. *I have done much today and want food. Meserv gets all the food all the time He wants.*

"Meserv is fat."

Phyll's whiskers twitched. *And slow.*

She picked him up and carried him into the kitchen. "I'm proud of the help you give me at the HealingHall."

Everybody loves Me there, Phyll said.

With a Word, she opened the cat section of the no-time food storage unit and dished out his special diet. "You will eat nutritious foods and become a strong, long-lived cat."

I am stronger than Meserv. Phyll cocked his head. *But no one is as strong as Holm Holly. I like him. We will see him often. Meserv and I will play together, and I will win.*

He started eating.

Lark stared at him, wondering how she could convince everyone, including herself, that she didn't want Holm Holly.

*H*olm stroked *Meserv's* head with his forefinger and contemplated the closed doors of the Green Knight Fencing and Fighting Salon, wondering if his Uncle Tab still locked the place against him. He needed to work off the pulsing energy of his lust.

He didn't know how he'd managed to stop from taking his Bélla's sweet body when she'd called a halt to their lovemaking.

Even so, he cursed himself. He'd been too hasty and come on too strong. Faults he'd never had to curb before. Faults that could cost him his HeartMate if he didn't check them now.

The first time they'd been together, he'd jumped on her.

He shook his head to banish erotic images as much as to regret his lost skill and sophistication with women. He sensed all his suavity was gone for good with his HeartMate. Lord and

Lady knew how he was going to scrape through this situation with any sort of finesse.

He'd simply jumped on her.

Served him right that he ached up to his teeth.

At least he hadn't pushed the telepathic bond.

He grinned. No, he'd been too completely wrapped up in the physical to be coherent enough to reach for her mentally. A good thing. He suspected the punishment for melding them together in a HeartBond without her consent was dire.

He tested the doors of the Green Knight, and accepted the small shock. Still barred from fighting. He'd have to swim.

There were both advantages and disadvantages to being the member of such a physical Family. He hurt now, and would probably suffer for some time with frustrated passion until he could seduce his Bélla.

But at least he'd be concentrating on the physical bonding, instead of impelling her into a HeartBond. No doubt it would take several extensive, heated sessions in bed with Bélla before he'd even think of progressing from physical consummation to the emotional, mental, then spiritual. In their bond he'd experienced qualities that drew him to her—her willingness to spend her energy to Heal, her compassion. And her sense of honor as strong as his own. Most of all he liked the deep serenity that soothed him. Serenity he could ruffle, passion he could ignite until all they'd think of was loving.

Bed. Bélla. He tensed at the idea. How soon could he win her, even moving fast? He recalled now the news that she could be moving to Gael City. That was a problem, but it didn't bother him as much as his own failings.

He teleported home and to the conservatory.

After many laps in the pool and a call to D'Rose to order a gift, Holm was calm and refreshed enough to satisfy his curiosity. He lay on a longchair with Meserv snoring beside him and contemplated the ever-expanding verdant flora.

"ResidenceLibrary," he said. "What is the punishment for telling a person you are HeartMates?" He fought his nature on this, trying to be patient.

And he was scared. Opening himself to another, sharing all his thoughts, emotions, experiences, even for the short time of the HeartBond, was enough to daunt the bravest.

The ResidenceLibrary spoke in somber tones with an edge of warning. "The punishment is a five-year courtship of the person or until the wronged one states in front of three heads of First-Families that she or he accepts the HeartMate status—"

"Puny Earth years or long Celtan years?" asked Holm.

In even more disapproving tones, the ResidenceLibrary answered, "HeartMates, HeartGifts, and HeartBonds were unknown on Earth. They are Celtan phenomena."

"Ah."

"To continue, the wronged one must make a statement that she or he accepts the status, *and* repeat it five times."

"Repeat it five times? Why five? Five isn't a magical number," Holm grumbled. "Not good." Not for an impatient Holly.

A few seconds of silence passed, then the ResidenceLibrary said, "Laws of Celta, topic twenty-four: the origin and philosophy of HeartMate laws—"

"Stop," Holm ordered. The ResidenceLibrary obviously had a two-hour lecture in its memory. "What is the punishment for HeartBonding with a HeartMate without telling her?"

"It is not known whether the HeartBond can be forced—"

"Not forced! Ah, persuasion, seduction, uncontrolled passion—"

"My interrupt feature is now engaged since the topic is Celtan law. It is not known whether the HeartBond can be forced," ResidenceLibrary said in a volume that echoed off the glass panes. "However, punishment of a nonconsensual Heart-Bond is exile of the offending party from within eighty kilometers of the victim for a period of five years—"

"After they have been HeartBonded? After they are mates and their feelings and minds melded?"

"Correct."

"This is impossible," Holm said, still feeling the semiarousal of his encounter with his Bélla. "I will never last." The blue pool lapped and reminded him of something else. "Close ResidenceLibrary. HollyHeir addressing the Residence."

The atmosphere around him changed in an aspect he couldn't define, and the voice of the Residence, deeper even than T'Holly's, addressed him. "Here, HollyHeir."

"Please set the temperature gauges on my personal waterfall fifteen degrees cooler."

"Done," T'Holly Residence said.

Holm could not depend upon his control with Lark, and to push her would be to lose her—if not forever, at least for too long of a time for him to endure. He smiled grimly. It had reached the point where just a few hours spent away from her set an irritation humming along his nerves.

To keep his control, he'd have to bolster it with meditation, autosuggestion, internal bonds. He sighed. The sleep-teleporting to the Great Labyrinth and the long walks out of the place had prepared him, but there was only one place he could set such strong ties in place.

"Residence, is T'Holly scheduled for the HouseHeart this evening?"

"No."

"I request the sole use of the HouseHeart as is my right as HollyHeir."

"You are allowed a half-day—fourteen septhours—in the HouseHeart every month. It has been thirty-four days, two days longer than a month, since your last use. Your request is granted," rumbled the Residence.

Holm stood, donned his sorbaroot robe, and picked up Meserv.

The kitten whuffled. Meserv slitted open his eyes until sapphire gleamed.

"You're coming to the HouseHeart with me where we will cast some spells."

Meserv opened his mouth in a yawn that turned into a grin. *Phyll helps Lark. I will help you,* he said smugly.

"That's right." Holm teleported to the main floor and the first door leading to the secured corridor which wound down three levels to the HouseHeart.

The HouseHeart was a small room, carved from bedrock by the first colonists. Only six meters square, the room would still take a large Family to circle it with hands clasped. The colonists had come from large families. Earth had had a population problem—too many people. Celta had a population problem—too few people. It would take a millennium or two before the Earth colonists covered this planet in civilized cities and large towns.

Under rich wall tapestries were marks of the chisels and machines that had come before Flair.

A thick, sweet-smelling grass grew underfoot in the odd light that approximated Earth's sun. There were holly bushes along one wall, with spiky leaves and red berries that looked nothing like any Celtan flora, tinted some essentially different hue of green. Tinkling chimes sounded at uneven intervals as a draft of air found and flowed through the stone conduit into the room. The altar of the Lord and Lady stood in the middle of the chamber, along with the most ancient ritual tools of the Family.

Meserv walked across Holm's bare feet to explore another wall—each had a symbol of the four elements: the holly bushes for earth; the air duct with chimes for air, as well as incense; the small fountain for water; and, naturally, a hearth fire.

Holm had left his robe outside the final, most-bespelled door of Holly Residence and stood naked.

He breathed deeply.

Here he could feel the weight of generations upon him, all the previous T'Hollys, D'Hollys, Heirs, presumptive Heirs. For years the GreatHouse Holly had only two children per generation, though Holm had heard some of the other branches off the original Holly tree had a higher birthrate.

"HollyHeir," acknowledged the HouseHeart's whispery voice, different from the Residence. No one knew who this particular Holly had been, or even whether he had been male or she had been female. To Holm, it was the spirit of the Family itself.

"HouseHeart, I request a personal lock upon this Ritual. No information or report of this time may be made to anyone else, including T'Holly."

"You have never requested this before," sighed the voice.

"This is an extremely personal matter regarding myself and my HeartMate. As such, it should not be accessible to T'Holly." Holm thought that sounded like a good reason.

After a short silence the HouseHeart spoke. "Correct."

Holm let out the breath he'd been holding.

"A HeartMate!" The breathy voice warmed, almost lilted, the fire leapt, the fountain splashed, rich incense wafted, and leaves rustled. "That is very good. A HeartMate had not been predicted for this particular Holm Holly."

"I had to grow to meet her," Holm explained.

"Such a union is a Blessing of the Lord and Lady on the Family. You have done well."

The warmth of pride heated Holm.

"I lack a little control around her," he said.

"Naturally." The HouseHeart sounded amused. "We are all impatient. It is one of our charms."

"Speaking of charms, I need a spell to bolster my will, Words to remind myself of the final goal."

"Words will help, but they won't prevent an impulsive action."

Holm sighed. "I know that."

"Sit, and pray to the Lord and Lady for the Words that will still your ardor and increase your determination to follow the HeartMate laws—not to tell her of HeartMates, not to seduce her into a HeartBond."

"That's what I need."

He sat on the grass before the altar and used meditation techniques to sink deeply down into himself, where—somewhere—he was supposed to have a calm center. He'd never quite found it himself, except in FirstFamilies RitualCircles when he'd been linked with the group will.

Slowly the words surfaced. When they came, he wasn't surprised they were those that he'd tried to follow all his life, with an addition of one or two. *Honor. Pride. Control. Triumph.*

Finally he wove them into a mantra. "My honor and pride will give me self-mastery over my sexual need. I *WILL* triumph by protecting my HeartMate from everything, including my own lust."

For hours he spun the spell, trying to anchor it within, as an unconscious curb that would check him when his passion ran hot. After a long time the HouseHeart gently nudged him to complete wakefulness, blessed him, and sent him on his way.

He repeated his mantra at every step.

After Holm left her apartment, Lark spent the rest of the evening mixing her own medicinal herbs, bespelling them, and placing them fresh in the no-time storage box. All to rid herself of reckless energy and unresolved sexual tension and avoid questions that nibbled at her mind. Grinding with the mortar and pestle was especially therapeutic. Phyll dozed on his kitten perch in the corner.

Just as she packaged the last herb, her scrybowl jingled. "Here," she said.

"Lark Collinson?"

"Yes."

"GrandSir Bunt D'Rose. I have a delivery for you."

"I'm uncoding the doors," Lark replied.

She went and opened the door. In a few seconds the legs of a man and a woman came into sight. Their torsos were hidden by huge bunches of flowers. Roses. Lark simply stood by the door, mouth hanging open, until one of them grunted an "Excuse me, please." She stepped aside and watched them set six bouquets of a dozen roses each on three small tables.

She cleared her throat. "Shouldn't you space them out?"

Bunt looked her up and down, raised his eyebrows, then exited, whistling. Lark turned to the woman.

She scowled at Lark. "Four more deliveries, compliments of HollyHeir. Strict confidentiality spell invoked." She left.

Lark put a hand on the nearest wall and leaned against it, head bowed. Roses, the man sent her roses. How did he know she had a weakness for the blooms?

The two human Roses trooped in and out, delivering flowers. The bouquets ranged the spectrum from pristine white to deep purple. Several arrangements held flowers that changed tint from stem to tip, other blooms were edged in contrasting colors.

Scent hung heavy in the air, and Lark opened her tall, arched windows to the summer night.

"That's it." The Rose daughter dusted her hands. She glanced around the room and shook her head. "You're going to have to arrange them better, of course. There are bouquets in every room. Merry meet," she ended abruptly.

"And merry part," Lark responded.

"And merry meet again." She dipped her head and left.

Before GrandMistrys D'Rose could shut the door, Lark's neighbor, Trif Clover strolled in. "I *thought* that was Holm Holly I saw leaving earlier. You know, of course, that Holm Holly is *the* most sought after man in Druida. He is *supposed* to be the best lover a woman . . ." Trif's mouth dropped as she got the full effect of the multitude of roses. For the first time since Lark had met her, Trif was speechless.

"HollyHeir being here means nothing," Lark said.

Trif Clover shot out a hip, put her hand on it, and stared at Lark in patent disbelief. "Oh, entertaining Holm Holly means nothing. I believe *that*!" She inhaled audibly, then looked a little dizzy as if the heavy scent of the roses overwhelmed her.

Lark sighed and opened a few more windows to mix the scent of the ocean a few kilometers away with the verdant power of the flowers. Thinking that she'd have to craft some spell to circulate fresh air, but let the scent of the flowers linger, she closed the hall door and took a seat on the couch, watching her neighbor, prepared to be amused.

The Clovers were not a restrained or shy Family. Particularly since they were the most abundant Family in Druida, multiplying just as humans were supposed to have done on Earth.

Lark always felt more than a single decade older than Trif. She was a cheerful, exuberant woman, loved and spoiled by her middle-class Family.

"I've heard that women have *fought* to have Holm Holly in their bed." Trif glanced at where Lark sat on the couch and stilled, her eyes opening wide.

Lark winced. She knew that look of Trif's. A flash of the young woman's uncontrolled Flair washed over her. Trif "saw" events of the past. From her expression, it was an event of the very recent past, like Lark's passion with Holm Holly on the sofa. Trif hadn't yet suffered through her third Passage that would give her the power to control her Flair. If she survived that Passage.

Tremors shook Trif, and Lark hurried to steer her to an oversize chair. "Sit." Lark summoned hot tea from the no-time and curved Trif's hands around the pretty mug.

"Drink," Lark ordered, setting her fingers gently on Trif's temples. Trif sidled back, obviously not wanting Lark's exploratory Healing touch.

Trif drank deeply and continued where she'd left off. "Yes. Women have fought to have him in their beds. Or on their *sofas*."

"I didn't have him on my sofa."

"Oh, didn't you?"

"Not exactly," Lark muttered, summoning hot tea for herself, in a matching cup, made by her sister-in-law, Painted Rock.

Trif drank. "From what I saw, it was close enough."

"Trif!" Lark choked and set aside her drink.

The young woman opened her eyes wide. "What? You don't want to talk about it? *Not* surprising." She sipped, her face serious. "Look, Lark, don't you think it's time you get on with your life?"

Lark scowled. "I have gotten on with my life. Contrary to what most believe, the worst of my grief is gone." Her breath hitched at the thought of the pain fading, along with the image of her lost husband. "Can you see me, *me,* with Holm Holly?"

Six

❤

*T*rif *narrowed her eyes. "Yes."*

"What?" Lark threw up her hands and plopped back down on the sofa. "Do I look like a woman who'd have a fling with the 'most sought after man in Druida'?"

"Why not?" Trif cradled her mug in her hands, tilting her head. "You're both firstborn of the colonist FirstFamilies, so you've known each other a *long* time. . . ."

"Known *of* each other."

Trif shrugged. "So? You have a lot in common."

Lark shot her an impatient look. "Including the fact that our Families have been fighting for as long as I remember and I'm a *Healer,* and he's a—"

"Warrior," Trif said.

Lark jerked. "Warrior? Where did you hear that word? We don't have wars."

Trif shrugged again. "I study the past. I have to, to try and make sense of my Flair. Old Earth had terrible wars." She shivered. "I've had dreams, I've *seen* them. Our little duels are bloody and wretched, but nothing like—"

"I don't want to hear this," Lark said tightly. "Fighting, maiming, wounding, killing. Large or small scale, it's wrong."

Sighing, Trif leaned back in her chair and finished her drink.

To set her mug on the sidetable, she had to push aside two vases. Then she shut her eyes for a moment. When she opened them, from the depth of her deep green gaze, Lark knew they were back to the topic of her love life. She grit her teeth. A love life she hadn't had before that afternoon.

Trif snuggled in the chair, making herself comfortable for a long chat.

"Do I look like a woman who can handle an affair with Holm Holly?" Lark asked.

Trif's gaze sharpened. "I think you can do whatever you *want*. There isn't a woman I admire more."

"But an affair—"

"All right. Do you want me to say you don't seem like a woman who has affairs? That's true." Trif stabbed a finger at her. "But why not take a chance? Why not enjoy yourself? What can you lose? Sounds like you already think the whole thing is *doomed,* so you've already shielded your heart." She swept a hand around her. "It's obvious you made an impression. And I *think,* if I want to recall that little scene I *saw* with my Flair, he made quite an impact on you, too." She pressed a fist to her heart. "My, my, what moves, what fire! Don't you want to explore that, just a *little*? Tell me true."

Lark's body wanted to explore that much more than a little, to the utmost limits of ecstasy and beyond. Her mind lagged behind. The relationship between them was so complex. "Maybe."

"Maybe?" Trif wiggled her eyebrows. Her eyes brightened. "Let's approach this another way. Say you've been on a restrictive diet for a *long* time. So you go into a café and order ice cream. Do you order a small bowl of whitesugar cream or do you order something exotic like dark cinnamon with whitemousse topping and nuts and cocoa sprinkles. . . ." She waved a hand, indicating complete decadence. Cinnamon was only grown on the starship *Nuada's Sword,* and the rage for the spice had swept the city for the last couple of years.

The analogy tugged a smile from Lark. "I understand you."

"Good. You go for the point of the pyramid! Otherwise why bother? You take the special. What could it hurt?"

"I could get sick from so much richness," Lark said dryly.

Trif flashed a grin. "But it would be worth it, right?"

Tempting. Tantalizing. Luscious. Holm Holly.

Lark blew out a breath. "Maybe."

Raising her brows, Trif studied Lark and asked, "What else is rattling you?"

Heat rose to Lark's cheeks, and she looked away. "I don't have a great deal of experience . . . only Ethyn . . . and now Holm. . . ."

Trif tsked. She shut her eyes briefly and flushed, popped her eyes open, and stared at the roses filling the apartment. "Yeah. Thinking back, you don't believe he was at all *affected* by you, was he? He didn't dump *you* on the floor."

"That's enough, Trif. Absolutely no more peeking."

"All right." Trif's hand flew in a fencer's gesture of concession. "I'll do my best not to *see* anything. But the flash and fire is between you and Holm Holly, and you'd be a fool to ignore it." She stood. "It would be so *good* for you, Lark. To have a man show you how beautiful you are outside and in, and not only as a Healer. To have someone share your life for a while, give you loving. And the sex, *hmmmm-mmmm*. Do it."

Phyll appeared at the threshold of the door between the bedroom and mainspace. He chirruped and yawned.

"Greetyou, Phyll kitten," Trif said.

Phyll rumbled a small, polite purr.

"Thought I was seeing double earlier today. Two Phylls." Trif cocked her head at Lark.

Lark gave up, knowing what she said would only reinforce Trif's idea that this connection with Holm was good. "Phyll has a brother, Meserv. He's Holm Holly's Fam."

Trif rubbed her hands. "Better and better."

Lark huffed. Phyll came and jumped onto her, purr revving.

"You keep me informed, now," Trif said. With one last wistful glance at the roses, she headed for the door.

"Wait," Lark called. "Take the white ones. You know I don't care for white."

"Oh, *yes*." Trif traipsed back to pick up three huge vases at the end of the rainbow of colored flowers. "Thank you." Her happy carol was muffled by the blooms, as was most of her body.

"Want me to 'port those for you?" asked Lark.

"No!" Vases tipped as Trif parted them to stare seriously at Lark. "You've been doing too much, lately. Working too long.

When we share rituals, you are almost too tired to do your part."

Lark frowned. Had everyone noticed the deep rut she'd carved and followed without peering out over the edges?

"That's another reason to allow Holm Holly into your life. He'll certainly give you a sense of the *right* priorities. And reshuffle your timeschedules." Trif grinned again. "And provide excellent entertainment and play. Blessed be."

"Blessed be," Lark replied, and opened her outer door with a Word before Trif reached it to sail out.

*H*olm leaned against the brick wall of *AllClass Healing* Hall, Meserv firmly anchored by a spell on his shoulder, stretched out and sleeping as usual. Holm idly scanned the street and late afternoon pedestrians as he waited for Bélla. His personal glider, a two-passenger model, stood ready, bespelled for a trip.

He knew it was too soon to see Bélla again, that he should delay a couple of days, but he couldn't. The yearning for her had overridden all his strategizing logic.

His hunger bordered on need. He'd had nightmares of failure and fighting and had sleep-teleported again. Just being with her would soothe him. It had been hard enough enduring the septhours before her shift ended.

This time he'd be smooth and charming. This time he'd avoid the topic of feuds until she only thought of him as a person, a man she was attracted to. This time he'd impress her.

He knew that after a long shift at the AllClass HealingHall she had no energy to spend on teleportation, and she usually took a public swiftgo to the AllClass Maroon beach on the southwestern shore of Pict Peninsula.

A few minutes later he saw her.

She left the building, not looking as exhausted as she'd been the day before, but still very tired. His gut tightened. Even with the autosuggestions reinforced by the HouseHeart, he experienced immediate arousal. He longed to take her into a cool, dark room and drive them both to the brink of madness with tender lovemaking. Just as well that his protective instincts around women came to the fore. That protectiveness had been bolstered by the HouseHeart to help him keep control.

He narrowed his eyes, gauged the three meters, and 'ported

Lark's bag into his hands. It mewed and wriggled. "I have you, Phyll," Holm said. The tabstrip at the top of one end gaped open, and a dark rose-colored nose surrounded with whiskers snuffled at him. Holm smiled down at the little cat, then focused his attention back onto his HeartMate.

"Thank you for the roses," she said softly.

He smiled in satisfaction. "You liked them."

"Was there a note? I might have missed one."

For once, facile, pretty words had escaped Holm. Everything sounded stilted or trite. Nothing he could say could express the delight he felt at just being in her presence, and he wasn't about to announce his sentiments for Bunt Rose to relay. "Sometimes notes aren't good enough. Actions are better," he said, sliding the straps of her bag over his left arm and taking her hands. Raising one, he kissed the backs of her fingers, then turned it over to taste her palm.

She drew back. "Stop that."

Holm merely repeated the action with her other hand and noted her pulse quicken in the blue tracery of her wrist veins. A few more licks and her heart might be racing as rapidly as his own. "Bélla," he said, lilting it, making it exotic and rich as she was to him.

"I'm Lark." She pulled on her hands.

"A pretty bird. Being a Holly, I favor the robin. Robins have done well on Celta." Unobtrusively, he tried to send a bit of his strength to her.

"And stop that, too!" This time she managed to jerk her hands from him.

His palms curved her lovely face. "You noticed my sending."

"It wasn't at all subtle," she huffed.

It was. He'd done the same to his mother and brother countless times, and neither had noticed. But he had a feeling that Bélla would always find him out, read him accurately, and generally know what he was thinking. Fearsome thought, being HeartBound and so vulnerable to someone else. Yet, even now, some of her own personal energy seemed to have transferred to him, and it felt as if she nestled close to his heart. He'd never be alone, or lonely, again.

Meserv yawned and turned his head to face Lark, brushing soft fur against Holm's throat.

Lark's gaze went to his neck and the bruise on it. Holm had worn a collarless shirt to remind her of the passion generated between them, and flaunt his lover's mark. She pinkened.

Greetyou, Lark Healer, Meserv said, opening wide blue eyes.

She ducked her head in acknowledgment. "Greetings, kitten Meserv." She took her bag from Holm, freed the rest of the tabstrip, and lifted Phyll out.

Greetyou, Mmmmmmesserv. Greetyou, Holly, Phyll said.

"Here, let me." Holm took Phyll and draped him on Lark's shoulder. He overflowed. "Let's try something else." Holm bowed the complacent kitten around her neck, lifting her hair and touching her sensitive nape as he did so.

She glared at him, but didn't move. He stretched his fingers over her nape—an intimate gesture that made him control his breathing and hope that she didn't look below his waist to his tight body. He touched her, in public, in a place where no one else touched her.

Phyll nipped his thumb.

"Ouch." He moved his hand and Phyll took its place, purring.

"Serves you right," Lark muttered.

Holm stepped back—their personal fields were mingling, and the heat and sensuality between them would soon be too much for him to handle. He feigned shock. "You would say I deserve to be hurt? You, a FirstLevel Healer?"

She raised her chin, studying the minute indentation of kitten teeth on his thumb. "Yes."

Holm grinned. "We progress. You are becoming less gentle and more realistic about fighting and life."

Lark narrowed her eyes. "*I* progress?"

"And I am becoming less bloodthirsty," he said smoothly.

Now she looked surprised. "You?"

"Me," he said. "Hollys find the adrenaline rush of fighting addicting, but as with all addictions, it can be fought and lessened. Or, my personal favorite, something new and even more wonderful can be substituted."

Lark shook her head. "This situation is impossible. I have no intention of having an affair with you."

Seeing her mouth set in stubborn lines, and that the discussion was garnering more attention than he wanted, Holm held out one hand and gestured with the other to his glider. "Let's not talk about this now. Spend a little time with me. I know you like to walk on AllClass Maroon Beach after work. My glider's already spelled for that destination."

She looked at the glider, at him, at Meserv.

Let's go play! both cats cried at once.

"Meserv hasn't been to the beach yet; has Phyll?"

"No," Lark said.

Phyll increased his purr, fluttering tendrils of her black hair. Meserv amplified his purr until it rumbled loudly.

Holm smiled smugly. "Meserv's purr is better than Phyll's."

She exhaled a laugh and placed her hand in his. Meserv's purr reverberated even louder.

At her touch, everything in him leapt. He wanted her, but wanted even more to ease her burdens. "Let's have fun," he said. As her fingers curled around his, he knew he'd been wise in choosing a public beach during a summer afternoon for their next tryst.

"All right," she said.

"Good," he said. "You don't relax enough."

*T*he fresh sea wind whipped her hair and whisked her fatigue away. Or it might have been Holm Holly's presence and the effervescence bubbling through her at his touch. Each time they met, his effect upon her intensified.

He held her hand and it felt like a physical current of energy circled between them. This was a sharing, mutual thing, not like the strength he'd tried to slip her unnoticed before. But the cycling vitality between them, the mixture of his and hers, invigorated her, just as she sensed it rid Holm of some edgy tension he carried.

With the energy ran a thread of pure physical desire. Tempting. The pleasure of anticipating when and how and the amount of passion that would be freed made her giddy.

She gloried in the summer blue of the sky, nearly white; smiled as bar birds swooped and sang, savored tangy scent of sea and grass. And Holm. His silver-gilt hair, too, shone white in Bel's light. As strong and warm and uplifting as the sunshine.

"Why are you here?" she asked.

His mouth quirked up at one corner. "To spend some time

with you, to have you become accustomed to seeing me and having me in your life. Every day," he added, lifting her hand to his mouth and brushing her fingers with his lips. Then he stopped and faced her, taking her other hand. The circuit between them hummed with exhilaration. "To experience this—this powerful connection—between us. And let you experience it, enjoy it and my company." He smiled lopsidedly. "And enjoy me."

She stared up at him, his silver hair a nimbus, his head outlined against the blue sky, his features clear-cut, refined, noble. Holm Holly, of whom she'd known as long as she lived. A man who seemed to have her as his goal.

She sighed. "This is not wise. And I don't like fighters, but perhaps until I hear about the Gael City position—"

He broke the circuit by raising a forefinger to her lips, but the energy continued to pulse between them as if they were still linked physically.

"Shh," he said. "No serious talk today. Just simple pleasure in each other's company, the beauty of the beach and ocean, the amusement of watching our kittens."

She told herself that she should stop this bond before it grew further, that she should not spend time with a man who would soon be spilling the blood of her Family—

"No!" Holm said, now placing both thumbs on her temples. She felt the spiraling of the bond, becoming more than physical, reaching for her emotions. She broke it, stepped back, and let Holm's hands fall from her face.

When she looked at him, his eyes were grave. "Do not question this short time we have together, please, Bélla. Can you not simply *be* within the moment?" He took her hand again and tugged gently, as he began to walk down the beach.

The summer's day was too precious to waste. He was right to remind her not to agonize about the future. Simply *living* was something she must do more often. So she surrendered to the day, to the fizzing link between herself and Holm, and to the man.

Seven

*L*ark *admitted to herself that she wanted these moments with* Holm. Even more, he gave her something she'd always yearned for—basic physical affection. Her father's Family had always been stern, polite, repressed, with a minimal of bodily contact.

Her mother's Family, trained as hands-on Healers, had kept touch as part of deepest intimacy and their careers. And Ethyn . . . her lost husband had grown up Downwind, equally unaccustomed to physical affection. There a touch was more often a slap or a blow than a caress. He hadn't seemed to notice that Lark and he only touched during sex or working together.

But Lark had. She'd begun to crave simple contact even before he'd died. She'd started wondering how to free herself and teach them both to give and take natural pats or hugs.

Now here was Holm, helping her from his glider, holding her hand as they walked to the beach; touching her casually, easily, often. How could she say no to him, even though she was frightened that she'd want too much or too little, or she wouldn't know how to return his touches, or the price of every touch would be too high, or—

"Bélla." Holm stopped and curved a hand around her face. Her heart thumped.

"You're thinking too hard." He sent a sizzle of energy through the link that evaporated her fuzzy worries.

She blinked, smiled, and deliberately relaxed. Soon the sun and sea and beach worked their natural magic to remind her of the value of life and the world around her.

The beach was dotted with small clumps of people. Phyll and Meserv danced around lapping waves, pounced on seaweed, raced and tumbled and hid behind small dunes and attacked each other. And made her smile and Holm laugh aloud.

He laughed and his head thrown back drew Lark's notice to his muscular neck, and the red-violet bruise she'd placed upon it the afternoon before. Tingles rippled into waves of sweet sensation within her, growing despite her resolution.

"Ah, here we go, seats." Holm gestured to several pale logs set on the beach, denuded of their bark, smooth and shiny with use. He sat down. "Come, take your shoes off and let's walk barefoot in the sand."

She smiled and settled beside him, slipping her shoes and liners off, laughing and wiggling her toes that looked milk pallid against the maroon sand.

When she glanced at him, he'd gone completely still. Deep emotion gleamed in his eyes. She looked back down at her feet.

"That's the first time I've heard you laugh," he said, a rough note in his voice.

Startled, she looked up. "Surely not."

Now he smiled. "Surely so. Boots off!" he ordered. His foot-gear and liners vanished. Then the brown furrabeast leather boots stood at attention beside him. Holm wore full-cut breeches that ended at his knee, showing athletic calves with fine hair.

The kittens tumbled to their feet and fought with tiny growls and hisses.

Holm laughed, took her hand, and tugged her up as he rose himself. He glanced at Lark, and freed his hand from hers to form a fuzzy pink puffball in the air, larger than both kittens. The delicate Flair-construct looked like a huge, pale pink dandelion gone to seed.

Lark smiled back at Holm, but felt a little pang. He'd made the toy so surely, so easily, that she knew he'd often done it before. His Family must have often played with the creation. Or—she thought as she eyed the puffball's airy, bouncing path—they continued to play with it. Holm had a younger brother.

Meserv leapt for the ball and missed, Phyll twisted in the air and sent it whirling with one small paw. It zoomed through the air to hit Lark in the face, and she laughed at the tickling softness of the thing. She snagged it as it rebounded from her head, then frowned, sniffed. "What's that smell?"

Holm looked wicked. "Catnip."

She lowered her brows even more. "Drugs for the cat? D'Ash's instructions—"

"Don't lecture." Holm ran to her, swung her around, and kissed her. His eyes darkened. Seeing his passion rise, she pulled away, but his hand slid down until he held her fingers, which he lifted. He nibbled on the tips. "We can play."

Sweet sensation tingled from her hand to spread through her. The puffball floated on the edge of her vision. She tugged her hand away and swatted it, feeling her lashes lower and a curve shape her lips. "We'll play with the kittens."

Holm shook his head and placed a hand over his heart. "The lady prefers play with kittens to a different type of 'play' with me. I am devastated. My ego is in ruins."

Lark laughed again and realized she felt more lighthearted than she had for years. And she'd laughed more in the last few minutes than all of last month.

Play! Phyll said, jumping for the ball hanging just out of paw-reach. His leap was the epitome of feline grace and beauty.

Play!! Meserv said. With a grunt he managed to spring a centimeter higher and bat the ball down and to his twin.

They both attacked it, sending it back and forth.

Lark blinked. "That's odd, I just noticed, though it happened yesterday, too. I can understand your kitten—"

Fam, Meserv corrected, tongue lolling as he panted.

"—perfectly." She frowned. "Phyll must be closely linked to his brother, and I, being linked to him, get an echo effect—yet, it didn't sound—"

"You must be right," Holm said. He opened his mouth, hesitated, then said, "It might be additional Flair in this new generation of cats. Danith D'Ash has set up a screening and breeding program to enhance various characteristics."

"Ah," said Lark, distracted as both kittens shot between her legs after the ball.

As the septhour wore on, the playing evolved into a game of "keep away" with Lark and the kittens against Holm.

Lark shook her head as she realized it. Three competitive males. Of course, what else had she expected?

A complex bond spun between them all at various levels. She had a hard time masking her thoughts from Holm as she and the kittens devised a strategy. At a nod from her, Phyll and Meserv executed their plan.

Meserv teleported to cling to Holm's sleeve while Phyll nipped at Holm's bare ankles. He gasped with laughter. While he was diverted, Lark ran to him, hooked her foot around his other ankle, and brought him down. He even fell gracefully. He appeared completely shocked that she'd do such a thing, she noticed smugly.

The kittens pounced on him. *We won. We won! WE WON!!* they screamed with delight. Meserv collapsed atop Holm, closing his eyes. Phyll followed the puffball, caught by a wayward breeze, down the beach.

Holm lay there, looking outrageously male. The sight of him stopped her laughter and made her heart lurch. His body was perfect: the broad line of his shoulders, emphasized by his white shirt against the deep red sand. Then the masculine line narrowing down to lean hips; solid thighs outlined by his breeches; and his naked, sturdy calves and feet. The sun turned his hair to silver, and the rest of his skin looked golden tan from the long summer days.

She just stood, relishing the sight of him. This sought-after man wanted her. The gleaming humor in his eyes had changed into dark hunger as her perusal lingered.

His shoulders shifted as if he was about to rise, and Lark whispered, "Don't." She was a meter and a half away, and he couldn't have heard her, but he must have seen her lips form the word, because he subsided. More, he flung out his arms in open invitation for her to study him as much as she wanted. And she didn't know if the thundering in her ears was the rushing of her blood or the pounding waves against the shore.

Sprawled, arms wide, he should have looked vulnerable, but didn't.

The moment spun between them. Lark became aware that a sea breeze had risen and shaped her clothes against her. His gaze lingered on her full breasts, dropped to study her equally full hips. Sexual desire licked her insides with small flames.

He wanted her. There was no doubt of that. For the first time in her life she allowed herself to stare at a man's groin. From the lowering of his lashes, the flush creeping beneath his skin, he liked the way she looked at him, how her own body obviously reacted to his arousal.

Holm was so incredible. And he wanted her. This powerful, wealthy, highly Flaired Heir to a GreatHouse wanted *her*.

Memories of seeing him at other times, reflecting his sophistication and rank, paraded before her. As a striking youth, the right hand of his father T'Holly, active in FirstFamilies Rituals, Holm's Flair had been strong and true. As a man, laughing with a group of male friends, he'd looked more virile than them all. Once, kissing a woman's hand, his easy and elegant moves had told of his attraction to and affection for women. She thought of yesterday, Holm lounging on her red sofa, before and after they'd almost made love, outwardly casual, yet with smoldering emotions pouring from his eyes.

The most engaging image of all was the laughing, gentle man playing with kittens, but it was his affection when he'd first held her that had opened her heart to him.

Now he lay before her, desire evident, waiting with dilated eyes, watching her.

She knew he wanted her and reminded herself that she didn't want a husband. That she'd worked hard to apply for the head of Gael City HealingHall. That if she got the post, she would leave everything behind.

As for Holm, since his death-duel Passages foretold no HeartMate for him, he'd look for a woman less committed to her career than she for a wife, a woman entrenched in her Family. He'd seek a FirstFamilies Lady who'd bring good connections and a favorable alliance to GreatHouse T'Holly.

Holm lifted his hand to stroke Meserv, who had promptly fallen asleep as soon as he'd climbed on Holm's chest.

Phyll was out of sight. She tested her telepathic bond with him and found him down the beach, stalking a wayward branchlet of dried twigs.

Her gaze went back to Holm's hands. Large and strong. Calloused and warm. Gentle and exciting.

The long minutes bred uneasiness as she sensed his demand

for more than she wished to give. Trying to find words to end this interlude, she opened her mouth to speak, but couldn't.

His stare captured hers and the link between them doubled and redoubled, spinning from a thread to a braided band. Physical—the sparkling energy that circled between them, laced with undercurrents of passion. Emotional—she felt his desire, not only sexual, but the echo of something deeper, something even more insistent that could sway and command her own emotions. Danger, there. Mental—his mind nudged hers, asking for a clear telepathic connection.

The day had taught her to trust, to risk. She opened to him.

Look at me, he said, his mental voice dark and rich. *You like looking at me, don't you?*

Yes, she replied in the equivalent of a mere whisper.

His lips curved. Again he lazily surveyed her. His hips shifted restlessly, and again her eyes were drawn to the front of his straining breeches. A warm, damp tremor rippled through her.

I like looking at you, Bélla, seeing your excitement. I like feeling you near. I like speaking to you intimately. Gently he lifted Meserv and placed him in a nearby hollow of sand. The kitten grunted, curled tighter into a ball, and slept.

Come to me, Holm said. The words were spoken with lazy power, with the full intention that she would do as he bid, laced with sexual promise.

It was a public beach. She looked around. They were quite alone. She touched her mind to Phyll's. He sensed no one else, either. She looked at Holm.

He smiled and raised a hand, palm up, fingers cupped in expectation.

She dug her toes into the sand. She stiffened her knees. She wasn't ready.

He grinned. He'd heard her thought and he grinned. One of the continuing pulses of desire inside her turned into pique.

I'm ready. His brilliant silver-gray eyes were lost to her as he looked down his own body. *Give me a chance, darling, and I'll make you ready for me. Quickly.*

She hesitated.

Come to me, he said, and now there was additional will behind his words, a mesmerizing call from his mind to hers. She shook it off.

He frowned, sent a burst of energy to her that flamed up her nerves, so odd and male and vital. She jumped.

Feel what we have between us. The circuit between them sizzled with cycling energy.

She found herself panting, caught her breath. She'd never handled this sort of Flair before, the powerful Flair of a virile man who wasn't a Healer. She should have fallen from the force of the link, cringed hurting into a fetal ball, hated it. It flowed through her, invigorating her, and as it swept through her and back to him, it changed. She saw his eyes widen as the power came back to him, transformed, female and—

Passionate, he completed her thought. *Female and passionate and delightful. The energy is complementary to mine! You suit me like the Lady suits the Lord.*

Instead of stepping forward, she stepped back, and broke the link. Coldness enveloped her. His words were true, and frightening. So she took another pace back.

Holm's hand flopped back on the sand as if in frustration or despair. No, it could not be despair, just male disappointment.

She tried to make her tones light as she put her hands on her hips and raised her eyebrows. "Did you think I'd jump on you like a woman wild with passion?"

He opened his eyes and they were still the dangerous, hungry silver signaling desire. "I could only hope. You showed great promise when you marked me." He touched the bruise on his neck.

Warmth flowed through her. "I, I—"

Holm held up a hand to stop her, then easily rocked to his feet, reminding her he was a fighter, and of all the differences between them.

She shut up and stepped back.

"Don't," Holm said. "Don't ever run from me. Do you think I could ever hurt *you?*"

Lark blinked at his emphatic tone and shook her head, as much to try to clear her mind as to instinctively deny that he would ever harm her, at least physically.

"Good. We Hollys cherish women."

She licked her lips. "Yes, everyone knows that." Lark stiffened her spine. "I will not let you fog my mind again."

His lips twisted in an ironic smile. "Easier said than done, I'd imagine."

Screeching hit her mind and ears at the same time. Phyll shot toward them, a small orange blur.

Meserv woke, bolted toward his brother, then was firmly fixed on Holm's shoulder, 'ported by him.

Lark began to run to her kitten, heart pounding.

"Stop!" ordered Holm.

She couldn't. Something in the waves matched Phyll's speed. A white sinewy tentacle whipped out close to the kitten.

Lark teleported her Fam to her chest. Phyll hooked all his claws into her tunic. She winced at the sharp pain, started running backward up the beach.

A huge beast rose from the waves, gathering substance and bulk as it towered over them. Breath squeezed from Lark as Holm 'ported her to the seagrass dunes. A spitting Meserv joined her.

Gasping, Lark watched as Holm drew his sword and challenged the advancing creature, attracting its attention. Mottled white and brown, the monster looked like a cross between a lizard and a toad—warty, with six eyes. Lark panted, trying to think.

Holm scanned the beach, saw it was deserted near a rocky outcropping to the north. He ran to the empty area, whipping mind probes at the monster. No effect, but it followed him. The thing hulked over him. Holm concentrated on swiping at three darting tentacles. Greasy ichor spurted, then melted into the sand. He scrambled to the top of a rock and screamed a war cry. One flick of his fingers brought the blaser in his glider slapping solidly into his hands. He fired.

The bloblike thing took the hit, hesitated, stretched into misshapen grotesqueness. Holm's breath caught in his chest. Something was wrong. Instead of reacting, instinctively fighting, he began to think.

Nothing on Celta had six eyes. "Stop!" cried Lark, jogging to Holm, the kittens clinging to her.

He scowled at a small figure beyond her—a boy. He swore. A Word sent his blaser back to the glider. He sheathed his sword, jumped from the rock, set his jaw, and marched back down the beach.

Lark met him, panting out words. "Six eyes. No entity—Celtan, Earthling, or hybrid has six eyes!"

He jerked a nod but continued past her to confront the maker of the illusion, the young GreatLord Vinni T'Vine.

"Just what do you think you are doing?" Holm thought himself a model of control given the fact he wanted to rage at the boy for interrupting Holm's sweet moments with his Bélla. With a sinking heart, he knew his plan to be gentlemanly and non-threatening had gone up like the stream of illusory smoke from the nostrils of the fake beast.

The boy paled, but stood his ground. "I was just having a little fun."

"Were you?" Holm smiled with all his teeth.

Vinni dug the toe of his boot into the sand. His mouth turned mulish. "Well, maybe my Flair got a little out of hand." Gazing up at Holm, Vinni's eyes took on an amber hue as if wiser than his years. "We all prefer to show ourselves at our best, spinning illusions."

Holm winced inwardly at the accurate hit.

Lark and the kittens joined them. Meserv sniffed and began grooming granules of dark red sand from his orange fur. Phyll stalked around Vinni, snuffling loudly. Tension radiated from her. Holm ground his teeth; he'd have some explaining to do.

With an awkward bob, Vinni bowed to Lark. "FirstLevel Healer, I wanted to ask about Avellana Hazel. Nobody tells me anything."

She nodded. "Avellana was released from PrimaryHealing Hall this morning. She's as well as can be expected."

Vinni chewed his lip. "I'd like a copy of her records."

Lark stared at him. Holm sensed her muscles relaxing as she concentrated on her work, her mind settling into even rhythms.

Vinni drew himself up and threw out his chest. "As a Great-Lord, I can make one request for medical records of an allied House—"

"I'll 'port a copy to your Residence," she said.

Vinni's eyelids half-closed over green-gold eyes. He sucked in a breath. "Can you send it to my sitting room in the T'Vine MasterSuite instead?"

"Yes."

Phyll jumped to Vinni's shoulder and nipped his ear. The boy winced and patted the kitten. "Sorry for scaring you."

Phyll hissed. Vinni rubbed Phyll's head, but met Holm's gaze. "A *feeling* sent me here."

Holm liked this less and less.

"There are many facets to each of us. All should be treasured," Vinni said to Holm. Then the young GreatLord turned to Lark. "And *you* must remember that he was defending his loved ones. That he was putting his body between you and danger. That he'd give his life in defense of another."

Lark gasped. She hadn't viewed it from that perspective.

Vinni detached Phyll from his shoulder and put him on the beach. "Merry meet," Vinni said.

"Merry part," Holm and Lark said together.

"And merry meet again." He vanished with a pop. Holm wondered if the lordling had the Flair and energy to teleport the long way back to Druida, was 'porting in stages, or had a glider.

Lark frowned. "He's back at T'Vine Residence."

Holm scooped up Phyll and arranged him around his lady's neck. "How do you know?"

She shrugged. "He was the first child I ever delivered. I have a small connection with him. A link develops sometimes. I have one with Avellana Hazel, too, since I worked so long on repairing her brain."

He didn't want to hear that, but he didn't want the conversation to veer into argument, either. He took her hand and brought it to his lips, drawing her gaze to his. As he kissed her palm, he matched his breathing to hers, reached for the cycling of her energy, and steadied it to duplicate his—to spin and pulse between them.

She withdrew her hand. "Thank you for the outing, Holly-Heir—"

"Holm!"

"—but a personal relationship between us will never work."

"Of course it will."

She ground her teeth. "We are too far apart, in ideals, in reactions, in hopes. It's not only the feud between our Families that separates us, or that I may be leaving soon, but our very natures. Your first instinct is to fight. Mine is to Heal." She spread her hands. "How can we possibly overcome that?"

"*Our* first instincts are to *protect*."

She scowled.

"Lark, what are you doing with *him?*" A woman's accusatory voice had Lark stiffening.

A tall, angular woman approached.

Eight

"*I thought you'd be here after work, Lark, and wanted to* talk," the woman said.

"Hello, Painted Rock." Lark greeted her former sister-in-law. "This is—"

"I know who he is, a *noble*." Her lip curled. "A noble *fighter.* Holm Holly. HollyHeir. A noble fighter specializing in killing other nobles."

"I never killed another noble," Holm said. He bowed to Painted Rock. It didn't remove her sneer.

"This is Painted Rock, Ethyn's sister," Lark said.

"Ah. That explains the hostility." He offered his hand, then dropped it. "A most gifted Family, Ethyn a FirstLevel Healer, and you a fine artist. I admire your work."

Her face mottled. "I don't admire yours. If you work."

"Painted—" Lark began.

Holm stopped her with a gesture. "I work. Family business."

"Feuding," Painted Rock spat.

"Not our choice," Holm said.

"No? You fight. You own a salon to teach others. Maybe you haven't killed other nobles. Maybe you only kill those you don't think are as fine as you. You had death-duel Passages Downwind, didn't you? Killed Downwinders?"

Holm's jaw clenched. "I never started a fight Downwind."

"Never?" Lark blurted.

Blazing silver lit Holm's eyes. "Never. I don't lie." Turning back to Painted Rock, he said, "Yes, during my Passages, Downwind's brutality called to me and I didn't gainsay my emotions. I let them carry me to Downwind. I suppose you never did anything you regretted during your Passages."

Painted Rock flung up her chin. "Your brother, Tinne, wiped out a gang Downwind just a couple of years ago, didn't he?"

"He was attacked, too."

"Oh, poor nobles slumming Downwind, forced to fight."

"That's enough, Painted Rock!" Lark said.

Painted Rock turned, and Lark was surprised to see the tears in her sister-in-law's eyes. "You betrayed us." Painted Rock's lips quivered. "You're one of them *again*. I told Ethyn not to marry you, but he did. I came to like you. I thought you were different from most nobles. I thought you cared about others. I thought you cared about him and me. You don't. Oh, maybe you hurt after he died. But now you're with *him*." She pointed at Holm. "You don't care that he kills. You'll just Heal him and let him go on his way. You don't stop to think that you're opposites. He kills, you Heal." She sucked in a breath and turned her back on them, walking hunched-shouldered away.

"Oh, Lady and Lord," Lark said, finding tears rising to her own eyes. She hurt. She liked and respected Painted Rock. "She won't forgive me."

"She's bitter," Holm said.

"As I am."

"No, you've worked through it." He reached for her hand, but she sidestepped.

"Some. She's right about us. It won't work." Painted Rock's words had vanquished the last tendrils of sexual haze in Lark and made her face stark reality.

Shades and layers of reality. When Holm fought, his handiwork gave *her* work. Without fighting and violence there wouldn't be as much need for Healing. Yet, he was willing to defend and protect with his life—an admirable quality.

Her vision of the world had tilted and cracked. Not only her ideas about her world, but about Holm—and herself. She no longer considered life as black or white.

Holm spoke persuasively. "Painted Rock is wrong. She doesn't know you or me and can't see the bond between us."

"There is no bond between us." Lark picked up Phyll and started back to the log that held their clothes.

Holm reached for her with his mind, not his hands. She kept all her shields closed against him, ignoring the tiniest thread still stretching between them.

"I won't let you deny it. I won't let it break," Holm said.

She stalked up the beach in silence. He matched her pace easily. Then a long, low tone echoed in the evening. Lark hesitated. She'd forgotten that AllClass Beach held evening prayer. She struggled between the need to escape Holm and the faith that was the basic tenet of their culture.

Holm saw her waver. He grabbed at the moment to try and bind them together once more and strengthen their link.

"Do you ignore the prayer bell?" He made his voice even, nonjudgmental. When she looked at him with hurt eyes, and he sensed again the limits of her strength, he couldn't prevent himself from holding out his hand. "Let us do this together." It would remind her of the past. It would deepen their connection. It would bring them together in something other than sex. He needed a hold on her that she couldn't slip out of. Even if she got away later, he'd have this moment.

She shook her head in confusion. "I can't. I don't know—"

He took her face in his hands. Comfort he could give, endlessly. "Don't try and figure out all the problems now, dear heart, my Bélla. Tomorrow is soon enough to worry."

Singing wafted to them on the light breeze, from others performing rituals. He let her go. Smiling, he faced the beach. From the corner of his eye he saw her do the same.

Lark didn't know what to think or feel. But Holm had touched her heart, and gave good advice. A small ritual would uplift her.

He inhaled deeply. The very air around him blurred as he released emotion. A whisper of wind brought the sound of subvocal muttering. Lark strained to hear, caught the rhythm, and smiled. He chanted a mantra! Her own mantra came to mind, as she faced the sea.

The sun, Bel, was setting, sending streamers of coral and red across the sky. The ocean had darkened to midnight blue with white froth. The mysterious scents of the coming night edged out the bright ones of a summer day. Brine and sea fragrances tossed on the waves spoke of Celta's deep oceans and far shores—depths and beaches she'd never experience. The maroon sand released a pleasant tang as it gave up the heat of the day.

The moment demanded recognition, praise. Lark raised her hands. "Lady, She that holds the oceans in her hands, the eternal flow of sea that reflects the eternal Love encompassing All."

Holm joined in, his voice deeper than she'd ever heard it, and more reverent. "Lady, Dancer of the Tides, beat of wave and pulse, let our lives manifest as Love in all."

He held out his hand—whether as participant in the Ritual, friend, or lover, she didn't know or care. As she took it, the bond between them flowed as steady and powerful as the ocean itself, and she felt that he had meant the gesture to include everything—participant, friend, and lover.

Hands joined together, she found new words. "Lady, strong and ceaselessly loving, send forth your tide of caring."

Holm said, "Lady, gentle and terrible; like water, changeable and changing, fill us with Your courage and Your Love. Touch us, change us, and make us whole."

They alternated. His words and the timbre of his voice resonated within her, as if setting up an internal vibration that spoke to her very soul and would never be stilled.

The kittens crept to sit at their feet, staring at the endless ocean and inserting a mew now and then, alternating as she and Holm did, Meserv after Lark, Phyll after Holm.

"We thank You for Your Presence, for Your Love, for Your Peace," Lark whispered.

Holm raised their locked hands to the ocean. "Blessed be," they ended in unison.

He turned to face her and caught her other hand. Again the circle of emotion between them was complete, and they experienced the same serenity. He kissed one of her hands, then the other. His eyes had deepened to dark gray, and seemed as bottomless and complex as the ocean. "I thank you for sharing your ritual for the Lady. We must find a moment to honor the Lord. I'll take you home," he said.

"Lark!" Painted Rock called.

Lark bit her lip and glanced toward the woman running to them. Painted Rock stopped in front of Lark, not deigning to glance at Holm.

"I wanted to give you this." Painted Rock panted as she dug into her artist's satchel and pulled out a piece of papyrus. Thrusting it into Lark's hands, Painted Rock slanted Holm a glance of triumph.

Lark stared down at a drawing of Ethyn. Her lost Ethyn, the face she'd known so well that had faded from her mind stared back at her. She moaned. This was the man who had shared her goals and her career. Not Holm.

Holm tensed. His jaw squared as he stared at Painted Rock. "What have I ever done to you that you should dislike me so?"

She paled and licked her lips, but didn't speak.

"Do you think I will take Lark away from you? That I would demand such a thing? That I could sully her relationship with you? Why do you believe she is so fickle?"

Painted Rock tossed her hair back. "You can't take her from me. I am her sister-in-law. She's leaving here anyway. I might just follow her from Druida to Gael City. Then you'll be the one left behind. You're leaving, aren't you, Lark?"

Lark felt the shock rippling through Holm at the news and found it difficult to meet his eyes. Why, she didn't know. Her campaign to head Gael City HealingHall wasn't a secret. She'd told Holm herself.

He looked at her, eyes glinting silver. "When will you hear about the appointment?"

Lark shrugged. "In a few days."

Holm's lips pressed together. The energy vibrating between them increased until Lark could hardly stand still.

"If you leave, I can't follow you—yet. My duty is here." Again his lips thinned. Then his grin flashed and he sent her a bolt of pure sexual desire through their connection.

He looked at Painted Rock, eyes sharp. For a moment he tottered between anger and pity. "I'm sorry for your loss. I can imagine how painful the death of a beloved brother is." His tone deepened with the chill of empathy. "I'm also sorry you can't set aside your grief to wish your friend Lark happiness."

Painted Rock flinched. Lark felt the blow, too. Ah, this man knew how to fight!—with words and actions and blades.

Holm gave Painted Rock a half-bow. When he spoke his voice was low and soothing. "I admire your work and respect your friendship with Lark. Should you ever have need of any of my services, please send for me."

The artist fled. Lark rolled up the portrait and slipped it inside the long pocket of her sleeve, then looked at Holm with wide eyes. Before she could speak, a singing mass of people swirled down a dune, joy and peace hovering around them. Ribbons of pink, red, and white rippled in the evening breeze. Tambourines and hand drums added gaiety. Lyrics spoke of love and betrothal.

Holm took her hand. With that affectionate touch Lark's doubts melted away and her earlier serenity returned. She and Holm joined the song as the party danced by.

Time eddied around her as they scooped up the kittens, retrieved their footgear, and entered the glider. Silence swathed the trip back to Druida. The peace that the ocean and evening had brought filled the quiet with pure delight that simply living in the moment brought.

At MidClass Lodge, Holm set the glider on steady and walked Lark through the courtyard gates, the tunnel of arched trees, the formal lobby, and down the hallway to her door. Meeting her eyes, he brushed his lips over hers. Their bodies touched only there, mouth to mouth, but desire stirred, as well as an underlying, more intimate emotion. "Merry meet," he said.

She started. She hadn't expected those words. "And merry part," she replied.

"And merry meet again," he said. He pressed his lips upon hers, then raised his head to catch her gaze. "Tomorrow, Bélla."

With Phyll curled around her neck and her bag in her hand, Lark opened her door. The first thing she saw was her scrybowl flickering ripples of purple-colored water. Her stomach clenched before she noticed the hue wasn't the dark purple of T'Hawthorn, but the lavender-rose of the other side of her Family, Heather. Heather-colored water. Her peace evaporated. The scrybowl held a message from her MotherSire, T'Heather.

She plopped a tired Phyll onto the red couch and went to the scrybowl, nearly hidden by several vases of roses. Taking a deep breath, she inhaled their fragrance while she repeated her mantra: calm and serenity, shield and acceptance.

Lark touched the rim of the delicate glass bowl. "Herc."

The image of T'Heather formed in the bowl. "Greetyou, Daughter'sDaughter," he said. "We would be honored if you joined us for dinner." His ruddy, square face looked out at her with a serious expression. "Please let us know. Blessed be."

Her father must have sent that wretched report to T'Heather. Now she'd have to face him and defend herself. Lark bit her lip, never doubting his words were more command than invitation. She glanced at the wall timer and winced. As Healers, T'Heathers ate early, to be ready for any evening emergency. She'd missed dinner.

"Scry T'Heather," she ordered her bowl, muttering words to smooth her hair before the water stopped swirling and showed her his face. "Greetyou, T'Heather, I just returned from restime at AllClass Beach." She kept her words unhurried and smiled under his penetrating gaze.

"Greetyou, beloved Daughter of Heather. We're sorry we missed you," he said. The unexpected, affectionate title relaxed her.

"Can I come for after-dinner drinks?" Lark knew her duty.

He nodded. " 'Port to the Library, we will be having caff, cinnamoncaff, cocoa, and herbals there in a quarter septhour."

"I'll be there," she said.

"We'll see you soon," he said and broke the spell.

Lark blew out a breath. As much as she hated it, she'd have to use a whirlwind spell. Now she appreciated Holm renewing her energy.

She inhaled, held her breath, let it out slowly, mentally listing her next actions. "Attention! Whirlwind spell, cleansing, dressing, hair arrangement, and minimal makeup consistent with the occasion of after-dinner drinks at T'Heather Residence." She snapped both her fingers, closed her eyes, and held completely still as her person was stripped, scoured by hot wind to clean her, underpinnings replaced, followed by an elegant dress with silver metallic threads that swirled onto her. Her hair separated into a hundred strands, yanked into intricate braids, wove together, and freshner makeup spritzed on her face.

After the four miserable minutes, she opened her eyelids to see Phyll sitting straight up on the couch and twitching his tail in fascination at her transformation. He studied her unblinkingly.

Pretty, he finally said. *Heather colors. Phyll is a Heather name,* he reminded her.

"Do you want to go to T'Heather's?" The words escaped her in a sigh at the battering she'd just endured. She'd like her Fam with her, and he might prove a welcome distraction. As far as she knew, no Heather had bonded with a Familiar animal.

Phyll shifted his muzzle, his whiskers drooped. *I would like some fizz-energy from you,* he said.

"Of course." Nerves had kicked in, making her edgy. Siphoning energy to Phyll would benefit her. She walked over to the couch, her toes trying to stretch in the stylish pointed shoes, and lifted Phyll into her hands. Lark met wide green eyes and their bond clicked into place. With the care that made her an excellent Healer, she funneled vitality into the kitten.

"Ready?" she asked.

He'd perked up to lick a patch of hair. *Ready.*

Lark teleported to T'Heather Residence.

Minimal security spells impinged on her awareness, more from exiting MidClass Lodge than entering the inner walls of a GreatHouse.

The Heathers were the Celtan Healers and kept their doors symbolically open for anyone hurt and in need. No moat or locked greeniron gates barred the estate. It wasn't set on an island in a lake, like D'SilverFir Residence, or reached through several small gatehouses like T'Holly Residence. Modeled after a French chateau, it was less a fortress than a home.

The library was the most comfortable gathering room in the Residence. Two stories tall with bookcases and a ladder on each wall, the old-fashioned room engendered calm—from the furnishings, the memories of good times that breathed in the room, and the centuries-old spells.

Lushly cushioned furniture in textured materials showing threadbare at the seams boasted wide, welcoming arms. Two large wooden tables, scarred and dented, glowed with scented lemon polish and enabled the Family to work together. A huge globe of Celta floated in the middle of the room, dominating the library. Its surface was bespelled to change as exploration updates were reported, and it slowly turned as the planet itself rotated.

Lark released a breath as she landed on layered Chinju rugs

in the corner of the room designated as the teleportation pad. She patted Phyll, who curled around her neck.

The mellow golden light of the chamber, reminiscent of a world with a dimmer sun, also instilled comfort. Yet, her eyes went first to a gleaming brass door on the far side of the room, and the alarmlight above it. The light glowed green. The emergency Healing Room was ready, if necessary.

When she returned her gaze to him, T'Heather smiled at her—approving that she, as any Healer, would check on the state of a Healing facility first.

He held out his hands. "Greetyou, Lark." His brown eyes were surrounded by white squint-lines. He looked more like a farmer than the premier Healer of Celta.

Lark gave him her hands. "Greetyou, MotherSire." When they touched, the old link between them—he as her last Teacher and household head—smoothly connected them. He studied her, then nodded and dropped one of her hands, leading her with the other in a courtesy that a nobleman used with a noblewoman. "Come, your MotherDam is here and wishes to see you, too."

Lark hadn't expected anything else. Heathers often Heart-Bonded, and T'Heather and D'Heather were HeartMates.

Her MotherDam rose as Lark approached. D'Heather, a plump woman with prematurely silver hair and bright blue eyes, also studied Lark, then in an unusual gesture, pulled her into a warm, soft embrace.

Lark felt tears sting.

"It has been too long since you have visited us, Lark," D'Heather chided.

"Yes, Dama," Lark reverted to the childhood name.

D'Heather tssked and tapped a finger on Lark's cheek. "Make sure you include us in your busy timetable, Lark. It is very important to keep Family close." She turned and walked to one of several conversational groupings of furniture set around the large room.

Lark's smile froze and her step hesitated as she saw Cinerea, her cuz who specialized in Mental-Emotional Healing, sitting on a twoseat and sipping cinnamoncaff from a tiny cup painted with sprays of heather and rimmed in gold.

Lark dipped her head and continued on. "Greetyou, Cinerea.

It's lovely that you are joining us tonight. How is your husband, Culpeper?"

A thin, elegant woman with russet hair, Cinerea smiled. "He's very well, immersed in his research as always, and not of a mind to spend any time with us. He sends his regards."

Just thinking of Culpeper made Lark's smile widen. Abstracted but kind, he was interested in the process of Healing as well as studying and developing new medicines. "And your children?"

"All three are thriving," Cinerea said with a laugh. "Nicholas is fostering here with T'Heather. T'Ash Tested Nick and he has the Heather Healing gift," Cinerea said proudly. "It's his first week here. We thought to start him as soon as possible."

"He's seven, isn't he?" Lark relaxed as she heard the reason for Cinerea's visit. Her presence wasn't *solely* to observe Lark. Lark smiled. Though the day had had emotional ups and downs, she still felt more relaxed than she'd been for a long time and knew her inner peace showed clearly.

"Yes, Nick's seven, and settling in," Cinerea said.

Phyll mewed politely.

Cinerea started, then focused on him, and Lark realized that her new hair arrangement had hidden the kitten.

"Who's that?" Cinerea placed her tiny cup in an equally tiny gilded saucer and rose.

Lark drew Phyll from her neck and put him on the rug. T'Heather and D'Heather came to stand and admire him.

"This is Phyll, my Fam," Lark said.

T'Heather shot her a shrewd look. "Phyll's a Heather name."

"I didn't name him," Lark said more sharply than she wanted.

D'Heather crouched and crooned, holding out a hand to Phyll. "What a precious baby. What lovely colored fur. What intelligent green eyes."

"You'd think she didn't have enough children calling her Dama," muttered T'Heather, "gushing about an animal."

Lark blinked. T'Heather's descendants were numerous for a noble Celtan Family. He had two children, four grandchildren, and seven great-grandchildren. She was the only childless grandchild. She ignored the thought.

Noise came from the hall off the open door. Several teens passed. One glanced in and squealed. "A kitten!"

Lark thought the girl was Linga, of the Family's Montain branch. Like most GreatLords, T'Heather liked as many relatives around him as he could persuade to live with him. The Residence, built for huge Families, was yet a third empty.

But T'Heather and D'Heather bound their Family with ties of love, not the chains of cold duty T'Hawthorn preferred.

The youngsters tumbled into the room, immediately surrounded Phyll, and dangled ribbons or rolled spell-balls. Phyll cast one smirking glance at Lark, to assure himself she was untroubled, then turned to accept adoration.

Cinerea laughed at D'Heather's pout when the kitten played with the younger ones. "Come, let's talk a bit," Cinerea said, taking her seat again. With a wave of her hand, an elegant silver pot appeared and decanted hot cocoacaff. Lark found herself inhaling and appreciating the rich cocoa scent touched with a whiff of bitter caff.

"Do you want cocoa with your cinnamon sprinkles, Lark? Cinerea teased, knowing Lark's taste as well as Lark knew Cinerea's.

Lark smiled more naturally at her cuz. "Yes." This wasn't the Hawthorn Family, she reminded herself. Cinerea *liked* her. And Cinerea, as a Heather, would stand beside Lark. If Lark had problems, Cinerea wouldn't discuss them outside the Family, and if Lark asked, wouldn't discuss them with T'Heather or D'Heather, either.

Lark lifted her chin. Despite her father's opinion, and despite the report T'Hawthorn had commissioned from GreatMistrys Shwif D'Sea, Lark was fine. Perfectly fine.

Defiantly she took the seat next to Cinerea. Let her cuz scrutinize and discreetly probe as much as she wanted. Lark was *fine*. And she was a FirstLevel Healer, as only two other Heathers were. Let them all remember that, too. They needed her. Celta needed her. They'd all know that.

Lark took a mug of cocoa topped with a mound of cinnamon sprinkles melting into it. Gingerly Lark sipped the hot brew, allowing her relatives to observe her and their gentle surface mind-touches to skim across her as they checked her health.

"You are rested and happy," T'Heather finally said. "Yet it would trouble us less"—he touched D'Heather's arm—"if you would move here into T'Heather Residence."

Nine

❤

T'Heather expected to be obeyed. Her wishes were less im-
portant, as always, than his.

The old bitterness at her class and their preoccupation with
their own concerns seethed through Lark. T'Heather, a Great-
Lord more generous and less hide-bound than most, still could
initiate potent spells with a Word, issue a command and expect
his will to be instantly enforced. He'd never had to struggle for a
decent life or to fulfill his Flair and destiny as her lost husband,
Ethyn, had done. T'Heather had only to ask and what he wished
would be given to him.

He'd never truly accepted Ethyn, and when Ethyn had died,
Lark sensed T'Heather had felt that a blotch on the Family tree
had been removed. He'd respected FirstLevel Healer Ethyn
Collinson, but never knew or appreciated the man.

And Ethyn, after all, wasn't Lark's HeartMate whom the
Family *must* accept. Ethyn had been merely a husband. That an
association with such a lower-class man was now gone relieved
T'Heather.

Lark fought the tide of resentment. Negative emotions had
dictated far too much of her life since Ethyn's death. Her feelings must be accepted as part of the grieving process, but denied
any further power to taint her future.

She noticed their concerned looks and forced herself to smile, reminding herself that these people cared about her. Perhaps they hadn't shared her grief, but they ached for her loss. And they *were* asking as opposed to using intimidation to bend her to their will, like her father.

"Yes," her MotherDam said, "please come and stay here."

Lark sighed. "I can't. I wish to remain on my own at this time." Part of that wish was an increasing need for the company and pleasure Holm Holly could give her. She didn't want to try and explain that connection with anyone.

T'Heather frowned. "You will promise to be *very* careful. As a Hawthorn, you could be a target."

"The Hollys would never harm a woman or a Healer."

"Not intentionally." He changed the subject.

"T'Hawthorn has spoken to me about you." T'Heather paused. D'Heather leaned her head against him as if giving him support. For an instant, Lark wished for that sort of bond with Holm, then pulled her mind from foolish notions to concentrate on the danger of the moment.

T'Heather sighed. "Your father is displeased with you, Lark." He waved with his other hand and a papyrus decorated with seals appeared on his lap.

Lark's heart beat hard.

"He sent me this report on you by Shwif D'Sea." T'Heather shot her a look from under lowered brows. "Did you ever personally consult with Shwif?"

"No," Lark replied with a dry tongue.

T'Heather shook his head. "Still, the conclusions are interesting. When I considered it, you are the sole unpartnered adult female of T'Heather Family. And no T'Heather woman ever lived her entire life without a mate."

Lark forced her mouth to stretch in a brief smile. "I am over the worst of my grief," she said softly, "but three years isn't considered a long mourning period." A corner of her mouth quirked in amusement. "I wouldn't think you'd worry about my single life for another year or two. And I *am* a Hawthorn. Hawthorns are made of stern stuff."

A thought struck her. She caught her breath and her hand came to her throat. She tried to master the dismay her face might have shown. "Perhaps," she said slowly, "my father wishes to use me in another alliance. I will not be bartered. I didn't allow it before, and I will not allow it in the future. Not by T'Hawthorn"—she sucked in a deep breath—"and not by you."

Now T'Heather's eyebrows raised. "I don't recall any alliance I need badly enough to promote a marriage tie," he said with arrogant unconcern. Then he looked down on his Heart-Mate. "Do you know of a man—" he started.

D'Heather looked up at him indignantly. "Of course I know of a man who would be good for our Daughter'sDaughter, I know several. There's—" Her words disintegrated into a mumble as T'Heather put a firm hand over her mouth.

"Matchmaking isn't one of your Flaired skills. Leave it to the Willows," he said.

D'Heather just giggled behind his palm, her eyes dancing bright above his hand. Then she plucked it away. "We are concerned for you, Lark, but you are a strong, lovely, sensible woman, and we trust you will follow your head and your heart."

Lark didn't want to think about following her desires. A vivid image of Holm Holly in her bed came to mind.

"You will find your own path, in time," D'Heather continued, "and we will give you that time."

"Thank you," Lark said, breathing easier.

"There is one thing that bothers me a bit." Now Cinerea spoke. "You *haven't* been attending either T'Hawthorn or T'Heather rituals. . . ."

"I've been at every Healing Ritual the NobleCouncil has called," Lark pointed out. "As for the other Rituals, I've been celebrating them with a friend."

Odd that as she spoke the words, she thought of Holm and the small ritual that evening, and not of herself and Trif and the many rituals they'd celebrated together.

She definitely thought of Holm as a friend. How strange to think of such a virile man so, a man who had such an amazing effect on her senses. And strange, too, that she knew he thought of *her* as a friend. She wondered idly how often he had friends as lovers or made lovers friends.

When she felt the brushing of minds against hers, the touch of emotional fields gliding past her own, Lark knew she'd been silent too long, lost in reverie. But when she looked at T'Heather and D'Heather and Cinerea, she found only smiles.

T'Heather touched D'Sea's report on his lap and sent it away—probably to his desk in his ResidenceDen. He eyed her. "As Captain of the Healers of Celta, I am formally notifying you that you should take each and every restime due you, from now on. You are working too hard. Furthermore, I will be observing you to ensure you don't overdo. A person who ignores her own health is not one I'd care to see as the head of Gael City HealingHall."

Lark understood the warning. "I'm afraid we'll all be working hard soon. The Hawthorn-Holly feud is heating up."

T'Heather shrugged large shoulders. "Skirmishing between those Families has been going on for thirty years."

"It's going to get worse," Lark replied.

T'Heather sat up straight, staring at her. "You know this?"

Lark's mouth thinned until her lips hurt from pressing them tight. "Yes. We'd better prepare Primary HealingHall and the Healers for emergencies. Fights. Blood."

Everyone stilled.

T'Heather tapped his fingers on D'Heather's thigh. "I'll speak to the FirstFamilies Council about this at their meeting."

"That's next month," Lark said. "That might be too late."

He stared at her. "There's something else you must know. T'Hawthorn hired two of my best journeymen Healers—your cuz, Garis Heather, and Vera Aloe. They will be living in T'Hawthorn Residence. A precaution for injuries from this feud, I see now. Yet I've given my word on this, and the young ones are eager to go. He's paying them top gilt and for their last year of training sponsored by the NobleCouncil."

"Generous," Lark forced out around the lump in her throat.

"I don't like it," T'Heather said.

At that moment the wave of teenagers and children surged back into the library. Linga held a limp Phyll.

"We seem to have tired him out," she muttered, not looking any of the adults in the eyes.

"Really, Linga!" D'Heather scolded.

"Sorry, Dama," Linga muttered.

Lark stood and took her seemingly boneless Fam wrapped in rose, purple, and white ribbons. She chuckled. "It's been a long day for both of us. The days ahead may be even longer." Cradling Phyll in one arm, she hugged and kissed D'Heather,

Cinerea, and T'Heather. D'Heather and Cinerea both stroked Phyll until he purred, and even T'Heather gave the Fam a pat.

"Stay in touch," D'Heather said.

"I'll be keeping an eye on you," T'Heather said.

"Blessed be," ended Cinerea.

Linga grinned and walked over to Lark, sending a look at a male cuz of about the same age. "Here, Cuz Lark, we'll give you a boost home."

Taller than she, her two young relatives framed her on each side, then glanced across Lark, still smiling.

"Ready?" they asked.

"Ready." Lark grasped Phyll firmly.

"We know the coordinates of your mainspace. One, and ready, two and set, three and go!" They cheerfully propelled her home. Lark landed just inside her door with a little "Whoof!"

She smiled. She'd passed the mental examination. The people who could influence her career and her life would leave her in peace—for now.

Her smile faded as she realized the only reason she'd been relaxed and serene enough to pass their scrutiny on the physical and emotional planes was the simple fact that she'd spent a few golden hours with Holm Holly. A shiver traced down her spine. If she'd had to answer the questions raised by that wretched report of her father's yesterday, or even this morning, she might not have managed. Then T'Heather would have demanded she return to live with the Heathers or the Hawthorns, unpalatable options.

He'd have seen it as providing her safety and support, but for her it would be a demotion. He held her future in his hands.

The outstanding question remained. An issue she'd ignored until now, and something both Families would watch her for. *No Heather woman has successfully lived more than three years alone.*

She'd be under constant scrutiny. How often would she be tested? How long would she be allowed to live independently? When would her Family insist she return to one of their Residences? Was the report right? Bouts of loneliness had become more frequent and more intense. Phyll mewed sleepily, calling her back from nibbling worries. She dismissed the issue, yet felt it sink to lurk at the back of her mind.

The emotionally full day crashed down on her. She checked securityspells and glanced at a timer. The Heathers ate early, it was barely mid-evening. More civilized Families would be just sitting down for dinner.

She wondered what Holm was doing, thought again of the link between them, and didn't know if the thin thread still spun between them, or if she imagined it. She remembered how he'd looked at her body, with hunger and intent. Recalled how he felt next to her emotionally, strong and supportive. Thought of his lips upon her own, persuasive and tempting.

She set out a small dish of snack food for Phyll, then undressed, washed, spell-cleaned her mouth, and fell onto her bedsponge.

Sleep swooped down upon Lark like a huge, dark bird, and in its deep-piercing claws it brought blood-filled dreams.

*H*olm chewed his *Barbq Furrabeast,* barely noticing the tangy taste as he contemplated the painting on the dining room wall he faced. The artwork was fully two meters by three and featured several dead animals hung around or laid out on a table to be prepared for dinner, a topic some long past Holly considered appropriate for the formal dining room. Holm thought the "still life" might be enough to rob a sensitive person of an appetite, or convince him to become vegetarian. He wondered how he was going to hide the thing if his Bélla ever came to dine. On either side of the painting was a geometric pattern; a circular one made of daggers, and a diamond shaped one of throwing stars.

His mother gasped and everyone looked at her.

Her own stare fixed on the darkening shadow of the bruise only partially covered by the wide collar of Holm's shirt. "Oh, dear Holm, you're courting," she said, a luminous expression adding to her beauty.

His father sent him a wicked glance. "More than courting, looks like."

"Grandbabies!" Passiflora D'Holly exclaimed.

Grandbabies! The melodic word from his mother reverberated through Holm's brain. He shuddered. Not yet. He wasn't ready. Bélla certainly wasn't ready. He glowered at his Mamá. "I told you, she's not going to be easy to win."

His mother applied herself to her meal with gusto. Holm noticed that her chair faced a view of the gardens.

"You said she is a Healer. That's a little problem. . . ." She frowned.

"A *large* problem," Holm said again, hoping he could control the conversation. He didn't want to reveal Lark's name and spoil his parents' good mood. Further, they'd *interfere* and that could ruin everything.

His father shrugged and grinned. "His wooing will take a little longer, then, and be all the more fun for the fight."

"A Healer," Tinne said quietly, his eyes narrowing. He stared at Holm, then dropped his fingers to his thigh, as if remembering his recent wound and the Lady who mended it.

Holm caught his breath, shook his head infinitesimally at his brother.

Tinne's mouth twisted in irony. "I think Holm's right. It isn't going to be easy getting a Healer to wed a Holly. Especially when the Hollys have no intention of changing their penchant for fighting."

Their father looked surprised. "Why should we?"

"Healers often have a dim view of bloodshed," Holm said.

"We only shed blood when necessary," T'Holly said virtuously.

Everyone laughed. "Oh, yes," Holm's mother said.

G'Uncle Tab looked at Tinne and Holm with considering eyes. "An' it won't be easy t'get a woman t'move inta T'Holly Residence, neither," he said. Tab lived over The Green Knight and preferred his solitary ways. That he took dinner with them tonight was a singular pleasure they all appreciated.

"There is *nothing wrong* with T'Holly Residence." T'Holly leapt to the defense of his position, as always.

"It's damp an' gloomy. Only good housekeepin' spells keep it from a-molderin'," Tab said, sharing a glance with Holm, who was grateful for the canny old man's diversionary tactic.

Holm waved to the painting he'd been considering. "Not to mention our decorations."

"That painting has hung in that spot for the last two hundred years!" T'Holly said.

His HeartMate turned her gaze on the thing, as if observing it for the first time in a long while, and winced. "It is a little *depressing,*" Holm's mother said.

"Then there's all the weapons," Tab continued. "The Great-Hall—"

"Our armory!" interjected T'Holly.

Tab quashed him with a look. "Weapons in patterns are fine for the fightin' salon, but hundreds of swords an' shields an' blazers an'—"

"Poignards and shortswords and spears—" continued Tinne irrepressibly.

"—and throwing stars and slings and knives—" Holm added.

"—all arranged in designs on every wall of T'Holly Residence, might give even a woman less kindly-minded than a Healer a qualm or two." Tab nodded shortly.

Holm's mother blinked as if realizing again how much of the decor of T'Holly Residence celebrated fighting. "They are very attractive patterns," she said weakly, obviously having not looked at the components of the figures for a long time. She lifted her chin. "Besides, T'Holly Residence is a very *masculine* house, and so it should be."

T'Holly sent her an approving smile before he scowled at the rest of them. "It hasn't been changed in decades, and I like it that way. It shows a sense of tradition, of regard for our ancestors, of—"

"—a lack of grace an' style an' beauty." Tab speared his fork at T'Holly. "This GreatHouse has been male for so long, any feminine softness has up an' disappeared. My FatherDam's Dam hung some pretty tapestries along the second-floor corridors. Where are they now?"

"Storage," T'Holly muttered, glared around the table. "I like the Residence as it is." He looked to his HeartMate. "Passiflora has never complained."

Tab snorted. "Passiflora has her own suite. Her rooms are as beautiful as any in her former Residence, T'Apple. Apples appreciate beauty. An' you, Holm senior," Tab waggled his fork, "traipse in an' outa your HeartMate's suite at will. All the rest of us,"—Tab gestured to the table of men—"are stuck with this bleakness." Tab scowled right back at T'Holly and deliberately clinked his fork on his plate. "You're facin' a new daughter-in-law, and a Healer ta boot. What are ya gonna do ta welcome her? Or do ya expect her ta stay in her suite? You'd better think about it," he ended.

After that, conversation languished. It was unsuitable to say that a GreatLord sulked, but Holm would have wagered that was what his father did.

His mother moved her chair a little closer to her HeartMate, and Holm believed the HeartBond between them carried soothing comfort from her to T'Holly, underlaid with music.

Tab ate placidly, a smile touching the corner of his mouth, glad, no doubt, that he'd retire to his own home—comfortably and exotically furnished with items from his sea days.

Tinne seemed lost in his thoughts. A line of concentration knit between his brows. Holm warily suspected that his younger brother had guessed the name of Holm's lady and was deliberating on the ramifications of a Hawthorn-Holly feud and a Hawthorn-Holly HeartMating. The situation Holm found himself in didn't appear to please Tinne.

But then the circumstances weren't satisfactory to Holm, either. Even the "dinner" painting across from him was more cheerful than pondering the tangle of feuding and loving. So, of course, he returned to thinking of his Bélla, her immediate and fiery response to him. The growing connection between them, so extraordinary and intimate, with the cycling energy that sizzled and echoed the emotions between them, the passion between them, was something he didn't think he could do without. And they weren't HeartBonded yet.

Finally T'Holly pushed himself back from the table. "We have matters to discuss. Let's talk in the ResidenceDen. Relatives of T'Hawthorn Family are increasing their presence in Druida and their attacks on us. We had three skirmishes today. It looks as if our disagreement is getting serious."

"The Holly-Hawthorn feud's been serious since ya both fought an' broke the GreatSeal in the Guildhall," Tab said.

T'Holly winced. "That was thirty years ago."

"Neither of ya have forgotten," Tab pointed out. "Neither of ya have made any peace overtures. NobleCircle Rituals have ta choose between havin' T'Holly or T'Hawthorn for Council workin's."

"And they usually choose me," T'Holly said.

Tab snorted. "The problem with you, Holm the Elder, is that ya can't admit a mistake, from the decor of your Residence ta breaking the GreatSeal. That'll cost ya someday." He glanced at

D'Holly, who'd been playing with Meserv next to her chair. The kitten batted at a bright blue ribbon dangling from her fingers. Tab snorted again as the ribbon swung out of Meserv's reach and he failed to follow and pounce.

"Have a good evening, Passiflora." Tab ducked a nod.

She lifted her gaze from the kitten and smiled sweetly. "The music muse is whispering in my ear. I'll work a while at my craft." She sent an intimate smile to her HeartMate as she rose from the table and the men stood, too. "And you all will work at yours." Her glance touched Holm's throat and softness came to her eyes. "Don't dawdle in your wooing, dear. I'd like to be a MotherSire before the year ends."

His father looked at Holm gravely, as if considering the escalating conflict with T'Hawthorn. "I agree. The sooner the next generation of Hollys is bred, the better."

Holm gritted his teeth, but still smiled at his Mamá.

Tinne shot Holm a concerned look.

Holm deliberately placed his napkin upon his plate and rose. "About the feud, I'm sure you're right, it's heating up." He touched his brother's arm as he passed Tinne, and nodded to G'Uncle Tab. "We definitely need to strategize."

Tab said, "The cuzes from the countryside are doin' well, an' should come here for further trainin'." He smiled briefly. "It's always been the reward for passin' the first test, ta be accepted at T'Holly Residence ta live and drill." He followed T'Holly and Holm from the dining room. "Tinne will be workin' with me at The Green Knight with my other students. That means you, Holm, will give our five cuzes intermediate instruction."

Holm nodded, but his heart clenched a moment in revolt at switching his thoughts from love to war.

Ten

Lark awoke to music. Soft and soothing, yet holding an underlying lilt of exuberance—almost a dance. It complemented the heady fragrance of the roses perfectly.

"Bélla? Wake up, my delightful Bélla." Holm's voice issued from the scrybowl. His tones contrasted with the music, deep and sensual. Just the sound of him caused her skin to tingle. How *could* he have such an affect on her?

"Bélla?"

She decided to ignore him, burying herself in the permamoss bedsponge and drawing a fluffup pillow over her head. But that muted the music, and it was simply too exquisite to dismiss. It refreshed her spirit. She'd slept poorly, tormented by dreams she couldn't, wouldn't remember. Dreams that featured street fights and blood.

"Bélla?" The ace street fighter whispered.

Lark sat up and threw the pillow at the wall.

"Bélla, my Bélla?"

"My scry and viz location are coded, GreatSir. They should not have been available to you." She raised her voice so it carried to the mainspace and her scrybowl.

"You don't like the music?" He sounded hurt.

"I don't like Nobles who think that laws, and even common

rules of courtesy, don't apply to them. It's the Noble class's most serious and dangerous flaw. It lacks respect."

The music continued, but Holm remained silent for a full minute. "Forgive me. Done." He disconnected and the bewitching music stopped.

Lark rose with a sigh and rubbed the back of her neck. Phyll and the fitful sleep had left her with a headache. She summoned PainRelief from the medicinal no-time storage unit, unwilling to spend the most minor Healing energy on herself.

Grumbling, she stripped off her thin silkeen nightshirt as she went to the waterfall and bent her neck beneath the wet heat. She hadn't been on call and today was a restday so she hadn't dressed in quilted pajamas.

When she emerged from her shower, a luscious aroma of freshly baked pastry filled her apartment. Phyll danced around her feet with ever-increasing yowls. *Food, food, FOOD!*

Lark plucked a robe off a bedroom hook and tossed it on, then walked to the mainspace. Streaks of soundless red lightning emerged from her scrybowl. An urgent call.

A quiet bell rang at intervals from her collection box.

Holm Holly scried. He sent Food and music, Phyll said.

That wasn't all he sent. As she opened her collection box, an angry, ruffled Meserv jumped out. He pounced on Phyll and they immediately became a whirl of growling, rolling kittens. Lark watched helplessly, not feeling up to separating and scolding them, particularly not for acting on natural instincts.

The mouthwatering scent wafting from a white carton demanded immediate action. She lifted the top of the thin box and licked her lips when she saw an assortment of muffins, tarts, turnovers, and pastry horns filled with cocoa and sprinkled with siftsugar and cinnamon. The man was diabolical. She broke off a piece of berry tart and let the flaky pastry dissolve on her tongue. The sweetness of fruit filled her mouth. Shutting her eyes, she savored.

A top-of-the-line baker had created such delicious masterpieces, someone from the Family of T'Wheat or D'Maple. Celtans as a whole had sweet tooths, and Lark was no exception. She hadn't had a pastry like this since the last time she dined at T'Hawthorn Residence.

Grabbing a bespelled cleantowl to erase every trace of food

from her fingers, she lifted a translucent green flexistrip from
the box. Music. No title or composer showed on the slip. Lark
put the flexistrip in the entertainment slot and activated it. The
music she'd awakened to filled the room with peaceful joy.

Phyll and Meserv trotted over. Phyll sported a scratch on his
nose, Meserv one by his ear.

Food, they chorused.

Lark eyed Meserv's bulging tummy. "Holm was awake and
active. Didn't he feed you already?"

Big sapphire eyes in a tiny kitten face exuded innocence.
Food! Phyll pawed at her foot.

She picked her kitten up. "Very well. I'll get some hot
furrabeast bites and greenmix from the no-time." Phyll wiggled
in her hands and looked around her arm to where the collection
box stood open. *Cocoa mousse!*

Lark frowned. She gazed into Phyll's emerald eyes and
said, "D'Ash's feeding instructions said nothing about cocoa
mousse."

Phyll scrunched his face. His whiskers twitched. Then he
opened his eyes and smiled a sly cat-smile. *Milk. Cocoa mousse
made from milk. Milk es-sen-tial for Cats. Milk builds strong
bones, strong bodies.*

Calcium. She narrowed her eyes at Phyll. "How do you know
that cocoa mousse is made from milk?"

I visit T'Ash chef with Sire.

Lark sighed. Everyone in Druida knew Phyll's Sire, Zanth,
terrorized the T'Ash chef. "Two spoonfuls of filling, that's all.
No pastry." She put Phyll down on the kitchen floor and pulled
his gently steaming breakfast from no-time.

Pastry never good at T'Ash's. Phyll attacked his food.

"Not with a nervous chef." Lark put her hands on her hips.
"Your food won't vanish in two seconds if you eat slower."

Cocoa mousse will. Meserv.

Horror hit her. She ran for the collection box. A small
orange-and-cream tail waved above the edge of the box. When
she reached it, Meserv had each of his front paws in a tart and
his nose buried in a cocoa mousse pastry horn.

She laughed and lifted him. As she did, her hand brushed a
message button discreetly attached to the side of the box. A holo
of Holm Holly formed.

He inclined his head, his face serious. "Forgive me for intruding, Bélla." He opened his mouth, closed it, shrugged. "I am an impatient man." He shrugged again and tried a charming smile. It warmed her. "Please invite me for breakfast." His image raised a hand. "I have a full day and will not be able to see you again until the ball tonight."

The ball tonight? Memory tugged. Another charity ball—this one for the Downwind shelters funded by T'Ash. She had promised to go. Damn.

Holm's holo winked out. Her scrybowl jingled, clashing with the music that had transformed into a long, romantic melody plucking at her heart.

Lark crossed to her scrybowl of prismatic glass. "Here," she said. The water in the bowl swirled, and once again Holm looked out at her. He smiled. But what impressed Lark was the instant pleasure that had lit his eyes when he first saw her, then another emotion, a flash of uncertainty.

"Bélla?" His smile went wry. "How many times must I apologize?" His gaze fixed on her mouth. "You have a berry stain next to your lips."

"That's all the pastry I've had," she said in mock exasperation and bent down to scoop up Meserv and hold him above the scrybowl so Holm could see. "This cat of yours . . ."

Meserv's nose looked like a blueblackberry. Orange and red stickiness coated his whiskers. A gob of cocoa mousse decorated one ear. He opened huge blue eyes. And burped.

Holm laughed. "He's a charmer, isn't he? Mamá can't refuse him."

"I didn't let him feast on purpose. He took the opportunity when I fed Phyll a *nutritious* meal."

"Good strategy, Meserv," Holm said.

Meserv rumbled a purr.

Now Holm's gaze looked as innocent as his kitten's. "I can be there in an instant. With more pastries. Please invite me to breakfast, Bélla."

She hesitated.

"Do I have to apologize again, Bélla?" he repeated.

She sighed. "No. Come, then. For breakfast *only*."

He grinned. "I'm there." The scrybowl went clear.

Lark hastily placed Meserv on his paws. Her hands reached

for her hair, then she stopped and her lips compressed. She would not primp for the man. If he wanted to visit her, he could take her as she was. No, that wasn't good phrasing. If he wanted to visit her, he'd have to look at her commoncloth robe. She glanced down and found her nipples peaked against the thin fabric. She raced for her bedroom and a thick velvet dressing gown that matched her eyes.

A couple of minutes later she heard a knock on her door and smiled. It hadn't occurred to her that he'd 'port to her hall. She thought he'd show up in the mainspace. The location of that room and the sofa would be imprinted on his memory.

She smoothed her rich, purple velvet robe, drew in a breath, and opened the door.

Holm cocked his head. "You're playing the music."

"It's lovely."

"It's a gift for my— for you."

"Thank you. Who composed— Ow!" Lark cried out as Phyll nipped her bare foot.

Meserv eating ALL THE MOUSSE! Phyll shouted loud enough for anyone telepathic in the building to hear him. He hopped up and down on all paws. *I can't get him!*

Lark whirled and ran to the mainspace, Holm laughing behind her. Meserv had wedged himself and the pastry box within a ring of vases burgeoned with blue-to-lavender roses.

Between laughs, Holm whisked his kitten from his treasure and hiding place and teleported him into the kitchen. "Clean yourself up, Meserv, or I'll take a wet cloth to you."

Meserv hissed.

Holm crouched down in front of Phyll, who stared at the table as if calculating his jump. "I have more." Holm's voice lilted. Phyll whipped around and Lark noted the box in Holm's hands for the first time.

With a gentle touch for the fragile carton, Holm opened it. Scents drifted from it and Lark's stomach grumbled. Holm laughed up at her. "Ah, my own sweet is human, then."

"Very," Lark replied.

Holm lifted out a pastry horn stuffed full of cocoa mousse. Phyll whined and sat, now eyeing the treat and Holm's large fingers as if he might try to snatch it. Lark's mouth watered.

"Don't think you can win a fight with *me*, GentleSir Phyll,"

Holm said, but dipped a finger in the horn and held it to the kitten.

Phyll licked it.

"That's unsanitary," Lark said, wishing he'd offered her the first bite—just as he had to Phyll, with his finger. She could imagine the taste of cocoa mousse and Holm, then swirling her tongue around his finger, taking it into her mouth. The thought nearly made her swoon.

Holm raised his eyebrows. "Who are you concerned about, Phyll or me?"

"What?" asked Lark.

Holm stood and broke off the other end of the pastry and popped the thing into her mouth. Light, rich cocoa taste exploded in her mouth. Textures caressed her tongue—frothy mousse, flaky pastry, slick siftsugar and cinnamon.

"I think I've found a secret weapon to discombobulate my own delightful Bélla. Cocoa mousse."

Me, too, said Phyll. *More for Me.*

Lark gathered her wits. "Two spoonfuls, only." She went toward the kitchen, licking her lips.

"Bélla, you can have two entire pastries." Holm's dark voice tempted her.

The last, lingering note of the music was spoiled by the sound of retching. Lark and Holm ran to the kitchen threshold as Meserv vomited on the floor.

Lark looked at the regurgitated food, appalled. "That is *your* kitten. That is *your* problem."

Holm sighed. "Not again."

I never throw up, Phyll said virtuously, trotting in to look at the puddle and Meserv.

"Watch and learn this spell," Holm said, taking Lark's hand. "It's easy." His mind brushed hers and Lark opened to him. She gauged the amount and variation of Flair. He spiraled their hands together and intoned, "Mess begone!"

The vomit vanished.

Lark pulled her hand away, still staring at the floor. "There's a stain on my carpet." The deep blue pile showed a dark brown spot.

Holm shifted his feet. "I'm afraid you'll have to take care of that yourself."

Lark watched Meserv trot to examine Phyll's empty bowl.

Holm must have felt her dismay. "Don't worry about the kitten. Stomach upsets are common among cats, especially kittens, and once they get the stuff out of their bellies, they're usually perfectly fine." She heard the echo of a feminine voice in her thoughts and knew Holm had spoken to D'Ash.

Lark blinked, thinking back to the brief scan she'd made of Meserv's vomit, now analyzing it as a Healer. "There were no greens in that vomit. Did Meserv eat his greens today?"

Red tinged Holm's cheeks. He glanced away. "I don't know. My Mamá insists on feeding him."

Lips thinning, Lark turned and poked a finger into his chest. "D'Ash provided me with sprouting greens. I give them to Phyll at the intervals she instructed. You make sure that you, *you,* the FamMan of this animal, the caretaker, feed him."

"Yes, my Lady." In a quick move he'd captured her hand and rained noisy kisses on it. "Forgive me, my Lady."

Hot embarrassment prickled her face. "Stop that, you fool."

"Bélla" His quiet, low tone was the only warning he'd changed the topic. "You know I want you to call me 'Lover.' "

"No," she choked.

Again he caught her hand and lifted it to his mouth, this time brushing his lips back and forth across the back. His soft nuzzling lips caused heat to spark inside her. She quelled the incipient blaze by drawing her hand away and stepping back.

Food! Phyll yowled.

"Yes, food," Lark agreed. "Greens for your brother there—"

And two spoonfuls of cocoa mousse for Me. Mousse I will enjoy. Mousse that will stay in My stomach. Mousse that will pass through My in-tes-tines. Mousse that I will—

"That's enough, Phyll," Lark said, shoving a bowl of greens from no-time to Meserv, and hurriedly plopping more than two spoonfuls of mousse in another bowl for Phyll.

Holm grinned. "You can tell that kitten's been spending time at a HealingHall."

"Yes." She washed and dried her hands and turned to the pastry box. "Have you eaten? Do you want some of these?"

"Do I want to breakfast with my Lady?" Holm rephrased her question. "Of course I do." He plucked a berry tart for himself. "These are not the circumstances I wanted for our first breakfast, but I am a reasonable man, I will take what I can get." His voice held that dark note again.

"Milk, caff, cinnamoncaff, tea?" Lark asked.

"Milk," he answered.

Before she busied herself with getting the small meal together, Lark nodded to the floor. "Remove that stain."

He frowned.

"I would have thought that now and again you would have seen a blow to the stomach that caused such a reaction." She pulled down a cobalt blue platter painted with bright summer flowers, put the platter on a large wooden tray, pastries on the platter and fussed with blue linen napkins.

"So, we're talking about my fighting?" Holm asked casually. "Yes, I've seen vomiting. I just never had to clean it up. Blood, now. I can get blood out of wood or stone." He went over to stand directly beside the stain.

"Vomit, blood, urine, they're all protein stains," Lark said tightly. "My carpet is hybrid Celtaearth wool, so it's organic like wood and stone. Try the spell."

His mind brushed against hers, like a large hand sliding down her back, soothing her. She remembered he'd touched her like that, comforting. It eased her.

Then she felt the intensity of his thoughts, the leap and twist of his Flair. A whiff of fresh herbs wafted through the kitchen, but was overpowered by the scent of the roses. When Lark looked at the carpet, the stain was gone.

Holm lifted his head, and when his eyes met hers, they were steel-gray and serious. "I'll take that," he said, picking up the tray. "Why don't you get the drinks?"

She'd automatically pulled two cylinders of cold milk from the no-time, and they stood on the counter.

Now his eyes were gentle as was the curve of his lips. "We don't have to talk about my fighting, Bélla, not now. I know it's a large problem between us. It can wait a while." His eyes darkened. "But we do have to talk about other things: this morning, my actions and your reaction, and I'll apologize again. This evening and the ball, and how we will be together."

"I don't think—"

"I don't think you're a coward, Bélla. We have concerns

between us that need to be discussed." Carrying the tray, he went into the mainspace.

Lark watched as his body filled the doorway from the kitchen to the mainspace, then as he went to the sofa—the long, wide red sofa that they'd rolled on together in passion.

"I said I was a reasonable man, Bélla, not a patient one." His smile quirked lopsidedly, and he held out a hand.

Eleven

❤

*H*e set the tray to hover by the sofa. *That offered hand was* becoming like an endearment between them. Despite all inner warnings, she found herself placing her hand in his. Immediately the mind-bond between them strengthened. The circuit of energy between them snapped shut, and Lark rocked back on her heels at the strength of it.

Taking advantage of her momentary confusion, Holm drew her to him, then settled her down on the couch beside him and moved the large tray to cover both their laps.

"Very smooth," Lark said, when her voice returned, still feeling the buzz of cycling vitality, trying to simply control it and move on with common actions. His mind felt as close to her as his body, outside surfaces touching. Warmth and strength and sheer vigor emanated from him, impinging on the atmosphere around her and fizzing through their bond. "I had anticipated putting the tray between us."

"Now, Bélla, what made you think I'd allow anything to come between us on this sofa?" He patted the red leather. "I have very fond memories of this sofa, with only a few clothes between us, as now." He nudged her knees with his own, causing the milk to slosh in the cylinders she'd just put on the tray.

"And"—he grinned, taking a large bite of berry tart and

licking his lips as efficiently as Phyll—"I anticipate having other, even better memories of this sofa in the future." He grinned at her, shameless and charming and amused at both himself and her. The pure joy of life and humor circled from him to her.

Lark decided to ignore his grin and his comment and eat. She closed her eyes as she savored the cocoa mousse in the light cinnamon-dusted pastry horn. "Who made this wonderful treat?"

Holm's wicked chuckle had her eyelids flying open. "A younger son of D'Honey became the T'Holly chef. He has a minimal amount of Flair, can only work the spells common to all Celtans, so his Family didn't value him. They overlooked his other skills, and now he's been adopted into our Family." Holm leaned back and watched her. "He's not a bad hand with a short-sword, either."

The casual reference to fighting made her stiffen. Lark sensed he watched her reaction, and felt her withdrawal. He frowned.

Two polite mews came from the kitchen doorway. Two orange-and-cream kittens stood, tails identically crooked. One stared out from wary green eyes, the other from lazy blue. The blue-eyed cat was fatter.

Human talk, Phyll concluded. *Boring. We will go play in the bedroom.* He trotted away.

Meserv swept a stray sprig of green from his muzzle with a tiny pink tongue and burped. He followed his brother. *Or We will sleep.*

With a Word, Holm cleaned his fingers. He slipped his arm around her waist. "Now, my dear one, my Bélla. We will talk."

His gray eyes remained steel-serious. His fingers stroked the nap of her velvet robe, and she perceived the pleasure he took from its texture and the flesh beneath. She became aware she was naked beneath the robe.

"I'm sorry I trespassed on your privacy this morning."

"It's my restday, I wanted to sleep in," Lark mumbled, setting the pastry down. The shadow of nightmares loomed in the back of her mind. She wished that her night had been like previous ones, tossing and turning because of Holm Holly.

"What's this?" With his free hand Holm nudged her chin up. "You had nightmares?" He frowned as if trying to grasp the wisps of recollection ghosting through her mind.

"That's right. Of fighting. You are in a feud with my Family, if you recall. Your brother, your cuz, and you were in a street fight just a few days ago." She pushed his hand away, tried to stand, but he pulled her closer. Though she felt his intention to comfort, it wasn't what she wanted. "Let me go!" She backed it with a snap in her thoughts.

He released her immediately, frowning. "When you speak in that tone, when your thoughts go flash-white, you can't bear restriction," he said, puzzling it out. "It was like that this morning. My knowing your scry locale bruised a tender spot. Some place within you that is hurt and angry."

She walked stiffly away from him and tried to close shields down against him. With effort, he kept a golden stream of emotion and thought connecting them.

"No, Bélla," he said. The light from the tall, arched windows behind the sofa highlighted the sculpted bones of his face. He looked noble and powerful, yet something about the elegance of his bearing, his concentration on her, caught at her heart.

"No," he repeated. "You choose. Keep the mental-emotional link between us open and our bodies physically apart, or sit next to me, my arm around you, and the link shut. One or the other."

She scowled at him, but heard the adamant in his words. One or the other. Her body chose for her. She was accustomed to linking with others to practice her profession, but she was all too needy for human touch. Even Trif, an affectionate person, had taken Lark's unspoken and cool manner at face value, and hugged her only occasionally. She walked back to the couch as if under a spell, fascinated by the line of his shoulders, the clean muscularity of his torso. His darkening eyes held hers, even as he teleported the tray to the kitchen, where she heard it click onto the counter.

When she sat, it was facing him. With one hand, he brushed her hair from her face, his fingers on her cheek infinitely gentle.

He bent and kissed her. The need that spiraled from him held a tide of pure lust. She cut the link.

Holm drew back, cheeks flushed, eyes dilated, and breath ragged. She knew if she looked down at his lap, she'd see his shaft hard in his trous. His arousal had quickened with a speed and urgency that surprised her.

"You distract me far too easily," Holm smiled, the genuine smile that pleased her more than all his practiced, charming ones. Not bothering to hide his trembling fingers, which beguiled her still more, he traced her closed lips.

"Your thoughts are soft now," he said.

Lark realized that somehow there was still a tie, something barely there on the unconscious level, something she'd never known before. And Holm distracted *her*. She couldn't think or analyze it right now, when he looked as if she might taste better than his berry tart.

He shoved himself back on the sofa, the depth of it accommodating the long muscles of his thighs, and he clasped one of her hands within his own.

"When your mind reaches flash-white you will not be held or bound by thought or hand—or reason? Why is that?" He played with her fingers, as if the action made him think better. "It sparks a hurt and angry reaction. Let's see. What did you say this morning?" He fell silent.

"Holm, it's nothing to discuss or worry about. This situation is hopeless," she said, trying to convince herself.

He shot her a stern look. "This 'situation' is not going away, Bélla. It is real, it is here and now, and it will continue. You must think I'm a fool if you believe I will walk away from such a strong bond between us. You're—" He stopped his own words by pressing her fingers to his mouth. The tip of his tongue tasted her. She tried to wiggle her fingers away.

"None of that," he said. "We had a bargain, physical or emotional-mental contact. Earlier this morning, you said: 'I don't like Nobles who think that laws, and even common rules of courtesy, don't apply to them. It's the Noble class's most serious and dangerous flaw. It lacks respect.'"

Hearing the truthful bitterness of her own words made her flinch.

"You see"—Holm squeezed her hand—"a physical reaction of pain."

Her lips pressed together in anger. "You are a very powerful Noble. You have great Flair and rank and gilt. Most people with great Flair and rank and gilt do not think of the laws as applying to them."

"People like you, Bélla? You have great Flair and rank and gilt."

"I consider myself a commoner."

"No! You are the only daughter of a FirstFamilies Great-House. That's the blood running through your veins, that's the gene pool you come from. Your husband was born Downwind but rose above his disadvantages."

She wanted to move from the couch, stand up and pace. She tugged at her hand. He held on tight.

"Physical or emotional-mental, Bélla."

Giving him a scathing glance, she opened the turmoil of her emotions to him and leapt to her feet. He wanted contact with her, did he? She waited for him to recoil. Nothing happened. Curiosity replaced a little of her anger.

After a few seconds, the hint of a smile curved his mouth. "Strong, turbulent emotions are standard amongst the Hollys, Bélla."

She hissed.

His smile broadened. "You sound like Meserv or Phyll." Holm inserted a lilting, hypnotic note into his voice; the same effect swirled through their tenuous bond. "Now, tell me why you cannot bear to be held or restrained at moments."

"I had a very restricted childhood."

Holm raised an eyebrow. "And? There is more."

"Since I had no HeartMate, I was expected to marry at T'Hawthorn's orders."

"You chose someone else." A rough note had entered his voice, and a thread of pain twisted through his thoughts.

"I chose Ethyn. My father raged and stormed and threatened. He was furious. I broke off relations with T'Hawthorns."

"You had T'Heathers."

Lark assayed a small smile. "They're a FirstFamily, also. They disapproved. No one respected my choice or respected *me* enough to understand and welcome Ethyn."

"Everyone tried to bind you to their will." Holm frowned as if trying to sort her emotions out.

"I was still a journeyman Healer, in my last year. Being a potential FirstLevel, my Masters loaded me down with work and timeschedules and examinations. . . ."

"So you fought free of one cage, but had to abide with the other if you wished to fulfil the potential of your Flair."

His emotions now cushioned her own, bolsters she could rest on, strength she could rely on.

She made an abrupt gesture. "Life was hectic, but manageable and satisfying."

His head lifted as if he'd caught the whiff of something. She felt a gentle probe and let it disappear into her emotional storm. Yet his eyes narrowed as if he were trying to judge the relationship between her and Ethyn and weigh it with that between himself and her. She hurried on with her story.

"When I lived with Ethyn as a commoner, as students in a shabby part of Druida, I saw how far above the rest of the people the Nobles are—"

"Seemed," corrected Holm.

She turned a puzzled face to him.

"We're human and have the same emotions as everyone else."

She gave a ladylike snort. "You cannot understand how your great Flair and rank and wealth and power isolate you from reality." Her lips pinched a moment. "Then Ethyn died in a stupid street fight, trying to help Nobles who wanted nothing of him. Helping men who hadn't prevailed against odds to win laurels as he did, but took all that came their way, even the death of a Healer in their fight, as merely their due." She shook. "When someone flouts the laws at my expense and for their own profit, I'm infuriated. I don't put up with it. I am a FirstLevel Healer and powerful enough in Flair that I can win my way when I want."

Lark laughed shortly. "Except with my father. When I'm with him, I revert to the child. I can barely hold my own against his will." Her mouth turned down. "I can only hold my own by distancing myself. And he will never change, never value my wishes. He will always seek to manipulate and intimidate me into his mold. I don't wish to live where I will never gain the respect I'm due." She lifted her chin defiantly. "That's why I applied for the Gael City HealingHall."

"Bélla—"

She rounded on him. "Then you stroll into my life and believe I should give you anything you want."

"It's not that way! There's a bond between us." He rose to keep pace with her, striding up and down the mainspace with her, not touching her, only keeping the bond steady. "I'm sorry I scried and vized without formally getting your number from you. I thought only of contacting you, of being here with you, of renewing our bond. When I asked T'Holly ResidenceLibrary for your scry locale, I didn't ask if it was coded. That is my fault, and I apologize for invading your privacy. I respect and value you, no one more!"

She didn't believe him. Scowling, she pointed her finger at him. "And you, Holm Holly, HollyHeir of the GreatHouse Holly, of the FirstFamilies"—she almost mocked him as she recited his rank—"have you never failed to receive what you wanted?"

Holm stared at her incredulously. Anger flickered in his eyes. He shook his head. "You seem to have forgotten that my brother Tinne and I were stranded in the harshest landscape on this continent. It took more than an eightday to trek to the nearest town, then make it back to Druida. It wasn't an easy journey, I assure you. Luck was with us and we survived."

Though he didn't project them, Lark received emotions and images—the smallness of the lifepod, the horror of his brother and himself as they catapulted through the sky, orbited the planet, then plummeted down.

His voice grew softer. "I've experienced the cold, hunger, thirst and lack of shelter that Ethyn might have known."

Lark saw it all. Holm and Tinne in shock and abandoned near the foot of the 241 mountain range, already winter when Druida was still late autumn. Sleeping together on a featureless plain, shivering, trying to conserve warmth and life. Trudging through the rugged landscape, battered by the screaming mollyck wind that insinuated defeat into their minds if they didn't keep their shields up, melting snow to slake their thirst.

Then a horrible misstep as Tinne fell into the Great Washington Boghole—something especially hurtful edged that memory, flashing by before she could analyze it. She only knew it had changed both brothers and their relationship.

Holm's words interlaced the pictures. "I've also endured the fear that I might never see my home and Family again, the knowledge my Mamá and father would be sick with worry and grief."

She knew that had been the worst. The spending of Flair by each of them and both linked, trying to contact their kin, frustrated by the mollyck, until they were exhausted and in worse shape than before.

"I've known leeches from the boghole, animal attacks. Tinne and I gave exhibitions of fighting for meals and supplies at an outpost or two between Lake Meraj and Ragge Town. If we hadn't been who we were, Hollys and carrying more than one weapon apiece, we wouldn't have survived."

The trip came to her in flashes—dark smelly camps of men where they provided entertainment, hiring out as guards for a merchant from Ragge Town to Tory Town, haggling and pawning their daggers to convince a freighter airship to fly them to Druida.

He fell silent and Lark sifted through her own memories of the day they'd arrived back in Druida. A day that would never be forgotten in Celtan history, House histories, or those who lived through it.

She'd been called to Heal that horrible day when a Fire-Bombspell swept the Council Chamber, a spell that consumed flesh and couldn't be stopped. Though she'd focused on minimizing the deaths, draining her Flair recklessly to save and Heal, she vaguely remembered a pair of shabby men who'd helped carry the wounded, lay out the dead. Holm and Tinne Holly.

Holm gasped. For a moment they both remembered the slaughter in odd, disjointed images from different angles; the carnage, the smell of burnt flesh and urine and blood and death. The helplessness to stop the plague. Grief.

They had shared that experience.

Lark covered her face with her hands. Holm led her back to the sofa to sit within the circle of his arms. "I'm sorry." Her voice came out muffled.

"You had cause to reproach me," he said. "Both before and after that little expedition I've been as arrogant and complacent as you accused. From now on, you'll scold me and remind me of my flaws, but you'll also know that I, too, have experienced deprivation. Adversity did me a deal of good."

Lark felt his large hands on her shoulders, then they inched down, slow and caressing, to her elbows and up to her hands. He lifted her palms from her face without much effort.

"Your emotions are not flash-white. I can hold you, and comfort you and—"

An appointment globe appeared. "HollyHeir reminder. Quarter-septhour notice. The five new cuzes have been welcomed to the Residence and chosen rooms. Your first session as Master for intermediate training is due to start in Sparring Room Two in quarter septhour: lessons in coordinating defensive sparring and unusual techniques." It clicked a bit. "After the training, you are allotted a septhour to refresh and review the legal affairs of the House before your quarterly meeting with Legal Adviser T'Yarrow." With a flash the sphere disappeared. Holm winced. "I hate that thing."

Lark smiled. "You have a busy day."

"An appointment with T'Yarrow," Holm grumbled. "Guaranteed to last all afternoon."

"An Heir's duty," Lark said.

He snorted. "Only because Father argued with T'Yarrow, and used that as an excuse to hand over the dry stuff to me."

Rising, Lark opened the door for him. He stood slowly, his steps to her equally leisurely. When he reached her, he shut the door and framed her face with his hands. The bond between them tugged, vibrated, as he tested it.

"You can feel that, can't you, even though we aren't consciously linked? It's not something I've ever had with anyone else, with *anyone* else, and I'm not going to walk away from it. I want to test that bond. Experiment," he whispered as he lowered his mouth to hers.

Even before his lips touched hers, her heart hammered hard in her chest, anticipating the swirl of feeling that would envelope her. The desire to be with this man in every way could become an addiction. She'd have to be careful. Then his mouth closed over hers, caressing, and her mind fogged. His lips opened hers, his tongue sliding against hers, probing. She shut her eyes. The taste of him was all that was masculine and vital, another thing that could become addicting.

He groaned and his hands glided down to pull her hips against his rigid flesh. She moaned at the feel of him, reminding her that she was a woman and the intimacies of passion she could share with him.

His hands squeezed her hips a final time and he tore himself away from her. When she opened her eyelids and her glance met his, the light of desire turned his eyes silver.

"I must go." His voice was thick. "It's a good thing I have five young men who'll work the tension from me." He wrinkled his nose. "Sparring Room Two, it's only slightly less scented with sweat than the others. Meserv," he called.

The kitten ambled from the bedroom.

Holm stooped and picked his Fam up. Holm's index finger stroked the top of the kitten's head and Meserv purred. "Petting Meserv also helps to keep me sane. Still, this breakfast was worth my suffering."

His stare pinned her as she stood, the current between them charged with sparking energy. "You know that however complicated this situation is around us, I will not be deterred in seeing you. You know that the attraction between us is more than simple lust, there is the bond. You have accepted me into your life." He dipped his head in courtesy. "That is great progress. Blessed be."

"Blessed be," Lark echoed, still shaken from the force of the truths he'd just spoken. Before she could think to say anything else, he disappeared.

For a moment, Lark considered returning to bed, but knew it would be futile. As she tidied up the mainspace and kitchen, she thought of the gifts he'd given her that morning: fabulous music, exquisite pastry, a minor spell, spine-tingling kisses, soft caresses, a strong link she could rely upon. He'd listened and tried to understand her, then given her the most important gift of all, acceptance of her feelings and herself *as* herself. Respect.

During his recital of his trek she'd sensed the hurt—a pain like the sore mass of spasmed muscle. It centered around Holm and his brother and the Great Washington Boghole. She could help there, if she dared and he allowed. She knew enough about Holm by now to understand that some things he'd push to the back of his mind and expect them to vanish or resolve themselves without effort. If they were together, she could help him Heal that hurt—

Her hands twitched as her blood still hummed with the energy they'd raised between them. She couldn't sit at home and rest, but walking the beach would only remind her of Holm. There was only one thing to be done—she'd go to T'Horehound's garden and practice her primary creative skill, and make a gift for Holm.

Twelve

♥

$\mathcal{A}$ *few moments later Lark wandered in* T'Horehound's huge estate garden, nerves calming. She'd chosen to live at Mid-Class Lodge for the large courtyard garden, but after a few months, she'd been frustrated at the lack of floral variety she needed for her art. She'd approached T'Horehound, a close friend of Culpeper, and T'Horehound had graciously given her leave to use his garden. She hadn't been there since the start of summer and wondered why she'd been so overcome by work that she couldn't take the pleasure of simply rambling the paths.

Now she studied the plants with an eye toward her craft, a basket on her arm. Even as she touched one plant, then another, testing the fragrance they left on her fingers, Lark called herself a fool. Getting involved with Holm Holly was stupid, foolish, idiotic.

Then she reassured herself. She might be able to get away with a passionate affair with Holm Holly. A *short* lusty fling. If she was very, very discreet, her father would never find out and use the knowledge against her.

She heard kitten whufflings and saw Phyll leap from a leafy bush to attack a stray twig on the path. Flipping it into the air, he let it fall and pounced again, tossing it, pouncing, catching it in his claws, and finally chewing it.

Wistfully she plucked a strand of flamingbells and carried it to her nose, inhaling the scent that reminded her of Holm's. Perhaps she could indulge herself this once, without thought of Family, or Family interference. Her father would intervene, completely, finally, and even fatally, if he found out she bedded Holm Holly.

She placed stems in her wide basket and continued on, choosing blooms and requesting the plant's permission to pick, then gently severing the flower, and in thanks saying a simple spell to Heal the plant and send it energy to grow.

By the time she reached the work arbor, she'd convinced herself that the foolish act would be ignoring Holm's offer and turning him away. No woman in her right mind would refuse sex with Holm Holly. She grinned. From all accounts, he was perfect in bed—at least that had been the rumor for years. Just thinking about rolling around on bedsheets with him made a low ache settle in her core and her blood simmer.

Yes, keeping their association on a quick, physical basis would be just the thing. She dismissed the fact that with touching of minds, with simply speaking to each other of weighty matters, they had passed the point of being simple bedmates.

As for making this gift for him, it wasn't truly a gift—more like a test. Would the fighting Holly accept a floral headpiece from her? Would he wear it?

She had no doubt he was solid in his own masculinity and self-worth. The only real question was whether he'd accept such a personal gift from her, a gift made with her own hands for him alone. Would that be more than what he might want from her? It was a risk.

She smiled again as she recalled their last kiss. No, he wanted more. He yearned for ecstasy, just as she did. Surely something so hot and tempestuous would flame high, then burn itself out. It couldn't possibly last. It would be secret.

That sent an additional thrill through her. A secret. Something for herself alone, shared only with him. If she was careful, she could even keep Trif guessing.

How delicious. A forbidden affair. Something else to give spice to the idea. A secret, forbidden, flaming fling. The words made her lips curve further and her fingers fly in crafting the wreath, intertwining the stems, angling and showcasing certain blossoms, and the cluster of Holly leaves that meant "foresight" in the language of flowers. As much as she needed foresight, she didn't seem to be able to act on reason.

She pulled silver seagem beads from her tunic pocket and threaded them through the whole, then stepped back and admired the effect. Almost perfect—just a twitch or two here and there . . .

"Perfect," a cool voice said from behind her, "as always. You have a true gift, my dear."

Lark turned to see T'Horehound standing in a shaft of sunlight, holding a quietly purring Phyll. A tall man with gray hair, his body was almost attenuated in its thinness. He wore a long simple robe the same green as his plants.

"Greetyou, T'Horehound," Lark said. "Thank you, as always, for letting me use your garden." She reached out and corrected a drooping alstroemeria.

A smile touched his mobile lips. "And I thank you for your thanks." He nodded toward the flowers on the worktable that she'd culled from her pickings for T'Horehound's own wreath.

He looked at her wreath and sighed. "I see that it is no use in continuing our standard conversation with a request that you wed me, or my Heir, or my Heir's Son. You have found another mate, again and at last."

Lark blinked and frowned in confusion.

T'Horehound gestured to the wreath for Holm. "Look at the flowers you wove for him, my dear Lark. They include two-hearts, deep red carnations, blue violets."

She stared, noticing her choices, now. Blood drained from her face and hands, making her fingers clumsy, then still. "No," she whispered. "No. It cannot be any more than a simple romp."

T'Horehound lifted his thin gray eyebrows. "My dear Lark, you are not the woman for a simple romp. I know it. You know it." He indicated the headpiece again. "I'm sure he knows it."

The GrandLord's brows lowered in concentration. "He must. The style you have woven is for a Nobleman, of taste and elegance. A passionate man. A man of honor who will not bruise something as fragile as these blooms or your heart." T'Horehound raised his eyes to meet hers.

Lark stuck her bottom lip out and jutted her chin. "I could be a woman for a quick tumble. If I wanted."

He smiled, showing even teeth, then shook his head.

She lifted her chin one centimeter more. "I could. That's what I want."

T'Horehound's laugh matched Phyll's cat-chuckle.

Lark grabbed the rest of the flowers and started weaving them efficiently, almost automatically.

"Another thing," T'Horehound said, rubbing the side of Phyll's muzzle. "If you have any influence with D'Ash, my dear, I would like you to put in a word for me. I wish for one of these." He lifted Phyll and examined him as if he were an infinitely amusing and precious object.

"I'm sorry," Lark said. "I received him from young Vinni—T'Vine."

A shiver coursed down T'Horehound's long body. "Thank you, no. No need to mention my whim to that boy. I would rather not meet him." T'Horehound lowered Phyll to his paws. Her Fam gamboled over to her.

T'Horehound studied her for a moment, then smiled sadly. "I will leave you to your work, my dear. Merry meet."

"And merry part," Lark said.

"And merry meet again," T'Horehound said, strolling down a stone path bordered by weeping sylvias and soon lost from view.

Lark finished her offering for T'Horehound, then scowled at her wreath for Holm. Ruthlessly she plucked the ferns and flowers signifying love—almost a HeartMate love, and she knew she had no HeartMate—from the circle and set them aside to weave a small headpiece for one of the T'Horehound children.

Now she prowled the garden, studying and selecting blooms that spoke of desire and passion and brevity, and not of eternal love. She mixed anemone and asparagus fern—expectation and fascination, added An'Alcha and yellow iris for passion, jasmine for sensuality, poppies for evanescent pleasure. Around it all, she inserted fluffy and fragile celtan momentaryflora. The flower she used the most was different-colored tuberoses—dangerous passion—as a warning for herself.

Bel rose high and wafted heavy scents of the garden to Lark as she worked, creating three other wreaths besides the one for Holm. The pure pleasure of the mingled fragrance satisfied her since she'd been breathing roses for days. Her fingers slowed and her eyelids drooped until she finally halted. When she stood back to admire her offerings, she smiled. They never matched her perfect vision, but sometimes letting her hands work unconsciously provided interesting and appealing results.

Before she could think better of it, she sent the wreath to Holm—a challenge, a test, and a message.

At the desk in his sitting room, Holm breathed deeply of the incense he'd commissioned and just received. When he'd contracted for it, he'd told D'Ivy that he wanted a scent for self-control. She had blinked, then made some comment on the spiraling feud with T'Hawthorn and the ever impulsive character of the Hollys. Holm was sure the stuff would work just as well for sexual self-control. As he caught the smell of sage, overwhelming the plantain and echinacea, he repeated his now well-known mantra and tried to sink deeper into meditation.

Half a septhour earlier he'd finished individually tutoring his cuzes in advanced swordplay. The group included Eryngi, now back to normal after his great Healing, cracking fewer jokes and paying more attention to his footwork.

Spread on Holm's desk were new annotations for their wills from T'Holly, Tinne, and Tab. Holm was to review and seal them as a witness and give the documents to T'Yarrow.

Just looking at them made his jaw clench and teeth hurt. His heart beat in a heavy rhythm. One slip of the foot, one moment's inattention, and any one of them could be dead. How could he keep his father, brother, and uncle safe? How could he save them? He didn't want to fail in this, too.

His fingers stroked his favorite bauble, a baroque pearl, and he thought of Bélla. Was she dreaming her own dreams or had his nightmares impinged on her through their connection? Dreams of fighting and the feud, she'd said. His lips thinned. They'd been her own dreams last night. His had been of failure.

When he'd awakened in the Great Labyrinth *again* in the deep of night he'd been trying to save Tinne from suffocating in the boghole, sinking himself—and had failed, as a brother and as HollyHeir.

Before that awful dream had been one about the first time he'd nightported. There'd only been that one small episode in his life, when his Aunt Leea and his Blackthorn cuzes had succumbed to the deadly virus and he'd been so devastated he'd sleep-ported to their estate. The estate that stank of corruption and death. A Healer had 'ported him to his parents' suite with instructions for grief treatment. The rest of the winter he'd spent hours with a mind-Healer.

Now he'd be HeartBound to one of the greatest Healers on Celta. She'd probe at those dreams if he let her. But he didn't want her to know of his imperfections and failures. The long walk out of the labyrinth hadn't yet calmed his mind, taught him how to reach the still central core of himself. He shook his head. A *minor* issue, especially compared to winning the feud and wooing his HeartMate.

Finally his glance focused on the wills. He wanted to set them flaming with a twitch of his finger—denying the possibility of death. Instead he scanned the papyrus and made notations of the changes, sent copies to the ResidenceLibrary and to a sealed file in the Guildhall.

The incense and the soft gleam of his pearl worked on him. He cheered a little. He'd definitely made progress this morning with Bélla.

A knock came, and his Mamá cracked open the door and peered inside. When Holm met her glance, she smiled and traipsed in.

Holm pushed the smoking brass incense burner to one side. "You looked pleased."

"I am. Work went wonderfully well." Her dimples flashed. "The muse gifted me last night and today with several compositions. I'm ahead of my commissions and will be dropping them off this afternoon. It's a beautiful day for walking. I saw you training with our cuzes outside."

She scanned his rooms. "Though it's quite comfortable here. You've furnished your suite with elegance and style, I hadn't noticed." She sighed. "And not to your father's taste."

"They are my rooms."

"Of course, and I'm glad you have your new conservatory. That was well done of T'Holly."

She came and stood next to his chair, ran her fingers through his hair, as she'd done so often when he was a boy. "I'm afraid I was wool-gathering last night during dinner, and not paying you as much attention as I should."

She hadn't been as sharp and quick with questions as usual, and he'd been grateful. He took her free hand and lifted it to his lips. "You are the Holly's treasure. You give us joy, and we're glad you practice your art among us. We prize your music and creativity." Why did smooth words flow from his mouth for every woman except his Bélla?

Passiflora patted his cheek. "All my men make me feel cherished." Holding his gaze, she spoke: "I wanted to tell you how proud I am of you. How fine a person you are. You are my son, and a man, and soon to give your heart over to another woman. It's a moment that must be recognized."

Holm put his hands over hers. "Thank you, Mamá."

She shook her head in wonder. "Where did the years go? It seemed just yesterday your father was asking me for a dance." She began to hum an ancient waltz. "We wed an eightday later. You should be able to do the same." She tilted her head, looking at him. "I know my sons. I think you worry overmuch."

The knowledge of the rough days ahead took a bit of the shine off her words of praise. He *didn't* worry overmuch.

Passiflora rested her hand on his shoulder. "You will find that each time you meet with your HeartMate, the link between you will grow stronger. Even before the ultimate consummation of the HeartBond, she will be with you."

She touched her breast. "Your Father was like a song in my heart." She chuckled again. "And in my head. I *heard* him, the rhythm of his thoughts ran as an undertone to mine when we were courting." Now she placed both hands on his shoulders. "From the evidence on your throat, you must have met your lady enough times for that to have developed. Rest your head against the back of your chair. Shut your eyes. Relax. And *listen.*"

Holm did as she bid. First he became aware of the light beyond his eyelids, golden spellballs that softly lit his sitting room. He dismissed that sight and concentrated on the exact hue of black of his love's hair, the violet of her eyes. Next came the lingering scent of the incense he'd been burning and his mother's familiar apple fragrance. He shut that away, and when he inhaled he thought of hawthorn blossoms instead. His fingers rested lightly on his desk blotter and the thick suede feel changed to the commoncloth trous-suits his Healer wore. He wanted to dress her in the most expensive of silkeens.

Finally he sank into the image of her, how she looked, laughing, on the beach, and the link between them. He strengthened that bond, visualizing it as deep purple and green intertwining, then changing from House colors to silver, then gold. The connection pulsed with the energy and the life that circled between them. With every pulse a whisper came to him, then a beat, then a flow of not-quite-melody, something like the humming of his own thoughts mingled with notes of birdsong, and finally the ancient cadence of the ocean and the heart. His Bélla was a Healer, her lifeforce beat in the same meter as a human heart, the same song.

"Ahhh," said Passiflora, and broke the spell.

Holm opened his eyes and she took her hands from his shoulders. "You see?" she said. "You are bonded and can sense her even now."

His mother blinked rapidly, sniffed. "My son will soon wed." She sniffed again. "It is good."

When she looked at him, tears dewed her eyes. Again she touched his hair. "Silvergilt hair, the Holly legacy. It looks just as good on you and Tinne as on your Father."

"But we are better looking. Finer features—your genes helped out there."

She laughed and shook her head again. "The Hollys have always been wildly handsome and irresistible, each generation, in their own way." She tugged lightly at his hair, then dropped her hand, to bend down and lightly kiss his cheek. "My Blessing upon you and your HeartMate, son Holm."

He inclined his head, his chest tight. "Thank you, Mamá."

With one last smile, she danced from the room.

Holm's lips were still curved when his personal chime sounded. "A private and confidential delivery for T'HollyHeir," a low, incredibly sexy voice said.

Holm's smile widened as he heard the seductive voice of his announcement. It was the first time in a long time that he actually noticed the voice he'd bespelled for his rooms as an adolescent. The voice belonged to his first lover. Now his smile turned reminiscent. An older woman, she'd been patient, demanding, and inventive. He'd chosen well.

The chime and voice came again, pulling Holm from nostalgia. "Personal acceptance is required for the delivery to remain," it added. The unusual stipulation snagged Holm's interest.

"Who's it from?"

A small pause followed. "To release such information, the delivery spell has requested I verify your personal password and your voice print."

Holm raised his brows. Odder and odder. "Sex," he said, reflecting that he'd have to change the password and the voice soon if he won Bélla and she came to live at T'Holly Residence.

"You were always very good at that, my dear," his personal voice purred in programmed response.

The chimes tangled. "Final notice of a delivery, scry locale unidentified, but sender identified herself as 'Bélla.' "

Holm shot to his feet. "Accepted. Immediately. Is there a scried message?"

"Playing the message," his room voice said.

"I know you must have increased security measures, so I'm confirming that I personally crafted and teleported this gift." Lark's tones whispered through his rooms and the lilt of it, so dear to him now, and deeply reverberating to his core, was infinitely sexier to him than the previous voice.

There was a pause of several heartbeats. "Bélla." The message ended.

Holm grinned. Just hearing her acknowledge the name he'd given her, the name no one else in the world called her, was gift enough, but what was her present? He allowed himself a moment of luxurious anticipation and tried to recall if he'd heard of any hobby of Bélla's.

He shook his head. He couldn't remember, and nothing that had passed between them had told him of her skill. His own talent was calligraphy, but he hadn't used a brush in over a year. He'd better start practicing if he wanted to give her a gift.

"Save the message until further notice and teleport the gift to my desk at once," Holm ordered.

"Don't I always do what you wish?" murmured the standard response.

With a small *whish,* a magnificent floral wreath appeared then settled gently atop his desk.

Holm stood, stunned at the offering. He'd often given flowers to various women, but had never received them.

The mixture of blooms and herbs and ferns showed true artistry, as did the mingling of their scents. Bélla's aura permeated the wreath, lingering and refreshing the tendril of connection that ran between them.

With one whiff, he was fully aroused. Unsteadily, but with infinite gentleness, he picked up the wreath, and knew with the touch that she'd thought of passion and surrender when she'd crafted the present. He narrowed his eyes as he read the language of the flowers—passion, surrender, and a brief affair. It was not enough.

It might have been enough with another woman in the past, but it was not enough for him and his HeartMate. She must know it, to spend such time and energy on a gift. This wasn't a gift to a onenight lover or even a eightday fling.

Now was the time to inform her of—some—of his intentions. Pleased and irritated, he donned the wreath.

Just as he visualized the hallway outside Bélla's apartment, T'Holly Residence announced, "T'Yarrow has arrived and is waiting in the Mistletoe Room."

Holm swore, picked up the instructions for the new family wills and his notes, and swept from his chambers. T'Yarrow wouldn't like being shoved the papyrus and hustled away, but the lawyer had just fallen to the bottom of Holm's priorities.

His blood was up, he had to see his Bélla, and not to talk. He could not wait a micron longer.

Thirteen

❤️

Lark tidied her apartment with a small housekeeping spell and lounged on the red sofa, lazily listening to a musicbroadcast. She stared at the ceiling and tinted it a light blue with wispy white clouds.

Satisfaction, tingling anticipation, and a small ache of sexual tension fizzed through her as she thought of her decision to be free and spontaneous and indulge in a wild affair with Holm Holly. She'd see him at the ball tonight.

A hard rapping came on her door. Blinking away daydreams, she sat up and put a grumbling Phyll on the floor, where he ostentatiously decided to groom himself. She smiled, then crossed to the door and opened it.

There stood Holm Holly, wide shoulders emphasized by an open-collared, billowing-sleeved shirt. He wore deep green breeches and boots. And her wreath.

She caught her breath at the sheer masculinity of him, sharply contrasting with the fragile, colorful blossoms on his head. As he entered he brushed his body against hers, and a low, prowling craving started in her center.

Lark gulped, shut the door, and retreated to the sofa.

He stared at her, and she became aware of the fine trembling of her body. His mind brushed hers, and she opened her own emotions and thoughts almost instinctively, like a flower opening its petals to the sun.

For a long moment he studied her. An irritation she felt on the edges of his mind calmed, then focused, then he made a decision. His eyes narrowed, a flash of calculation appeared and vanished before she could wonder what it meant. Not that she was thinking. His desire stormed back to her, bubbling in her pulse and sending heat washing through her until all she could do was feel. And wait for his touch.

Carefully he removed the wreath from his head and touched one finger to a huge red blossom with purple leaves. "I received your gift." He stroked the bloom. "It pleases me." He lifted the wreath to his nose and his nostrils widened as he drew in the scent, spicy against the heavy perfume of the roses. "Immensely." His eyes darkened nearly to black. "As you do, Mayblossom Larkspur, my Bélla." A dark flush highlighted his cheekbones.

Lark snapped her mouth shut before she drooled, knowing her knees were now too weak to stand, she was so bedazzled by the sight of male hunger. She fumbled for words. "I thought you were too busy to see me before the ball tonight."

He shrugged. "Papyrus can wait." He smiled again, more wolfishly. "I received your message, too."

"My message?"

He cocked an eyebrow. "I'm fully conversant with the language of flowers, Bélla. So you choose to take me as your lover," he said quietly, caressingly.

Lark licked her lips and realized her mistake when his gaze fastened on her mouth. He set the wreath gently on a table. "One question," he said.

Just one? she thought. "Yes?"

"Did you put a stayfresh spell on the wreath?"

She'd wanted to, but the wreath symbolized a brief, passionate affair, so she hadn't.

"No."

A spell from Holm made the wreath last as long as his life. Lark suffered a pang at the phrasing.

"Also," Holm narrowed his eyes and pointed at the wreath. "Kitten-proof!"

Lark's eyes widened. She giggled. The delicate stems of

fairybelles would lure a cat to play. She eyed the wreath. Some of the edible flowers might tempt Meserv's appetite.

The wreath rocked on the table, taking the spell. Holm lunged for it and replaced it on his head, then picked up the musicstrip and inserted it in the entertainment slot, setting it to continuous play.

The romantic melody started quiet and lilting. Her heart contracted as the music flowed into her, making her mind and heart ache for Holm as much as her body.

Soon his warmth and strength and vitality would encompass her. Soon she would be held and petted and fulfilled. Soon.

He strode to stand before her, eyes intent. Through their bond, Lark felt the fast pumping of his blood, the control he used to keep his breathing even and his outward manner casual.

As she absorbed the sight of him, large and strong and virile, she realized he waited for her to make the first move, to tell him to stay or go. Just as on the beach, he was offering himself to her for her pleasure. She'd make the decision to be intimate. His body was hers to use as she wished.

Her own breath clogged and dizziness swirled as her senses became unbearably acute. The scent of roses and him wrapped around her, the energy field surrounding him took on the gilt of his hair and was almost too bright for her eyes, the music intensified to pure sensuality with the power of an orchestra.

The pulsing of his heart set up a deep liquid beat within her core, a rising tension transmuting to an ache.

When his whisper came, it was harsh and low. "Say the Words to undress me."

That delicious thought tightened her insides. She licked lips dry from anticipation and the heat of her desire. "Holm's clothes off," she said. His garments folded next to him, atop the feet of his boots.

Now he stood before her naked, magnificent, the wreath on his head only emphasizing his masculinity and making her feel as if she'd won a great prize.

She stared at the well-defined muscles of his shoulders, his arms, his broad chest lightly haired so blond as to be silver. Her breath quickened as she let her gaze wander to his stomach and hips, then snagged on his jutting shaft.

"I want you, Bélla."

It was obvious; she couldn't tear her gaze away. She reminded herself she was a Healer and no body should make her tremble. But all she knew was a craving to have him cover her and move with her and climax together.

"Bed, Bélla," he rasped.

She didn't know how he could speak, the link between them throbbed with red-hot lust, clouding all thought. Each centimeter of her skin was sensitized, her inner hollowness begged to be filled, her nipples contracted. She slipped into the depths of the sofa. It took all thought to mentally order her own clothes gone, but instinct alone to open her thighs.

A groan ripped from him as he strode across the room. His weight pressed her deep into the cushions of the couch.

His erection pressed against her core, and she didn't know how she could stand the sensation.

He panted and tangled his hands into her hair, and she whimpered in delight at the slight tugging and how it tingled her nerve-endings to settle in her very core.

"Bélla, my Bélla, do you want me?"

"More—" more than she could say. More than she wanted anything else.

He moved slightly, his chest hair teasing her nipples until they ached, her body sending more demands for fulfillment to her dimming mind.

His hands slid under her bottom and he poised himself at her entrance. "I can't wait. I can't."

She gloried at the wildness of his eyes, the probing of his manhood, and the powerful thrust that joined them.

Her eyes shut and she whimpered with the delight of having him in her.

"Look at me," he said, and she didn't know if it was a harsh whisper or a rough mind-call. Either one, she couldn't refuse. She opened her lashes to blazing mercury eyes in a taut face.

"You were ready for me," he said. "Wet. Hot. Tight." He shuddered and she felt it deep inside. An answering tremor racked her. The fine tautness of his muscular body on her, and the sheer sensual expectation of what was to come when he started to move, made her pant.

"Bélla," he said, and brushed her mouth with his own. Her lips were swollen, ultrasensitive.

"Please," she whispered.

He lifted himself on his elbows. "Yes! Now."

The inner sound of his control snapping was an instant warning of the withdrawal of his body. She cried out at the loss.

Then he plunged into her and everything except sensation tore away. The glide of their bodies together, the riptide of passion reverberating between their mental link, the sheer weight and scent and energy of him were her world. Red desire led her exquisitely up the shining crest of a wave she'd never experienced, then plummeted her down until she shattered.

An instant later a long, low moan echoed from Holm. He surged and she screamed again in awful rapture. Their climaxes mingled and flooded together.

When he collapsed on her, she could only wonder how she lived through the passion. She clutched at him, not able to let him go. A moment's clarity hit. What had she done?

Holm groaned. This time not in ecstasy. This time in self-disgust. What had he done? He'd disgraced himself, not made the loving perfect for her.

He'd lost every shred of control and simply jumped on her, mating like the primitive male he was instead of showing any finesse, any civilized recognition of her own needs.

He tested the tie between them and shuddered as he experienced the same small white bursts of pleasure still streaking through her. Lord and Lady, so good. So incredible!

His own body jerked in one last pulsing spurt of rapture.

He wanted to take her again, needed her. The coming together had been too fast, over too quickly. He had to strengthen the bond between them until it could never be broken. And he must pay more attention to that link. Before—just moments before—he'd only been aware that it sizzled passion between them, each stroke of his body escalating into unimaginable ecstasy as he felt the delicious sensations she knew. Now he wanted the bond to send more than lust, he wanted to affect her emotions.

Again he examined their bond. Only dazed completion throbbed from her. Relief lightened his heart. He had another chance. Next time he'd be suave, sophisticated, spin the loving out until she accepted that there was more to their relationship than physical desire. Next time he'd be a perfect lover.

So his heart was light. His body wasn't. He crushed her into the sofa. He winced. More care was needed there, too. Taking her fast, uncontrolled on the sofa, he hadn't considered her delicate body except to feel it beneath his, around his.

Still, he'd never experienced anything more powerful in his life than his release. He didn't know how he could keep away from her now. He'd forgotten every syllable of his mantra of control and suspected that he'd remember the words only out of her presence. With her, he would always fight for restraint, and he feared it would be a constant battle he'd always lose.

When he could move, he stood. His brain was too scrambled for the complex calculations required to port them to her bedsponge. He looked down at her and all his blood pooled in his groin. His mouth dried.

The bright red couch framed her pale, dainty body. He'd been too gripped in passion to notice anything but the creaminess of her rounded thighs and the heaven that lay between. She was well-made with small bones, full breasts, narrow waist, welcoming hips. Her thick black hair tumbled to her shoulders, contrasting with the purple of her eyes, the rosy crowns of her breasts. Near the edge of his vision was a rose the exact same shade as her lips, her nipples, the flesh peeking through the black triangle of hair.

Stretching, he plucked the rose from the vase, stripped it of thorns with a Word, and tossed it upon her. Droplets of water beaded on her abdomen and she shivered. His aim had been true. The full blossom lay just above her tight right nipple.

Desire started a drumbeat cadence within him. The sight of her seared the memory of every other woman from his mind.

"Yes," his voice came thick. "Exactly the same color."

She blinked, and the cloudiness in her eyes cleared as she glanced down. And she blushed. Her cheeks, still pink with passion, flushed redder, and the blush flowed down her torso.

Delight mixed with desire in him. He bent and scooped her into his arms. "This time, the bedsponge," he managed. He decided if he hurried, kisses could wait. If he started kissing her here, it wouldn't be the sofa again. It would be the floor.

At least he hadn't tumbled her to the floor. He ran to her bedroom, got an impression of a coral bedspread splashed with red poppies before he tore the thing aside and placed her on cream-colored sheets.

He caught his breath. Now the only color he saw was her hair and her eyes, the rose matching her nipples. He moaned, feeling his sex thicken and throb and rise, ready again. He'd been sure he could go slowly this time. He reached for the wisps of his mantra that eluded him when her eyelids lowered and she licked her lips.

Kissing. He remembered that much. His lips ached, nearly as much as his shaft, for the taste of her. He'd never kissed her after she'd climaxed. Surely her fulfilled passion would change the taste of her mouth and her skin.

He settled himself on his side next to her, groaning as his sex brushed her thigh. He held himself still until he regained a shred of discipline. He wanted to love her slowly. He hoped he could. His fingers traced the curve of her shoulder. Her body was beautiful, unflawed. Unscarred. Suddenly he was aware of his many scars, scars that emphasized the differences between them. She, a Healer, would never scar. He, a fighter, would gain scars by the year.

She touched his cheek with fingertips. "Holm," she said.

His name on her lips, spoken with tenderness and desire, shot through him, moving him as nothing ever had before.

"That's my name," he said, slipping his hand behind her head to encompass the nape of her neck, raise her head, and bring her lips close for his mouth. He caressed her lips and tempted her to open them, then his tongue plunged into her mouth to conquer just as his body had claimed hers moments before. The need to bury himself again in her and link them physically, intimately, rushed through him, and he grabbed at self-restraint.

He opened the bond between them, wide, and found what pleased her most. When he sucked on her tongue, her whimper of pleasure pushed him to a new level of heated desire.

Slowly he withdrew from her mouth, and she raised her head to follow him, to rub his lips with her own, to tangle tongues in his mouth, and he knew when she trembled in delight at his taste.

It nearly undid him. Every second tested him.

He lifted his head, breaking the kiss, and glided his lips down the curve of her jaw to the hollow of her throat. Skin damp with perspiration greeted him, a touch of perfume and her own elusive taste. Not enough. Other places of her body would have their own tastes, and he needed to imprint them on his memory, to know in his soul every aspect of her taste. Something Heart-Mates knew, he now understood.

He would learn every note and tone of her voice. Every tint of her skin. Every scent of her body. Every millimeter of her under his hands, every sensation of her skin against his.

And he would start with taste.

Her heart slowed a bit and she shifted in surprise as she realized his intentions. Pink embarrassment fuzzed her mind.

He took in the fragrance and sweetness of the top of her breasts, touching on the tips and swirling his tongue to know this taste, reveling when her body arched to his mouth. Ah, he could tempt her with the pleasures he could teach her, he thought triumphantly—with wonder she was so unschooled in the many levels of passion.

Her essential taste was slightly stronger between her breasts and on the underside of them. He spent some time there, then nibbled with questing tongue to her belly.

Her hands curved around his shoulders and tugged. Her embarrassment was endearing, but irrelevant. He was on a mission.

From her thoughts, he knew that her husband had never tasted her womanflesh, never cherished it with his mouth, never brought her to ecstasy in that way. And she'd had no other lover.

Through his own thoughts he let her know the challenge was too much to resist, that nothing would stop him, that he would touch her as no other man had, body, mind, and heart.

His hands caressed her, exploring the curves and dips of her body, liking the fine turn of her collarbone, the soft smoothness of her skin, and the velvet plush of her nipples. He reveled in the sensations he gave her. She'd never forget his mouth or his touch.

She tugged on his hair, exciting him more.

He chuckled as he tasted more sweet Bélla-essence below her hipbones, held her wriggling body and sent the bolts of lust he felt through their tie until she quieted and her breathing came ragged and her heart pounded in the same beat as his own.

The scent and taste of her at the apex of her thighs pulled a growl from him. He smelled her, his woman. And he smelled himself, his mark on his woman, his seed, the results of the ecstasy they found together, and it was the most perfect smell in the universe. Once more his primal nature swamped all reason.

She lay still as if his emotions pulsing through their bond overwhelmed her. No remnant of embarrassment, only surrender to his touch and his will mixed with the rising passion twisting inside her.

Moving his hands from her hips to her thighs, he spread them wide. Up close he admired her womanly folds and the glistening proof of their union. He recalled the rose that matched the color of her most intimate flesh and 'ported it to just above her sex. He trembled at the sight.

With the utmost delicacy, he traced her with his tongue and her perfume exploded in his brain, demolishing all control. He reveled in the scent and taste and renewed moistness and softness against his face and arching of her body against his lips and the thundering in their blood and the swelling of his shaft and the demand of his own sex until she screamed and he tasted her climax and the instinct to mate seized him.

He rose and watched himself surge into her. The ripples of her body clasping him ignited the firestorm of orgasm.

As soon as his brain cleared from the most magnificent event of his life, Holm rolled to his side and pulled a limp and unresisting Bélla into his arms, curving his body around her. Shocks of renewed pleasure shivered through them both as their skin touched. He noted the wondering and sleepy tone of her mind and decided a nice little intimate nap would foster the complete bond that continued to weave them together.

"Sleep," he whispered in a dark voice he knew could mesmerize. The fog of gray creeping over her thoughts thickened. "Sleep, you are safe with me, Bélla."

"Safe," she murmured.

"Cherished," he said.

"Cherished?" Her mind started to spark with thought.

"Welcome," he amended.

A slight laugh came from her. "You're welcome, too, Holm." She snuggled a little and fell asleep.

Finally relieved from the sexual pressure of the last several days, Holm slept.

He woke a septhour later with Bélla still in his arms. It was a very good sign that she hadn't moved away from him in her sleep. Unconsciously, she must know they were HeartMates. Now all he had to do was convince her mind. He wished he'd thought to initiate the HeartBond, but that took one more thought than he'd had.

Unable to keep his hands to himself, he curved one hand around her hip and cupped her breast with the other, calculating how much more of the afternoon he could afford to while away with loving. Something furry moved against his hand on Bélla's breast, and he recognized Meserv, also cuddled against her. From the foot of the bedsponge came Phyll's quiet snuffling.

Under his touch, Bélla awoke and stretched. When Holm brushed her mind, she refused entrance.

She was going to be difficult.

Fourteen

♥

Holm sighed, then caught sight of the wreath that one of the kittens had dragged from Lark's mainspace to the bedroom's threshold and frowned. If he hadn't placed a spell on the piece, it would have been ruined.

She hadn't protected it. She'd made the wreath with particular flowers signaling that she was willing to have an affair with him, no more. He scowled.

Lark drew away and he turned her to face him. At least she didn't resist that. Her expression showed vulnerability before she shuttered it, and tenderness welled.

"The blooms are wrong, Bélla," Holm muttered. He reached out to toy with glossy black strands of her hair, assessing how soon he could love her again and what position he'd try.

"Hmmmm?" she said, shifting. Her breasts plumped out on the bedsponge, and made his voice fail and thoughts vanish.

He sucked in a breath to savor the lingering scents of the room, his woman and himself and their joining, the fragrance of roses and the faint hint of the spicy flowers that graced his wreath. Ah, the wreath.

He cleared his throat. Her deep purple eyes met his. "Your wreath speaks of desire."

She smiled smugly and her eyelids dropped. The tips of her

fingers touched his chest, trailed against him as if enjoying the consistency of his hair. "Yes," she said. "Flaming desire. Hot passion. Greedy sex, or sexy greed." She laughed up at him, tilting her head. He appreciated the smooth line of her long white throat. "I'm a little befuddled," she ended.

He'd never seen her so soft and relaxed and open. So he hesitated to bring up a subject that might push her away, but he wanted her to know that he'd be in her bed that night.

He inhaled again and refused to let the exquisite scent distract him. "Yes. Passion. Desire. But"—he narrowed his eyes as he tried to recall the flowers that spoke of something more. The quickly fading flowers. The short-lived flowers.

Catching her chin in his fingers, he watched her eyes open wide and note his seriousness. "But intertwined with the An'Alcha passionflowers are dayferns, fragile Moonbeams. Flowers that die in a few hours."

She arched her brows. "Yes?"

"This is not a simple affair, Bélla. Not short."

Wariness came to her eyes and he hated putting it there.

At that moment the music swelled from soft and steady to singing joy.

"The music," he said, working for smooth words to say to a woman for the first time in his life.

"It's lovely," she responded as she had earlier in the day.

He looked steadily at her. "It's new. Composed by my Mamá just last night when I informed her I was courting a woman to be my—wife."

Shock jolted through Lark. "Wife?" she squeaked. She squeezed Meserv too hard and he mewed a protest. She didn't know what to think. Of course Holm would need a wife to carry on the Family name.

"I'm serious, Bélla. And my intentions are honorable."

She caught her breath. "Our problems are insurmountable."

He opened his mouth.

"No," she said. "I don't want to have this conversation naked in bed with you. This is serious."

"Of course it's serious, but I do my best persuasion in bed." He smiled with patent charm.

She shook her head, but felt heat creep into her cheeks. She suspected that he could persuade a woman to do anything if he was in bed with her. She wondered how long she could keep him satisfied, then blinked as she remembered that they were actually discussing marriage. He'd be a faithful husband, the Hollys always were, HeartMates or not.

"I'm going to the waterfall," she said, using Flair to 'port to the cubicle. At a Word, the waterfall shot over the wide granite ledge above her and poured down. The music D'Holly had written matched and mingled with the water.

Marriage! She'd been married before, married for love—or what she thought was love, but Holm—she cut that thought off at the start. Marriage. Ethyn.

Ethyn Collinson had been the most innately gentle man she'd ever known. Now she understood it had been the contrast with her Father's inflexibility that had drawn her to Ethyn.

His sweet smile, his intelligence, and the strength of his Healing Flair that so complemented her own, all combined in one man; a common man with no Noble arrogance had proved to be impossible for Lark to resist.

She was being tempted—when her tumbled thoughts were not being swayed by her weak body—with an actual marriage offer from one of the most confident, virile, and powerful men on Celta. A man she wasn't even sure she respected. Oh, he had Flair enough, and cleverness, and honor— She stopped. Ah, the quality that redeemed him, his own sense of honor. An honor she believed he'd never betray. He'd follow all the rules and laws that governed everyone on Celta.

But marriage? How could such a blazing passion between them allow for anything other than a short affair? Not to mention the feuding of their Families. She winced. She'd actually forgotten that basic fact the moment Holm stepped into her apartment.

His mind reached for hers. "Bélla," he called from outside the door.

She refused to let him have an open current between them, yet knew there existed a link on a basic level she couldn't reject or deny.

"I'll be right there!" she replied, using a whirlwind spell to dry and clothe her.

When she walked into the mainspace, he was lounging on the sofa, stroking its arm, with half-lidded eyes and a smile quirking the corner of his mouth. She tried to dismiss the hard thump of her heart at the sight of him. His shirt was open at the chest, but his breeches and boots were on. She knew they could vanish at a word.

The kittens stretched out on the back of the couch.

She summoned two icyblacktea cylinders from the no-time and brought one to him.

His eyebrows rose as he took it, making sure their fingers touched. "Being a hostess, Bélla? Retreating behind manners?"

Lark compressed her lips and chose a chair at an angle to the sofa. She was *not* getting on that couch again with Holm.

They sipped in silence, and Lark found herself too restless to sit. Leaving her half-full drink, she stood and drifted to a window. She didn't really see the courtyard gardens, but was intensely aware of Holm.

She heard the small click as he set his own cylinder down, then the slight intake of his breath.

"Open to me, Bélla."

"No." But she turned to face him.

He smiled lopsidedly. "Our previous rules of engagement, Bélla, physical or mental, but one connection."

She hissed. The kittens looked at her admiringly.

With complete grace, Holm stood and strode to within a handspan of her, dominating her space. "You can order me from this apartment, and I will go, but it will not change the fact that there is something very, very strong between us. Do you want this unresolved before we meet at the ball, tonight?"

His scent crept into her nostrils, dazing her mind with remembered images of their passion. If he touched her, the craving for him and what he could give her would begin again. And if he held her, without passion but with the tenderness she felt underlying his demands, she would surrender utterly.

Appalled at the emotion he drew from her, she knew she'd gone too far to be cautious with him ever again, and too deep to be able to play a superficial lover. What had she done?

She couldn't retreat. "Please," she said unsteadily, not meeting his eyes. Lark edged open her mind and their bond flashed between them, golden and pulsing and strong.

She felt rather than saw him narrow his eyes and come to a decision. He withdrew to the sofa and she found she could breathe deeper and could meet his pewter eyes.

"No flash-white sparks from my Bélla. I am not pushing too hard," Holm murmured.

He was right. She felt slightly constricted, but not the feeling he'd ever hold her against her will, that he'd cage her until she was wild to escape.

"Now, Bélla," he tapped his long, elegant fingers against the sofa arm. "Marriage."

She met his gaze squarely and lifted her chin, denying all the yearning that swelled up inside her. "Make it easy on yourself, Holm, choose another woman."

His lips curved in a smile. "What ever made you think the Hollys want it easy?"

"Is that why you're pursuing me? Because it's difficult?"

Holm looked annoyed. "Well, men don't want to have their courtship as complicated as mine, either. I simply want you to know that I won't be backing off because of anything that happens between our Families."

Her brows lowered. "Your Family doesn't know you're courting me."

"Of course—"

She lifted a hand. "No, I believe they know you're wooing someone, but not me, not a Hawthorn."

The muscles in his shoulder shifted a minute amount. It was enough for Lark. "They don't know," she repeated.

His gaze remained steady. "You're the woman, the *Lady*, I want as a wife. No other. My Family must accept that. Will accept it."

"How can you say that. You love your Family—"

"And you don't?"

"Of course I do."

"So you know how much it hurts when you're estranged. I'm sorry about that, Bélla."

She ignored his gentleness. "This won't work."

"My Family won't hate you because you're a Hawthorn, Bélla. They don't see just a Family when they look at a person, they see the individual."

"They'll disown you."

"No, they won't."

She sighed in exasperation. "This won't work."

"I'll make it work."

Another thought struck her. "Are you wooing me because I'm a Hawthorn? Is this how you want to mend the feud?"

His mouth tightened. He cut the stream of energy between them. "I need to touch you."

Lark retreated a step and lifted her palms. "No sex."

He stood and looked down his straight nose. "I'm perfectly capable of restraining myself when I must, but I need to touch you."

Holm walked over and curved his hands to frame her face. He searched her eyes. A smile played around his lips. "Would it impress you that I'd marry to stop a feud?"

Her eyes widened. "Perhaps."

"To impress you I might say that. But I don't run from fights, Bélla, you know that."

"Marrying to stop the feud," she said, consideringly.

His hands dropped to her shoulders and he gave her a little shake. "Don't think you'll marry me for that reason. I won't let you."

She shook her head. "It wouldn't stop the feud, anyway. My Father would disown me. Our relations are already strained."

"I'm sorry for that."

"Find another woman, Holm."

"I'm going to marry *you*."

"Why?"

He opened his mouth, closed it, then sent her an easy smile. "The simple reason is that I want you, Bélla. Very much. More than I've ever wanted any other woman. We match, physically," He pulled her against him, and moved his hands down her back stroking. "We match mentally. Our connection is effortless and strong." His mind skimmed against hers, containing just enough sensual hunger to fire her own. She couldn't refuse him.

Seeing nothing but disaster in their future, she pressed her face against his shoulder and allowed herself a whimper.

"Don't, Bélla," he whispered in her hair. "If we are careful, we can make this work."

Sardonic humor quirked her mouth. "I am known to be a careful person. You are not."

"I am if the stakes are high enough. These are the highest stakes there are."

His words stirred her hair and tickled her scalp. She stepped back. He kept one hand on her upper arm and clasped her fingers in his other hand. He put her palm on his chest, pressed his own palm against the softness of her breast to feel the pace of her heart.

"Open to me, Bélla."

He held her with such care, she couldn't refuse. The tie between them opened, redoubled, surged, until their hearts beat in time, they breathed together. "We have this bond, Bélla."

She cut the link.

He caught her shoulders. His eyes darkened to storm-cloud gray. "I'm not an inexperienced fool, I know how precious our connection is, how strange and powerful and wonderful. I'm not going to let you deny it, or refuse to act upon it."

"You want the bond."

He tunneled his fingers through his hair. "You want it, too. Should want it. Me."

"What I want isn't my only consideration."

"You would throw away something special because of this— this feud between our Families? Time for harsh words, I think. Did you have a bond like this with your husband?"

She flinched. That arrow hit solid and true. Her lips were dry. "I won't speak of my husband with you, Holm."

"Just this one question, Bélla. I think you owe me that."

"I don't know what I owe you. I don't want to owe you, I don't want you to owe me! I don't want—"

"We are lovers. Not onenight lovers, not reckless lovers involved in a fling, but two who care for each other, more than affection, more than—"

"No!" She put her hands over her ears, then angled her fingers to massage her temples.

Silence simmered for a long moment. She sensed the impatience prowling inside him, but he didn't move from where he stood. Perhaps he longed to push her with words, with caresses, with the strong will of his mind, with the emotional attachment between them, but he didn't. He refrained. Because he didn't push, she found the strength to answer his questions honestly.

When she looked at him again, his face was taut.

"No, Holm, my husband Ethyn and I never had such a link as the one that's developed between you and me." She shook her head in confusion, puzzling how such a thing had sprung so quickly into being. Then she took a deep breath and continued. "And no, I never reached the sort of sexual climax with him that I have with you. We never— He never—" She stopped.

Holm's eyes gleamed. "I think there are many ways of loving you've never tried. Time to expand your horizons—our horizons. I promise—"

"Holm, please. We've only met a handful of times. We've just become lovers. Can't you give me some time? Not only is the resolution of the feud between our Families uncertain, but I'm uncertain of the suddenness of this attraction—uncertain of myself." A gleeful thought pounced and she gave it voice. "Since you insist on comparisons, I knew and worked with Ethyn daily for over two years before we married, and we didn't become intimate until our wedding night."

Horrified amazement appeared in his widened eyes. He paled and cursed softly. She didn't quite catch his mutter, but it sounded like "The man was an idiot." She ignored the words.

Then his spine straightened and his head lifted with all the arrogance and pride inbred in a Nobleman. The mannerism irritated her, but not as much as before. This was Holm, after all, and Holm only took himself seriously sometimes.

He set his fists on his hips and studied her intensely.

It looked as if this was one of those times.

"You and I linked and participated in GreatCircle Rituals for *three* years when we were younger, Bélla. We've known of each other and our Families all our lives. We've become lovers and reached a level of sensuality and a sexual height I've never known. We have a strong, emotional, and intimate connection."

And it sounded as if he'd thought about their relationship seriously.

"I need time," she said.

Holm frowned, rocked forward as if he wanted to stride over and snatch her up, then settled back into his solid stance.

"I'll give you as much time to answer my proposal as I can. But I won't let you deny the bond between us, emotional, spiritual, or physical. I'll be here in your bed tonight, Bélla."

"We must be discreet," she whispered.

He grimaced and jerked his head in a nod. "Yes. Much as I hate it, we must be discreet."

"I'll see you at the ball."

His shoulders slumped in exaggerated dejection even as his fingers snapped Meserv from the couch into his hands. He cradled the plump kitten gently, and Lark felt another bit of the shield surrounding her heart from this man crumble. He shifted Meserv to one broad shoulder.

Holm 'ported his wreath to land on his head. He looked incredibly sexy, a manifestation of the Green Man or the Green Knight of their culture. Breath stopped in her throat.

"I owe you a gift from my own hands. Be sure you'll receive one from me." The way he emphasized the words, she'd have thought he offered a HeartGift, but neither of them had Heart-Mates. She wondered what his creative talent was.

As Holm lifted his fingertips to his lips and sent a kiss her way, his hand brushed the collar of his shirt aside and the bruise of her bite showed. She stepped forward and lifted her own Healing fingers. "Your throat. Now that we're lovers, you'll let me Heal—"

Holm fended her off. "No, no, no. It's your lovemark and I intend to wear it proudly. Just be glad that formal wear covers it, otherwise I'd flaunt it at the ball tonight."

"Holm Holly with a sex bite on his neck," she said dryly. "Now, that would be surprising."

His brows rose. "Yes, it would be. I've never showed one before. And, Bélla, be prepared to meet my parents tonight, because I fully intend to formally introduce you."

She gasped. "You can't. You said your mother created that music . . . they'd be bound to guess."

He frowned. "I don't want them to interfere, but I do want them to know you. I'll think of something. Is your father, T'Hawthorn, going to be there?"

A short laugh escaped her. "T'Hawthorn supporting centers for Downwind youths? No. Of course he won't be there."

Holm closed the space between them in two gliding strides, grasped her hands, and lifted them to his lips, kissing each in turn. "Think of me, Bélla. Until tonight, at the ball, and later. It will be an eternity until we meet again."

The words sounded as if he'd said them to others, but the punch of feeling behind them was like he believed this situation unique.

"Go with the Lady and Lord," she said weakly, adding a little wave as he left.

Marriage. He'd proposed marriage. She hadn't answered. They'd had incredible sex. "Reached a level of sensuality and a sexual height I've never known," he'd said. She began to accept that he really meant to have her as a wife. The daughter of his worst enemy.

*M*idClass Lodge *was exclusive and set just outside "Noble* country," and Holm decided to walk the short distance home.

He whistled snatches of the melody his mother had written for Bélla. His suit was progressing. She hadn't experienced those dangerous flashes when he'd spoken of marriage.

Rolling his shoulders, he was conscious the underlying tension that had invaded his muscles was finally released in absolutely phenomenal lovemaking. If this was the passion between Heart-Mates, he hadn't been giving his friend T'Ash and his father enough credit for getting out of bed every morning. Of course, he thought, they had their women in bed every night. And at hand during the day.

He grinned. He wondered if Bélla would consider him domineering if he spent every night in her bed. Hard to keep that discreet, though.

How would he handle the ball? Someone from the Willows could attend. It wouldn't be wise to single Bélla out and alert D'Willow of his HeartMate. D'Willow would act on the knowledge for her own ends. Once the Willows knew, rumors would spread to the rest of the Nobles. Even now, he was far from sure how soon he would win his mate.

Then there were his parents. He'd deliberately kept Bélla's name from them so they wouldn't meddle. Yet he wanted them to know and value her. Perhaps he could introduce her to them as the Healer who saved Tinne's leg. They'd know she was T'Hawthorn's daughter, of course, but they'd see that she was more Heather than Hawthorn. Like all gossip, it was common knowledge that T'Hawthorn and his daughter didn't get along.

Holm stopped whistling. He didn't know how he'd get around that thorny issue, make some sort of peace with his father-in-law after the Hollys won the feud. Especially since Holm didn't like the way T'Hawthorn had treated his daughter, resulting in problems for Holm by causing her to react with white-flashes.

He lengthened his stride, letting his legs loosen and muscles stretch. He hadn't felt this good in a long, long time.

Never.

Surely his mind and emotions were eased enough that he wouldn't sleep-port tonight—after more incredible loving with Bélla. No. Positively no chance he'd nightport from Bélla's bed. Making love with her would solve all his problems. He grinned, free from the bothersome past at last.

"Holm, Tinne," T'Holly mind-called just as Holm came within sight of T'Holly Residence. *"Sparring Room One in quarter septhour."* Holm smiled ferally; just what he needed.

Fifteen

Holm teleported to Sparring Room One and sent Meserv to his suite. Tinne and T'Holly were already present and dressed in practice garb of stretchy trous over bespelled groin-guard. With a Word Holm whipped his day wear off and his fighting clothes on.

Tinne wrinkled his nose. "You could have cleansed before you came."

Holm only lifted a brow, glanced at T'Holly. "Want me to?"

"Whirlwind spell," T'Holly grunted.

Holm made a sour face. "Yecch. I hate those things."

"Who doesn't?" T'Holly said. "I haven't used one in years."

"Women use them all the time. Several of my lovers do." Tinne smirked.

"It's not as if my odor will add to this stench. Despite every housekeeping spell, the Sparring Rooms all stink," Holm said.

T'Holly narrowed his eyes. "Are you criticizing my Residence again?"

Holm grinned, showing teeth, settled into his balance, and shook his wrists out. "That's right."

Tinne tensed.

"Go!" T'Holly yelled, leaping for Holm.

Tinne swept a leg at Holm's legs.

The fight started.

None of them spoke. Grunts, occasional swears, and fighting yells peppered the quiet, but they saved their breath for battle. Holm heard the sounds of body hitting body, thuds of bodies on ground, the whisper of rolls and ducked blows. He saw blurs of darting arms and feet, the stars of shock and pain as hits landed. He felt his own blows connect against the tough muscle and sinew and flesh of his kin. Sweat trickled down him and slicked the skin under his hands as he threw his father or brother. Holm tasted salt, but not blood.

The zing of life and adrenalin flashed through him, the delight of fighting, of practicing his skill. Yet even as his body dodged and tumbled, he knew that this pleasure dimmed beside that he'd just found with Bélla.

The thought of her distracted him for an instant and he took a clout on the shoulder he should have parried. He retaliated and jabbed Tinne nicely in the ribs.

"Stop!" T'Holly cut the air with his hand. Holm altered his fist's direction so the blow missed his father. Tinne, more committed to the battle, had to drop and roll in a somersault. They ended the session equal in points.

"Towels," ordered T'Holly, and an instant later all three had thick green towels around their necks. T'Holly mopped his face. "Well done. We'll rest for a few moments. Sit."

Holm and Tinne collapsed onto the tough, springy mossbed and sat cross-legged, looking up at their father. The familiarity of their positions made Holm feel like a boy again. He shared a grin with Tinne.

"The Hawthorns are resolved to feud." T'Holly paced to the end of the mat and back.

"Do we call in our allies?" asked Tinne.

"No. We'll handle this matter within the Family. But I've decided I'll call in the younger sons from the branches of Winterberry, Blackdrink, and Mounthol who have weathered their second Passage and have an aptitude for fighting. It's Family policy that all Holly boys, no matter what branch, and no matter how remote, are trained in fighting from the age of three Celtan years. I studied the list of names, and we should have twenty new men as additional Family Guards. The last will arrive no later than two eightdays from now."

Tinne whistled tunelessly. "A nice number. New friends, how fun."

The gravity of the feud oppressed Holm. How much distress would it cause Lark? Would she let him comfort her? And could they comfort each other?

"I anticipate deaths, but not a bloodfeud. We should be able to keep our tempers enough to win, and win well. Try not to kill T'Hawthorn's son or grandson."

T'Holly stopped and stared at each of them in turn. "We are the best fighters on Celta. It is bred in our very bones, but the reason we are the best is only one." His gaze speared Tinne, awaiting the proper answer.

"Because we are men of honor," Tinne said.

"And because we are men of honor, we follow rules stricter than the Noble's Feuding Code," Holm murmured. He had spoken those words to the five men in his own lesson that morning.

"That's right." T'Holly nodded shortly. "Remember it. We'll do defensive street fighting this afternoon. Dismissed."

As soon as *Holm left, restlessness imbued Lark, and her* brain picked at the emotions he'd ignited in her and what she should do.

So she cleaned her apartment by hand instead of by spells and got a certain satisfaction from the physical movement.

As she scrubbed the many windowsills, she finally decided that the issue came down to love. She should marry for love and nothing else. There was no other acceptable reason for marriage. Even if she wanted children, it would be bad for everyone concerned if they were raised in a loveless marriage.

She plopped the rag back in the bucket and moved on to the next shelf. She halted in mid-swipe as her logic came to a conclusion and jolted her.

The truth was, she didn't believe in a deep, abiding love for herself. Perhaps because her parents hadn't been HeartMates, or in love. Her father's parents had also married for alliance and gain. FatherDam still lived on T'Hawthorn estates, long after her husband's death. HeartMates died within a year of their spouses.

The influence of her father, and her father's House, had never been mitigated by the visits to T'Heather. That set of HeartMates didn't publicly express their devotion, though it was evident, particularly on an emotional plane.

Of course, when she'd married Ethyn, she'd taken the risk, had hoped to find a true and abiding love, if not a HeartMate. But the depth of the emotion she'd expected had escaped her like sand through her fingers and her heart had gone back to disbelieving in love between two people.

There wasn't a HeartMate for her in this lifetime. She hadn't experienced any metaphysical connection to another person during the Passages that had freed her Flair, and that was the prime indicator that a person had a HeartMate—a link during Passage. No, her Passages had been stormy, but controllable, and with no outreaching to touch another's soul.

Knowing this, she hadn't hesitated to marry a fellow journeyman Healer. A man with the potential to be a great Healer, a Downwind man who'd triumphed over his rough childhood. To Lark, the violent manner of his death at the hands of Nobles had been as great a wound as his death itself.

Of course Holm Holly would believe in love and HeartMates, his parents were such. He'd grown up in a household permeated by the love of HeartMates for each other and their children. Lark frowned. T'Holly's sister had been a HeartMate and had bonded with T'Blackthorn. *And* Holm's best friend, T'Ash, was HeartBound to his mate. Holm had taken part in that courtship, seeing how HeartMates courted and joined, contemporaries of himself.

Though it was common knowledge Holm had no HeartMate in this life, he'd think marriage would bring love. He'd consider that with caring and affection and passion, a deep and life-long love would come.

So he believed.

She didn't.

If she was entirely truthful with herself, there were also the doubts of her own nature. What about her attracted Holm so? His conquests from all classes of women, his gallantry and affairs had become nearly legendary. Why would he settle for an estranged daughter of a FirstFamily? A woman who cared little for Nobles and their intrigues. How could he prize a Healer, when his own Flair and that of his Family from the time of the Colonists had been for fighting?

Oh, yes. Lark could believe in lust, in the sexual attraction that sparked between them whenever they came close to each other. She could accept that there was a complementary harmony in their natures that established between them an easy mental and emotional link.

She could admit to those stimuli with Holm.

She could even admit that love between men and women could be deep and satisfying. But she couldn't see such a love developing between herself and Holm.

Perhaps for others, but not for herself.

And she couldn't even understand why this thought seemed so odd to her. Didn't she believe that she could be loved?

Ethyn had loved her. She knew that. But she knew the basis of his love had been because she had been a Healer. She knew the trials, problems, and joy of Healing. She could understand him, match him in that. Lark acknowledged her great Flair, confident in it and in the status of FirstLevel Healer.

But did she have such a poor opinion of herself as a person, as a woman, that she didn't know what the Heir to a GreatHouse would find to love in her?

Yes.

She wasn't even sure who she was as a person other than a Healer. That was the basic tenet of her soul, the way she defined herself, her image of herself—Lark, the Healer.

She sniffed in disgust at herself and emptied the last bucket of dirty water down the drain. She shook her head in disbelief at her low confidence.

Recalling the passion between herself and Holm, her blood sizzled. Obviously the man desired her. Obviously he thought her beautiful and worth spending time with. Obviously nothing would deter him—not even a feud, so how could she doubt herself?

Rationally she couldn't. But emotionally, when she thought of the emotional ties—or the lack of them—she'd had all her life, she doubted in her heart. The only true great emotional bond she'd had was with Ethyn, and next to the vitality of Holm, it seemed pallid.

A clumping sound came down the hall. Trif in her fashionable new clunky shoes. Lark smiled. She had a bond with Trif. Lark would give Trif a little time to relax after her work day before visiting.

Right now Lark needed a bath. She soaked her aching muscles then dressed in a loose gown and meditated half a septhour. She sank deeply into herself, finding her center and the calm there that would lead her to inner truths, and they, in turn, would help her decide what to do about Holm and his astonishing marriage proposal.

When she rose from her contemplation, she felt as if a deep, central well had filled with peace. No answers had come, but her unconscious would provide them in time. As she straightened her robe, her eyes lit on the colorful multitude of roses, and she decided to take another bouquet to Trif. She thought of the rose she and Holm had shredded between them in their last act of sex, and blushed.

No, she'd keep that particular color, but Trif would like the blue ones.

Stabbing pain hit Lark in burning waves, crumpling her.

She pressed a hand to her side, where the lick of fiery torment had started, but now felt numb. Streamers of agony spiraled out, threading through her body.

Yet another, emotional, blow arrowed through her—the terror of four shocked and desperate souls.

Lark struggled to block the empathic-telepathic feelings and forced her inner shields up. She panted and ignored the perspiration trickling down her face.

Phyll clambered upon her, mewing and licking her face.

She gasped, wondering at the connection. These weren't Heathers, the resonance wasn't right. She had no close bonds with the Hawthorns, not even her brother. Who? She groaned.

One of the four was dying.

Without moving from her curled position, she teleported herself and Phyll to Intake at Primary HealingHall.

Raging shouts, screaming fury battered her. Myrrh helped Lark to her feet and snagged Phyll, ignoring his hissing. Myrrh shoved Lark into the nearest cleansing tube. "Thank the Lady and Lord you are here. D'Holly was knifed. Wound should have been bad, but Healed. Something's wrong." Myrrh lifted her voice around the whooshing of scouring air. "Your nephew, young Huathe Hawthorn, did it in a street scramble."

"Laev?" Lark gasped.

"Who?" asked Myrrh.

"There are three Huathe Hawthorns. We call my nephew by his middle name, Laev," Lark explained, blocking pain and pushing past Myrrh. Lark ran to the tumult surrounding an emergency bed. Three solid men were in her way, she poked the smallest with her finger. Nothing happened.

"Move!" she used her tone of command.

Tinne Holly shifted so she could squeeze through. Roiling fear and despair billowed from him. His emotions were echoed in her Holm and T'Holly.

D'Holly lay pale and still on the raised bed. T'Heather himself had his FirstLevel Healing hands on her abdomen. His daughter and Heir, Ur, stood beside him, her hands curved over D'Holly's rib cage.

"Lark, put your hands on her heart, keep it pumping evenly," T'Heather said, not even looking up, knowing she was there. The Healing link between the three snapped into place. Lark felt how quickly energy and strength drained from the other two. This wasn't a normal knife wound.

She stood opposite them and placed her hands on D'Holly's chest. Her heart beat erratically. Frowning with concentration, Lark evened the rhythm.

T'Holly jumped forward. "I won't have filthy Hawthorn hands touching my HeartMate," he snarled.

Strong arms restrained him. Holm.

"Holm Senior, you want my Daughter'sDaughter's hands off your Lady, she dies in minutes. Quiet or go away," T'Heather said.

A green glow of Healing energy encompassed D'Holly from the Healers. While the Holly men murmured amongst themselves, the Heathers consulted telepathically.

I Cleansed and Healed the wound, but there is still something wrong. Let's do an in-depth overview. Lungs, Ur? asked T'Heather.

Whatever it is, it's affecting her breathing, Ur said.

Her heart, too, Lark said.

Thought so, T'Heather said. *Let's examine the wound at a cellular level. The dagger punctured her left kidney. You can see I mended the cells; there's a shadow where the wound was.*

What's that yellow-green trace? Ur asked sharply.

Sweat beaded T'Heather's forehead as he sharpened the focus, angled the view, and magnified the cells. He zoomed in on a line of hideous chartreuse that spread into filaments and split again into minute threads as they watched.

T'Heather swore. "Poison!" he whispered aloud.

Lark felt the Hollys stir, but refused to be distracted.

"Poison?" T'Holly shouted. "What are you talking about?"

"Shut up, Holm Senior," T'Heather said. "Let us work."

I don't recognize this pattern, Ur said, gnawing on her lip.

I don't either, Lark said.

Nor I. We need an expert. "Myrrh, get Culpeper here, stat!" ordered T'Heather.

Myrrh's floral scent brushed Lark as she hurried out.

"Nep!" T'Heather called for his second-in-command, the Primary HealingHall administrator.

"I'm here," Nep's cool voice answered.

"Notify all the Flaired PerSuns on our roster that we'll be needing them. Set up shifts. I don't know how long D'Holly will need life support."

Struggling bodies impinged on Lark's notice. "Is she dying?" For a moment, Lark didn't recognize T'Holly's voice.

"I don't know," T'Heather said. "Not if we can prevent it, but there are unknown factors here. Will you keep quiet!"

"Sir, if you need energy to Heal, or my Mamá needs strength to live, we are ready to link with you and provide it." Lark knew her Holm spoke, yet had never heard such fierce, controlled intensity from him.

"Save your strength, young Holm. You'll do your part," T'Heather murmured. Linked, the Healers decreased the magnified view of D'Holly's kidney until they could see the whole thing. *Look at that,* T'Heather transmitted grimly. Threads had multiplied until a yellow-green pulsing web encompassed a bottom quarter of the kidney.

It's getting worse, Ur said. *We must keep it from spreading.*

The shock of the wound continues to affect her lungs and heart, but at least the threads aren't jumping organs, Lark said with more calm than she felt. Deep in her mind panic chittered. She'd never seen anything like this. Had no idea how to Heal it.

Keeping D'Holly's heart beating normally meant constant attention. Moment-by-moment life support wore out Healers at an alarming rate. Even the PerSuns—Flaired individuals who linked to the Universe's stream and easily transferred and stored energy—would be hard pressed to keep D'Holly's body functioning.

Lark poured energy into the woman, striving to keep the heart rhythm normal. She gulped when she recalled the woman under her hands had fashioned the wonderful melody Lark had listened to all day. Swallowing again, she realized part of the music's underlying tempo had the cadence of a beating heart. The back of her gown clung damply to her body.

Look! Your Healing isn't the only thing that left a shadow. Breathing hard herself, Lark showed the others what she meant, a scattered sickly-yellow pattern.

Propulsion spell! T'Heather said. *Built into the poison to spread it. I've seen it once before. We can Heal the specks of poison—take the left third, Ur, I'll do the middle, and Lark the right. The original damage wasn't too bad, but with a propulsion spell the poison will return, and spread.* Horror filled his thoughts.

No damage at all to lungs, just an interference in function, I'm eradicating the specks. Ur's projection dimmed, but the delicacy and the detail of her Healing held steady.

Lark shut her eyes. It took too much energy to keep them open and Heal, and it was her inner eye that needed to see. Yet she knew her Holm was still near. She'd never forget his scent.

"PerSun?" asked T'Heather as the lines of their combined energy wavered.

"T'Cayenne, here," rasped a deep, calm voice.

"Ah, the GrandLord himself," whispered T'Heather.

"I asked him to come," T'Holly said.

"A three-generation alliance with T'Holly GreatHouse is a boon for any House," T'Cayenne said. "My GrandHouse is at D'Holly's service."

"We need your contribution of energy for Healing and life support," T'Heather said.

Lark gasped as a new, strong power fortified her own and coursed amongst them. With renewed vigor, she finished Healing the yellow shadow-specks. With infinite gentleness, she withdrew her control of D'Holly's heart. It beat by itself. Lark smiled.

"Her heart's fine," she said.

"It wasn't before?" snapped T'Holly.

"Her lungs are fine," Ur added.

"What's going—" the rest of T'Holly's sentence was muffled.

Let's look at the kidney, T'Heather said.

The chartreuse web had continued to grow.

Poison. Nausea rose in Lark. *My nephew Laev couldn't have set a propulsion spell on the knife. He's only thirteen, too young to master his Flair, and that's not a spell he would know.*

T'Heather grunted. *Spell and poison was on the knife when he got it, then. Do Hawthorns keep such weapons?*

I don't know, Lark replied miserably, trying to recall the few times when she visited T'Hawthorn armory, or heard discussions of weapons. Her memory held nothing.

Deal with the effects, first, Ur said.

Let's see if we can stop it, T'Heather said.

Droplets of sweat rolled down Lark's spine, dampened the hair at her temples. She heard Ur panting. The poisonous threads writhed under their assault, but didn't die.

Halt, said T'Heather several minutes later. Immediately the strands began to separate into new fibers. *We're going to need a Healer and a PerSun, just to keep her kidneys functioning properly, let alone to try and stop this.*

For how long? asked Ur.

He didn't answer.

"T'Culpeper, here," said a cheerful voice.

Lark heard him rubbing his hands. What was a desperate situation to the Healers, and a devastation to the Hollys, was a fascinating problem to T'Culpeper. At least now, before he knew the extent of the dilemma.

"Join," ordered T'Heather. The cool blue of T'Culpeper's personal energy joined them.

"Lark, can you handle the review? I need to deal with other matters," asked T'Heather. His voice sounded strained, and Lark wondered just how long he'd been Healing D'Holly. Ur would be flagging soon, too.

"Yes," Lark said. Surely she had enough energy for that. T'Culpeper needed to be shown a detailed visualization.

She braced herself for T'Heather's withdrawal. The shifting current threw her a little off balance and she fumbled the link and the view of the kidney. "Sorry," she muttered.

"That's fine," said T'Culpeper absently, "that line of green-yellow there? Is that what I must analyze?"

"Yes," Lark said. Ur labored, but held steady.

"What are you talking about?" demanded T'Holly.

Can you telepath, Culpeper? asked Lark mentally.

Now T'Culpeper bumbled. *Bet-ter not. Less en-er-gy loss for all if we speak.*

Lark sighed. "T'Heather, can you please brief T'Holly?"

"Yes, Lark. As the freshest FirstLevel Healer, you're in charge. You Hollys, come with me, and I'll tell you what I can. T'Culpeper will update us as soon as he's done."

"I'll stay with my HeartMate," T'Holly said. Even across the room and blind, Lark could feel his burning anger. And fear.

"To be blunt, Holm Senior, my Healers don't need your disturbances. Every minute counts. Don't disrupt the only FirstLevel Healers I have. Soon we'll be calling in all the Second-Levels to take shifts for your Lady."

"That bad?" came a stunned whisper.

"Not good. Come, friend." T'Heather's tones were those he used with his smallest youngling.

"I'm staying," said the familiar voice of HollyHeir Holm, Lark's Holm. Through all the commotion she'd still sensed his presence, and the bond between them.

"Hmmmm," said T'Culpeper as the incremental magnification Lark had been providing finally enlarged the faint tendril the size of a finger-width. "It's organic, all right. Continues to grow like a virus, though. . . ."

"Propulsion spell, we haven't been able to stop it," Lark said, knowing Holm would want to hear the worst. He moved behind her until she could feel his heat and his strength and his vitality. All the things his mother would soon need from him.

"Nasty. Propulsion spells can be very individual. If you don't know the creator it's a difficult spell to stop."

"It wasn't my nephew Laev," Lark choked and cleared her voice. "He doesn't have that kind of Flair yet."

"Looks somewhat like a firespell. Hawthorns aren't noted for any ability in that line," T'Culpeper said.

Lark wasn't surprised he'd already heard what happened, by now ten thousand rumors would be rounding the Noble Houses.

"The poison?" Holm's voice had an edge to it.

"I'm studying it, HollyHeir. Hmmmm. No. I'm very sorry. I don't recognize it."

"Ahem." T'Cayenne coughed.

"Yes, T'Cayenne?"

"My namesake spice has been known to cause kidney failure in large amounts." The words seemed pulled from his raspy throat.

"Not cayenne," T'Culpeper said. "Definitely not. Something else, I don't know. Lark, can you 'freeze' the image for me and copy it to Primary HealingHall and T'Culpeper ResidenceLibrary so it's on file and I can study it further?"

Her knees weakened. "Yes, of course." She dragged in air. Large hands curled around her arms. Strength streamed into her.

No, Holm, she projected only to him.

Yes, my Bélla.

Your mother will need your—

Right now, my Mamá needs you, and you need me, he ended with a decisiveness that stopped any further questions.

Lark "froze" an image of the poison. At the end of her strength, Ur cried out and crumpled to the floor. The circle of power fluctuated wildly. Lark grabbed it, then vized the picture to Primary HealingHall, and T'Culpeper's Residence. Myrrh and three other SecondLevel Healers joined the Healing circle. Lark regulated the new energy and melded it with T'Cayenne and T'Culpeper. With one last effort, she gently funneled the current to a trickle between the others and herself. Then she fell into Holm's arms and darkness.

Sixteen

$\mathcal{T}$*he black hole in Holm whirled deeper when Lark col-*
lapsed. He picked her up and cradled her close against his chest.
GrandLord T'Culpeper retrieved HeatherHeir Ur from the floor,
while T'Cayenne and the three new Healers continued to supply
strength to D'Holly.

At that moment T'Heather strode in with T'Holly and Tinne
following. Holm's father looked haggard as he gazed upon
D'Holly, his wife, his HeartMate. Holm tightened his grip on his
own HeartMate, needing her comfort if only in the warmth of
her body and the press of her flesh against him.

A great, roaring wind had whipped into his heart when his
Mamá had fallen, scouring his emotions until he felt raw. He
walked, he observed, but the heart blow was so hard, no emotion
could be summoned.

T'Holly held one of D'Holly's limp hands, then he smoothed
back her bronze hair.

Holm trembled at the loving gesture and concentrated on the
returning color in Lark's cheeks.

"Remember, Holm Senior," T'Heather admonished. "Send
only a small amount of your strength and energy to her. This isn't
a time for impulsiveness. Not all your energy nor your sons' combined would Heal her, and she's too fragile for a Great Ritual

Healing; the poison is too entrenched. You hear, Holm Junior?"

Holm cuddled Lark and jerked a nod. "I hear."

"You hear, Tinne?"

"Yes." Tinne's face appeared as colorless as his hair, and Holm knew his brother had been violently ill.

T'Heather crossed to T'Culpeper and placed a hand on his daughter's forehead. "Ur is too weary to work further, even linked with a PerSun. I'll send her home by HealingHall glider." He swept a look around the room. "We all must conserve our energy until this is resolved. Even with additional PerSuns from Cayenne and with you Hollys providing life support, this case will be very difficult."

"The Apples will contribute strength, too," T'Holly added. "I called her brother, the GrandLord." T'Holly stroked his Heart-Mate's hand. "No one wants to lose Passiflora." He choked and continued to caress his Lady.

T'Culpeper's mouth pinched. "I'll take Ur to T'Heather Residence, then port home from there to work on identifying the poison." He opened his mouth to speak, then shook his head and left at a quick pace with Ur in his arms.

T'Heather glanced at Holm. "There's a small cotspace just outside behind the green door. You can put Lark there until she wakens." The Healer sighed. "This was her restday. No doubt she expended her energy instead of saving it to Heal. I'm surprised she did so well, but she's a consummate Healer."

When Holm thought how they'd "expended" energy, heat rose to his cheeks. Then he found Tinne studying them. Perhaps his father and T'Heather had been too preoccupied to notice, and T'Cayenne and T'Culpeper too unaware of Holm's character, but Tinne surely knew the difference between the touch of a lover and that of a courteous man. Holm held his woman like she was *his,* now and forever.

Tinne frowned and Holm noticed fine lines etching themselves in his younger brother's forehead. Lines that wouldn't fade after the feud ended. Holm wondered how the circumstances would age him, and his Bélla.

He had a very bad feeling about how Lark would react to this tragedy, both as Healer and his enemy's daughter. T'Hawthorn was his enemy now, no doubt of that.

Holm nodded to the others and exited, carrying Lark to the

cotspace. Though tiny, the room held only the finest furnishings: three layered Chinju rugs of dark, brilliant colors; a carved redd-wood frame supporting a thick permamoss sponge and several covers of the softest llamawoolweave. A premier entertain-mentspell whispered soothing tones and matched them to pastel colors tinting the walls. Holm smiled grimly, this was Primary-Healing Hall. Such comforts weren't available in AllClass Heal-ing Hall near Downwind, where Lark donated her time. That brought the recollection of the ball. His heart tightened in his chest so he could barely breathe.

Now, right now, he should be holding Lark in his arms, danc-ing, not cradling her after she dropped from exhaustion. He should be listening to his Mamá's music and introducing Lark to his parents. Not wondering whether his Mamá lived from one moment to the next and thinking how he might comfort his father.

He sat on the cot and buried his face in Lark's hair, inhaling her fragrance and roses. As much as he tried, he found no trace of the scent they'd made together. So he contented himself with brushing his face against the silkiness of her hair until she stirred.

She stiffened. "Holm," she said.

He only clasped her closer.

"Actually," she continued in a dusty voice, "I should call you 'Holm Junior.'"

"Call me 'Lover.'"

She pulled herself from his arms. He didn't want to let her go. He needed her more than he could say, but he'd never hold or constrain her.

Twitching her gown into smoother folds, she avoided his gaze and turned to the open door.

"Don't go," he said roughly.

Before she could answer, a youngster appeared at the end of the corridor. He stopped as he caught sight of Lark, then ran to her, an ungainly boy awkward in his growth. He skidded to within a handspan of her.

"Laev," she said.

His gaze wildly ranged to Holm, then back to Lark. "I didn't mean to hurt her. I never meant to hurt a *Lady*. She's tall, but she's skinny, and her clothing and colors mixed with the others and the fight lurched around and—" He caught his breath and pretended to cough, not to sob.

Holm was glad his emotions were frozen. He was deathly afraid that if he felt something it would be killing rage at this boy.

"I never meant to hurt her. I didn't really mean to fight at all, but that Eryngi taunted me. . . ."

"That matches Eryngi's story," said a new voice, Tinne's. Laev jumped and Holm started. For an instant, he'd thought it was his father speaking. Tinne's voice was usually smoother, lighter. "He's blaming himself, too. I imagine we all are, in some way or another—T'Holly for not accompanying her on her errands, the rest of us for not sending better guards with her. . . ." Tinne lowered his eyes. Holm felt the same self-blame.

"You'd better get that whelp out of sight before papa kills him," Tinne said, not looking at anyone but the boy.

"You're right." Lark's voice wasn't normal either.

She took the youngster's hand and led him down the hallway. Words floated back to Holm. "I'm needed now. Why don't you wait for me in the chapel? You know where my den is. . . . I'll join you shortly." She watched as the teen obediently walked away.

When she didn't turn back to them, Holm stood up. "Lord and Lady." The prayer-curse shot from him with unusual violence.

Tinne eyed him warily, then looked at Lark's ramrod back. "I'll report to T'Heather that his Daughter'sDaughter has awakened. They have four SecondLevel Healers with Mamá." He shook his head. "Four!" A tremor rippled through his body.

Holm dipped his head. "I need to speak with . . . Mayblossom."

He made no attempt to muffle his footsteps as he came up behind her. Even through her loose gown he saw her shoulders tense. He hesitated, but knew she didn't intend to turn and confront him, so he circled her. "Bélla—"

She cut him off with a chopping gesture, her face set in stern lines. "Your Family needs you. Your mother and your father."

"And I need you."

She raised both palms. "Stop. Our association was irrational, foolish, doomed. It's done. We can't go any further without hurting ourselves and others, and I won't do that."

"Our 'association'?" His own voice grated with a note he'd never used with a woman, but as red hazed over his vision, he knew his anger at her words and her rejection was too deep for manners. Better anger than pain. When the horrible numbness around his emotions wore off, he would have two great wounds in his heart.

He was a fighter. He'd fight. "I won't listen to you now," he said through clenched teeth. "I won't give you up. You will be my He— *wife*!"

Her released breath was more scream than sigh. Her nostrils widened and he saw her stance brace and her lips move silently. A few seconds later she said far too calmly for his temper, "Find another wife, Holm."

He ground his teeth. Far too much had happened. Time to tell her she was his HeartMate, damn the consequences.

"Mild silence spell on Holm HollyHeir!" she commanded, and his lips clamped shut, emitting only garbled sounds. He reached for her mentally, but all her shields loomed high and strong.

"You listen to me! I will not be forced, in any way." When he noticed white flashes emanating from her, he was relieved she'd gagged him. "Everything is different, now. How can you stand there and say we could marry?"

Her question to him released the spell. He battled down the fury and panted until he could control his own voice. "My parents promised. By their Words of Honor I could have my wife, whoever she might be."

Lark raised her eyebrows. "And when was this?"

"Before I went wooing," he said deliberately. "As Heart-Mates, they were sorry I had to take only a wife."

She flinched, and he cursed hurting her. But he continued. "So they gave their solemn Words of Honor, Words that cannot be broken to the detriment of the GreatHouse."

Her face softened an iota, and she was more his passionate Bélla than the FirstLevel Healer. "Holm, Holm"—she shook her head—"our—affair—"

"Loving," he said.

Again her chest rose with a deep breath and she dropped her eyes. "Our loving before was difficult. Now it's unimaginable."

"No."

Red tinted her cheeks again, and she gestured to where his Mamá lay. "Can you tell me that T'Holly would welcome me into your Family? Can you tell me that there would be no rift between you *now* if you did?"

"You are more Heather than Hawthorn," he muttered.

She only tugged a lock of black hair. "I am T'Hawthorn's *daughter.* He will always seek to influence me. I will always be Mayblossom Larkspur Hawthorn Collinson."

"You will always be Bélla to me. I will have you!"

"Why?" She flung up her hands. "Why? When any sane man would walk—run—from our liaison."

He was cool enough now not to tell her the truth. "We have a special bond." Though she might not let him in, she could do nothing when he enveloped her in a field of tenderness. For her, he'd dig inside himself for emotions. In her presence he could experience feelings in spite of his own great wound of his injured Mamá. So he gently settled a cloak of soft love, unthreatening love devoid of passion, around Bélla.

She turned her head away from him and sniffed. Her lips trembled. "Find another woman, Holm," she whispered.

"The bond between us is strong and good. And right. Can't you tell how right it is?" he, too, whispered.

Her mouth curved down. "The bond is right, the time is wrong. Let it go, Holm."

"I can't. They promised."

Her chin came up in passion. "How could you hold them to such a promise now?"

He didn't know if he could, but it seemed like the only thread of hope he could hang on to.

At that moment Tinne appeared, carrying a pair of drooping kittens. A ring of white rimmed his mouth. "Meserv and Phyll insisted on trying to help." He stepped between Lark and Holm, facing her. Tinne sucked in a breath of air and blinked rapidly. "They did well. Both of them." He handed Meserv to Holm and Phyll to Lark with a bow.

Tinne continued to keep his body between them. "I think you must be very weary, FirstLevel Healer," he said evenly.

"Yes." A small, sad smile flickered across her face. "It's time for me to go. I'll be here tomorrow to—to help."

"Tinne—" Holm started.

Tinne didn't turn to him. "Father is asking for you."

"Blessed be, Holm HollyHeir and GreatSir Tinne Holly," Lark said, and Holm knew her retreat into formal manners was to put as much distance between them as she could. Reluctantly he dissipated the field around her. She shivered, then shrugged and hurried away down the hallway.

"Don't say anything, Tinne," Holm warned his brother's back. "I don't want to hear a word."

"You wouldn't listen anyway." Tinne sounded muffled.

"Damnable situation," Holm smacked his fist against the nearest wall, hard enough to make a satisfactory sound and sting, but not do any damage.

"Yes," Tinne said.

Lark took a shortcut through a Healer's corridor to the chapel. On her way, she stopped by her den and found Laev huddled in the twoseat.

"Laev?"

He lifted his face, this time not pretending he hadn't been crying, though the tracks of his tears showed only faintly in the dim light. "I stayed in the chapel a while, it smelled nice and felt good, but there's a holo of the Lady, and she looks just like the one I hurt—" His voice cracked.

Lark winced inwardly. She'd forgotten that a woman of the Apple Family had posed for the portrait, some ancestor of the present Passiflora D'Holly, no doubt.

Lark shut the door behind her and advanced into the shabbily furnished little room.

"So I came here," Laev said. He hauled a softleaf from his pocket and blew his nose. Since the tissue was a pale peach color, Lark knew he'd gotten it from the bowl on her desk.

"You have fash music." He waved to the entertainment slot. Lark shivered. He'd spelled the system to play several of Passiflora D'Holly's pieces. She didn't know until Holm had left her apartment that morning how many flexistrips of D'Holly's music she'd collected.

"Will she live?" Laev asked with the bluntness of youth and guilt.

Lark petted the sleeping Fam in her arms. "I don't know. No one knows. It seems your blade had a propulsion and poison spell."

He turned very white and shuddered. "I didn't put it there. I didn't. I didn't know. I wouldn't have used the knife if I'd known!"

"Where did you get it?"

Now color raced to his cheeks. "I picked it up in the street, about three years ago outside the Guildhall, but it was a real gang knife. It had symbols and everything."

"Oh. I think someone needs to look at it. GrandLord T'Culpeper or T'Heather."

Taking a chance, she went to the twoseat and sat, placing Phyll in her lap and putting her arm around Laev. He stiffened, then leaned into her. She stroked his hair. His mother, bless her, had been an unusually demonstrative person to marry into the Family and had taught her son how to touch and be touched.

After a few moments he said, "She might die."

"Yes," agreed Lark.

"And if she dies, *he* dies. They're HeartMates, aren't they?"

"Yes."

A racking shudder went through him at the thought of killing the great T'Holly, even indirectly. Laev had spoken the words no one in the HealingHall had wanted even to think, let alone say aloud. If D'Holly died, T'Holly would follow within a year, since HeartMates were so bound together.

"That's bad. That's horrible. I don't ever want to be a Heart-Mate," Laev said.

She ruffled his hair again. "I hear there are compensations. And it's a few years before you'll know yet."

Once more the silence stretched between them. Laev wrestled with some thoughts. Another time she believed they'd get on well together, something she and her brother had never managed. She liked this boy, and could come to love him as one should love Family.

"You know what's the worst?" he whispered.

"What?"

"Papa and FatherSire are *proud* of me. And FatherSire, he's *glad* that T'Holly might die, and that I did it by mistake. It makes me feel sick."

Bitterness welled up in her, but not surprise. Lark wondered how to handle this. She didn't want to criticize their Family, no matter how wrong they were, that might make Laev react out of loyalty and stop him from thinking. "What would your mother have said about this?"

Tremors rocked him, and she took his hands and put Phyll in them. "Here, pet my kitten, Phyll. It will help both of you."

"Mama would have said I was stupid and now I'm suffering the consequences of my own foolish actions. But the results shouldn't have been as bad as this." He snuffled and laid Phyll on his lap to use the softleaf again.

"She sounds like she was a wise woman."

"She was a Grove."

"Then she was wise."

"I don't think I like feuding."

"Hawthorns aren't very good at the fighting part," Lark said carefully. "Groves and Heathers aren't even good at the grudge part. I've never heard of either a Grove or a Heather feud."

"Before I did this, Papa and FatherSire said the feud was just business. It seemed exciting."

"And now?"

"How can it be just business if people die? That's not what business is about, is it?"

"Not to me. But I don't think Tryskel Pass is worth dying for, either. There's enough land on Celta. I'm not sure I know what is worth dying for."

"I don't, either," he said miserably. "We could die, too."

"That's right. I worry about you, your father, FatherSire—and Cratag."

"Cratag fights all the time." Laev petted Phyll faster. "He's been Healed twice. He says he fights to keep his place in T'Hawthorn Residence, but I wouldn't make him fight. I like him."

"I like him, too."

This time the quiet that spun between them was companionable, and Lark treasured the notion that she finally connected with her nephew and found in him someone she could feel affection for.

"When I'm T'Hawthorn, I won't feud," Laev announced.

"There are better ways of settling disputes," Lark agreed. "From what you've already suffered, that's a wise decision."

His expression tensed with fear. "What can they do to me?"

"Who?"

"The NobleCouncil."

Lark raised her eyebrows. "Your FatherSire will never let anything happen to you, and the informal laws of the feud protect you, as well as your youth. It was an accident."

He jerked his head in the direction of Intake. "Do *they* know?"

"The Hollys? That it was an accident? Yes, Eryngi told them he taunted you."

"He did, but I should have been able to ignore it."

Lark hid a smile at his too-high-minded tone, encouraged that his teenage sense of drama had returned.

"Hindsight." She sighed. "How are you feeling?"

His face lightened a little as if at any other time he might have smiled. "Not good. But better. Thank you for helping me in the Intake and speaking with me."

Lark inclined her head. "I know you have some Heathers living at T'Hawthorn Residence . . . if you have nightmares—"

"Nightmares!" Laev shivered. "I hadn't thought of that. How am I supposed to sleep?"

Lark 'ported packets of chamomile tea and tucked them in his shirt pocket. "This tea will help you. If you need to talk further, go to Garis. He's a good, solid Healer and won't tell anyone of your conversations."

Laev slid his eyes in her direction. "Vera Aloe is cuter."

Lark chuckled. She took his hand and offered a mental-emotional link he immediately accepted. "Anytime you want to talk, or anything else, just call me mind-to-mind."

His spirits lightened a little. "Yes." Laev lifted a now-purring Phyll and put him back on Lark's lap. "I channeled some energy to him. Papa comes, time for me to go." He said a small spell, and his clothes were tidied and face and hands cleansed.

Lark pressed her lips together at a pang of memory. Everyone in T'Hawthorn Household learned that spell as soon as they could speak—the one that would always make them presentable to their elders.

When Lark caught sound of her brother Huathe's heavy footsteps on the floor outside her office, she straightened her spine and practiced her mantra: calm, and breathe, and serenity, and shield, and breathe, and acceptance.

Seventeen

The door opened and Lark's brother, the younger Huathe Hawthorn, walked in. "Sulking in the dark? Lights on."

Both Lark and Laev blinked.

"Oh, it's you, Mayblossom."

Lark gritted her teeth. "It's my den."

Huathe nodded and shut the door behind him.

Laev stood and bowed formally. "Greetyou, Father."

"Son. This trip was unnecessary. I hope you realize that."

"As you say," Laev replied.

A spurt of pride in the boy warmed Lark. He'd be able to stand up to his father, and someday his FatherSire. She wondered if it was because he knew he would be T'Hawthorn, being a male, or being half-Grove. She only wished she'd learned the trick at his age.

As Huathe put a hand on his son's shoulder, Lark thought it might be that her brother was—slightly—less intimidating than her father.

Still, when he turned a cool, purple-eyed gaze on her, she raised her chin.

"How does D'Holly?" Huathe asked.

"I don't know. I haven't seen her for a while. You should speak to T'Heather." She wouldn't give him any information to plot the damn feud.

Huathe raised his brows. "I've never known you to be so uncertain of your Heather skills, Mayblossom."

She shrugged. "D'Holly is T'Heather's patient."

"Give me an estimate of her condition."

"I'll do better. I'll take you to her, so you can see how a woman with a poison knife wound looks. I'll give you an inner view of the disease inside her—the color, the morbidity, the effect on her organs—"

A strangled cry came from Laev. Lark bit her lip.

"That was uncalled for," Huathe said.

"I'm sorry, Laev," Lark apologized.

"No need." But Laev brushed a hand across his eyes. "I saw her. Father, if you want a report—"

"Not right now," Huathe said, quickly enough for Lark to wonder if he was in the habit of receiving reports from his son, and on what issues. She suppressed another sigh, remembering her own childhood when she stood before her father every evening to detail her septhours.

"Laev should go to bed. He's had a long day," Lark said.

"So have you, I imagine," Huathe said in subtle question.

"It was my restday. I was called in." No need to say how. She hunched a shoulder. "The days will be long for all Healers for a while."

Huathe narrowed his eyes, and the quiet now was like bitemites, invisible and stinging with challenge.

"Father, is Cratag with you?" asked Laev.

"Yes. HealingHalls are neutral ground, he's just outside the door."

Lark circled around her brother and nephew and opened the door. "Good evening, Cratag."

"Is it?" replied the scarred man in a tone gentler than she recalled. "I don't think many believe so."

He wore formal clothes. Lark cocked her head.

He half-smiled. "I came straight from the ball."

The charity ball for T'Ash's Downwind Centers. The ball, and the consequences of being seen there with Holm, that had loomed so importantly a few septhours before.

Lark's smile came easier than expected. "You look very debonair."

He stared at her.

"I wouldn't have thought you the type to attend a ball."

"I like to dance," he said mildly. "It was for a good cause."

That was it. He supported the Downwind Centers. Lark nodded.

"Is this witty dialogue done?" asked Huathe. "It's past time to go."

Cratag stepped back into the corridor and Lark followed. "At your service, HawthornHeir." Cratag bowed his head.

Huathe didn't spare him a glance. "Laev is here with me. He's fine."

"How could he be otherwise, in the hands of a FirstLevel Healer?" Cratag asked, and Lark believed it was actually an indirect compliment.

Huathe gestured for Laev to precede him, then stalked into the hallway and to the nearest exit.

Cratag dipped a nod to Lark. "Merry meet, Lark."

Lark shut her eyes briefly. She could *not* follow with the words "merry part," and hear his "merry meet again." Not when she was a Healer and he a fighter. "Blessed be, Cratag. Go with the Lady and Lord."

"And you, Lark." He cast one glance down the hall and lowered his voice. "This has been an ill day for all. D'Holly, the boy—" He shook his head.

"I gave Laev some herbs. Garis Heather is at T'Hawthorn Residence if either you or Laev need him. Laev and I have a bond. If you need me, tell him, or scry or viz and I will come." She'd brave her father for Laev.

"A very generous offer." With another nod, he strode away, easily catching up with her brother. As she watched him move, she knew that Holm moved in much the same way, with a fencer's grace. Fighters would make excellent dancers.

The night in his *Mamá's* Intake room stretched eternally, with new Healers and PerSuns every three hours. Holm had teleported Meserv home to his bedsponge, but neither Holm nor

Tinne were capable of leaving, and T'Holly seemed permanently installed in a seat at his HeartMate's bedside. Now and
again an ashen T'Holly ordered his sons home. Then the three
would have a heated, whispered disagreement that only ended
when a Healer stated D'Holly turned restless at their voices. Finally, when it was obvious there'd be no immediate improve-
ment in their Mamá's condition, Holm and Tinne agreed that
they, too, would take watches. Tinne left at midnight, to return
during the late morning hours, and Holm accepted the afternoon
shift.

He dragged himself to T'Holly Residence an hour before
dawn. Though lights were on, he avoided everyone in the household who still kept vigil. He embraced the exhaustion that continued to mute his feelings, particularly the pain of two heart
blows. His steps lagged as he went to his suite. After the bene-
diction of sleep, he'd wake and memory would crash upon him
and the pain would be fresh and new and unbearable.

Eventually he reached the sanctuary of his rooms, stripped
and let his clothes fall to the floor of his sitting room. In the bedroom he carefully put his dagger and blaser on the table next to
his bedsponge. On his way to the bathroom and waterfall he
passed the open doorway of his den and something lying on his
desk caught his eye. He went to his desk.

Bélla's wreath sat to one side, as beautiful and fresh now as it
had been when she'd made it. It hurt to look at it and know
everything, *everything* had changed.

Next to the wreath was a large, rolled parchment tied with a
green and gray ribbon and a stack of flexistrips. Music from his
mother. His trembling fingers knocked them askew. Through
blurred vision he saw the titles: "Holm's Courting Melody,"
"Meditation for Spellwork," "Joy for the HollyHeir," and the last
one, simply: "My Son."

Somehow he found his chair. He buried his face in his hands,
and shudders ripped from deep within his chest.

His Mamá was dying and the men of her house were alone.
He yearned for Bélla.

During the next four days, Holm felt as if he lived within
a nightmare, populated by irrational and desperate people,

including himself. All effort of T'Holly Household centered around D'Holly lying still and deathlike in Primary Healing-Hall, all schedules revolved around Healing shifts. Despair and an edge of panic infused the atmosphere.

Holm could not say what he ate or when, and the only reason he ate at all was to fuel himself so he could send energy and strength and *life* to his Mamá. He lived in a half-world of men, communicating with grunts, avoiding eye contact so they would not see any horrible truth in another's gaze. Even Meserv drooped, starting at shadows or burrowing into Holm for companionship. The Fam was unusually quiet, the hush of the Residence burdening him, too, and he lost some baby fat. Now and again Holm would wake to the kitten's retching. He mastered the clean-up spell so he could do it in two seconds flat and half-asleep.

T'Holly's rage and weariness hurt Holm on several levels. He hated seeing his father, the strength of his childhood, helpless and suffering and alone, without the always-present love and support of his mother. T'Holly appeared gaunter and more desolate with each passing moment.

The thought of his Mamá dying tore at Holm, shredding him, and, he feared, the fabric of the Holly Family.

Tinne's cheeks hollowed, his eyes sank deep into his head. Tab's brusque manner became taciturn.

And Holm had no peace or comfort from the sight of his HeartMate. Somehow Mayblossom Larkspur Bélla Hawthorn Collinson had always just finished her long hours at the Healing-Hall and left before Holm arrived for his heartbreaking duty of keeping his Mamá alive. He'd have welcomed the most impersonal Healing link with his love.

Unrelieved desire, now worse because he knew how wonderful fulfillment with Bélla could be, tormented him physically. Since T'Holly men released anxiety by fighting, there was never a lack of a sparring partner. Family members from distant branches trickled in and were assigned to train with Tab or Tinne or Holm.

Holm heard that some of the men, even the T'Holly cook, prowled the streets, scouting for T'Hawthorn colors. T'Hawthorns moved through the city warily and in large well-guarded groups. Skirmishes between the two clans erupted daily.

Rumor said one wing of T'Hawthorn Residence had been converted into HealingHall, with an attached courtyard as the essential Healing Grove.

With every gram of Flair needed to sustain D'Holly, Holm, Tinne, and T'Holly used gliders to go to and from Primary HealingHall.

Holm survived the days like an automaton, suppressing the agony of his two wounds—losing his Mamá and Bélla's rejection. The only time he felt truly alive was at his Mamá's bedside, holding her hand and channeling her strength.

She did not improve. She barely stayed alive.

If she died, the Hollys would become a Household of men. If she died, T'Holly would, also.

That scared Holm. To be bonded with another, to feel such a wrenching loss that it literally ripped an integral part of you away so you couldn't survive, was something he didn't want to contemplate.

Why would he wish to have a love so deep and encompassing that he'd die without it? Yet his feelings for Lark became more intense and compelling each day. He lusted after her soft and full body. He yearned for the sweet energy she mixed with his. He craved the closeness of his heart and emotions to hers, those that complemented and completed his own.

But putting his heart and his life in the hands of another seemed madness. Could he draw back, this close to her? How strong was their connection?

Should he draw back? Live his life alone, perhaps barely contented with a wife and an alliance when he could have the deep soul-sharing experience of a HeartMate?

His thoughts scrambled time and again at the questions, most particularly when he took his shift in the dim, luxurious room at Primary HealingHall, holding his Mamá's limp hand and seeing her lovely face devoid of all animation.

However he resolved his inner turmoil, he'd soon be pressured to take a mate. T'Holly, with the future of the GreatHouse in question, would turn his thoughts to his Heir, and the fact there was no third generation yet on the way to ensure the line. His father wouldn't be patient and casual regarding Holm's wooing now. T'Holly would order Holm to proceed with his duty immediately and demand a daughter-in-law be installed in the

Residence and impregnated at the earliest possible moment. Holm winced at the cold words that would come from his father and strip Holm's marriage of any passion or love.

Holm practiced his calligraphy to make a gift for Lark and dreamed of creating a HeartGift to win her as he struggled with his decision.

What of his own Bélla, as he called her in his heart and when they were alone? She'd been shocked and horrified at the twist the feud had taken. He'd felt her disbelief, and angry guilt that such an injury had been done by her Family to his. She'd withdrawn from him. Used all her skill and strength and Flair powers to Heal his mother until Bélla herself was drained, but she had still withdrawn as if this horrible event had raised an impenetrable wall between them. He'd been furious at her nephew, her father, her House, but not at her. Never at her, not that kind of vengeful, plotting, destructive anger for her.

He squiggled a line, made it into an acceptable glyph. He still wanted her. When his emotions were on the pendulum side of taking his HeartMate, other feelings boiled through him at the thought of her. Anger that she'd think her walls would keep him away, keep him from steeping himself in her when he needed her so, keep him from seeing her. Never.

A determination infused him—a refusal to let her turn from him, become less than lover, friend, companion—turn into an acquaintance, a woman with whom he'd had one afternoon of passion. Those septhours of passion that he had never equaled in the past and would never match in the future without her.

Dread of the future if he let her go. He could see her fade, turning into a Healer and nothing more, moving to Gael City and out of his reach. She might even avoid everything else life had to offer—love, children, family, home. Two ugly blots fell from his brush. He crumpled the ink-darkened papyrus and threw it to join others littering the carpet beside his desk.

The rumor that he'd overheard in the HealingHall tugged at his mind. Bélla had been the subject of a report—and the conclusion was that a Heather woman had never lived longer than three years without a mate. The Healers had discussed it as if it were an interesting tidbit to divert them from the awful gloom of D'Holly and the feud that raged outside their walls.

Bélla wed to another, in the arms of another, moving under

another man than he. The idea made him wild, savage. Never. Never! *Never!*

The brush fell from his fingers and rolled across clean papyrus and blotter, ruining them all.

He thrust down the stupid images of Bélla with some other man, banished and flung them far away into the ether, beyond Bel and the stars, not to torment him again.

She was his. His HeartMate. He would not let her go, even if the bond scared him, even if she wished it.

For a moment he found some peace. He'd decided: make her his. His mouth twisted in a wry smile, and he sponged up the ink mess with softleaves. He could still use the sheets for practice. He'd need a lot more to make a gift for Bélla.

The problems in courting her mounted, piling one atop another. Her feelings for him and the feud; the emotions the feud would engender in his own Family for her and hers; the pressure for him to marry.

T'Holly would insist Holm claim his HeartMate, yet what would his father say when she turned out to be a Hawthorn? Would T'Holly command Holm put aside all love for a Heart-Mate and woo and wed a wife? Even at the same time T'Holly loved and feared for his own HeartMate? Holm would not submit to such an order. In defying his father, how would that affect their relationship, Holm's with Tinne, and Tab, and Eryngi?

Too many questions. Too much brooding over vaporous might-bes, and not concentrating in the now—evident as more blotches dribbled over his papyrus. He steadied his hand. His strategy of wooing would have to be adjusted, again.

At least now he knew. His feelings for Bélla were acknowledged and sure. He was too far along this tightrope stretched over a chasm to turn back. He must negotiate it as best he could.

A knock came on his door in Tinne's pattern. Holm raised his voice, "Come."

Tinne opened the door and shoved his head in. He looked a little red-faced, a bead of sweat on his brow. "I've requested a discussion with T'Holly in quarter-septhour in the Green Room. I'd like you to be there, too."

Surprise and wariness shot through Holm. This sounded serious. His brother appeared tense. "Of course."

A muscle flexed in Tinne's cheek. "I'd like your support."

Holm nodded. "You have it."

Tinne's brows rose. "You're not going to ask for what, or why?"

Holm set his calligraphic brush down. "You're my brother. We stick together."

"Against our father?" Tinne muttered, then said under his breath, "I did it for the Family. It was the right thing to do."

Holm didn't question him, but addressed his obvious anxiety. "I doubt you could do anything that would earn you disinheritance." Not like Holm loving a T'Hawthorn woman, choosing her over his Family. He continued. "We're brothers and we're close. Our journey made sure of that."

Tinne's expression eased, and his mouth curved slightly. It was a wonder to them both that they hadn't killed each other on the trail back to Druida.

"Thank you." Tinne shut the door.

Holm gave his face one last scrub, then noticed the ink stains painting his hands. He decided to leave them, signs of good work, and better than blood.

"Mirror," he called. When the construct hung in front of him, he scanned his face. No ink. A small shadow showed on his throat. He opened his collar wide to study it. The lovebite Bélla had first put on him was fading. He would have to make sure she marked him as her own again. Soon.

A few minutes later Holm stopped with his hand on the doorknob of the Green Room. T'Holly Residence hadn't been redecorated in generations, but unlike all of the other public rooms, the Green Room reflected a woman's touch. His Mamá had spent many septhours here, and since her absence, the Family tended to congregate there.

The room had been built inside the main courtyard of T'Holly Residence, again as a boon to a Holly bride, so it had windows on three sides. The strips of solid walls were tinted with subtle shades of green ranging from the palest sea foam to the darkest forest, and many-paned windows let in dappled light.

The room would forever echo of his Mamá.

He opened the door. In the sunny room Tinne stood tall and pale, with his arm around Genista Furze. An uneasy tingle shot up Holm's spine.

Tab and Eryngi lounged in chairs with a game of holostrat

hanging between them. Holm could tell by the gleam in Tab's half-lidded eyes and the tapping of Eryngi's foot that both were primed for revelations.

T'Holly stood, his back against the light of the window behind him, straight and as stern as an Earth patriarch.

"Father, I want to introduce you to my wife, Genista Holly," Tinne said.

Eighteen

*H*olm gasped like he'd taken a gut blow. Buzzing filled his ears. Tinne had done this for him, of course. His brother had figured out that Holm wouldn't be bringing an acceptable bride to T'Holly Residence soon, and Tinne had acted instead.

But Tinne had a HeartMate, he knew it from his last two Passages. The idea repeated in Holm's mind. Had Tinne decided loving a HeartMate wasn't worth the pain? Holm dismissed that. Tinne would never be so cowardly as to reject the best of life's pleasure to avoid pain. Holm's smile quirked. He should have realize that when he'd been fretting. He finally noticed the silence and that his father hadn't moved.

"I know Genista, of course." T'Holly's voice was rusty. His eyes burned as if drawn from despair to face something distasteful.

Holm repressed a wince. Everyone in noble society knew Genista, and her reputation. At least T'Holly, being a HeartMate, would never have slept with her. Holm reminded himself that it had been years since their brief affair.

"Then you will welcome her into the Family," Tinne said.

Holm admired his guts, even as he felt his own twist into knots. Tinne had done this for him!

Genista smiled and tossed long golden hair that fell to her curvaceous hips. Holm was relieved that her sensuality left him unmoved, and that he couldn't remember any details of their fling. Tall and well-endowed, with lovely eyes and lithe grace, she looked good next to Tinne. Perhaps he hadn't made a mistake.

Holm had to move. He had to say something. All he could do was think Tinne had sacrificed himself.

Tab came to his feet and crossed to Tinne and Genista. Tab lifted her hand and kissed her fingers. "Welcome you are to the Holly Family," he said.

Eryngi bolted from the room.

"Thank you, GreatSir Holly," Genista said, cheeks flushing.

Holm set his feet in motion. The smile he tried came easily. He shouldered his G'Uncle Tab aside, took her fingers, and brushed them with his lips. "Welcome, sister."

She smiled and fluttered her lashes.

"I think—" started T'Holly in repressed tones that Holm knew preceded a scathing indictment.

"—that I should lead this lovely lady to your suite, eh, Tinne?" Tab ended. "She can look at your rooms, and her suite. There's a-plenty of redecoratin' she'll need to be doin'." He placed Genista's hand on his arm with deferential care, then heaved a great sigh. "What a charmin' addition to the Family, 'tis almost enough to make me move back ta the Residence." As he led Genista to the door, he swept the rest of them with glances. Holm got a stare of admonition, Tinne one of encouragement, and T'Holly of warning.

Tab continued to compliment Genista as he escorted her from the room and let the door whisper close behind them.

"What have you done!" growled T'Holly. "That creature . . ."

"Don't call her that," Holm said. "She is your son's wife, to be respected."

T'Holly snorted and thundered at Tinne. "Your brother, my Heir, has a HeartMate he'll be wedding. He'll fulfill his duties as HollyHeir. This rash act was unnecessary!"

Tinne flinched, but didn't give way. "I'm married and will start a Family at once. That's a fact." His gaze slid to Holm.

Holm made sure he stood shoulder to shoulder with his brother. "She's Genista Holly now, for the rest of her life."

T'Holly opened and closed his mouth. Then stared at Tinne. "You have a HeartMate. Why would you wed Genista?"

"We all have HeartMates," Tinne said. "Do you really want to talk of HeartMates, now?"

It reminded them all of their anguish.

"And you might consider the ramifications of alliance with T'Furze," Tinne said.

T'Holly said, "Furze has been trying to get rid of his youngest girl for years."

"Father," Holm said. "That is unworthy of you."

Tinne spoke. "She has the glamor. She gathers luck and good fortune to her."

"She gathers men to her," T'Holly said.

"The Furzes are known for their fertility," Holm pointed out. "They're the only FirstFamily that usually has three children or more. They're abundant and rich. Richer than we."

"Greater Flair runs in our Family," T'Holly muttered. "They aren't known for wedding HeartMates."

"HeartMates can rip you apart," Tinne said with fervor. They all flinched at the resonance of that truth. T'Holly's HeartMate was dying, Holm's HeartMate was presently beyond his reach. What had happened with Tinne?

Only their breathing made sound for a moment.

As if regaining some sensitivity, T'Holly said, "Forgive my words about your wife." He bowed his head to Tinne. "Genista Furze isn't a woman I had in mind for either of my sons."

"She is my choice," Tinne said stiffly.

Holm noted his brother's phrasing. Holm wanted to question Tinne, but wouldn't in T'Holly's presence. Holm itched with curiosity, and guilt felt like a thorn in his side.

T'Holly's eyes darkened, his shoulders slumped, he waved a hand. "It is your decision and your life. You will live it as you please, and well, I hope."

Holm and Tinne shared a glance. Holm clapped Tinne on the shoulder, jolting both his brother and father. "Tell us of the marriage settlements."

"T'Reed is the financial genius of the FirstFamilies, but the Furzes . . ."

"No one can match the Furzes' fortune," Holm agreed, making sure his father would accept the marriage. "At least that's what I've always heard." He angled his head to T'Holly.

"How much did we get?" asked T'Holly.

"Enough, but the gilt isn't important here," Tinne said.

"No?" T'Holly asked.

"ResidenceLibrary, present globe, magnifying the area around Triskel Pass," Tinne ordered.

"Look. The pass is ours, the western side and middle of the valley south is Hawthorn's, but next to him on the east, all the way back to the other range of mountains is . . ."

"Furze land!" T'Holly exclaimed.

"Not anymore," Tinne said.

"We got gilt and the land?" Holm asked.

"Yes," Tinne said.

"In exchange for?" T'Holly proceeded.

Tinne's face tightened. "That was her dowry. As evidence of my good faith to be a responsible husband, I deeded to T'Furze a small portion of my own property, and stipulated a large monthly stipend from the Hollys for Genista."

"What portion of your property?" asked T'Holly.

"The warehouses on the dock."

"They're a bit far from the main harbor, very old but in good repair." T'Holly nodded. "Well done."

Tinne let out a breath. "I thought so. Yarrow came, too."

Holm thought of the bill he'd get from the lawyer. He shrugged. It didn't matter. Tinne did very well.

"And," Tinne continued, "my oath that the Hollys will consider Genista a Holly, will support her the rest of her life, will give her a household of her own upon my death, and find her another husband, if she wishes."

T'Holly's eyebrows raised. "Not very different from the standard arrangement."

"You'll accept her, then." Tension laced Tinne's voice.

His father patted him on the shoulder, T'Holly's gaze fixed on the holo map. "She is my daughter."

Tinne's lips smiled, but his eyes were haunted. "Yes."

The golden oak door opened, and Tab rolled into the room with a seagoer's gait. "I've ordered champagne for two sent to your suite, young Tinne."

"Thank you."

"Brother, I'd like to talk to you," Holm said.

Hands in his pockets, Tab came to stand and look at

the globe. "Your time at Healing Hall's a-comin' up, Holm."

Holm's stomach lurched. He hadn't forgotten his Mamá, but Tinne's marriage had stirred Holm's emotions into a mess.

"You didn't invite us to the wedding," Holm said through stiff lips.

Tinne glanced at him impassively, shrugged, put his hands in his trous pockets. "We wanted it done quickly and quietly. Gen didn't want a big fuss like her two older sisters. Priestess D'Peony and Priest T'Scullcap took care of the formalities at Courtyard Grove behind GreatCircle Temple. I promised Gen a big reception . . . later."

With a trembling hand, T'Holly dismissed the globe. "Yes. A big party. Later. She is a lovely girl to look at," he murmured. "It's always good to have a pretty woman around."

Holm's jaw clenched. Tinne had married for the Family, not for himself. What of Tinne's HeartMate?

Holm would woo and HeartBond wed his true mate. Tinne would not. Tinne was tied for life to a woman who would never fulfill him like a true HeartMate.

Tinne met Holm's eyes. "We'll talk when you get back from HealingHall."

Tinne had sacrificed for Holm. The second time the younger brother had proved to be stronger than the elder. What could Holm do to ever repay that?

Holm bathed and changed before taking the glider to Primary HealingHall and his declining Mamá.

Emotions racked him: desperation, guilt, fear. He had to see Bélla again. He could not survive the day or the coming night without her.

After spending time with his Mamá, Holm ghosted through the HealingHall, using senses honed by fighting to elude others. He'd discovered that Bélla's schedule would bring her to the HealingHall no more than two septhours after he usually left— and being conscientious, she'd show up early—he sent his glider away and walked as cat-footed as Meserv to her den.

Seeing her things, breathing in the fragrance of her, absorbing the lingering *atmosphere* of her through his cells didn't calm him as he thought it might. His edginess increased each moment the den was empty of her. Seconds ticked away in heightened anticipation.

He crossed to the window, hoping the sight of the lush Healing Grove, ancient and awesome with spells, would settle his pounding heart. To no avail. The glade and towering trees just reminded him of his nearly nightly 'porting. Holm grimaced. Since his Mamá's injury, he'd been sleeping with a DepressFlair bracelet that kept him from nightporting though it disturbed his sleep on a different level. He hated the armlet.

He still hadn't been able to find his true center and calm his mind. In his sessions with the HouseHeart, it almost sounded amazed that he could fight so well without such depth of inner balance. The HouseHeart had gone so far as to test his reflexes and skills and pronounced him the best fighter the Family had ever had. Holm shook his head. Just what he needed to be while wooing a Healer.

He calmed his blood, clenched his shaky hands until he knew when he opened his fingers they'd be steady. He could not leap on her and take her away. All his impulses warred with his brain. From the moment he'd recognized his HeartMate as Mayblossom Lark Collinson T'Hawthorn, he'd had to strap down his reckless nature and use his head. He didn't like it. He much preferred leading with his heart. Or even with a more unruly part of his body situated lower. He'd always lived up to the expectations of a HollyHeir. He'd always mastered whatever consequences had befallen him—except for that one little time when he'd nearly killed himself trying to save Tinne from the Great Washington Boghole and Tinne had rescued them both.

But he needed to see Lark, and he must be calm about it. He'd lure her, tempt her, ensure she renewed her mark on him. He could live without her minute by minute if he felt the bruise on his throat, saw it in the mirror, had others tease him about it.

He wanted to grab her and run to T'Holly Residence, throw her on the bed, and forget about everything but loving her for months. All his muscles tensed at the images that flowed into his brain and set his blood to sizzling. That's what he wanted. But a HollyHeir couldn't do such rash things that would endanger the House.

His skin felt tight, his sinews hummed with a fine tension.

The door opened behind him, and her essence wafted in to envelop him. The tie between them looped around his heart, encasing it, wholly hers.

When he saw her, the hit he took dazed him. How could he have thought he could forsake her? He sank into his physically balanced stance. "Come to me."

Her eyes were huge and wide, with shadows under them. He held out a hand. "Come to me." None of the facile, pretty phrases he'd used with other women came to mind, ready to fall honey sweet from his lips. He tried. "You are so beautiful. Inside and out." He wanted to tell her what she meant to him, but he could only say with a dry mouth, "Come to me."

She hadn't moved a step, let alone within reach of his fingers. The gap between them seemed infinite. He couldn't move. Something in her eyes—weariness, unhappiness—kept him frozen. No smooth moves or charming words with this woman. "I need you," he croaked.

Lark stared at Holm. She couldn't help it. She hadn't understood she'd been starved for the sight of him. Passion bloomed in her core, loosening the muscles in her body. She noted distantly that her breathing had quickened and her pulse throbbed in her temple.

A fierce aura surrounded him. When a patient felt intensely, she could see their aura. She blinked. He *did* need her. She sensed his hunger, mental and emotional as well as physical. He'd always radiated strength and vitality. Now she observed desperation and despair.

Her body reacted to his. Her nostrils widened to breathe in his scent, her skin tingled as she recalled the skim of his hands down her. Insidious desire diffused into her bloodstream, causing a liquid heat within her.

She looked at his hand, and it trembled.

"This is madness," she said.

That broke the spell between them. He strode to her and swept her into his embrace, enveloping her with strong arms, pressing her close to his hard body, dropping butterfly kisses on her face. He lifted her until their mouths were even. As she gasped, his tongue surged into her mouth. The bond sprang between them. His desire enfolded her, transferred from his body and his emotions through their bond, demanding she reject thought and only *feel*.

With one last effort, she pulled her lips from the pressure of his. "I can't."

She tipped back her head and his dark gray eyes, flecked with silver, captured her.

Need. It pulsed from him to her, a craving so deep and powerful she couldn't deny it. She brought her legs around his waist and settled the aching place between her thighs against his rigid sex. She couldn't tell who moaned. She didn't know who whispered the Word that removed their clothes. Only the fact that they were tangled on the twoseat, his hands on her breasts, sending licks of hot sensation to her core mattered. Only the feel of pliant skin over tough muscle under her fingers mattered. Only the starkness of his handsome face, the craving in his eyes, the slickness of body against body, mattered.

Surging emotions—passion, need, pleasure bordering on pain—broke over her like a wave, and she was lost in a maelstrom of sensuality. His fingers speared through her hair, and he pressed her face to his throat. She tasted him and went mad. The salty, primal essence of him was something she needed more than anything else in her life. She bit him.

He lifted her hips, drove inside her, and the link of body and mind was so close and so right she surrendered utterly. He felt wonderful inside her, stroking her until they raced to reach ecstasy. The rhythm between them matched. Their heartbeats, their breathing, their spiral to the ultimate peak. His energy and intensity burned her, setting her nerves afire with lust and life. His thrusts increased until she thought she'd die from the ferocity, yet she matched him, held him, and with a cry, reached rapture with him.

He arched against her and emptied into her, and she felt the flood of not only his seed, but all his emotions into her in a great tsunami.

And when her wits returned, she shriveled. What had she done? She had acted from impulse, from emotion, from pure physical lust. She could not believe it of herself. "Madness," she whispered, disappointed and disgusted with herself.

She'd just renewed a bond she'd vowed to let wither and die, just made matters worse for them both at this awful time. She sensed the determination in him to claim her and keep her. A determination that matched her stubborn logic to stay apart.

She cut the exquisite mind tie between them and felt *cold.*

"Don't withdraw from me," he said.

Embarrassment flooded her, flushing the skin on her body. She didn't look at him. "No withdrawal. You are *inside* me."

He stroked her head with unsteady fingers. "I need all of you, Bélla, the emotional connection most of all."

"We *can't do this!*"

"Please, Bélla," he whispered and gentle mind-fingers brushed her, requesting the link. That tie was stronger than ever, Lark *saw* it as a golden cord as thick as her index finger. Each time they met it grew stronger.

She opened her surface thoughts and outer emotions as she raised herself from him and went to a tiny cubby that held a small waterfall.

Holm followed. She didn't dare look at him while she washed, but his mind-soothing, his renewed optimism showered over her like the water. "Bélla, my Bélla, what we have is right. It may not be the best moment to find each other, but it is *right*."

Feeling better than she had for several days, she drew on a robe and steeled herself to face Holm.

He'd used the small basin and a sponge to clean himself and lounged in the doorway. Naturally. He looked good. Better than good. He looked fabulous. His eyes were clear, the worry hounding his life shoved deep to wherever he kept his secrets—and he had them, she knew that now more than ever. Something long-term bothered him that he wouldn't speak of.

No matter, she chided herself. The present circumstances were worry enough for the entire city of Druida, and they wouldn't be together for long, anyway.

She lifted her chin. "I will not let this liaison continue. It is inappropriate and completely stupid at this time of our lives." Brushing past him, she dressed and glanced at the timer. She had twenty minutes before her shift.

Holm's thoughts fell into a "strategizing" pattern.

"No!" she said aloud.

Again he followed her, this time stopping behind her so she could feel the warmth of him at her back, the tickle of his breath on the top of her head. "We will continue to need each other, on many levels. Why deny ourselves the comfort of each other? It's not good for either of us to be apart."

Lark rolled her eyes. "Such logic!"

"Let me come to you tonight."

She turned and met his gaze with difficulty. "No."

"Bélla—"

She didn't want to hurt him, but knew her next words would. "I sleep in T'Hawthorn Residence tonight."

Nineteen

Holm's face settled into a mask.

"My nephew needs me, as does my FatherDam. I spend time with them each day," Lark said.

He laced his fingers through her wet hair and said a Word to dry it. The affectionate, caring gesture made her heart clutch.

"Family is very important. I'm glad that you haven't severed such bonds. You always give of yourself despite the cost. You're wonderful," Holm said.

"You exaggerate," Lark said. The thought of Family weighed like a heavy burden. She chose her words carefully. "I don't visit with my father or brother. We avoid each other because we disagree so."

Every night T'Hawthorn scried and asked about D'Holly's condition, the visitors she had, the general countenances of her Family. Lark replied with evasions about her health, protestations of ignorance as to the callers, and information regarding the Apples. With her words her father's eyes would chill, his expression would harden, and in that smooth voice of his he'd remind Lark of the unsatisfactory report on her.

She dreaded the scries. When she'd made an attempt to cut them short and stop them, T'Hawthorn merely frowned and said she didn't look well. He would send Cratag over—alone—to check on her. Further, T'Hawthorn would speak to T'Heather about her health. Perhaps Lark worked too hard.

His less-than-subtle threats, all issued in smooth tones, always defeated her. She could never tell if he cared for her or not, and when he finally ended the scry, she felt stupid and angry that she'd responded to him as she'd been taught all her life.

Holm traced her mouth with his finger. "You're frowning. Let me help."

Lark scowled. "We can't talk without differing, either."

He grinned. "No, we can't *talk*. But we communicate incredibly well in other ways—where we are in *full* agreement."

"Thank you for the rose every evening," she said.

He dipped his head. "I want to ensure you remember me."

No chance she'd forget. He caught her mental comment, and his teeth flashed again in a smile. Then he angled his chin to flaunt the mark she'd put on his throat, ruby and purple. Lark winced. She lifted a hand to touch the bruise, then decided against it.

Too late. He took her fingers and kissed them. "We are learning about each other. You know that I will wear your lovebite proudly. And I, *I* learn to let you go even when I want nothing more than to keep you near." He ended on a serious note. "But I won't stay away forever."

She sensed layers of meaning and secrets and determination in his voice, and trembled inside. "I have to go."

"Yes. For now. Merry meet."

Lark closed her eyes in pain. "I can't say that. I *can't*."

His lips brushed her eyelids. "No, it's not a 'merry parting,' since I don't want to part. But we will meet again."

"That's not the first time you said that." She opened her eyes, released herself from his grip, straightened her shoulders and walked to the door.

"That's because I mean it. I'll see you again, soon." He put a hand over his heart. "I'll be with you if I have to beg for the pleasure."

"What!" She glanced back at him. He looked tough, but his smile was sweet.

"You don't think I'll beg? I will."

She just stared at him. His eyes heated and the connection between them rippled with desire. Images of lovemaking swept from him to her and back. They were taking turns begging. She fled.

*H*olm's amusement at *Bélla's* shocked look buoyed him a moment, then the creeping fear of his Mamá lingering at the entrance to the Wheel of Stars of death and birth oppressed him. He took a quick shower and 'ported home, directly to his new pool. His sanctuary.

Tinne found him there and the sight of Tinne's uncertain expression sent the guilt Holm preferred to ignore blazing through him. So he spoke too sharply. "What have you done?"

Tinne lowered himself to a lounge near the pool and gave a wide grin.

Holm looked behind it to see the flash of inner pain that matched his brother's somber eyes.

"Why did I marry Genista? Her bloodline is good, she has minor Healing abilities, and she's the sexiest noblewoman around. We're hoping to engender the next generation of Hollys immediately." Tinne waggled his eyebrows.

"You have a HeartMate! You know you have a HeartMate. You always felt so and had inklings during your first Passage. Why did you marry? There's no divorce in a dynastic marriage like this. You fool, why didn't you wait for your love?" All the loneliness Holm had gone through when he thought he had no HeartMate, all the frustration he'd felt waiting after he'd met Lark and felt the pull, all the fury he experienced trying to woo her, exploded in his words.

Tinne shrugged, then lifted a serious face. "I'm sorry you haven't won your HeartMate. Leave this alone."

Nausea rolled in Holm's stomach. He gripped the back of a longchair to keep from shaking his brother. "I can't. You fool. You should have—"

"She's wed!" Tinne burst out. "My HeartMate's Family married her off before she experienced her third Passage and knew for sure she had a HeartMate. I was waiting for her to grow up a little more. I didn't know her marriage was planned. A quiet ceremony took place four days ago."

Just after their Mamá had been struck down. When Tinne had been distracted.

"So you thought to help me—" Holm started.

"I guessed Healer Lark was your HeartMate. Father is desperate for a grandchild. You couldn't marry. I could." Tinne cut the air with his hand. "My HeartMate's wed and now so am I. I don't want to talk about it." His stormy gaze nailed Holm. "I don't ever want to discuss this again. Understood?"

Holm staggered under the blow fate had struck his brother. And he, Holm, thought he'd had romantic problems! His lover wasn't married—she struggled against their bond, but she wasn't completely lost to him. And he hadn't managed to get himself married before he'd found her; something in him had always demanded he wait and wait and wait.

He released his grip on the chair and bowed deeply toward his brother.

"Please, go," Tinne said, his stare fixed on the waterfall cascading over the rocks. "You were right to build the conservatory. It's a good place. The water is soothing." He smiled crookedly. "I'd rather live here with Genista, instead of setting up an estate of my own now, and after I inherit The Green Knight. Do I have your permission?"

Holm nodded and crossed over to his brother, who had returned to contemplating the waterfall. "Yes, T'Holly Residence is your home, always."

Holm gripped Tinne's shoulder. "Don't give up. Don't tempt your luck in fights. For the Lord and Lady's sake, and my own, don't get yourself killed. There is always hope."

A corner of Tinne's mouth lifted, but he didn't look up. "The Hollys usually believe that. I used to think so, too."

*T*he night was as long and restless as all the others. Meserv whined at Holm's tossing and slept as far as he could from the DepressFlair bracelet. T'Holly spent the darkest reaches of the night with his HeartMate, knowing that most people slipped away from life in those septhours. Holm could feel his father's mind-numbing grief, his hope draining millisecond by millisecond.

In the morning T'Holly summoned Holm to the Residence-Den.

He took a seat in the loathed wingchair before his father's

desk. T'Holly appeared to have lost twenty pounds, and his skin was tight over a drawn face.

He looked old.

"My HeartMate, your mother, is dying." T'Holly laced his fingers together, but they trembled. "The Healers cannot halt the spell. It is only a matter of time." His facial muscles crumpled for a moment, then firmed into iron rigidity. "I have revised my will. The lifespan of a widowed HeartMate has never exceeded the circle of the year."

His lips trembled. "That fatality rate includes my sister, Leea, who died with her husband T'Blackthorn when he succumbed to that damned Blackthorn disease."

T'Holly drew a harsh breath and went on. "The only Heart-Mate who ever lasted a full year was engaged in a bloodfeud—as we will be. You, as the FirstSon and strongest Flaired Holly, will become T'Holly as we've expected all your life. But before I embark on the Wheel of Stars of rebirth, I will see those Hawthorns in the Cave of the Dark Goddess." His eyes blazed with mad fervor, and he bared his teeth in a wolflike grin. "We will fight and we will win! I want your HeartOath that the Hawthorn Family will be destroyed, every last one of them."

"No!" Holm jumped to his feet. His father's words freed Holm's roiling emotions. He leaned over the desk and used his own fury backed by fear to combat his father's will. Only tenacity from the bedrock of his being could deflect T'Holly in this. "Not the women."

"Everyone! Women! Babes newborn! All!" His father rose and roared his grief.

Holm sucked in a breath and refused to let his own despair tip him over into the same madness. "Not. The. Women. We are not Hawthorns who fight women. We are Hollys *who cherish them.* No child under sixteen. The children to be fostered with T'Ash."

"All!"

Holm did something he'd never done before, never even considered. He struck his father open-handed on the cheek.

T'Holly rocked back. His mouth opened.

Holm beat him to speech. "Don't spew what you feel. Stop. Think. Our Family would be destroyed by the FirstFamilies Council, all of us sterilized and the line and name to die if we followed your vengeance stalk. It's the oldest rule on the books, and the reason the Rue family is no more. That happened in your lifetime, don't you recall? One son, one, attempted to destroy the T'Ash line, and all the Rues were held accountable, and forfeit. There are no Rues now, and never will be again. Do you want to take my future from me, and from Tinne? From Tab, Eryngi, Ruscus, the rest of this House? You've always acted in the Family's good, only a fligger like Bucus Elder—"

A thought struck Holm. A dizzying thought, a memory of the young prophet—Vinni's—words. A sickening thought because it brought bright hope. His mouth dried, but he managed to mutter words anyhow. "Ruis. Ruis Elder. *The Ship.*"

T'Holly turned white and gripped the desk, but his whole body shook. "What?" His whisper rasped. "What are you thinking?"

Holm shouted at the top of his lungs. "Tinne, Lark Collinson, meet me at Primary HealingHall!" He knew the anguish, and wrath, and hope that propelled his telepathic thought would reach the two anywhere. "ResidenceLibrary," Holm snapped. "Is the starship, *Nuada's Sword,* and Captain Elder aware of our situation?"

"Captain'sLady, Supreme Judge of Druida, Ailim Elder, has of course been informed of a feud that could lead to bloodfeud and serious municipal tumult. She held a private session with the Hawthorns. T'Holly refused to see her," the Residence said.

"Inform Ruis Elder and *Nuada's Sword* we'll be there with D'Holly within half a septhour."

"What are you thinking?" T'Holly whispered again. The hope lighting his face tore at Holm.

"Ruis Elder is a *Null.* He can stop spells. Be glad you didn't execute him two and a half years ago."

T'Holly sank to the desk with his head in his hands. Tears slipped down his face.

Holm 'ported to Primary HealingHall and found Tinne in abstracted conversation with Lark. Holm wanted to grab her, squeeze her, hold her until he felt better. But an image came of the hourglass of his Mamá's life, sand plummeting. So little time. Too little time. "Good, you're here. You're both coming with me. Now." He pushed past to his mother's room, and without looking at her—he couldn't afford to break—pulled the silkeen covers around her and lifted her in his arms. He tried not to notice how little she weighed.

"You can't take her. Stop!" Lark cried.

"Take over her life support," Holm ordered coolly.

"I won't."

Holm moved away from the permamoss bed, away from the three gray-faced SecondLevel Healers and PerSun who strove to keep D'Holly alive. "I'm taking her to Ruis Elder at *Nuada's Sword.*"

A heartbeat passed before Tinne grasped their Mamá's hands. "I can do life support. The Null, Lady and Lord, the Null."

"Let me," Lark said, elbowing Tinne aside. "You are too clumsy. A fighter will never be a Healer."

Holm said, "The Null stopped one spell-driven deathplague, he can do it again. Hold on to me. I have the coordinates and am 'porting in three seconds. Countdown. One fantastic Holm Holly. Two fantastic Tinne Hollys. Three—we go!"

They materialized a few yards from the starship, and Holm felt a touch of vertigo as the huge Ship loomed over them. The surrounding park rustled with birds and avians, whirring insects, and held the scents of high summer grasses and flowers. His Mother felt smaller than ever in his arms.

He looked at Lark. "She's well?"

"She lives."

"Good." Holm led his little party up to the northeast portal of *Nuada's Sword.* "Announce us," he asked Tinne.

Tinne's voice sliced through the lethargic summer air. "GreatLady Passiflora D'Holly, FirstLevel Healer Mayblossom Collinson, HollyHeir Holm, GreatSir Tinne Holly requesting entrance to the Ship and an interview with Captain Elder," Tinne shouted.

The shining metal door rose and showed two people, Ruis and Ailim Elder. "Greetyou," Ruis said. "Sick bay's been notified. This is the closest entry. Let me take her. I understand she suffers from a propulsion poison spell."

Holm shuddered as the Null, a man who could stop any Flair, gently accepted the light weight of D'Holly. The Captain aimed a lopsided smile at Lark. "No need for you to try and keep her stable, GreatMistrys, your Flair has no effect around me."

Tinne, Lark, and Holm all faded back a couple of meters from Ruis for mere comfort. Captain Elder strode through the hallways of *Nuada's Sword.*

They came to a door marked "Sick Bay" in old Earth writing and followed Elder through. He placed D'Holly on a strange-looking bed.

"Diagnostic bed. Results, Ship?" commanded Elder.

A female voice sounding uncannily like Primary HealingHall answered. "As with most things on Celta, the poison-spell is a mixture of the psi power called Flair and technology, or in this case, organic chemistry. The propelling spell already shows signs of slowing, due to your Nullness. You can halt its spread by 100 percent. The poison, however—"

"Analyze the poison, please," Elder said, and climbed up onto the bed to lie next to D'Holly and encircle her with his arms. Reflexively Holm and Tinne lunged.

"Stop them!" Ailim Elder cried, grabbing Tinne.

Lark's arms went around Holm's waist from behind, tight. Nothing in the world could have stopped him but that. Tremors swept through him at the press of her body against his.

"Can't you see, he's enveloping her in his Null field. It's the only way to stop the poison. Look at her color—it's better already," Lark said.

Holm took a step toward the bed, and Lark's arms dropped. He clamped one of his own arms around her waist and drew her to his side. If she offered comfort, by the Lord and Lady he'd take it. He'd take anything he could get from her at any time. Let her explain his touches to herself as grief or need or anything else, as long as she let him hold her. "Yes, she looks better."

"As if she's sleeping," Tinne said.

Before their eyes, a tentacle from the bed attached to D'Holly's arm, pressed, then wiggled away.

"T'Holly comes," Ship said.

The door opened and T'Holly shouted and plunged to the bed. Tinne and the women jumped on T'Holly, carrying him to the floor.

"Always distrusted. Never appreciated. I am damn sick of this Society," Ruis Elder muttered.

"What would you do, if you found a man lying with your HeartMate?" Holm asked.

Ruis turned his head to smile at Holm. "Kill him."

"And if he was Healing her?" Lark shouted in T'Holly's ear, then boxed it. "There's been too much violence already."

T'Holly groaned. Sitting up, he dislodged his attackers. He rose and shook himself. When he glanced over at the bed, his face darkened.

"Ship, report on D'Holly's condition," Ruis Elder ordered.

"The spread of poison has stopped, but the effects linger."

"Prognosis?" Lark snapped.

"The poison has been verified as Colchicum Autumnale, in Earth words, autumn crocus. Since colchicine retards cell-division, a propulsion spell was used to ensure its efficacy. Ship estimates a very strong dosage, probably created in FirstGrove by Nightshade three years ago."

"A poison Hawthorn blade," Tinne raised a fist. "I'll settle with them."

"Young Laev found the blade in the street. He's just thirteen. He didn't know it was poisoned," Ailim Elder said.

"Debate that later," Lark said. "Silence! Ship, please continue with the prognosis. Can D'Holly be Healed?"

"Ship believes her condition and the nature of the poison makes it unlikely that native psi talent, Flair, can Heal this patient at this time."

"The tubes," T'Holly ground out. "The suspended animation tubes that brought the colonists here. Can you use those?"

Holm stared at his father.

"I toured the Ship as a child, before we closed everything but the museum rooms," T'Holly said.

Again Ship politely waited until all speech ended. "The tubes would keep the Lady just as she is now. However, there is a 90 percent chance of total recovery under certain conditions."

Twenty

♥

"What are the conditions that will save my HeartMate?" T'Holly demanded.

"If the one functioning lifepod on the Ship is activated and maintained by the Captain—"

"Elder, I beg you," T'Holly turned to the former thief, "anything—"

"Ship, continue with prognosis despite any human talk," Lark said impatiently.

Ship made a little noise, then started again. "A kidney must be donated by a close relative to replace her poisoned one, to invigorate and cleanse her body—"

"Anything, anything of mine," T'Holly said.

Holm knew his father wasn't thinking. He'd gone to his HeartMate and held her hand in both of his.

"—a kidney from one of her sons would do," Ship said.

"Mine," Holm said, beginning to strip.

Tinne slapped Holm's fingers from the tab groove of his shirt. "You're Heir. If D'Holly dies, if—" He looked at T'Holly and back to Holm. "Use my kidney!"

"A replacement for the donated organ can be grown in Our vats, then restored to the donor," Ship pointed out. "We await your decision."

Holm pushed his younger brother aside. "I'll donate. I'm not letting you run around dueling with only one kidney. And we are feuding, aren't we?" he asked T'Holly.

T'Holly's blazing eyes and wolf grin were back. "Damn right."

"It is not necessary—" began Ailim Elder, the judge.

T'Holly's mouth hardened. "I've had no apologies from the Hawthorns, no offer of reparation, no indication they care that they tore the heart from my Family. We fight."

Ailim's expression turned grim. She gave a slight nod, obviously unwilling to broach the subject again.

T'Holly swept them all with a simmering gaze. "Tinne's right, Holm is heir and next in line to be T'Holly. He cannot be risked any more than necessary. My SecondSon, Tinne, will donate a kidney for my HeartMate. The Ship will heal my HeartMate and grow a new kidney to replace Tinne's as soon as possible." T'Holly's gaze rested on Holm, still heavy with anger. "As for you, you will marry immediately and begin engendering sons."

Tinne snorted behind Holm.

Holm smiled his father's own feral smile back at T'Holly. " 'Courting and feuding take all a man's time,' " he quoted an old saying. "Which would you rather I do?"

"Fight," his father bit off.

"Yes." Holm nodded, hoping, somehow, that he'd be able to win his own HeartMate, and soon. She looked very distant now. "Ship, give me a scry line to T'Ash."

"Ship runs on nanotech, not Flair," Ship's voice said primly.

"I know you can create a visual and audio communication; please do so," Holm said, not taking his eyes from Lark.

"Very well," Ship acknowledged.

A few seconds later T'Ash looked out of a holo. He sat at his ResidenceDen desk, a writetool in hand. "Holm," he said.

Holm grinned again. "We fight. I need a protection amulet for my brother."

T'Ash raised heavy black brows. His swarthy face showed no surprise. "I suggest he wear the main-gauche I made for that purpose."

Tinne gasped in irritation. "You did what?"

"I want something more," Holm said. "Something that will

automatically teleport him to a HealingHall if injured. He'll be fighting without a kidney."

T'Ash looked past them, as if studying Sick Bay. He pushed away papyrus covering his desk. "I see. A feud with the Hawthorns. Do you want my arm in alliance?"

"You've offered that before," T'Holly said. "My answer is the same. No. Only amulets, one for both my sons."

T'Ash inclined his head. "It will be done."

Holly knew his friend would work his body and Flair into exhaustion to make them quickly.

T'Ash continued. "I can create the amulets within six septhours of receiving an object for the pendant. I have the chains and will work the spells into them, but I suggest you use gemstones from the Family vault as focusing pendants. I know the Holly jewels. There is a cylindrical stone of Earth hematite that resonates to Tinne. Send that one to me for him. I will use all my skill, but for additional protection and the 'port spells, you should also give it to D'Alder to bespell."

"I agree," T'Holly said.

A brief smile flickered across T'Ash's lips. "All of you, carry your main gauches I crafted. Tinne's isn't the only one with a protection spell." That brought a short laugh from T'Holly, who stroked his HeartMate's hand.

"As for T'Holly . . . my HeartMate, Danith"—T'Ash's smile widened in love—"has been working with a hunting cat, a gift for you, T'Holly."

"My thanks. A hunting cat is always useful in a fight."

T'Ash studied Holm. "The jewel I'd choose for your amulet is the baroque pearl. You know the one I mean."

Holm scowled, a flush heated his neck. "Not the pink one."

T'Ash's eyes lit in unholy amusement. "That's right, the thumb-length baroque pastel-*pink* pearl. I'll use it for your amulet. We should talk."

The pearl had always fascinated Holm. "I'm not wearing a pink pearl as an amulet when I'm fighting."

"Yes, you are," T'Holly commanded.

"Yes, you are," Tinne chortled.

"I'm sure it won't compromise your virility." Lark looked coolly at him, lips thinned.

Holm sighed.

* * *

*H*olm *rarely brooded, but when he did, he came to this* dungeon chamber. It was a perfect place to brood, able to depress even the most exuberant spirits. Like many rooms in T'Holly Residence, despite the brightest light, cleansing spells and technology, it had a tendency to remain dark and damp, with a Celtan lichen-moss growing from the floor up the walls and imparting a pungent odor. But this room always stayed that way. It had no windows, only spell-lighting.

He crossed to a tank of water on the far wall. Though the water was perfectly calibrated to suit the inhabitants, and one in particular, it looked murky. Algae floated on the top. Sea fronds waved muddy brown streamers, and in the layer of sediment sat an oyster as big as his forearm.

It was his oyster.

He'd been responsible for it since he'd been a small boy, when he'd been fascinated with its crusty shell, that it could project its basic needs telepathically, and even recognize him. Its origins weren't noted in the Holly histories—the Family had always been impatient and it had been several generations before an adopted son recorded the vanishing stories of their early years on Celta—but legend had it that the oyster had originated on the Ship, *Arianrod's Wheel.*

Holm called it "Clam." When young, the thing that had engrossed Holm the most was the few times he'd seen Clam completely open, and inside sat a ravishing, incongruously petal-pink pearl. Eventually, Clam had made it clear that the pearl was too large an impediment and should be removed. So Holm had done it and kept the gem.

Like Clam, the pearl had been unique: pink and as long as his thumb and twice as wide. T'Ash had seen the jewel, admired it, confirmed its vast value.

"It's all your fault," Holm said to Clam.

T'Holly rested upstairs after submitting to a sleep spell, new hope in his heart. Tinne had remained at *Nuada's Sword,* lounging in the wondrous Greensward, taking it easy after the removal of his kidney. A new one was budding in a vat that looked remarkably like this tank.

Holm sensed a slow, chill regard emanating from Clam.

"Maybe I should return you to the Ship. You might like it better there. It might be more like the home you originally knew," he stated. "It's because of you I have to wear that pearl. It was *your* pearl. Do you know what sort of trouble that pearl is going to get me into?"

The oyster's lifeforce quickened, and it used its jetspray to move closer to the glass where Holm stood.

"But you can redeem yourself," Holm said. "I haven't checked lately, but it's been years since I took that last pearl from you. Maybe you have a new one that I could use in the amulet instead. White. Or black. Black would be good. And shaped better." Holm thought a moment and grinned. "A heart-shaped pearl would be fabulous. I could wear it, then later give it to my Bélla as a gift—I wouldn't even mind a pink heart. Do you have a pearl?" He rapped his knuckle on the glass.

Clam settled. Cold watery consideration enveloped it. Slowly a crack appeared in its shell.

T'Ash comes, T'Holly Residence stated. *I informed him you were here, and reminded him of the way.*

"Thank you," Holm muttered, watching with awe as Clam's shell yawned wider and wider.

By the time it finally opened, T'Ash stood beside Holm.

"Pink again," Holm choked.

"I'd call it more of a dark coral color. That oyster has a remarkable facility for making pearls that look like body parts," T'Ash commented.

The tops of Holm's ears burned with embarrassment. "This one's worse than the other. It looks like a man's cock."

"And almost life-size. Very valuable. You don't want it?"

"No!"

"I'll be glad to take it off your hands, payment for fashioning your amulets."

"Good."

"Hmmm." T'Ash surveyed the pearl. "I think I'll give it another year or two to grow."

Clam disagreed. It wanted the pearl out as soon as possible. Holm passed this on to T'Ash.

T'Ash considered the oyster. "Very well. It's large enough for a small sculpture to be fashioned."

Holm choked again. "All right. You're sure you want it?"

T'Ash raised his eyebrows. "There's a market for sensual jewelry, the same as for every other sort of erotic art." He squeezed Holm's shoulder, and a white grin broke the olive tone of his face. "Count your blessings. This could have been the first pearl, then you'd be wearing it."

"Not a chance."

"As if this wouldn't have caught your attention as a boy."

Holm coughed, but couldn't deny it.

"That's why your pearl will be the centerpiece of your protective spell. It's the jewel you're most linked with. You've toyed with it when thinking. You've carried it in your pocket. It sits in your suite, on your headboard or on your desk. It's you." T'Ash made kissy noises.

Holm took him down. They landed on the stone floor with grunts and began a satisfying fight.

Damn it, Holm thought as he shot an arm out and caught T'Ash's jaw, grinning himself now. *I'm going to have to wear a pink pendant that looks like lips pursed for a kiss.*

He'd be fighting a lot.

A *few moments later they both lay on longchairs in the con-*servatory at the top of the fortress, drying off from an after-fight swim. Meserv snored gently by Holm's side. The soft fur of the kitten felt good against his skin. Sunlight streamed through the glass dome and bounced off the deep blue pool water, then vanished in the layers of greenery.

"Nice," T'Ash grunted, sporting a standard quick-heal bandage on his jaw that should Heal the bruise in a couple of septhours.

Holm pressed a painease spellcloth to the cut by his mouth before he replied. "Thanks. I'm the only one who likes it."

"Tinne?" T'Ash asked.

"He spends a little time here. Mamá tolerates it—" How wonderful to be able to talk of her casually, knowing she wouldn't die. "Father resents that I've altered an ancient and miserable attic storeroom, making it into a place of beauty."

T'Ash just grunted. Holm knew he thought of his own lost Residence, burned to the ground when T'Ash was six. Sometimes Holm envied T'Ash the freedom he had to design and build a brand-new home, consulting only his taste. But Holm knew T'Ash didn't see it that way. Holm could barely move a chair without hearing about it. Now. But his time would come.

Idly he wondered what his lady would change about T'Holly Residence when they were wed and HeartBonded. Her apartment had been light and airy, with cream-colored walls and vibrant-colored furniture. He smiled in anticpated glee. In one of the storerooms, well-wrapped, were brightly colored tapestries that he could hardly wait to hang. She'd like those.

The chair next to his creaked and Holm turned to see T'Ash's eyes narrowed at him. "You look different," T'Ash said. "Softer."

They stared at each other for a moment.

"A woman," T'Ash concluded, propping himself on an elbow.

Holm felt his mouth twist. "A HeartMate."

T'Ash's eyes widened. "I didn't think you had one, didn't think you ever Connected during your Passages."

Holm's smile became even more sardonic. "It's hard to think about anything except staying alive when your Passages consist of death duels."

T'Ash nodded. "Especially Downwind."

Holm shifted Meserv to his chest, where he could pet the kitten. Meserv's purr vibrated against Holm's chest wall and soothed him even as the Fam's small snuffles tickled Holm's hair. "My parents sent me to D'Willow for a matchmaking consult." From the corner of his eye he saw T'Ash's brows rise.

"Expensive."

"She confirmed that I'd had to 'grow' to match my Heart-Mate. I think that little trek across the country with Tinne was responsible for my 'growth.'"

"Hmmm," T'Ash said.

"It's not going to be easy to win her."

T'Ash gave a crack of laughter. "When is it ever?"

Holm shot him a look. "It shouldn't be difficult. My parents had it easy."

"The older generation." T'Ash fell back into his chair and stared at the leaves of the tree above him. He chuckled. "Just make her a HeartGift."

"Your little joke," Holm grumbled. T'Ash had gone through

hell to make a HeartGift and win his HeartMate the easy way. Holm felt certain that particular tactic would be just as futile for himself as it had been for his friend. "She's Mayblossom Larkspur Hawthorn Collinson."

T'Ash's groan and laughter mixed. "Lord and Lady, you have a worse situation than I did. And I thought mine was doomed." He turned sky-crystal blue eyes to Holm. "Seriously, consider a HeartGift."

"What can I offer her that she'll accept? I haven't continually practiced my artistic Flair like you," Holm snapped. His efforts with the calligraphy brush continued to be ugly.

T'Ash swung his legs off the chair and faced Holm. "I know that feeling. My HeartGift was the least of what I was, and reflected the man I'd been seventeen years before. But you do yourself an injustice. Your artistry will return with practice."

"Even if that's so, most HeartGifts are backed by the power of Flair being freed during Passage. That's what makes them so potent. My three Passages have come and gone. I could make her a gift, but it wouldn't be the same."

T'Ash's brows lowered. "Wrong. There are Rituals. I know that now. I was wrong, myself, when I thought only a forced Passage would create a HeartGift."

Holm couldn't sit still. He lifted Meserv, who opened a sapphire eye and mewed. Holm draped the kitten over his shoulder with a small Word to keep the Fam balanced and comfortable. Meserv shifted to lie lengthwise on Holm's shoulder, gurgled and rolled over onto his back, paws curved over round belly.

T'Ash blinked. "That's a sight."

"Don't distract me." Holm began to pace. "I've looked at Rituals to create a HeartGift. There are some, granted, but they aren't as powerful as Passage."

"Nothing's as powerful as Passage."

Holm ran a hand through his hair. "And the ones I've studied call for about two eightdays of fasting, purification, and dedication—"

T'Ash laughed. "Hard for a Holly to practice patience for a septhour, let alone an eightday."

Holm ignored the truth. "—then the Ritual itself takes a full day, in the HouseHeart. When the twinmoons are no more than a septhour from waxing to full."

"It's just the beginning of Hazel, next full twinmoons and the start of Apple is more than twenty days away," T'Ash said.

"Yes."

"You're sunk."

"Yes. I can't enter a time of purification when I'll be fighting. Neither the Hawthorns nor my father will grant me that time. I can't arrange for a full day in the HouseHeart for myself without requesting permission from my father. And Apple twinmoons is too long from now." Holm smiled bleakly.

T'Ash stood and shook water from his long, tangled black hair, spraying droplets as far as Holm and Meserv. Meserv hissed at T'Ash.

He grinned, strode over, and tickled the kitten's stomach. "You're not much like your Sire or Dam, young Meserv. You're lazy."

No reason to exert self, Meserv said mildly.

Holm ran his own hand along the kitten's plump body. "I think his twin got all his aggression—Phyll, Lark's Fam."

T'Ash rubbed a hand over his jaw. "You concentrate on dueling. Try not to kill any of her favorite relatives."

Holm winced.

T'Ash picked up a towel and dried off. "The power of my HeartGift scared Danith. It was a detriment and set me back. Your Lark impresses me as a very sensitive woman. FirstDaughter of a FirstFamily, and great enough Flair to be named a FirstLevel Healer. Your HeartGift won't need much power to impress her." He grinned again. "And like you keep telling me, most women admire subtlety. So a subtle HeartGift, swirling with power, Flair . . . It could very well do the trick. You"—he leveled a finger at Holm—"practice your calligraphy." Scooping up his clothes, he teleported home.

Later Holm followed T'Ash's advice. His brush strokes looked better, more elegant and less wobbly. His hand was relearning the motor skills needed for calligraphy as opposed to wielding a blaser or blade. He set his jaw. Tonight he'd create a piece and infuse it with all his power—as close to a HeartGift as possible.

He was inking his brush and considering the optimum time to arrive at Lark's apartment when T'Holly's viz appeared. The lines in Holm's father's face were more deeply incised than an eightday ago, but hope showed in his bearing and a gleam of battle in his eyes. Holm's stomach tightened.

"All available residents to SparringRoom Three for a free-for-all melée." T'Holly sounded cheerful. "Common bathing to follow, then a feast, then strategic planning for our feud, then a Ritual of Thanks in the Family Grove for the recovery of our GreatLady. Begin in ten minutes, count starting *now!*"

Holm stared at the space where his father's visage had hovered. Damn! It didn't look as if he could visit Bélla tonight. After what had happened that morning—an incident he hoped he and his father ignored and never spoke of—he must mend his Family ties tonight.

He gritted his teeth and dashed off a symbol. The ink glistened against the papyrus—bold and supple. "Your loveliness haunts me." He admired the character. Instinctively he drew another. That one looked good, too. "May I linger in your thoughts." Satisfied he could send her something of himself with his nightly rose, he 'ported the artistic papyrus with instructions to GrandHouse Rose. The ritual would give him excellent energy to make his HeartGift. He wondered what Bélla thought of calligraphy, hoped she admired it.

As he put away his brush set, it occurred to him that she might be expecting him that night, and a little distance—much as he hated it—might put her off balance. He grinned.

Doing a few stretches, he let his grin widen and go feral. He knew where he could release the sexual tension that prowled in him. He'd win that melée.

Twenty-one

❦

That night Lark went wild tinting her walls. She'd seen a striking sunset as she'd weeded the flower beds in T'Horehound's gardens, and frozen the image in her mind.

Just before darkness fell, the GrandLord had drifted near her work, and they'd shared an inconsequential conversation, as they had every night since D'Holly had fallen. Lark sensed the older man's concern, but she hadn't spoken of her own worries, and the gentle discussions soothed her as much as the physical work in his gardens. She'd scried Danith D'Ash and requested T'Horehound be placed on the waiting list for a rare kitten.

But that night was different. That night hope sang in her veins. The music would not be stilled. D'Holly would live.

Back in her apartment she was physically tired yet emotionally restless. So she tinted the long wall across from her red sofa to match the sunset and rippled the other walls with subtle bands of peach, pink, and coral.

Pleased at the effect, she lay on the couch and stared up at the ceiling of blue sky and white clouds.

The morning after her lovemaking with Holm, Lark had requested special spells and conditioning liquid from the Clover Family to treat her sofa and bedsponge to remove any trace of

Holm's scent. The new fragrance of the sofa was pleasantly reminiscent of good Celtan soil. She'd also given all the roses to Trif Clover.

When the white rose had come the first evening she and Holm were apart, she couldn't force herself to give it to Trif. These roses came after their loving—their sex. The new flowers came *after* D'Holly's awful wounding. Lark knew she shouldn't keep them, but couldn't throw them away. She compromised by putting them in a vase in a dim kitchen corner.

The jubilant news while in *Nuada's Sword* that D'Holly could be cured almost mended the yawning hole inside her at her denial of Holm. There was still no future for them. Neither Family would be able to forget what had happened, the feud still flourished, but at least she wouldn't be part of a Family that had committed the heinous killing of a GreatLady.

Lark repressed a tremor at the remembrance of Holm's touch earlier that day. Simply the brush of his hand against hers had caused her blood to race with the pounding of her heart, had flashed visuals of their loving to the forefront of her mind. She'd had to spend energy to control herself, and resorted to her mantra more than once.

She'd been surprised and displeased with the huge cavity of emptiness and hurt inside her now their affair was over. She grimaced in a parody of laughter as she thought that it had truly been a onenight, or a oneafternoon.

The last few days had been horrible. The PerSuns had been a blessing, giving her the strength to go beyond her usual range. She'd pushed herself to the limits every day.

And in the night she ached for Holm and wept silent tears that his tender arms didn't envelop her and never would again.

Lark whimpered and Phyll appeared. He leapt onto her stomach and changed her whimper to a grunt.

While you played in the gardens, Meserv and I played in a Ship. Very good place. Ship belongs to a Cat, Samba. She showed us many games. Phyll stretched out on Lark and she started petting him, noticing he grew larger each day and was becoming quite muscular.

He answered her general thoughts. *I am strong, but not as strong as Samba. She is a big Cat. Fatter than Meserv. Meserv got*

*sick after eating an earthplant in the Greensward. Tinne Holly
petted us. He does not have one kid-ney. The Ship is growing him
another. Do I have a kid-ney?*

"You have two, as do all mammals."

Dogs, also?

"Yes."

*There is a stupid dog on the Ship. We did not play with her.
She is much smaller than Samba. Tinne is a good Holly, but not
as good as Ours. When will Our Holm Holly come back?*

Hope warred with reason. She shouldn't want him to come
back. He *shouldn't* come back, for both their sakes. Pain
wrenched through her. "He's not coming back."

Phyll snorted and jumped off her to trot into the kitchen and
investigate his food dish. *You still have a string between you,* he
said before munching his crunchies.

The evening passed with relentless slowness. Lark kept an
ear tuned to the door and the scry, but the only break in her solitary pursuits was the delivery of the white rose. Curled around it
was a piece of papyrus. Lark unrolled it and her breath stuck in
her throat.

Calligraphy. Holm's creative gift was calligraphy. What an
odd, ironic thing.

She pivoted on her heel and swept into her bedroom. From
the top closet shelf, she floated down a large, heavy package.
With a Word, she banished the safespell that kept the glass clean
and unbroken. Deliberately she sent the three pieces of framed
calligraphy to hover around Holm's that sat on the table. She
took one pace back, two, then shook her head.

Her father, T'Hawthorn, held a Master's Laurel in calligraphy. She suspected that Holm had never completed formal training, or tested for his laurels in the art, but it was obvious he was
equally skilled.

But what a difference in style!

And what a difference in topic.

Her father's was a classic, distinguished hand and his symbols: Duty. Obedience. Family. Even his signature and the Family sigil were constrained and stiffly correct.

Holm's two characters showed grace and boldness. His note
spoke of memory and yearning, radiated affection and passion
and something more.

She banished T'Hawthorn's pieces back to the closet and paced the room. "Your loveliness lingers in my thoughts." Sincerity radiated from the papyrus. He truly thought she was lovely. She shook her head. "May I linger in your thoughts."

She set Holm's work on her desk under a paperweight by Painted Rock, one of her sister-in-law's early works and the reason she took her name.

If Lark was as nervy and fidgety tomorrow as she was tonight, she'd fret away her restday. She *would not* let the presence or absence of that man affect her so.

She scried Painted Rock. Lark had progressed beyond loss and bitterness and tried to help Painted Rock do the same. There was one thing they shared, a love of solar sailing. Painted Rock wasn't in, and Lark left a message in her cache. "I'm sailing tomorrow. If you want to join me, meet me at our cabana near ShipProws at ninebells. Love, Lark."

Impatient with herself for fretting about Holm, she decided to meditate. If she sank into herself, her mind would ease and her nerves would calm. What would come, would come.

Phyll gave up his pounce-on-papyrus-ball play and trotted to her. *We all have fine fate. Vinni said so.*

Lark picked him up and nuzzled him. "Of course you do."

You, too. And Meserv. And Our Holly.

Lark sighed. "If you say so."

Phyll rumbled a small purr. *I do,* he said smugly.

She laughed and settled into her favorite position to meditate, Phyll on her lap.

I will med-i-tate, too. I med-i-tate good. Meserv falls asleep, Phyll reported virtuously.

Her amusement at her kitten steadied her mood, and she was able to take them both into a deep trance.

*W*hen she awakened the next morning, her restlessness was back. This would simply *not* do, obsessing over a man.

So she'd occupy her mind and body with something nearly as exciting. Time to solar-sail.

She went to her bedroom cabinet and got her flying outfit, a onesuit of layered and insulated material. It unrolled in her hands, feather-light and thin, but strong and warm for sailing in high air. Automatically her fingers checked the suit for tears, but found none. She smiled. The clothing, as with all her solar sailing equipment, was expensive and fashioned completely by hand, with only minimal Flair.

She prided herself on her sailing skill—no Flair, only muscle and timing and expertise. Lark checked the large front pocket that curved over her breasts and opened near her collarbone. It was empty. She gauged Phyll's size and weight.

"Do you want to go solar sailing?"

The kitten knew she sailed. He'd found the suit in a cabinet drawer, and she'd been upset at his kneading it.

Phyll sat down and raised a back leg to groom. *If Lady and Lord had wanted Cats to fly, the Two would have given Cats wings,* he said as he licked fine bits of hair back into place.

Lark kept her smile to herself, then frowned as the cheerful melody of her scrybowl announced a caller. She went to the bedroom door and looked into the mainspace. The light that glowed from the instrument was Holly green.

Relief that he still cared warred with distress that she'd have to battle him—and herself—again. "I'm not going to answer, Phyll. I'm going sailing." Stretching, she tested her muscles. Lately the most physical activity she'd had was weeding T'Horehound's garden. Sailing sounded better every moment.

Lark slipped from her robe and donned her onesuit, stuffing her hair into the headcovering and tightening it with tabs. The sound of the scrybowl muted. She slid her thumb down along the rest of her tabbed seams to close them.

Phyll jumped onto the table that held her scrybowl.

Lark grabbed her bag and scanned the mainspace for anything she might need. Gilt, quickfood, and her Healing Tools were in her bag. A gleam of green caught her eye. The music flexistrip. She recalled the loveliness of the lilting music that she'd programmed to waken her. Music that held within it the very essence of solar-sailing—the swoops and the curves, intricate figures to soar through.

Now that D'Holly was healing, Lark could bear to listen to the music again. She plucked up the flexistrip and inserted it into her collar, pressing the tiny jewel to ready the spell.

You never let Me answer scrybowl. Can I answer now?

Phyll would delay Holm enough for her to leave. "Yes."

Circling the scrybowl with an orange paw to answer the call, Phyll mewed. *Phyll here.*

"Good morning, Phyll. May I speak with my Bélla?" Holm's voice caused a melting in her lower body, a softening of her knees. No, it would be a softening of her head if she continued to keep him in her life.

Phyll's head circled as if following the water before it stilled. His gaze slid toward her.

Feeling her temper rise, she decided to spend her energy in teleportation to the last public carrier stop departing for the jutting rocks known as the ShipProws. She popped from her space.

*H*olm *heard the distinctive whoosh of teleportation over the* scrybowl and set his jaw. He hurt and tried not to show it, tried to suppress it. He shouldn't hurt so, not over something so trivial. He felt as if he'd been ripped inside.

Phyll's whiskers quivered. *FamWoman gone sailing.*

Holm was glad of the translator spell he'd set on his scrybowl, and the practice with Meserv. "Sailing?" Holm's spirits lifted. His G'Uncle Tab had taught both Holly boys to sail well. Holm had a sweet yacht that would catch whatever craft Bélla rented. He knew she didn't keep a boat. Surely she'd prefer dancing over the waves in a tip-of-the-pyramid craft instead of whatever miserable rental thing she used. He'd be charming. He'd even promise to keep the length of the boat between them—until she warmed up to him again. He'd dazzle her with his yacht and his skill.

An enlarged paw dominated the scry-vision. If it touched the water, the call would end. There were many marinas along the coast. . . . "Phyll, wait! Where did she go?"

ShipProws. The paw dabbed the water. Phyll hissed and Holm's bowl went clear.

"ShipProws!" Holm repeated. The ridge of tilted sandstone rock to the south of Druida was an outshoot of the Hard Rock Mountains, named by the colonists for the upthrust triangular peaks that looked like starship prows. There wasn't a patch of water larger than a pond anywhere near there.

He shouldn't snoop into Bélla's life any further. He should save learning about her from her own words, from the link between them, from his hands touching her body. For a moment the thought distracted him. When tension coiled in his loins, he brought his mind back to the fact that he wouldn't even see her if he didn't solve the little puzzle.

Holm paced up and down the length of his sitting room. He'd been ready to beg to see her.

A simple question to the ResidenceLibrary wouldn't be prying into her life.

Showing up at a public place wouldn't be too pushy.

He hoped.

He cleared his throat. "ResidenceLibrary, please define the use of 'sailing' in relation to the ShipProws."

"The ShipProws are the center of personal solar-sailing around Druida," ResidenceLibrary responded.

Holm gulped. Personal solar-sailing. Flying on gossamer batwings. Naturally he'd tried it as a child, but his Family preferred water to air and yachting together to personal solar-sailing. Wherever his suit and wings had gone, he didn't know, probably to some cuzes, but they sure wouldn't fit him now.

Throwing off apprehension, he made his voice as strong as his resolve. "Don't we have a solar-sailing harness somewhere in storage?" He thought he'd moved a box or two from the storerooms that had been his new pool and conservatory to another area.

"Osmanthus Holly, three generations ago, solar-sailed. The equipment is in new Storage Room Six," ResidenceLibrary replied with disapproval.

"Ah, I knew it."

"The spells on the solar-sailing harness have deteriorated."

"I have the energy to renew them." The feast and the Ritual last night had energized everyone. Holm's HeartGift had turned out surprisingly well and had also given him power. He hadn't used the DepressFlair bracelet and hadn't nightported to the Great Labyrinth. He was rested and ready.

Holm rolled his shoulders and left his rooms to walk long corridors to the other side of the bailey square. He considered teleporting, but decided to save his strength. Solar-sailing after so long might be a little tricky.

"The solar-sail wings are of an old design and substance." ResidenceLibrary's admonitions echoed down the hallway, surrounding Holm.

"Osmanthus did it. I can. I'm smarter and stronger than he ever was."

"Osmanthus injured himself badly solar-sailing. There's blood on the sails. Techniques have changed."

Holm knew he couldn't escape ResidenceLibrary, not even turning corners and loping down the hall, but the action felt good. Any action that would bring him to Bélla felt good.

A mew sounded in his mind with an image of Meserv sitting with ears perked. *Solar sailing? Flying? Zoom like Samba on her Saucer? I want to go, too!*

Holm laughed and 'ported the kitten to his shoulder. "We'll go and impress Bélla and Phyll." He scratched Meserv's cheek.

"Osmanthus," the Residence warned in tones of doom.

"I have greater Flair. I can teleport to safety in an emergency. As for hurting myself, I'll be with a Healer." With luck. He'd ask if he could join her, of course, no need to cause those white flashes of hers. If she missed him as much as he missed her, she'd want to see him.

This time he wouldn't slip up and make a fool of himself like he had on the beach. The memory caused his neck and face to heat. This time he'd dazzle her. Everything he knew about solar-sailing would come back to him.

If she wanted to see him. He gritted his teeth. As much as he longed to spend time with her, if she refused his company he would leave—perhaps work his restlessness out on *sea* sailing. But how he yearned for her!

*B*y the time the public glider reached ShipProws Town, Lark's blood was buzzing with anticipation. It had been far too long since she'd experienced the complete freedom of solar-sailing. She treasured the long septhours of gliding as she angled her gossamer wings to Bel to power her flight, the skill of using thermals and cross-winds to soar in elaborate patterns that were the hallmark of the craft.

She hummed as she walked to the primary-colored cabanas where she and Painted Rock kept their gear. Her cabana was bright red. She snapped the security spell off with a Word, opened the door, and stepped inside, shivering at the cool air that preserved the molecular wings. They hung in ethereal swathes.

A few molecules thick, they shimmered with a lure of the only unrestricted septhours Lark had ever had.

She frowned briefly. Ethyn had never wanted to fly. He said he'd worked too hard to become a Healer ever to endanger himself. She had sailed less and less when she was wed to him, preferring to spend time with him and his hobbies.

"Lark? Lark?" Painted Rock called. She ducked into the cabana and closed the door.

Lark turned to her with a smile that faded. Painted Rock's tall, thin frame looked even more emaciated, her eyes more haunted. Her suppressed emotions over Ethyn's death could not be allowed to continue. Though not a mind-Healer, Lark knew enough from her studies that ignored emotions generated unhealthy results both physically and mentally.

Lark, herself, had been angry and bitter and grief-stricken, but she'd been open about the emotions and worked through them until they were in her past. She was sure Painted Rock never acknowledged her feelings—pushed them aside and hid them until they dammed up to eat away at her. Lark sighed. She could only do her best, try and link with Painted Rock, and hope the inner wound was ready to be lanced.

Brushing Painted Rock's mind with gentle encouragement and love, Lark stepped to her and hugged her tight. "I'm glad you came."

Painted Rock's brooding eyes searched her face. "I've been thinking about what you and *that Nobleman* said. I *do* wish you happiness. But I don't think you can find it with *him*," she ended defiantly.

Lark shrugged and kept her smile. Though the words hurt, they only echoed what her own reason told her. She took Painted Rock's hands. They were icy. Lark warmed them with a two-word and squeezed her fingers. "Let's not discuss that. Let's *sail!*"

They put on their wings, then checked in with the Solar Sailing Society and listed where they'd be sailing and the septhours they'd be in the air. They went to a high jutting hill where the updrafts would lift them into takeoff. They'd chosen a less popular area with trickier crosswinds and were the only sailors in the vicinity. The better to bond again, Lark hoped.

Running and laughing, they jumped off the cliff and were borne into the blue, blue sky.

Lark reached for the connection between herself and her sister-in-law, and for the first time in years, Painted Rock allowed it. Lark thumbed the jewel to start D'Holly's music and amplified it to Painted Rock to increase their joy. Using little Flair and the skill they'd learned together, they began with simple patterns and alternated the progression of each series until they swooped in the most intricate designs.

They soared together, reveling in the freedom of the wide sky above verdant Celta. Exhilaration passed between them and they grinned, but Lark sensed a huge black mass of emotional pain in Painted Rock. After this respite Painted Rock would return to that darkness—black grief and hurt that blocked her artistic talent to a trickle, causing even more despair.

For a while they sailed in silence, Lark trying to loosen and smooth Painted Rock's awful tangle of feelings. Then Lark's probing neared Painted Rock's deep hurt, and she found a great thermal flow, waved to Lark, and let the wind take her up and up.

Lark accepted the retreat with resignation and relief. Now she could truly enjoy herself. Concentrate on nothing but the moment and her own sensations . . . the soft chill of the wind against her face, the sight of playing hawks a kilometer away, and most of all the freedom to dip and sway and dance in the air to D'Holly's music. She cruised level, horizontal winds—soaking in the serene sight of lush fields and groves. Letting the greenness of healthy growing plants soothe her.

Half a septhour later Holm touched her mind with a gentle caress. *Bélla.*

Exactly what she needed to complete a perfect moment. *Yes, Holm?* The link must be very strong if she could hear him so well when he was in Druida.

Phyll told me where you were. May I join you?

She hesitated. Painted Rock was near, and troubled, but Lark had tried her best this morning to help her sister-in-law, and Painted Rock had flown away.

Lark wanted to play again with Holm. To enjoy time with him. She circled wide around lush fields as she considered. The last week or so had been hideous—mentally, emotionally, and physically exhausting. She deserved to have fun—and fun with Holm. She hovered in the bright blue sky, tipped her hand and spun gracefully on her wings. Here she was in her element and he would be at a disadvantage.

Brilliant, sparkling air flowed over her. Holm would add to the pleasure of the day, it was as simple as that, would gild the memory with gold. If Painted Rock appeared again—so what? Lark deserved some lovely times and memories. She couldn't live her life anxious about Painted Rock's problems which mirrored the fear and bitterness she'd left behind.

She swooped and still Holm did not press her for an answer. Good. She smiled. *Yes, Holm, you may join me.*

Then he was there.

His appearance startled her and she stared, hardly believing her eyes. Her mouth hung open until the wind dried it and she snapped it shut. He was obviously a beginner, augmenting his natural grace and balance in flight with Flair—and the rig he wore! A regular airstream circled her around the area as she studied him. Material wings! He flew with wings made of tissue-thin material, but material none the less, looking frayed with age. Incredible that he managed so well.

Even as she watched, he naturally learned how to shift and balance, use wind and solar power more and Flair less to sail. It amazed her.

A high cat-shriek of glee accompanied him. Again Lark stared. White whiskers twitched and a small red tongue darted out from an orange face as if tasting the air. Meserv hung in a holly-green pouch on Holm's chest. Lark laughed. In this one thing, Meserv outmatched her brother.

The link between herself and Holm had snapped open as soon as he'd appeared and now she sensed his pure exultation at mastering a long neglected skill. Too far away to match gazes, his mind-emotions touched hers in a light caress backed by excruciating tenderness that made her breath catch in her throat.

Then he began to climb in ever-narrowing circles around her. Caring welled within her as she watched him and the emotions pulsed up and down their bond, layering, deepening, becoming complex and intimate.

He wooed her. Drifting in close enough to flash a grin or wink, then drawing away. Even with his antique equipment he was more graceful soaring than any man she'd ever seen.

He danced in the air, and tempted her to angle her wings and dance with him, in the teasing game of courtship. All the while the link between them ebbed and flowed with intense, unspoken emotion. There was affection, desire, and even more, a yearning of the heart and soul.

Her pulse raced harder as he dived past her, pulled from the dive, and spiraled upward again—she gasped, but she'd watched hawks air-dancing too often not to know the male mating flights.

The man enchanted her.

He maneuvered close, within a long wingspan, and their tie throbbed with sensual images, the delight at hearing his mother's music, the scent of her that wafted to him, calling him.

It was as if the world was brand new and they created it by swooping and dancing. A wave of a hand birthed a spray of moons, the glide of a body seeded the planet with verdant growth.

Lark, how could you invite him, too? Painted Rock cried betrayal. Zooming in on a fast crosswind, she darted between them.

Holm was too inexperienced to handle the backwash of her wings, her stop, more rushing air as Lark compensated. His wing edges dropped, feathered the air wrong, and he careened into Painted Rock. She plummeted into Lark. They tangled and fell.

Twenty-two

❦

"NO!" *Holm cried. He hadn't the Flair to save them all.* No! Not to fail a loved one again.

Painted Rock freed herself, but they continued to plummet. Holm reached mentally for Lark, but she was concentrating and didn't bond with him. An updraft whirled Holm away, then sent him falling.

The women struggled to right themselves with skill, using wind and sun to control their fall. Both still dropped.

With effort and technical moves that amazed him, Lark set Painted Rock on a wobbling but safe downward descent. Lark pinwheeled down. Out of reach.

Then she reached for him, 'ported midair to him, and pulled him close. Her sheer willpower, strength, and soaring knowledge augmented by judicious Flair pulled them from their dive. Holm sent her energy, but she returned it to him, steadied him, and fixed 'porting coordinates in her mind.

Port! she ordered.

He did, teleporting Meserv home before landing hard and rolling. When he caught his breath, he looked for her.

She still flew, angling down to where Painted Rock huddled on the ground.

Talons of fear, anger, guilt, and complete failure sank into him with cruel sharpness.

*P*ainted *Rock had landed physically safe and emotionally* broken. Lark slipped off her harness and ran to her.

The woman had collapsed into a weeping heap, finally releasing all the pent up hurt and grief and fury at her brother's death. Lark sat down and put her arms around her, cradling her as she wildly sobbed, comforting her with gentle noises, stroking hands, and a mindstream of warm understanding. Several meters away Holm strode to them, fear and anger spiking his aura, as well as a dark smudge. Obviously the incident had stirred up deep feelings in him, rousing an old, suppressed problem. She didn't know how she'd cope with two of them tugging at her heart. Both needing her and unwilling to admit their hurt.

Others ran to them, including GentleLady Southernwood, the head of the Solar Sailing Society.

Lark said, "Shhh, Painted Rock, it's all over, and we're alive and fine. Time to set aside your grieving and *live*."

"He was the best of us. The best of *me*. He saved me from Downwind. He made me an artist."

Lark smoothed Painted Rock's hair. "Ethyn was a good and kind man," and why hadn't Lark loved him like the man who stopped near them now? Oh, Lady and Lord, she loved Holm! Disaster. "Painted Rock, Ethyn could not make you an artist. *You* have the talent. *You* are creative. Allow yourself to express whatever you feel and grow."

Holm's precise movements radiated control of roiling emotions. He crouched beside them, but didn't touch Lark. Didn't want her linked further to whatever he feared most, she thought. But he said, "Can I help?" in a low, calm voice. There was no hope for it. She was well and truly in love with him.

"I'm s-s-sorry," Painted Rock gulped. "I'm s-s-"

"Shhhh," Lark rocked them. "It's over and we're fine."

A starburst page burst near Lark. "STAT," PrimaryHealing Hall broadcast. "Two down in Hawthorn-Holly street fight, mortal wounds. Bergamot Square."

Painted Rock rubbed her wet face and pushed Lark away. *"Go!"*

GentleLady Southernwood helped Lark to her feet.

Another page showered sparks. "Holm!" T'Holly's voice rang out. "Coordinates here! Come. We need your fighting arm. Bergamot Square!"

Holm's tormented gaze met hers over the wide gulf that had opened between them.

Her mind fought with her clutching heart. She wanted to link with him, hold him, love him. Healing bag in hand, she 'ported.

*W*ith *a sweeping glance, Lark saw T'Holly and his men,* swords drawn, defending one corner of the square. The Great-Lord was planted in front of Tinne. Hunting cats growled and paced.

Winterberry, the Council guardsman, led a contingent of guards herding a less cohesive group of Hawthorns away from where two bodies lay. One in Hawthorn purple, the other in Holly green. T'Heather already stooped over the still men.

Lark ran to them. Healers were too late. She looked down in horror. Her cuz Whitey Hawthorn lay with his head half-severed from his body, his jugular ripped open, blood puddled under his neck.

Her gaze went to the other. A Hawthorn dagger protruded from Eryngi Holly's chest.

They both smiled as if fighting and dying had been the best sport they'd ever had.

Horror skittered through her. She caught her breath on a sob. Her heart ached for the loss of both of them—both had been strong and vibrant and young.

Holm ported into the square near T'Holly. Holm *reached* for her, but she sent grief and anger to him.

Her lips trembled as she said to T'Heather, "Eryngi Holly. No more than an eightday ago I Healed a fatal wound of his. Now he's dead."

T'Heather rose awkwardly to his feet and met her eyes. His anger matched hers. "Yes." He augmented his voice with Flair so it bounced off the brick walls of the buildings surrounding the square. "A waste of Healing energy and lives. A private feud or dueling is one thing—reprehensible but sanctioned by our laws. Street fighting, leaving dead in the squares, is another matter. The NobleCouncil will hear of this and *rule* on the issue."

T'Holly gestured Holm to take his place and strode to them, sheathing his blade, a large hunting cat with him. His voice, too, carried to all corners of the square. "I did not start this feud. I did not recently escalate it. But the fighting has sorely wounded my HeartMate, and no apology has been forthcoming. Let the NobleCouncil consider *that*."

Wild fury lived in his eyes and was outlined in every strong sinew of his body. With a display of Holly strength, T'Holly reached down and gathered up the fallen Eryngi, cradling the dead man in his arms. "By the Cave of the Dark Goddess, I will end this feud. The cost to the Hawthorns will be dear." His eyes burned as he surveyed the clump of Hawthorns. T'Holly jerked a nod to his men. They 'ported away in silence.

Lark narrowed the bond between herself and Holm to the merest filament, but knew despairingly that it was still too strong to cut. What would cut that thread? And how shattered would she be were it severed?

Lark's father, T'Hawthorn, walked to her slain cuz.

"Lark, you are needed at home."

To her surprise, T'Heather curled a large, warm hand over her shoulder. Strength, determination, and comfort flowed from him to her. "I think it best that Lark remain at MidClass Lodge or move to T'Heather Residence. A Healer is not to be involved in a feud."

T'Hawthorn scowled. "Will you recall Garis Heather and Vera Aloe from my home, too?"

Her MotherSire's nostrils flared in distaste. "You have contracted with them. That is between you and them." He shook his head at Whitey's body. "Lady and Lord knows you will be needing them if you continue with this foolhardiness."

Blood rushed to T'Hawthorn's pale cheeks. He stood stiffly.

T'Heather studied him. "There will be a Major Healing Ritual for D'Holly in GreatCircle Temple in two days' time, on quarter twinmoons. Will you show your willingness to end this feud, and attend, to Heal instead of kill?"

"No."

"Let this feud go, Huathe," T'Heather said.

Her father's lips thinned and whitened. With a wave of his hand he summoned a floating pallet for Whitey. "No."

Without further word or glance at Lark, her father marched away, the other Hawthorns straggling behind him.

Cratag crossed to Lark and T'Heather and stopped a moment. Lark saw a slash in the leather over his right biceps. "Let me Heal that."

He intercepted her hand and squeezed her fingers while ducking his head. "The T'Hawthorn Healers can take care of it for me. I'm sorry for your loss," he said, and dropped her hand. His eyes held troubled concern. He bowed to T'Heather. "I am sorry for all of us."

Pivoting on a heel, he easily caught up with the rest.

"I don't know what to do. What am I going to do?" The words escaped Lark. T'Heather slipped his muscular arm around her shoulders. His mind touched hers and knew her desolation.

"We will need you for D'Holly's Healing Ritual. After that . . . I will speak to the committee in charge of selecting the Head of Gael City HealingHall and ensure they decide *soon*." His tone indicated that there'd be no doubt Lark would receive the position she'd once longed for so much.

She'd thought of making a new life, becoming a new woman. She had partially gained her goal. T'Heather's support of her independent living had given her the respect she so wanted from *all* her Family.

But nothing could lift the pain of loving Holm, and the knowledge of imminent heartbreak.

T'Heather urged her from the site of death, circling around the dark blood that seeped between the cracks of the gray stones, staining the mortar red.

*T*here was another Ritual that night in *T'Holly* Sacred Grove. This one was not of thanksgiving or joy, but the last rite to release Eryngi's soul to the Wheel of Stars—the cycle of death and rebirth.

The Holly men performed the Ritual and the dispersion of Eryngi's earthly molecules into the ground and trees of the Grove with grief and determination. Only the presence of Genista kept their language moderate.

It was odd to see a feminine form not his Mamá in the Sacred Grove, but Holm sensed Genista was sincerely moved by the Ritual and shared her warmth and comfort with them all. Tinne had done better in marriage than Holm had earlier believed, and he was thankful for that. But his heart ached for Bélla.

A knot of emotions plagued him. To his shame the overwhelming one was failure. He was humiliated that once again someone he loved and tried to save had instead rescued him. Guilt ate at him that he hadn't lived up to his own standards.

He'd managed another calligraphic note to be delivered with his white rose. Like fighting, if he let his fingers form the symbols without thought, the ink flowed gracefully and well.

Holm hadn't known quite what to say. He was deeply involved in the feud, now. Nothing would stop that. And she stood on the other side of the canyon between them—a Healer. A Hawthorn.

Finally he'd closed his eyes and let his hand form the intricate glyph-letters. "I cherish you."

He didn't know how he was going to overcome his father's hatred of the Hawthorns. Worse, he didn't know how he was going to face Lark with the knowledge that *she* had saved *him,* or deal with his stupid feeling of failure.

Knowing of his stupidity didn't mean he could control the feeling. He'd even tried an hour of meditation in the HouseHeart under the guidance of the whispery voice to no avail. The deep peace that should have been his, the grounding of his Flair and merging of his mind, body, and emotions yet eluded him.

But he did know one thing with bone-deep knowledge. Nothing was going to keep him from making Lark his HeartMate. Not the feud. Not his Family. Not his own flaws.

And not Lark herself.

Holm waited until he couldn't bear the ambiance of the all-male household another moment before 'porting to Lark's door.

He knew he radiated violent desire and need—emotional turmoil he couldn't restrain.

Desperately he maintained control, knowing that, as always, he'd be lucky to make it to the bedroom with his Bélla.

More and more he thought of her as Bélla, not Lark. Lark was her name associated with her Families and her profession.

Those two areas were like an embedded thorn in their relationship—ready to fester.

He knocked on her door, sensed Phyll bounding to the other side, then the slower steps of his lover, his HeartMate.

Phyll, this time is for my Lady and me, go sleep. He nudged the kitten back to bed. Phyll grumbled but accepted Holm's direction.

Holm placed the fingertips of his hand on the solid wood before him and projected his feelings. *Bélla, lover, let me in.*

He could almost feel the warmth through the door as she set her hand opposite his. His throat closed with emotion and the red tide of passion heated his blood until it grew fast and pulsed in his ears. His breath was ragged.

Bélla.

She didn't open her mind or heart to him. When she spoke it was with hesitant words. "I want no fighter in my bed."

He absorbed the jolt. *Bélla. I have no blood on my hands, no fury to fight in my heart. I am your lover,* he caressed her with a soothing, whisper of gentle mind-voice.

"You are a fighter." Her choked tones gave her away: She was in pain, and he was wild to comfort her. His fingers curled into a fist on the door, but he kept the stream of emotion between them steady.

"You've fought before. You will fight again." He heard her more with his mind than his ears.

I need you. Will you reject me? He didn't like saying the words, but there was no way to hide his emotions. In his mind's eye his hand on the door pulsed golden, enveloped by the color of the bond between them. He took the aura and let it flow down to his wrist and encircle it—forming a marriage band.

Please! I told you I'm not ashamed to beg. He tried to overlay his desperation with humor.

As he waited the silence grew thick with reverberating desire. He sensed a weakness in her—her emotions, her loneliness—and pushed. He had no shame, no honor when it came to needing her. Not the perfect HollyHeir in this, either. He would use whatever means necessary to win her. And he would let her use him, his body, however she wished in return.

Let us be together. Take comfort from each other. Who else in the world knows how we are torn, how we feel? We match in this as well as everything else.

She withdrew and his gut clenched as he wondered if he'd gone too far.

But her muttered Word opened the door.

Her apartment was shrouded by night—yet he sensed that she'd changed it since he'd last been there. Because of him? Her own Hawthorn scent mixed with something spicier and less floral than the roses. He narrowed his eyes but saw no evidence of his gifts—the multicolored roses or the white ones he'd sent each night.

For the first time it struck him that he'd made the same mistake in wooing his woman that his bumbling friend T'Ash had made with his HeartMate—overwhelming her with gifts. He couldn't prevent a smile of wry amusement. He should have been smoother, more sophisticated than that, but no, he'd fallen into the same instinctive male trap—heap gifts upon the desired one. Lord and Lady how he ached for her—his HeartMate.

She stood before him, small, pale, troubled.

Holm said, "I can't stop this feud. Do you want me to step away from this fight with your Family?"

"Yes! I want you to step away from it—and all fights! But that isn't you, is it, HollyHeir? I can't ask it of you, I haven't the right. And I won't ask it of you. Would you have me step away from my Family?"

"No, never. Will you ask me not to harm your relatives?"

Her gaze dropped. "You must defend yourself." She turned and walked away, leaving him to enter or go as he wished. She hurt, and her pain twisted through him, stinging.

"I need you." He sent the words reverberating through the room, over the link between them.

She shrugged. "I want you, too." Glancing back, she wetted her lips with her tongue. "One last time," she said. "Our Houses are enemies, we can't continue this affair, but we can share ourselves with each other one last time."

He didn't deny her words. He just stepped inside, nudged her door shut with a foot, and swept her into his arms.

Just holding her, the press of her soft, curvy form against his, was enough. To start.

It was as he'd said. Comforting. The warmth of her and the sheer *affection* they had for each other seeped into him and smoothed his raw emotions. Circulating to her, they lifted her depression.

And he felt good. Simply good. He could give this to her as no one else did. He had succeeded in something at last today. The most important thing of all, pleasing his lover.

To Lark, Holm felt large and strong and comforting. More, he felt *right*. When the thought sent a bolt of dread careening through her, Holm caught it and vanquished it.

"None of that." His warm mouth whispered below her ear, and she shuddered at the dampness of his tongue on her skin. Once she was again enveloped in his scent and heat and strength. She reveled in their closeness, the energy flow that more than doubled as it cycled from one to the other. Merged, they were stronger than she'd ever experienced. Too right. She set her pain and grief and worries aside to cherish the moment.

At a word from him their clothes disappeared. Holm set her on her feet and stepped back. His eyes fixed on her with aching hunger that twined through the connection between them, adding sizzle, kindling a yearning in her—heating and flushing her skin from the inside out.

In his nakedness he was dazzling, as always. Tall, well-built, muscles developed to match his frame—a perfect male human specimen to study in an anatomy class. But the brilliance of his gray eyes and the glint of his silver-blond hair even in the room only lit by waxing twinmoons and starlight emphasized his vitality.

Her gaze went to the large, dark bruise on his neck, and she winced. He chuckled. The bruise she'd set on him as her mark— how primitive was that!—was larger and more livid than the first one.

He touched his throat. "I treasure the sting."

She felt his pleasure as he thought of her lovebite, and noticed the results as his sex thickened.

This was a beggar? She closed her eyes and shook her head. A soft brush of his fingertips against hers and a whiff of him told her he moved. She opened her eyes to see him circling her. His gaze held hers.

Open your senses. See the energy flow between us, he said as he caressed her temple, then glided away in a slide-step.

She did. A cascade of silver-gold spun between them, linking them in a complex weave she'd never experienced, never seen amongst others before.

*An intimate, **right** bond between us,* his mind whispered, but a small frown line appeared between his brows. She blinked, understanding that he struggled for words with her and that frustrated him because it was unusual. Her lips curved—then she noticed the knotted tangle of injury that he kept hidden was much closer to the surface of his mind-heart-emotions now. She could reach out and touch it, find it and smooth it and Heal it. What wounded *him*?

She gathered herself for a probe—and he touched the tip of her breasts. All thought fled.

He circled, and she turned, matching him in steps like the sensual dance they'd done in the air that morning, so very long ago in emotional time.

His fingers trailed down her shoulder, then away. She countered by testing his biceps, then twirling under his arm and out of reach.

His lips parted on a wicked grin, he sent his hands through her scalp to follow her hair to the tips, and she felt the rustling of nerves to the soles of her feet. She gasped.

His hands tugged free and his arms opened wide, he sidestepped, letting her enjoy the view of his aroused body, the intimacy of the dance.

Lark followed instinct. She took a gliding pace to him, skimmed the tips of her nails down his chest, lightly covered with gleaming blond hair.

He shuddered. His face tightened. His hand flicked out and his index finger followed the line of her collarbone, then his fingers fell away as she swayed. Her body readied for his.

She'd never seen anything like the hair on his body. White gold. Tempting beyond belief to explore, to discover texture and density. While she spun in the dance, trying to decide where to touch him next, his hands shaped her waist, darted in to cup her breasts, curved over her bottom.

A mist of glittering desire surrounded her, the sweep of

their energy, tender but incendiary, flaring red with passion.

He stepped close and their bodies grazed, skin against skin, her breasts against his side. They both moaned.

She grasped his shoulder, slid her fingers over his lean hip, but the soft curling silver-hair near his groin tempted.

Instead of stepping away, she stepped into his circling dance and grasped his sex.

He stopped, panting.

She looked up and what she saw in his eyes thrilled her. No calm and sophisticated Nobleman, but an instinctive male bent on mating. That she could bring him to this made her heart pound, her blood sing.

She tightened her grasp on the manhood that had brushed her again and again in the teasing dance. "Time to pay." She didn't know where the words came from, what they meant, only that she'd die if she couldn't have him.

He growled and grabbed her hips.

Laughter ripped from her as she bounced on the sofa, then he was atop her and his shaft was against her most needy flesh and she cried out in yearning.

Look! he ordered, and caught her gaze with his. His fierce eyes flamed silver.

Mine! he cried, twining his fingers with hers.

Now! he prayed and slid into her slowly.

Linked together, eyes, hands, bodies.

Emotions.

Chained together.

He surged and watched her, she surrendered and watched him, they rose and fell into ecstasy. Together.

Twenty-three

❤

"*Rrrrrow!*" *It was a demand.*

Lark opened her eyes to see Meserv pounce on Holm's clothes and drag a fine chain with something that gleamed white and pink and shone black. She watched in languorous amusement. As usual after a bout of loving with Holm, she felt incredibly good—totally a woman, totally *herself,* the woman she'd wanted to become and had thought to develop in Gael City.

Holm strolled in from the kitchen, carrying an elegant vase Painted Rock had made which held the white roses he'd been sending. His eyes glinted down at her and he smiled.

The last time. Her heart clenched. This was the last time she'd see him as her lover—she ordered her heart to believe it.

"No," Holm said, eyes narrowed at her.

Meserv dropped the chain on Holm's foot. *Put amulet on. Never off T'Ash says. Never.*

Holm transferred his cool gaze from her to his kitten. "Who is your FamMan, T'Ash or me?"

Meserv just sniffed.

Phyll trotted in from her bedroom, purring. *Meserv!*

Meserv rumbled his purr louder.

Lark smiled.

The two kittens touched noses. *Brother,* they said.

Holm took the chain and slipped the amulet around his neck, then arranged the roses and the vase to his liking on Lark's scry table. With a Word, he lit some lamps and bathed the room in a soft glow. He glanced at the wall opposite the couch where the sunset burst in all its glory and stepped back.

"Incredible." He grinned at Lark. "Your talent never ceases to amaze me, Bélla."

Lark stared, transfixed, at the amulet hanging from Holm's neck. After a few seconds she bit her lip to keep a chuckle from escaping.

He glowered at her. "Still think it doesn't affect my virility?"

She coughed.

He closed his hand over it.

"No, wait." She rose from the sofa to open his fingers. He stilled. Her gaze locked with his and she saw licks of fiery silver grow with the sensual awareness between them.

She wrenched her glance from his. "May I see it?"

His hand dropped away and she lifted the amulet to study. She bit her lip again. When she was sure she had her amusement under control, she said, "The pearl looks remarkably real." Soft, pink lips ready to kiss and be kissed. They even had tiny lines at the same intervals as natural lips. She looked at the jewel's setting, some unknown creamy-white material. "What's this?" She frowned as her Flair probed. "It feels like—bone." She dropped the thing. It should have felt distasteful, but it didn't. Somehow, she sensed that it had been prized and loved. Odd.

"It's called ivory, very old, from Earth. One of the few pieces that remain. T'Ash had it, of course. It originally came from an elephant."

"So that's ivory. I've heard of elephants." She smiled. Every child had heard of elephants. They'd taken on the legend of guardian beasts on Celta. The animals transported from Earth hadn't fared well, but their genetic code and samples were still available. Celtans waited for more Flaired descendants to be able to engender, raise, and assure the survival of ancient Earth animals.

She touched the amulet again, at the black that ringed the white. Holm's chest rose and fell beneath the pendant. "And what's this?"

"Unpolished obsidian."

"Ah."

Her mouth twitched again as the pink lips sent her an illusory kiss.

"I wanted T'Ash to mount it vertically, but he wouldn't."

She pressed her lips together, then cleared her throat. "The impact would have been lost." Her voice quivered. She arranged her expression and looked back up into his eyes. "I think it's beautiful," she said sincerely.

Now Holm studied her. "Do you? Then that's enough to soothe my pride—that I should make you smile and that you like something of mine." He trailed fingers from her hairline to the corner of her mouth and all the amusement in her fled to be replaced by rising anticipation and pure sensual pleasure.

"It's not an easy thing to wear—" he started.

"No?" Some note in his voice caught at her.

His own lips quirked. "Perhaps I should say, 'It's not an easy thing to display.'" He let out a rueful breath. "I must admit I've been fascinated by the pearl all of my life." He shrugged. "What's not to like? A kiss frozen forever on pink lips, female lips." An arrested look came to his eyes. He lifted the pearl to position it next to her lips. "Lord and Lady, a match. A perfect match," he whispered.

She pushed his hand away, feeling heat paint her cheeks. If she didn't watch out, she'd be as pink as the pearl.

"No, no," he said, raising the pendant again next to her mouth. "Now, come along, pucker your lips."

"No," she said.

"Perhaps this will help." He lowered his head to hers.

His mouth brushed hers, hesitated, lingered. It took only that for her blood to fire, rich sensuality to spiral from her core, the needs of her body to edge out thought.

She caught her breath as his tongue traced her lips, and felt her knees go soft and her head tilt back.

His hands gripped her shoulders and slid down to her hips to pull her against him. She exhaled a moan as she felt the heavy hardness of his body against her. Bubbling fizz entered her blood, sensations she could no longer deny, such passion had never tempted her, and she had no willpower to resist.

One of his large hands continued to curve her lower body into his, while the other tipped her chin up, stroked her throat.

They stayed that way for long moments until Lark realized she *had* to fight or surrender. She opened her eyes to be caught in a silver gaze fiery with need. Holm's cheeks showed a hectic flush. His lips looked plush and inviting as the amulet that had caused all this.

"Kiss me," he said.

They made it to the bedroom this time.

The moment she awoke, *Lark knew she and Phyll were* alone. She'd lived there long enough to know the daily sounds and energies of those who roomed around her. Phyll snuffled in his sleep near her head. When she looked where Holm had sprawled, there wasn't even the indentation of his body in the linens or the permamoss beneath.

Despite the summer heat, she was cold to the bone. He'd taken her at her word, then. The night had been their last. She didn't know how she could endure the pain. She'd never felt such emotional agony, not when her mother had died, not when her father had rejected her, not even when Ethyn had died.

She chanted her mantra and breathed through it. She *would not* allow bitterness or resentment or envy to ever sully her life again. Too much of her time had been wasted on suffering through and banishing those negative emotions when Ethyn died.

She'd chosen to have an affair with Holm knowing they were very separate individuals with differing lifestyles, that circumstances were difficult for them even for a brief fling. She *would not* regret their time together had been so short. He'd started her on her way to becoming the woman she believed she could be. If she hadn't been able to reach his knot of wounded emotions and help *him* in return as she'd wished—well, life wasn't fair. Healing taught that. Some died who should have Healed and lived, some lived who Healers had despaired of.

Still, she searched for a note from Holm and there was none. Only the white roses spoke of their affair, and only the short calligraphic pieces that came with the last several roses held his essence. Lark shrugged, stripped, and washed under her waterfall. She thought he'd have been courteous enough to leave a note or a token, but what did she know of the proper way to end a short, Noble liaison?

She scrubbed at her skin with herbal soap and ignored the tears trickling from her eyes. He'd finally decided it was best for *everyone* that they no longer be involved. He was right. She was right.

If she worked hard all day preparing the GreatCircle Temple for tomorrow's Healing perhaps she could ignore the deep, aching hope that a rose would come this evening, too. Stupid to believe when he left without a word, but the heart was a very stupid organ.

The knock on her door came just as she pressed the shoulder tab of her tunic closed. She sent a mental probe and was surprised at Painted Rock's emanations. The rhythms of her vibrations were true to Painted Rock's essential character, but markedly changed from the last three years.

Lark hurried to open the door. Painted Rock stood in traveling leathers, a large rucksack by her feet. She looked weary, scoured out by old grief, but at the same time her skin, the light in her eyes, and her very stance were healthier than Lark had seen in a long, long time.

"Painted Rock!" Lark stepped into the corridor and hugged her. Painted Rock stiffened a moment in surprise, then awkwardly returned Lark's embrace. Lark felt a steady vitality in her sister-in-law's muscles, sensed an unfurling of creative energy. A burden lifted from Lark, one she hadn't been aware of, the responsibility for the well-being of Ethyn's sister. Lark let out a long sigh of relief.

When she looked up, Painted Rock's lips curved in a half-smile, and her green eyes were bright. Eyes the same color as Ethyn's, now, but which had been muddy with unhappiness for so long. For an instant Lark almost caught a flashing image of her lost husband, but it vanished before she could grasp it.

"Not Painted Rock, it's Citrula," the woman said. A little color tinted her cheeks. "I chose that name in rebellion, when Ethyn and I struggled to make a life for ourselves out of Downwind. But that's behind me. I can finally let it go."

She inhaled. "I wasn't there to protect him and he died, but I am not guilty of his death. You weren't there to protect him and he died, but it's not your fault, either." She hesitated and though her mouth twisted and her eyes briefly gleamed with bitterness, her words showed new acceptance. "Nobles killed him, but Ethyn made a foolish choice, too, trying to interfere in a duel."

Lark choked. "We all make foolish mistakes. Come in."

Painted Rock looked over her head into the apartment. "I don't think so. I wanted to tell you I'm joining the new artist's community on Mona Island. I submitted some pieces and was accepted. I'm leaving, now." Her shoulders shifted. "I couldn't work before. Wherever I went, I'd take my own problems with me. Now I've confronted my faults and survived, I want fresh surroundings." Thin shoulders twitched again. "New scenery will stimulate me. That's why you applied for that position in Gael City, isn't it? I thought you were running away but you aren't, you're just getting a new perspective on things."

Lark blew out a breath and laughed. "When you decide to open your eyes, Painted Rock, you're very perceptive, and Citrula is a lovely name."

"Yes, names are very important."

Lark tried not to hear Holm's low voice in her mind calling her Bélla. She wondered how long that would haunt her. Forever.

"I wanted to stop by and let you know. Ah"—she shifted feet and ducked her head—"is *he* here?"

"Holm?" Lark managed to keep her voice from breaking. "No. That won't work out."

Citrula flushed red. "It wasn't any of my business to pass judgment on your relationship with him, or him—"

"No, it wasn't." A voice came from across the hall.

They both turned to see Trif Clover standing in her doorway, hands on her hips.

Citrula straightened to her full, bony height. "It's none of your business, either."

Trif lifted her chin. "Yeah, it is. Lark's my friend. I want the best for her. I want to see her happy. You've been dragging her down for years."

"Since we met, you never liked me," Citrula said tightly.

"No, I didn't, 'cause you never liked me. You were jealous of anything that made Lark more cheerful after Ethyn's death."

"That's enough from both of you," Lark said.

Trif tossed her long, tangled mop of brown hair. "It's true. I bet she and Ethyn used you to help move out of Downwind and become middle-class. Then he died and she blamed you."

Lark threw up her hands. "I don't think we need to discuss—"

"Maybe it is true," Citrula said in a low voice. Freckles stood out against her pale skin. "I don't know anymore. And I'm tired of picking apart every feeling I've had for the last few years. I'm ready to move on, and I wanted to let Lark know how much I love and appreciate her. You do that lately, Trif Clover?"

"Aaarrrgh!" Lark waved her hands. "Quiet, please!" She set her hands on Citrula's shoulders and rose to her toes to kiss her cheek. "I'm glad you're better, and that you're starting a new life. Whatever we've been in the past, we're still friends. Whatever I gave you and Ethyn in the past, I gave freely and willingly." She kissed Citrula's other cheek. "Go with the Lady and Lord. Blessed be."

Citrula ducked her head and glanced past Lark, as if expecting to see Holm. She sighed and met Lark's eyes. "I was jealous of him on behalf of Ethyn." She flipped an elegant, long fingered hand. "There he is, so handsome and rich and powerful and Noble and *perfect*. The golden son of a golden Family. I thought it made Ethyn a small nobody."

"Nothing could make Ethyn small. He was a FirstLevel Healer, *not* a nobody. He had the determination to develop his Flair. So did you. You'll go far. Merry meet, Citrula."

"And merry part." Citrula nodded to Lark, then to Trif.

"And merry meet again," Lark and Trif said in unison.

Citrula inclined her head, picked up her bag, and walked down the hall without looking back.

Trif crossed the corridor and stuck her head in Lark's apartment, then withdrew it and looked at Lark. "Holm Holly really isn't in there?"

"No."

"Well, *I'll* come in for a cup of caff." Trif traipsed into Lark's apartment.

Lark followed and closed the door.

Trif sniffed. "Not even a scent of the man. I know he came last night, but I didn't hear him leave."

"I didn't, either." Lark went to the kitchen no-time and pulled out two brimming mugs of hot caff.

Trif scanned the mainspace as Lark handed her a mug.

"No peeking!" Lark ordered.

Trif looked affronted and settled herself into the red sofa. Phyll trotted out from the bedroom to jump up and curl on the girl's knees. Her eyes widened as she saw the opposite wall. "Nice sunset. When did you do that?"

"A few days ago." Lark took a chair at an angle and looked at the sunset herself, just days ago and yet it seemed part of another life.

"So, tell me all." Trif wriggled into the deep cushions.

"There's nothing to tell. It's over."

Trif choked, sputtered a mouthful of caff back into her cup. "Over!"

"How can it be anything else now that there are deaths on both sides of our families? He's a warrior, and T'Holly's going to pursue this feud with all his might. Holm is sworn to obey his GreatLord, his father. He'll be fighting. I'm a Healer." She hated that her voice broke and her breathing went unsteady when just laying out the facts of things.

Trif shook her head. "I can't understand it. You two are so *right* together. It's wrong to just let circumstances stop a good relationship. Why, you two might be able to stop the feud."

"He left without a word. It's better that way. Besides, nothing will stop the feud."

"Your father could stop it."

"But he won't. T'Hawthorn *started* this up again. He won't back down."

"Have you tried, lately?"

Lark sent her a bitter glance. "You know I don't have any influence over my father."

"Have you tried?"

"Yes!"

"Lately?"

Lark hesitated.

"You see, try again!"

Lark just stared at her. Trif was a person who'd never give up, despite any odds against her. Lark wasn't like that. She sipped her caff. The acidity of the brew stung her tongue.

"Don't you want Holm?" Trif persisted.

"Yes." Her whole being ached to be with him.

"Then what are you waiting for? Go after him."

Lark's hands began to tremble. She set her mug down. "I can't. It's best this way. No one gets hurt further."

"You look pretty devastated to me now," Trif pointed out.

Lark hissed a breath. She shot to her feet and paced. "Yes, I want him. But I'm not putting myself or Holm in a position to be used against the Hollys by my father. *And* I'm not putting myself or Holm in a position to be used against my father by the Hollys. The feud is bad enough as it is. Mix in the affair and who knows what might happen!"

Trif finished her caff and set her mug down with a clank. Phyll jumped from her lap to the floor. Trif stood. She fixed her gaze on Lark. "If it were my man, I wouldn't give up."

"I'm not you. I'm me." Lark pounded a fist over her heart. "*Me*, Lark Collinson," not Bélla, not ever again. "And I'll do what is best for *me*. If it were a year ago or a few years hence—" She threw up her hands. "Some things are fate. They're not meant to be."

Trif looked at Phyll. "Catshit."

"What?"

I do not de-fe-cate in-app-ro-pri-ate-ly, Phyll lifted his nose in the air.

"What you said is just stupid. Some things *are fated* to be, despite everything. I think you and Holm are like that." Trif leveled a finger at Lark. "You think about *that*." She stalked from the apartment.

Bing-Bong-Bong-Ching. Lark's scrybowl sounded.

"Here," she said.

A small sour-faced man looked out at her. "FirstLevel Healer Mayblossom Larkspur Hawthorn Collinson?"

"Yes."

"This is Monkshood, Chief Clerk of All Councils. You are wanted immediately at Guildhall Committee Room One for questioning." He disconnected.

*H*olm strode through the greeniron gates of T'Holly estate, across the drawbridge over the moat, into the courtyard, and up to the front door muttering under his breath. Meserv trotted beside him, impervious to Holm's dark mood.

When he'd nightported, his clothes and Meserv had come with him. Lord and Lady knew what Lark thought of him.

The moment he'd stepped from the labyrinth he'd sent a mind-probe to Lark and found her talking with Painted Rock and Trif Clover. He swore then and he swore now.

He'd only paused to dress before teleporting himself and Meserv to outside the T'Holly gates. 'Porting to his rooms through the additional protective shields would expend more energy than he felt safe in using.

Why had he thought that being with Lark would prevent him from nightporting? Well, why shouldn't it? She was his Heart-Mate. They were lovers, bound together by desire and physicality as well as weaving a complex tapestry of emotional commitment between them. She should have anchored him, shouldn't she? Bloody Cave of the Dark Goddess, but this sleep-porting business was getting very, very tiresome.

Can we solar-sail today? trilled Meserv, sniffing the air like a connoisseur, as if he could tell sweet winds would blow.

"No!" He never wanted to solar-sail again. Water was good enough for him. He'd have to convince Bélla. He winced at the thought of trying to explain why—how—he left her bed so rudely.

He grabbed the door handle, but it opened. His cuz, Straif Blackthorn, FirstFamily GrandLord T'Blackthorn, stood in the doorway munching good white bread and cinnamon-sweet.

"Greetyou," Straif said. "I'd have thought the feud would have put a crimp in your love life."

Holm gave him a dark look and pushed past him. Maybe he could do a bit of calligraphy and have it delivered with a rose this morning before Lark left for work.

"And," Straif continued, "I also heard that D'Willow found a HeartMate for you, so that should limit your nightlife. Who is this fellow?" Straif lifted Meserv, who blinked big blue seraphic eyes at him.

"Mmmmmessssservvvvvv," the kitten rumbled.

"Meserv," Holm said, heading to the dining room.

"Right," Straif said. "I wouldn't have thought you'd have the balls to stroll home mid-morning."

"It's hardly past dawn," Holm ground out.

"Foooooood," Meserv said, fastening his mouth on one of Straif's sweet-sticky fingers and sucking.

"Right," Straif said. "Good idea. Maybe you weren't out

loving. Doesn't look like you had a great night. Do you know you have leaves in your hair?"

"What are you doing here?" Holm asked.

Straif raised sandy eyebrows. "T'Holly asked me to come for the Great Healing of Aunt Passiflora tomorrow."

Holm shut his eyes and scrubbed his hands over his face, flicked the leaves from his hair. When he opened his eyelids, his cuz was scrutinizing him.

"Tough times," Straif said.

"Yes." Holm managed a half bow. "Thank you for coming."

"All fighters to Sparring Rooms One, Two, and Three, as assigned," boomed the Residence through the halls.

Holm scowled and grasped Straif by the upper arm. "Has T'Holly asked you to feud?"

Straif raised a brow. "Not yet."

"Don't agree. Our lives are a mess. This whole thing is a rare brouhaha. Stay free of it, Cuz."

Straif dipped his head. "I'll consider it, Cuz. Go to the dining room and grab breakfast, I'll keep T'Holly occupied."

For the first time since he'd awakened in the Great Labyrinth again, Holm felt a slip of pleasure. "My thanks."

Men ran through the halls, footsteps loud, armor jangling. Holm shook his head. "A real mess."

Twenty-four

❦

*H*olm's *hasty breakfast didn't lie easy in his stomach. He* sat on the floor of Sparring Room One with the rest of the Holly men who would prowl the streets. Tinne sat to his right.

T'Holly dominated the room, his entire attention focused on winning the feud. "I commissioned GreatLord Furze to do soli-vids of our opponents. Furze, Tab, the ResidenceLibrary, and I have programmed the models with what we know of their fighting skills. We will train with these models, in single duels and street melées until we are all proficient."

With a wave of a hand he summoned the first soli-vid. "This is T'Hawthorn." The model was amazingly like the man—at least what T'Hawthorn looked like the last time Holm had seen him close. Lark would have been able to tell the difference, of course. He winced.

"We will probably not meet T'Hawthorn, especially not traveling in a small group." T'Holly flashed a lethal grin. "I've been told he only travels by glider. Yet it is wise to know his ways." His father seemed to enjoy walking around the stocky man, looking down at the shorter simulacrum.

"T'Hawthorn fights in the *Porthos* style of three generations past. He is old," T'Holly sneered. T'Hawthorn was a few years older than Holm's father, but damn sure not as supple. He had

Lark's hair and eyes. Holm suppressed a tremor. He would *not* be facing T'Hawthorn over naked blades.

"Capture of T'Hawthorn and ransom would be our goal, should we find him. Avoid killing if possible." T'Holly's words caused a little stir. There wasn't a man in the room who'd easily skewer a GreatLord except T'Holly himself.

T'Holly waved and the model moved to the center of the room. "Let's practice capturing T'Hawthorn. Divide into groups of five."

"*We* appreciate your prompt attendance, FirstLevel Healer Collinson," said GrandLady D'Grove, the Captain of the Council as she ushered Lark into a small room richly appointed with dark blue velvet cushioned chairs arranged in a circle. Lark's MotherSire, T'Heather, was speaking with GreatLord T'Oak in one of the corners. With a swift scan, Lark counted eight Great-Lords or GreatLadies who headed their Families.

"We are a very discreet committee doing a preliminary investigation into the feud between T'Holly and T'Hawthorn which is disrupting the city," D'Grove continued.

Lark quashed a curl of anger. Two men had already died, several had been seriously wounded, and Nobles now slowly moved to censure those of their own status. Lark's life had been changed beyond all recognition. So had Painted Rock's—Citrula's—just two of the common folk who'd been affected by this feud.

D'Grove raised her voice. "Since FirstLevel Healer Collinson is available, I would like to start this matter. On the record."

The people separated into two distinct groups, three Hawthorn allies and three Holly allies, including the formidable T'Ash.

"If you would take the center chair, please, FirstLevel Healer." Clerk Monkshood stepped forward. "And hold the truth stone shaped as a Quirin egg."

Lark had dressed for the meeting in an elegant robe of heather-colored silkeen with elaborate silver embroidery. She put her hands in her large, stylish opposite sleeves and lifted her eyebrows. "A truth stone? My word of honor is not good enough?"

"A formality only." Monkshood gave her a nasty smile.

Lark returned it with a gentle one. "If it's a formality, I don't see why it matters that I hold it. My hands are my primary Healing instruments."

T'Ash crossed over to where the milky-white stone lay on a blue velvet pad. He picked up the stone and it glowed. Meeting Lark's eyes, he said, "I made it. It's not highly calibrated, so it won't show nuances of feeling, won't react to nerves, only deep untruths. For instance"—he spread his large fingers so the stone showed through, "My hair is blond," he said. An instant passed, then the stone blazed. T'Ash turned his hand palm up and opened his fingers, letting beams of light brighten the room. "There's no heat associated with the light. There is no electrical or Flaired charge, no harm can come to you."

Lark stood tall and swept the nobles with cool scrutiny. "Why does this committee want me to hold a Truth Stone?"

A crack of laughter came from T'Ash. "I'd be insulted, too." He shrugged massive shoulders. "You're a Hawthorn."

"And"—T'Reed's pointed nose wiggled at the tip as he spoke—"because it's rumored you are having an affair with a Holly."

Lark felt as if she'd swallowed the stone and it had thudded to the pit of her stomach. Despite all of her and Holm's discretion, their fling was known. One too many sets of watching eyes and calculating brains. Somewhere. Sometime.

She looked at T'Ash. He knew. She didn't think he'd spoken of it. Not T'Ash.

Lark borrowed a smile she'd seen Holm use, one that showed teeth. "Apparently some of you doubt my word of honor. Well, I doubt your words that this will remain confidential. I'll hold the stone *after* you do and you swear you will tell no one what is discussed, including HeartMates." She inclined her head to the clerk. "You first, GentleSir Monkshood."

"FirstLevel Healer—" T'Reed sputtered.

"That's right. I am a FirstLevel Healer, matching anyone here in Flair. I am a FirstDaughter of T'Hawthorn, matching anyone here in rank. If I chose to apply for a GrandHouse of my own, GrandHouse Collinson"—briefly she thought what Citrula would think of that and smiled—"I would meet all the requirements and it would be granted, wouldn't it?"

They stared at her. T'Ash snickered.

She gazed at Monkshood, D'Grove. "It would be granted?"

"Yes," D'Grove said.

"Very well. My honor matches yours, my word yours. If you

call my word in question, I can call your words in question. T'Reed, do you wish to hold the Truth Stone first and swear confidentiality? Or would you rather ask your questions?"

T'Reed had flushed an unbecoming red. Lark studied him. "GreatLord Reed, I suggest you see your household Healer for a complete physical examination."

T'Ash coughed, strolled over, and wrapped the stone in the velvet and stuck it in his pocket, where it bulged and ruined the line of his costly trous. A face-saving gesture for everyone.

Lark spoke: "I can only see harm in stirring up the Hawthorn-Holly feud further, which is what any information from me could do. Of course, it is rare for someone to cross a Healer's wishes, especially a Heather Healer," she threatened as subtly as her father.

Her MotherSire came to stand beside her and place a supportive hand on her shoulder. "That's true. One usually doesn't want a Healer who might be irritated with one."

"And," Lark continued, meeting each person's eyes, "most people are willing to give Healers information—such as who leaked a confidential news story. A favor for a Healer is usually a wise thing." T'Ash's lips twitched. The other Nobles appeared affronted as if reporting to the news Families of Daisy or Bindweed was beyond their comprehension.

Having done as much as she could to keep the whole thing quiet, Lark prepared for the questions. "Yes?" she prompted.

D'Grove sighed. "An eightday or so ago you were paged to Primary HealingHall and treated Eryngi and Tinne Holly. Let's start there. . . ."

The memory was razor sharp, cutting into her peace of mind. Her fingers curled in her sleeves.

*T'*Hawthorn's soli-vid was a bit battered by the time twelve groups of Hollys "captured" it. But they'd all begun to work seamlessly together, discovering the best tactics to separate T'Hawthorn from his escort.

The task was more difficult because all knew Tinne fought without a kidney. Everyone kept an eye out for him and overlapped his defense. Through the bouts most of them ended up bruised, including Holm—Tinne emerged without a hair ruffled.

Holm slid his long dagger into his sheath as he rubbed his opposite shoulder and grimaced at his smirking brother.

Tinne just looked smug. "I'm grateful for the men's protection. Must keep up my strength and appearance for the marriage bed."

After a short rest and water, T'Holly summoned another simulacrum. "Next, Huathe Hawthorn the younger, HawthornHeir."

Sweat chilled on Holm's body. He liked this less and less. He eyed Lark's brother. The man was quite a few years older than she and looked almost as pompous as his father.

"HawthornHeir is a competent fighter in the *Athos* style. He is cautious, conservative, and does not take risks. He can be found in the streets of Druida during the usual course of his business day, and has been prowling the streets with other Hawthorns during the escalation of the feud. He was part of the party who wounded my HeartMate."

The air seemed to sizzle around T'Holly. All movement stilled. "Capture and ransom would be preferable, but do not hesitate to defend yourselves or fight to kill."

Holm's ears buzzed with the pressure of a headache. He glanced around. Most of the men were as grim-faced as his father, his brother, and himself. This was war, but it felt more like a massacre. How could the Hawthorns hope to win?

He didn't know what decision he might have made if the choice to feud had been left to him, but he feared his father was going in the wrong direction. Holm glanced at Tab. Tension showed in Tab's muscles, in the way he didn't quite look at T'Holly. Tab didn't approve of this vengeance stalk, either.

Holm angled his jaw until his uncle met his eyes. *Can we stop him?* he risked a thought on their private mental path.

No. Not at this moment. Perhaps if we can shape events—

"Holm, demonstrate a straight duel with HawthornHeir before we practice street fighting with the soli-vid," ordered T'Holly.

Holm jumped to his feet, jerked his head in a nod to his father, and concentrated on the model. The simulacrum's eyes weren't quite the right hue. Not the violet of Lark's at all. A relief. He took up his preferred stance.

"Begin!" T'Holly ordered.

* * *

*"W*hat *knowledge do you have of the Hawthorn-Holly feud?"* asked T'Recd.

Lark's palms sweated and she dried them on her sleeve linings. "I know the current feud is centered around Triskel Pass and the Hollys have kin that died there," she said.

"You don't know what T'Hawthorn wants with the pass?"

"No," she said.

"Did you give any information about the Hollys to the Hawthorns?" asked T'Reed.

"T'Hawthorn asked about the state of health of D'Holly. I referred him to T'Heather," Lark said.

"That's all?"

"I don't know anything further."

T'Reed leaned forward, his features sharpened. "Did you give the Hollys any information about the Hawthorns?"

"I've answered that question before. No. If you want to ask me all the questions again, I think it would be a waste of our valuable time."

"I agree," T'Ash said. "I'm a Holly ally. If it were necessary, I'd ask questions concerning the Hollys. The lady is a Healer, obviously not someone who wishes the feud to continue. Three simple questions, Lady, if I may?"

Lark nodded. T'Reed's lips thinned, but he nodded to T'Ash.

"FirstLevel Healer, did your affair with a Holly have anything to do with the feud?" he asked gently.

"No."

"You never passed any information to either Family?"

"No."

"Do you know anything that might help us stop this feud or determine the action to take regarding the warring Families?"

"No."

"That's done. Is there anything you'd like to say?" T'Ash asked.

She glanced around the circle of nobles. "My affair with the Holly is over." Whatever misty fantasies she'd had about continuing the fling had dissolved under the ugly questioning. She'd been right all along. It had been a stupid thing to do, something that would make the feud worse, have every Noble in the city interfering in her or Holm's life. She just wished it hadn't died so brutally, and that she didn't hurt so much.

Keeping her face and manner as serene as she had throughout the ordeal, Lark rose. "I can't tell you anything else. I wish you well in trying to find an end to the matter."

T'Heather took her left hand and tucked it into the crook of his elbow. "My Daughter'sDaughter has applied for and has been granted the position of Head of Gael City HealingHall. She will be leaving in a week to assume that post." He bent an encouraging look on Lark. He wanted her out of this mess.

T'Ash scowled.

Lark nodded.

D'Grove said, "I don't blame you. This is a dreadful situation." She glanced at the wall timer. "Let's take a break. T'Heather, can I speak with you about the Great Healing Ritual for D'Holly tomorrow, please?"

T'Heather squeezed Lark's hand and raised his eyebrows. She smiled reassuringly up at him. "I'm fine." She felt too scoured out by emotion to react to anything.

He let her go. "Of course, D'Grove, I am at your service."

T'Ash stepped up. "I'll see the lady home, T'Heather."

T'Heather nodded absently and walked off with D'Grove.

T'Ash took her arm and matched her pace as they walked from the chamber to the front of the Guildhall. He waited until she was settled in his personal glider and the vehicle spelled to MidClass Lodge before he spoke again. "Usually I wouldn't presume to mix in Holm's aff—uh, business."

Lark didn't look at him. She'd known him for years, when he'd been courting his HeartMate Danith and Lark herself had been bitter over the loss of her husband, but they had never been more than superficially friendly. "You shouldn't now, either, T'Ash."

He made a strangled noise. "Do you want Holm?"

That jolted her. Did she want Holm? Yes, holding her, running a hand over her hair, in her bed. Unbidden, the images rushed through her mind. "Want him?" she asked.

"Want him in your life?" T'Ash persisted.

New visions formed—walking down the beach, playing with kittens, eating breakfast, solar-sailing. Her breath caught.

T'Ash touched her cheek, requesting she look at him. She saw concern—for Holm or her, or both?—in his troubled blue gaze. "Fight for him."

"Fight for him?" She stared at the man.

"If you want him, fight for him. Don't let circumstances separate you."

"The circumstances are impossible!" she bit out.

"Fight for him."

All men could think of was fighting! "There is nothing I could do, right now, that wouldn't make the feud between our Families worse if I 'fought for him.' People are dying. It was madness to try and have an affair with him."

The glider pulled up to MidClass Lodge and hissed to a stop. The door raised.

T'Ash scowled again. "Love's more important than a feud or Families. He needs you. You need him. Don't go away. Fight for him."

Her mouth hadn't shut before the glider took off again.

Fight for him? She had a feeling that T'Ash's words would haunt her, though *she* was right. Their affair could only make things worse if it continued, bring the wrath of their families down on them, churn up tangled emotions more, create conflicts within the families themselves. She shuddered.

There was no going back. It was over. Nothing would make her induce more strife within the two Families. She'd deal with the hurt as she'd dealt with her grief, a moment at a time.

"*The last soli-vid.*" *T'Holly summoned the model.*

Holm's tension lessened a little. He'd feared that T'Holly might be so crude as to have one made of the boy who'd accidentally harmed their Mamá. That would have been difficult to handle. He hadn't known what he'd have done in that case.

"This is Cratag," T'Holly said. "The most dangerous guard Hawthorn has. He is a distant relative as most of you are, and grew up south in the jungles. Note his walk."

The model glided to the center of the room with the fluidity of a good fighter.

"Cratag Hawthorn was in the skirmish that wounded D'Holly. He protected the boy. He was also in the melée that killed Eryngi. Tab and I have spoken with those of you who have met him and taken your observations into consideration of the soli-vid's instruction. The loss of Cratag would greatly damage the Hawthorns. He must be seen as our prime target."

Holm sensed the increased alertness around him as the men focused on the simulacrum.

A level of awareness permeated him, too. He believed it came from his passive connection with Lark. He analyzed it and understood that she liked and respected Cratag. She valued him as a member of the Family.

Holm's headache grew. He looked around at the groups in the large sparring room. The Hollys were going to war. There were no guards the Hawthorns could field who would beat Hollys, unless Hawthorn hired mercenaries.

There'd be more clashes. More casualties. More blood running in the streets and squares. More deaths.

His fighting nature, which he'd tried to minimize with Lark, would be put on brilliant display. He didn't even need to be around for the lesson to hit home to her—his father, brother, and rest of his Family would illustrate a fighting Family in lurid, gruesome color.

He could help win the feud or win his HeartMate.

Twenty-five

❤

The next day Holm paced around GreatCircle Temple. Lark had returned the rose and his calligraphy he'd sent last night.

Straif Blackthorn had kept pace with Holm for a while, then went to the atrium to act as Doorkeeper.

The three FirstLevel Healers of Druida—T'Heather, Heather-Heir Ur, and Mayblossom Larkspur Collinson—along with T'Holly, were supervising the transfer of D'Holly from *Nuada's Sword* to the Temple. Tinne and his wife had gone along to check on the development of his new kidney in the Ship's vats. Holm patted his sides, glad he had both kidneys. Tinne had shown an unwholesome fascination with the progress of his new kidney's growth. Holm had the sneaking suspicion that Tinne *talked* to it, encouraging it to mature.

Holm himself was frustrated to the limits of his small store of patience. As usual these nights, he'd sleep-ported. Meserv had been dragged along and was vociferous in his disapproval of having to *walk* out of the Great Labyrinth. He'd sat on Holm's shoulder and complained every step—until he'd insulted Holm by falling asleep while *Holm* walked out—and snored in Holm's ear.

The nightporting had been a minor anxiety, but the trip out had let him brood about Lark. T'Ash had scried to mutter dark hints she'd been through an ordeal, but Holm couldn't get any meaningful details from his friend.

The entire night had set his nerves winding into a spring of tension under a sliver of control.

The rising babble of voices pulled Holm from his dour thoughts, and he stopped pacing to scan the crowd. A Healing Ritual was considered outside all alliances, so T'Hawthorn's allies were attending. All FirstFamilies Heads and their consorts except T'Hawthorn were there, and some Noble Council Grand-Lords and Ladies and GraceLords and Ladies.

T'Ash and D'Ash stood with their Fam Zanth in the middle of a knot of Holly's staunchest supporters. Meserv sat behind D'Ash's gown, peeking out at his sire, then at the door awaiting his twin Phyll.

The one who caught and held Holm's attention was the young prophet, Muin "Vinni" T'Vine. His changeable eyes held a glitter that screamed of a fateful gathering—setting Holm's hackles rising and his teeth on edge.

T'Holly strode in, carrying his HeartMate and the hall fell silent. To Holm she looked better than the evening before and much healthier than when he'd taken her to *Nuada's Sword*, but he could tell by the whispers that most were shocked at her thin body and her hair, which was now more silver than bronze.

She was placed on the large carved rainbowstone altar in the center of GreatCircle Temple which held a soft down-filled mattress covered in the finest llamawoolweave. The scent of fresh, healing herbs rose as D'Holly settled.

All three FirstLevel Healers attended his Mamá. Holm hurried to his Mamá's side and took her hand. She looked up at him with clear turquoise eyes and smiled. He smiled back, but his shoulders felt tight. His Father appeared worn. The long hours he spent on *Nuada's Sword*, where Flair only occasionally worked, had irritated him.

Holm turned his gaze to Lark, but she busied herself with his Mamá, and he couldn't interrupt. After the return of his rose the night before, she'd pinched their connection to the thinnest of microfilaments, thinner than a thread of her solar sail. It angered and worried him, but the fact that she couldn't break it let a small flame of hope burn within him.

T'Holly smiled down on his HeartMate and T'Heather

handed her a drink. He glanced at his timer. "We are progressing very well and have a half-septhour before the Ritual should start. Rest, GreatLady, and seek your inner core. That is needful for the Healing to work."

Passiflora smiled as T'Holly helped her drink, then nodded and subsided back onto the mattress, closing her eyes. T'Holly held her left hand and murmured love words to her. The aura surrounding them was so bright a gold it made Holm's eyes hurt.

An outraged yowl screeched above the hum of voices. Everyone turned to the southwest quadrant of the room. Zanth, a huge black-and-white tomcat, flung off small patches of orange and cream—the kittens. Each landed with a plop on a nearby heap of summer grasses, gathered for autumnal equinox a couple of months away.

Lark gasped. She and Holm converged on the scene. Holm grabbed her hand, but she sent him a shock that tingled his fingers. He stopped to stare at her and she flushed. She, too, was on the ragged edge of control. He sensed bubbling emotions, including the white flashes that bespoke resistance to any constraint. But fury and fear burned in him. She should not treat him so, her lover, her *HeartMate*.

He reached the kittens as Phyll stood, then wavered, then plunked down on his rump, shaking his head. Meserv rolled to his back and curled his paws over his round belly.

Lark scooped up her Fam and checked him for hurts. He extended all ten of his sharp little claws into her arms. *I am fine. Let Me down. Now!*

She carefully placed him on his feet.

"The little one is proud," chuckled T'Ash, joining them. "Quite a fighter."

Phyll sat, full of feline arrogance, and began licking a patch of fur on his shoulder.

Meserv cracked a gleaming sapphire eye, saw them, shut his eye and whimpered.

Holm sighed.

Zanth stalked over, dripping blood from a drooping, tattered ear. The other ear pointed up. He crouched near the kittens and rumbled a long growl.

"What's going on here, Phyll?" asked Holm.

Phyll twitched his whiskers and rotated his ears in disdain.

Sire Zanth say We are puny. And stupid. And slow. Tiny white teeth showed as Phyll lifted his lip. *He's not laughing now. WE got HIM!*

"You certainly did." Danith D'Ash, the sole animal Healer on Celta, shook her head. "You're bleeding on the floor, Zanth."

Still growling, the tom turned his head to look at D'Ash. *Reckless kits. Only trouble, trouble, trouble.*

Meserv gave a heart-wrenching sigh, then rolled over to sprawl on his side, his eyes wide-open with hurt innocence.

"Poor Zanth, your sons beat you up," Danith said. She turned a laugh into a cough, then knelt and held out her hand. The tom strode haughtily to her and butted her fingers.

Lark stared at Zanth. "There are pinpoint holes clear through Zanth's ear. Phyll!"

Phyll lifted his pink nose, a miniature of his sire's. *We beat him. We win. We speak better than he does, too. And just as loud.*

T'Ash winced. *Certainly, you can make your thoughts felt, youngling.*

"Poor Zanth," Danith crooned. "Let me see that ear." With a small lightball, she illumined the ear. The light reflected off a shining emerald ear stud.

Lark blinked.

Danith shook her head. "You know what this means, don't you? I'll straighten out that other ear, while I mend the tooth-holes, but not now. My energy is needed for the true Healing of D'Holly that will take place here today. You must wait until this evening, Zanth, and serves you right."

Frowning, she looked at Lark. "Did this little skirmish disrupt the energy flow too much?"

Lark looked at T'Heather, who appeared disgusted. Holm's Mamá seemed in a deep trance.

Holm made a half-bow. "With your permission, FirstLevel Healer, if we join, you can judge the power of the room." He held out a demanding hand. She fulminated but placed her hand in his, widened their connection for a heartbeat, then withdrew and minimized their link to a thread. Far too short a time for him to try and mend the rift between them.

"The Healing Energy builds. T'Heather has used the release of tension between these three to strengthen his initial Call to the Lady and Lord," Lark said briskly.

Zanth sat on his solid hindquarters and glared at his off-spring. Meserv curled into a ball.

To calm himself, Holm picked up his kitten, cradling him. "You're worthless," he said, but his forefinger stroked Meserv's head and he purred. At least someone liked his touch. "Danith, could you check my Fam, to make sure he has no hurt?"

Danith slid a sly gaze to Holm. "For a tableful of GreatHouse pastries."

"Zanth still terrorizing your chef?"

"Every morning." Danith shrugged. She turned her smile on Lark. "Fighters. You learn to live with them." Lark looked startled, but Holm blessed his friend's HeartMate. T'Ash winked.

Then Danith directed her gaze to Phyll, who studiously separated his pads to clean between them. "May I examine you, also, Fam Phyll Collinson?"

He stopped his grooming and sat up regally, curling his tail around his paws. "Yesssss," he vocalized. *But I am a HealerCat and I am learning My body. All My insides are fine. I am a most healthy Cat.*

"Your brother first, then." Danith took the purring but limp Meserv in her hands, then frowned in concentration. She darted a glance up at Holm. "His digestive system is not quite right. You must stop feeding him people food."

Holm grimaced. "My Mamá started it, and we can't, any of us, deny her whatever she wants. Lately the household hasn't been organized." He turned to glance at his mother and saw she was well-attended and deep in trance.

Danith's face softened. "I understand. I'll send you some treats you can substitute for the people food." She put Meserv down and scooped up Phyll. "Yes, you are a very fine kitten." She rubbed his head and put him down.

Phyll preened, then cocked an ear. *T'Heather calls Us.* The kittens trotted away. The Ashes followed.

Holm grasped Lark's arm and absorbed the shock she gave him. He didn't budge, searching for words. "The kittens will always be a bond between us, as they should be. We should be together."

Her lips pressed tight and she glanced up at him with angry eyes. "Please let me go."

He sent a caress to her, then released her.

Holm saw tears in her eyes before she looked away. "Holm, it's no use. Our love affair is over."

"No."

Lark shut her eyes briefly. "If our Families found out, it would make the feud more vicious. We'd be disowned and there'd be internal problems within our Families as members took sides. I won't be the cause of such strife."

"You overestimate the effect our—loving—would have," he said, but sensed he'd lose this battle and cursed himself for bringing it up when they both worried about his Mamá.

Mouth grim, he gave her a half bow and went back to the altar to stand to the right of his Mamá.

Since it was the month of Hazel, the FirstFamily GreatLady and GreatLord D'Hazel and T'Hazel were the leaders of all Rituals. They were HeartMates and Holm was glad of it, though last month had been Holly and next month was Apple, so either of those months would have helped his Mamá Heal better, too.

D'Hazel and her husband went hand-in-hand to the altar. "Merry meet!" D'Hazel raised her voice for attention. Everyone turned to her. "Since this is a Healing Ritual, we will turn the roles of Lady and Lord over to D'Heather and T'Heather. Our placement in the Circle, who will link with whom, will be maximized for the Healing of D'Holly and will be determined by T'Heather."

"And me!" piped Vinni.

Everyone stared at him. He smirked and adjusted his shirt-cuffs, the embroidery on them signifying his rank.

D'Hazel frowned at T'Heather, but the Healer just lifted and dropped his stocky shoulders. D'Hazel inclined her head to the boy. "As you will, GreatLord T'Vine."

"I will arrange people as *tynged,* Destiny, decrees," said the boy in a lower voice.

Holm wasn't the only one who shivered.

T'Heather stumped with his HeartMate to join D'Hazel and T'Hazel by the altar. "When I contacted each of you earlier, you gave me permission to sample your energy for this ceremony. Last night I drew up the Heart Circle that will be the most effective in this final Healing for D'Holly. With our energy, her new kidney will be totally accepted by her body, she will regain strength and be well on the way to complete recovery."

There was a murmur of approval.

"We will proceed," T'Heather said. To Holm's surprise, the first thing he did was place Meserv by his mother's left hip—the side of her new kidney donated by Tinne—and Phyll by her right hip. T'Ash's Fam, Zanth, lay next to her feet, and Tinne's fighting cat, Ilexa, curled around her head.

As Holm and Lark reached the altar there came a commotion at the door.

"Let him in," ordered Vinni, "It's Hawthorn!"

Another boy entered—the youngest Huathe Hawthorn, Lark's nephew, Laev, followed by the Hawthorn guard Cratag.

Holm eyed Cratag. He looked much tougher than the model they'd fought with the day before. Holm winced inwardly as he recalled how often the Hollys had practiced killing the man—a man Lark obviously liked and admired since she embraced him and he patted her back.

"T'Hawthorn?" T'Holly's voice boomed from several strides away, a mixture of fury and wariness in it.

Lark said. "Welcome, Laev." She hesitated, and Holm knew she wanted to hug the youngster, but was conscious of the boy's dignity. Her sensitivity sent a spurt of pride through him.

"T'Hawthorn!" T'Holly roared.

The boy flinched. Lark laid a hand on his thin shoulder. Laev trembled, then stepped away from his guard. When he spoke, his voice shook. "I'm Huathe, FirstSon and Heir of HawthornHeir. I was the one who hurt your Lady. I didn't mean to, I'm sorry, I—" he broke off and took a shuddering breath.

Holm admired the slight boy, barely a teenager. Thin, but with a shock of thick black hair and the violet eyes of the Hawthorns, his voice stilled by fear, yet he stood before T'Holly and admitted his fault.

"Come, Laev," Holm said. "And welcome. We are glad you attend. As the one who injured my Mamá, your presence will add potency to the Healing Ritual. The Hollys" —Holm shot a glance at his father who glared at Laev—"do not war on children. Do we, sir?" he asked T'Holly.

T'Holly's lips had thinned. "You wielded the knife that felled my HeartMate?" The undertone of anguish made his voice fill the building.

Lark moved to stand to one side of the boy, Cratag to the other. Both had supportive hands on his shoulders.

Laev opened his mouth, swallowed, then a squeaky "Yes" emerged.

For a moment mad fury lit T'Holly's eyes. His jaw worked, then he spun on his heel. "Hollys do not war on children."

T'Heather stepped forward. "The Healing Ritual is long and powerful. You are not of age yet. You have not experienced your second Passage. Does your Family know you are here?"

Laev sent a desperate look up to Lark. "FirstDaughter Mayblossom does."

"Laev has not been Tested yet, but the Oracle at his birth confirmed his great Flair, enough to rise to T'Hawthorn," Lark said. "As the one who wounded D'Holly, his presence and his remorse will be a potent spur to our spell."

T'Heather bowed to the boy. "It is a right and honorable thing that you are here. Come." He strode away. Laev heaved a breath and hurried after him.

Holm met Cratag's gaze. "Hollys cherish young ones, and women," he said softly. He waited until Cratag inclined his head, acknowledging that the Hollys were holding back in the duel, while the Hawthorns fought without such limitations. "T'Holly can loathe but understand the mistake of a poorly trained boy in a fight."

It was good for Lark to know the Hollys had limits to their violence and kept their honor in the midst of a bloody feud.

He suspected she'd finish the unspoken corollary to his thought. T'Holly can loathe, but understand, the mistake of a poorly trained boy in a fight. But had young Laev been trained by the Hollys, he would not have made such a mistake, even in the fury and excitement of a scrambling fight. The whole dreadful act that had shot the feud to new levels would have been avoided.

"Cratag, your strength and vitality will contribute to the HealingCircle," Lark said. "HollyHeir, I don't believe you've been introduced to my cuz Cratag Maytree, currently serving GreatHouse T'Hawthorn?"

"No," Holm said. He'd only skewered the man's simulacrum several times the day before. "I'm sorry to meet under these circumstances."

Cratag nodded and turned to scan the crowd. Lark slid her arm in his. "Let's find where T'Heather wishes to place you."

She didn't even look at Holm as she walked to the altar, but he was on her heels.

With a frown of concentration, T'Heather ordered the Nobles. HeartMates would always be connected, and the couples would be spaced at intervals to boost the circulating energy.

T'Holly held his HeartMate's left hand, and T'Heather and his HeartMate came after, then FirstLevel HeatherHeir Ur, then Tinne and Genista, Tab Holly and D'Ash and T'Ash.

It was obvious to Holm that he should hold his Mamá's right hand. "FirstLevel Healer Mayblossom Collinson should link with me," Holm said, extending his hand to her. They, as all HeartMates, should be together.

But Vinni T'Vine was there, leading a pale, thin young woman with limp blond hair. "No," Vinni said. "GrandLady D'Marigold will link with HollyHeir." He challenged T'Heather with a stare and T'Heather took a step back. Red touched his cheeks. He nodded and continued lining up the other side of the circle.

Forcing a smile, Holm bowed to the colorless Marigold. "A pleasure," he lied. Her light blue eyes sharpened, but she just nodded and set an unexpectedly firm hand in his. His amulet heated and Holm stilled. There was something strange about her Flair. He dropped her hand.

"D'Marigold, you link with Cratag Maytree," Vinni chivvied the large, scarred guard into place.

The lady looked up at Cratag with awe. He flushed and shifted.

"Laev," insisted Vinni, "over here, you take Cratag's hand on your left and Lark's hand on your right, I will link with Lark on one side and D'Hazel on the other." The GreatLady and her HeartMate T'Hazel came at the young prophet's gesture.

Everyone acknowledged each other, briefly clasped hands to test the connection with those on either side, then stood and waited for T'Heather to finish arranging the Nobles.

Even though the circle was not complete, voices hushed and a heavy, portentous atmosphere enveloped the room. If Holm squinted, he could see individual colored auras, the merging of a HeartMate couple's energy—that made him swallow hard—and the blur of color as they began to merge into a powerful whole.

Finally everyone was in their assigned place. The circle was more the form of a womb—the womb of initiation, or a heart with a rounded point. D'Holly lay on the altar, T'Holly on her left and Holm on her right started the upward curves of the heart, then the circle rounded out.

Holm's heart thudded one hard beat as he realized that they were the shape of the innermost path of the Great Labyrinth, at the bottom of the crater bowl. He *reached*, he *sank*, but could not find his calm center. He could not bear the thought of failure. He glanced at his Mamá. She lay serene, her skin rosy and her lips parted. She had reached her own essential self and dwelt in a stream of music.

His father looked more peaceful than he'd been since D'Holly had been wounded, but his face had trimmed down to stern lines that Holm regretted. He wondered if the laughing, loving father he'd known would ever return, or if something deep and intrinsic had changed in the man. Soon Holm would take his Mamá's hand and funnel all his energy, and the energy from others, into her. He muttered a prayer under his breath and saw other noble lips moving in the same fashion. He hoped with every fiber of his being that his Mamá's poison-ravaged body would accept Tinne's kidney and she would heal.

The light dimmed, the Temple charged with anticipation, and T'Heather began the Ritual.

Twenty-six

❦

D'Heather and T'Heather cast the circle and Called the Deities. A hum of powerful energy poured through the Nobles. Lark nearly gasped aloud at the potency.

It had been a long time since she'd participated in a GreatRitual Circle. The T'Hawthorn Rituals couldn't begin to equal this. Her father and brother were always restrained— perhaps unable to release their full power when linking with less Flaired Family members. But Lark thought it was something more, the strict manners and propriety with which all Hawthorns were ingrained might unconsciously limit them. Did that explain those "white flashes" she experienced, the fighting of her Flair against restrictions ingrained since she was a babe?

But the Heathers were used to freeing their Flair in their craft, as were the Ashes and Hollys. The exultation of working at her full potential, pouring her Flair into a merging of great power, dizzied Lark. Then she could separate and examine individual pinpoints in the stream of building Healing-Light.

The Hollys were by far the strongest, smoothest cluster. Lark sensed the great, intimate and long-standing Family bonds. They liked each other. They *loved* each other. Even the new bride Genista and the small Fam Meserv were welcomed and accom- modated in their Family tie. No wonder D'Holly had managed to survive so long with her fearsome wound. Her HeartMate and sons bolstered her with unconditional love and strength. The Apples, D'Holly's brother, nieces, and nephews, were second only to the Hollys in their bonding. They, too, were a close Family.

Lark choked back tears of sentimentality and longing for such closeness in her own Family. It wouldn't ever happen with her Father or her brother leading the household, but perhaps Laev could make a change. With the thought, she was conscious of his brilliant, surging Flair. She squeezed his hand and slanted him a glance.

He looked up shyly, eyes sheened with dampness. If he'd ever participated in a Noble GreatRitual, it was when T'Hawthorn had been present and the Hollys absent. He was touched by the complete bonding of the HeartMates in the circle, the solidity of the Hollys and Apples, the ties between himself, Cratag, Phyll and her, and through her and the kitten, the personal link with the strong and compassionate Heathers. Lark realized she'd unconsciously smoothed Laev's fluctuating energy—his Flair wasn't regulated since he hadn't experienced all his Passages. She also amplified and directed Cratag's meager talent.

The other odd note in the Circle was D'Marigold. Her Flair changed colors and *twisted* the current of power when it reached her. Lark closed her eyes to determine the differences, but couldn't ascertain them. She shrugged inwardly. It wasn't important. The spin D'Marigold put on the energy enhanced it.

Vinni T'Vine was a blazing starburst but had his great and singular Flair under control. Her heart skipped as she understood he was a "natural." He wouldn't undergo any Passages, his Flair was already integrated into every fiber of his body, his emotions, heart, soul, and life.

A continuous, small crackle from Holm disturbed the flow. Lark frowned. He was having trouble with D'Marigold's twist. He hadn't sunk into his inner balance and core like everyone else, even Laev. She fretted that it resulted from the conflict between them. His tension rose, and though he handled it, shaped it, and used it to boost the vitality he fed to his mother, it couldn't be easy on him. It would be a constant irritant to his nerves.

She wanted to link intimately with him. Badly. But that was unwise and against her decision to end their affair.

T'Heather spoke the first couplet of the Healing Ritual, demanding her Healing Flair and attention, and Lark turned her mind and heart to practicing her craft.

Holm set his teeth. He didn't know what was going on, but everyone in the whole damn Circle seemed at ease except him.

Mamá's Healing was going well. Linked to her as he was, he felt the plumping of her cells, the expanding of her tissues with life-renewing force. Her skin pinkened as they purified her blood. Though she was deep in trance, music pulsed from her to him and his father—small bursts that told them she was doing more than absorbing the energy, she'd started to participate in the Circle.

Sweat beaded at his hairline and trickled down his spine. He held on grimly. He could finish this rite, he wouldn't fail in this most important task. Meanwhile he counted the couplets of the Ritual, breathed, and danced the thin line of balance with all his skill.

None too soon his Mamá's chest rose in a deep breath and her eyelids fluttered open. She turned her head and smiled at T'Holly.

Her fingers curled around Holm's as she recalled where she was, and he doubled his effort to send her strength.

Finally the Heathers led the Circle in a short thanksgiving chorus, dismissed the Guardians, and ended the Ritual. D'Marigold dropped Holm's hand and swayed, and Cratag Hawthorn supported her with a brawny arm.

Only then did Holm notice signs of strain on the others. The funneling of such power was an exaltation but also tiring—as tools under the direction of others.

The Heathers all looked weary but pleased, including his Bélla. His mind and emotions *needed* the intimate cycling of energy between them, nothing but her touch would settle the tight strain within him.

Holm headed for Lark, circling around D'Marigold and Cratag, ignoring a glittering silver look from T'Vine. When the boy GreatLord stepped into Holm's path, Holm simply lifted him and set him aside, noting with pleasure how Vinni's mouth dropped open. Nothing was going to stop him from reaching his lady.

The young Hawthorn was talking to her. Holm nudged him

aside with a charming smile he dredged from his depths. "Pardon me. I need Lark."

"You need to speak with me?" Lark bristled.

Holm only widened his smile and brushed his neck where the still livid lovebite was covered by his collar. "No." He grasped her hands in his and lifted them to his mouth.

He felt a mental tug from his parents. He ignored it.

No, sent his father.

Holm didn't listen.

"No!" T'Holly thundered. "Holm, I will *not* have you associating with a Hawthorn, the daughter of my enemy." He followed the command with a sizzling disciplinary shock through their bond that Holm hadn't experienced for thirty years.

He looked at his father near the altar, cradling his HeartMate in his arms. Holm's ire rose with the jangling of his nerves. His father could claim and hold his HeartMate, but dared to forbid Holm.

"You will deny me the company of one of the FirstLevel Healers who just spent her time and Flair in Healing my Mamá?" He formed each word precisely. Everything in him rose in a great surge of denial at T'Holly's command. He met the older man's eyes. His father had been wrong before. He was wrong now.

T'Ash swung from a conversation and started toward Holm. Other Nobles stopped talking and stared at the Holly men. The kittens hopped from the altar and ran to them.

"Holm, please, let me go," whispered Lark, pulling on her hands. He kept them firmly in his own. Only the feel of her soft skin kept him sane.

T'Holly's gaze fired to molten pewter. He sent another jolt to Holm. Holm cut the connection between them. His Mamá made a protesting sound. Holm didn't care.

"No son of mine will consort with the FirstDaughter of the Hawthorns," T'Holly said. "Come attend your Mamá and me."

"No," Holm said. He looked down at Lark. "I need you. Now. Forever."

Her eyes widened and she looked scandalized at his increasing torrent of desire to claim her.

"Tinne, Tab," T'Holly said. Holm didn't know what mental order T'Holly communicated, but Tinne and Tab exchanged glances and slowly began to walk toward him.

"Cool, my friend," muttered T'Ash.

Holm swept an arm around Lark's waist.

"Let's take this outside," T'Ash said, grasping Lark's arm.

"I don't—" Lark started.

"Unhand my cuz," said Cratag Hawthorn.

Two frowning GreatNobles swept to them. "I will not have conflict in the Temple under my auspices," T'Heather said.

"Nor will I during my month," said D'Hazel. They shared a glance. D'Hazel, the more diplomatic, strode to the altar and Holm's parents.

"Unhand my cuz." Cratag rested a hand on his hip, near the empty sheath of his dagger.

"Go to hell, Maytree." Holm showed all his teeth.

T'Ash hissed out a breath. "Come *on*." He circled his black-smith's muscular arm around Holm's shoulder and pulled. The kittens whined.

Tinne and Tab arrived.

"T'Holly orders you to his side," Tab said neutrally. "Don't disobey him. He's in a volatile mood."

Not as volatile as Holm's.

T'Holly *stood* on the altar, holding his HeartMate close to his chest. "Give her up, Holm."

It was the last straw. "No," he called to his father. "She's my HeartMate."

"No!" yelled T'Holly.

"No!" cried Lark, wrenching herself from him, flinging T'Ash's arm away, too. She hopped back and color drained from her face. "No," she whispered. "This can't be. I don't have a HeartMate. Neither do you."

"We do now." He grinned, beginning to enjoy himself. At least the rasping anxiety of his nerves and the strain of keeping his secret was being released in the verbal battle.

"Uh-oh," said Laev. He picked up Phyll.

T'Heather stopped and stared, then shook his head.

Deep color rushed back into Lark's face. Her eyes narrowed. "I don't believe this. This can't be true."

"It's always been true and right between us," Holm retorted, stepping to her.

"No!" She whirled and faced her MotherSire, T'Heather. "I have been awarded the position as Head of the Gael City

HealingHall." Lark shot Holm a confused, betrayed glance. He
hurt for her. "I will be leaving within the week."

He absorbed the blow, the hurt, told himself that she was upset, that she would come around if he wooed her more, and right,
and openly, this time.

"No son of mine has a Hawthorn for a HeartMate," T'Holly
boomed from the altar. D'Holly tugged at the collar of his shirt,
but he paid her no mind.

Holm pivoted to meet his father's eyes. "Yes, I do. I love her
and I will have her. Mayblossom Larkspur Hawthorn Collinson.
My *HeartMate*."

"I disown you. I disown you. I disown you. You are no longer
a Holly son. You have no more rights to my name or my house,
my Family or my Residence." T'Holly issued the ritual words,
and Holm staggered, more from the abrupt snapping of all the
mental and emotional bonds with his Family than with the blows
of the words. His ears rang. He was no longer Holm Holly.

"I am *not* your HeartMate!" Lark cried. She took his hand,
opened the bond between them to its fullest extent, a large
golden rope, and sent energy to him. It sizzled through his
blood, pooled in his groin, burned upward to his throat.

She Healed the lovebite she'd given him, dropped his hand,
and strode away.

Rejection upon rejection piled upon him due to his failure after failure. Only willpower kept him from falling to his knees.
Meserv mewed and Holm picked him up and cradled him.

T'Heather and D'Hazel and another woman came over, Ailim
Elder, SupremeJudge of Druida. She looked at him and sighed,
shaking her head. "T'Ash, bring Holm to the back anteroom. He
has violated one of the most sacred laws of our society."

"Glad to get out of here," T'Ash said.

Holm was weak and blind. Emotional agony roared through
him. He had failed completely and utterly. He was nothing.

T'Ash kept him on his feet and stumbling in the right direction. Holm had lost everything. He hoped the small connection
with Lark was still there, but he couldn't feel it. Did his breaking
of the HeartMate laws sever that tie, too?

His throat closed.

Ailim went inside a small room, and the door closed after her.
T'Ash stopped outside the room. His concerned face, eyebrows

drawn, moved into Holm's vision, scowling. He shook Holm.

"Get a grip, man. This is no time to fall to pieces. Where's your charm and suavity?"

Those traits had belonged to HollyHeir. He didn't know who he was.

Holm smiled and T'Ash jerked back. "A corpse can smile better than that."

Another shake. "Pull yourself together."

Holm licked dry lips. "My Family ties . . ."

"You think I don't know what you're feeling? I lost *all* my Family when I was six. I remember." The big man shuddered. Then he curved his hands around Holm's face, locked gazes with him, and sent him a bolt of sheer strength and energy that lifted the hair on Holm's nape, zapped to his toes, tweaked his balls, then found his gut and settled there.

Meserv hissed. Holm rocked back and shook his head. Whatever else, he had one good friend in the world. He reached for his mantra, wavered. The mantra had been found in T'Holly HouseHeart, which he'd never see again. The mantra, too, belonged to Holm, HollyHeir, not to whoever he was now.

"Another jolt?" asked T'Ash.

"No." Holm straightened. His and T'Ash's Flair had never melded well. Holm rolled his shoulders, stretched muscles.

T'Ash sighed. "Good." He glanced at the closed door and winced. "I'll wait here for you." Then he shook his head and clapped his hand on Holm's shoulder. Holm nearly staggered. "When you lose your composure, you *really* lose it. I knew that impulsive Holly nature would do you in."

Shaking his head and testing himself for hurt—dreadful but manageable—Holm recalled how he used to stand, gesture, walk. The manner was no longer instinctive, but like an uncomfortable costume donned for a play. He didn't know how to move in it. Jerkily he opened the door and stepped through.

Ailim Elder sat in a winged chair by the window. T'Ash had spoken of composure, but he'd only seen this lady lose her serenity once, and he'd had a part in that. He winced.

She smiled faintly and he recalled that she was a telempath. "Please sit, Holm."

His knees gave out as he reached the chair. Meserv settled beside him, and Holm petted the kitten.

Now her expression was troubled. "I'm sorry for the turmoil you are going through, Holm."

He shrugged, put Meserv on his lap, and toyed with his fur.

"I can tell by your thoughts, and those of your friends and Family, that the announcement of your HeartMate is true."

"D'Willow confirmed I had a HeartMate. She didn't know who, but now she will." He smiled thinly. "Not that it will matter."

"She wasn't at the ceremony, but her Heir was. They don't get along, but she will hear the news from someone. All of Druida will know what happened soon."

Her words about D'Willow and her heir only reminded him of the emptiness inside him. Tinne was HollyHeir now.

Ailim continued. "D'Hazel and T'Heather got to me fast. T'Heather is particularly concerned about your—lapse. They would like this handled discreetly. It would be better for you to admit to your guilt now and privately than to schedule this for a hearing and a trial. As a matter of fact, I'm not quite sure what council would judge you."

He just stared at her. The intense pain ebbed and flowed through him at intervals, leaving him breathless and acting in spurts. He hoped numbness would come soon. It had when his Mamá had been wounded—but then there had always been hope. Now there was none. His father—T'Holly—had repeated the Disowning Words three times, as was proper. Holm had failed quite spectacularly. Razor-sharp claws of guilt bit in him at that, but not at his bald announcement.

"I acted hastily, and I am sorry for that, but I will not deny Lark is my HeartMate or that I want and need her."

Ailim's face softened. "Personally, it is awkward for me to chide you, since I, too, broke Celtan laws." She smiled lopsidedly. "But as a judge and the representative of the GreatLords in charge of this ritual, I must remind you that you have admitted breaking one of the most sacred laws of Celta. You have informed a woman she is your HeartMate."

Holm's stomach pitched. One more failure. He'd never broken any law that had brought him before a judge, let alone the SupremeJudge of Druida.

"Before a large assembly for a sacred Healing for your *Mother,* you announced that Mayblossom Collinson was your Heart-Mate. You surprised and humiliated her. You've placed her in an intolerable position amongst her equals, her co-workers, and her maternal Family."

He choked. He hadn't thought of that. Hadn't thought at all of *her*, just himself. He'd acted arrogantly again. He truly was despicable.

And he found he hated this wing chair as much as the one in front of T'Holly's desk. He preferred T'Holly's stern visage and D'Holly's sighs to these quiet words from this young, slender woman with the steady blue-gray eyes, who had told him how he'd wounded his HeartMate.

She continued to speak words that tore at him. "With that pronouncement, you escalated the strife between her and her Father." Ailim tilted her head. "And you have hurt yourself so badly it's as if you are bleeding inside. I know that. So perhaps it is good that the law will put restraints on you."

Ailim looked at him with sorrow and lifted a hand. "You will always be chaperoned while in the presence of your HeartMate. If no chaperone is available, you must remain at least three meters away from her. The restrictions are for five years or until Mayblossom Collinson states in front of three FirstFamilies heads that she accepts HeartMate status and repeats it five times."

The words rolled over him, sucking him into a swift undertow he thought would finish him. The roaring of his heart filled his ears. His vision faded again until he felt tossed about on a dark sea of fate.

Ailim's cool hand pressed his head forward between his knees. Meserv squeaked. "Shhh, Holm. It's not that bad. You live. She lives. You are HeartMates. This will work out."

He sincerely doubted that. He wanted to vomit. Blood rushed to his head and his clammy face heated with embarrassment. Meserv set sharp pointed little claws into Holm's thigh.

Pounding came on the door. "Holm? Holm? Are you all right? I'm coming in." T'Ash banged the door open.

Judge Elder sent a tingle of a calming spell to him that refreshed him enough to straighten and lean back into the chair. She went back to her own seat.

T'Ash strode in. "I'm here. Danith said everybody's been talking about the HeartMate laws out there"—he gestured to the Temple—"and she sent this guy to be a chaperone."

A large, long-haired cat swaggered in.

Holm choked again, surprised he could feel a jet of amusement.

The cat stopped in front of him and lifted his nose in disdain. At knee-level, golden eyes stared up haughtily at him.

Meserv gave a tiny squeak and tried to curl himself completely near the back of the chair.

The cat before them had an entirely black face, and his fur shaded only to a lighter dark gray down the rest of his form. His flat face did nothing to minimize the effect of his eyes.

The cat sat. *I am Black Pierre,* he said. *D'Ash loves Me.*

No news there; D'Ash loved every animal she saw.

Black Pierre narrowed his eyes and whipped his tail at T'Ash. The GreatLord rumbled back.

T'Ash is not an agreeable man. Zanth is not a Cat I care to associate with.

Another cat with attitude. There must have been furious cat fights in T'Ash Residence. When Holm narrowed his eyes, he saw two streaks of silver on a tufted midnight ear—healing scars.

Black Pierre looked Holm up and down. *I am a Superior Cat, strong and smart. Many people can hear my thoughts. I speak well. I am long-haired and beautiful.*

Meserv started a low-toned grumble and hiss beneath Holm's left elbow.

I wish a FamMan. A GreatLord would be appropriate. A warrior would be good.

Screeching, Meserv jumped from the chair to land in front of Black Pierre, back arched, hair on end, hissing.

I am Fam to Holm! cried Meserv.

Holm had never seen a cat sneer so well. Black Pierre lifted his black nose and curled his upper muzzle over one white and pointed tooth. With little imagination Holm could visualize blood dripping from that tooth. *Fat, puny kitten,* Black Pierre said, raising a paw and extending sharp, curved claws.

"That's enough," Ailim Elder commanded in her judge's tones. "I hereby retain Black Pierre as chaperone to Holm to ensure he is restrained in his courtship of his HeartMate, Mayblossom Collinson." She met Holm's eyes. "Black Pierre will follow you and keep me apprised of your movements."

I am sure I will find an acceptable FamMan. Black Pierre picked up a paw and licked dark pads.

T'Ash grunted. He stalked back to the door and opened it. "Better a cat than a human chaperone. Come on, Holm, we've got a lot to settle. Vinni T'Vine took Laev Hawthorn and Cratag Maytree to T'Hawthorn's in the T'Vine glider. Straif is waiting for us, too. Everyone else left to spread gossip."

Holm rose slowly. T'Ash was right. Better a cat pacing him than a man. He swept Meserv into his arms and carried him, wanting the Fam's loving warmth. When the kitten began to purr, a little of Holm's desolation lessened. His voice sounded rusty when he spoke. "What about Lark? Is she still here?"

He received a hard, comforting pummel on the shoulder. "Yes, but she's surrounded by the Heathers like a baby bird who's fallen out of the nest. Don't even think about trying to swoop down on her."

Holm grunted. When Lark's attention had been distracted, he'd managed to widen their connection. He knew enough about women to know that she was in no state to talk to him. The overwhelming emotion she felt was humiliation, then there was confusion and pure stubbornness. He winced. If he hadn't been a trained warrior—at least he knew that much about himself—he'd think about slipping away from the Temple through a back door. But he wasn't a coward. A failure, but never a coward. Still, for the first time, he dreaded seeing Lark.

Twenty-seven

❦

*W*hen *Holm stepped inside the round chamber of the Tem-*ple, followed by Black Pierre, T'Heather glared at him from across the room and herded his HeartMate, Heir, and Daughter'sDaughter—Lark—outside the main doors. Holm didn't know whether to be relieved or upset. The keen knife edge of pain had subsided into the aching emptiness of loss.

His cuz, Straif Blackthorn, and his brother Tinne joined them.

"Tab and Genista went in the glider with T'Holly and D'Holly and my hunting cat," Tinne said.

"Greetyou, HollyHeir," Holm said, the words hurting. Meserv stopped purring.

Tinne whirled. "Don't start on me, Holm," he snarled. "Cave of the Dark Goddess, do you think I want to be Heir? I don't. I don't have any great ambitions and don't want the responsibility. I wasn't groomed to be Heir, you were. And you were a damn good one until you shot yourself in the foot with your blaser by opening that big mouth of yours. Now my life is going to be hell! And Genista—" Tinne growled, walked away, and jerked his head to the others to keep up.

Holm didn't think he'd ever heard Tinne growl. It reassured him. "You'll be a fine Heir. Better than me."

Tinne's growl rose, then bit off as he snapped, "Don't be so stupid. No one could fill your shoes. I don't even want to try."

Curiouser and curiouser. Holm stroked Meserv's head. "I've been convinced since you saved us both from the boghole that you are the better man." The words were finally out. His guilt at not being able to rescue his brother. His shame at his failure and that his brother had succeeded when he had failed.

Tinne stopped and stared at him. "Don't be a stup. You were in deeper than I, you were more active trying to get to me. There was better footing where I was, and I managed to haul myself out, then you. Simple logistics. If you'd been where I was, you'd have saved us both, too."

Holm didn't know about that, but it was true he hadn't been able to reach the spot where Tinne was. Maybe it was true, that it had been shallower than where he'd started to sink. His throat nearly closed just remembering the quicksand. Meserv butted his hand, wanting more strokes. Holm obliged and the kitten started purring again, rumbling against Holm's chest, the sound vibrating in a comforting pattern.

Tinne hit him on the shoulder. "Come on."

His shoulder was beginning to hurt. He coughed. "Well, at least you're still my brother."

This time Tinne didn't even look at him. "Don't be an ass. We'll head home. By the time we reach there, Tab and Mamá will have worked on Father, you'll see."

"He's disowned me. Thrice." Holm knew it wouldn't be that easy. T'Holly would have to admit he made a mistake. He'd have to see through the fog of madness that had shrouded him since D'Holly had been wounded. He'd have to set aside anger.

They reached the atrium and rearmed themselves with the weapons they couldn't carry into the Temple. Holm curved Meserv around his neck and the kitten lay like a fur collar, continuing to purr and soothe Holm, looking down his nose at Black Pierre who padded beside them.

They stepped through the huge brass door and into the early afternoon sunshine. It was a beautiful day, but Holm couldn't bring himself to care.

He saw the Heathers, all dressed in Heather lavender, strolling a block away, walking to Noble Country, the section of Druida housing most FirstFamily Residences. His heart twinged. All three of the other Heathers expostulated to Lark. She just stuck out her chin and walked with serene grace and dignity. He wanted her badly.

Another thought struck him. What colors would he wear now? What belongings did he have that weren't marked with the Holly crest? Very few.

A couple of blocks later they turned into a narrow square.

"It's about time they showed up. There they are, get them!" HawthornHeir yelled.

Blades scraped from scabbards. Hawthorns were on them. Too close for blasers. Too entangled already to 'port away. With a Word, Holm sent Meserv to T'Holly's.

Holm spun and danced to meet the opponents, trying to keep his back to his brother and T'Ash and Straif for mutual defense. From the corner of his eye he tried to count the Hawthorns—many, maybe too many.

Adrenaline pumped through him fast and hard. Sword in his right hand, long dagger in his left, he let his body dip and sway, fighting instinctively. He slashed open an arm, kicked the Hawthorn guard away and out of the battle, plunged his knife into a shoulder and withdrew. Pivoted.

And faced HawthornHeir. Huathe came at him, teeth bared in a rictus grin. Holm fended off an attack from his left. Droplets of blood flew in an arc.

Screams came from the side of the square. Holm darted a glance. The Heather Healers stood waiting. D'Heather and HeatherHeir screamed. Lark stared at him with huge eyes set in a pale face. *Just like his dream. His dream of blood and death.*

Huathe feinted at Straif, lunged at Holm. He hesitated, beat up the man's blade. Half-turning, Huathe speared Tinne.

Tinne! Failure!

Screams.

Tinne only laughed at the slit along his side—the side with his only kidney.

Holm jolted.

A line of blood welled through Tinne's shirt. Tinne riposted, sliding his blade into Huathe's heart.

He died.

Screams.

Holm stared in shock. His brother had killed Lark's brother.

A bespelled forcefield encompassed Tinne, sending a

Hawthorn flying a meter away, shocked into a heap, breaking another's blade. Tinne winked from view, his protective amulet 'porting him to Primary HealingHall.

"Enough!" Holm cried, sickened of the violence, beating back the blades around him. *Enough. Fight to disarm!* he sent T'Ash and T'Blackthorn. There must have been enough injury and death to bring the GreatLords to their senses. *Let's force a truce!* The three of them could do it, with NobleCouncil help. T'Ash's and Straif's rhythm changed as they fought defensively.

Right, Straif said.

Yes. T'Ash's face was grim, sweat trickled down his brow.

"Enough!" Holm yelled, backing the command with Flair. He parried, elbowed an assailant in the ribs, then slipped on blood and went down. Two Hawthorn men landed on him. Black Pierre's teeth sank into Holm's leg.

" 'Port!" a Hawthorn panted.

The world went dark.

*H*olm woke. *Rough jags of pain shot through his head. He* sagged against stone that was cool against his back. His mind battled for comprehension. His vision was blurred and he was chained by his wrists to a wall. He couldn't port with chains on. He was attached to a stone wall and couldn't take the wall with him.

He wiped his head on his shoulder. Red stains marked his white shirt where he'd laid his head against it. Forehead wound. Stickiness. Blood.

Lifting his face, he saw he was in a castle courtyard. It had been a very long time since he'd been at T'Hawthorn Residence, but he recognized it. Of course, the coat of arms painted on the closed Earthoak doors helped.

He tugged on his wrists. Yes, chains. Looking down, he noted his ankles were chained, too. Holm cursed. More and more often he envied T'Ash his new Residence. Holm'd bet his new pool there were no chains in T'Ash Residence. Residences modeled after Earth castles usually had chains. T'Holly's had a multitude. When he was T'Holly—

Recollection rushed back in vignettes. *Tinne.* Holm closed his eyes and visualized his brother, down to his weapons and the

HouseRing he wore that would always locate him, the hematite amulet protecting him. *Tinne!*

Don't shout! Tinne grumbled. *Where are you?*

How are you?

Healed well enough. Where are you?

T'Hawthorn's.

T'Hawthorn's? Tinne sounded surprised.

"Well, HollyHeir, it's been a long time since we met." T'Hawthorn stood before him. Holm recognized the expression in his eyes and ached. For Lark. For himself. For the man.

His eyes were as grief-stricken and mad as T'Holly's.

"You killed my son," T'Hawthorn said, and raised a knife.

Holm shrugged. "T'Holly disowned me this morning. He won't pay ransom. Take your vengeance."

For the first time T'Hawthorn looked foolish. His mouth hung open, worked for words that didn't come, snapped shut. Finally he spoke. "He wouldn't do such a thing!"

Holm shrugged again.

T'Hawthorn's pallid, ravaged face twisted. "You killed my son. My heir!" he cried. Desolation and pain battered at Holm in waves. Holm didn't correct him.

The sharp tip of the blade slit through Holm's shirt, piercing his skin. Blood beaded against his chest. The hurt was nothing compared to the pain of his myriad failures, the rejection by Lark and T'Holly.

Holm met T'Hawthorn's wild violet eyes—the same colored eyes as Lark—and he flinched inside, bled inside, where it didn't show. "Your Son'sSon poisoned my Mamá near to death. I heard you rejoiced at the thought of my parents' deaths."

T'Hawthorn looked shocked. He shook his head, but Holm knew he couldn't deny it. The dagger withdrew from Holm' chest.

Their gazes locked. The knife slid lower to under his ribs, pressed at an angle. Holm knew he was going to die.

The Residence alarm shrieked as the inner courtyard gate exploded open.

"Stop!" yelled T'Ash and D'Ash together. T'Ash shouted a Word, but nothing happened. The courtyard was spelled for only Hawthorns.

"Silence!" ordered T'Hawthorn. The alarm cut off mid-note.

"This is murder!" SupremeJudge Ailim D'Elder announced.

"I'll demand feud!" shouted Straif Blackthorn.

Another door banged open to Holm's left. "No! *NO!*"

He looked up a set of stairs to a landing. Lark, Laev, and Cratag stood there. New despair rolled through him. He didn't want her to see him like this, didn't want her to watch him die by her father's hand.

He stared. Her aura was wild, sparking white, just as it had done whenever she felt constrained.

"No! *Don't!*" Lark shouted again, wondering that she could speak at all with her heart pounding in her throat. "How dare you! Look what you've wrought! My brother dead, my father, you, near crazed. Do you kill? Do you murder for *land?* Do you kill your daughter's HeartMate?"

For the first time in her life she realized what the "sparking" was, it was her own capacity for violence that she'd never dealt with, never acknowledged or channeled. She let it go—all the pent-up anger at the constraints upon her all her life. She let it free, but she directed it. She was no longer and never again simply T'Hawthorn's daughter. She was Mayblossom Larkspur Bélla Hawthorn Collinson, HeartMate to Holm Holly. She let the words roll in her mind, her name, her inner-core self, and backed her name with the force of her newly found fight.

The dagger whipped from T'Hawthorn's hand, flew against a wall and shattered, disintegrated into shards of gold and gems.

T'Hawthorn drew his blaser.

Lark shrieked, which she'd never done before. It felt good, so she screamed again. Her father gaped at her. She shouted, "He is my HeartMate! If you kill him I will die." She 'ported in front of Holm to shield him. Lark heard Laev's and Cratag's steps running down the stairs.

"You have not HeartBonded." T'Hawthorn slowly lowered the blaser, each word equally measured. "I am your father, I would know when you bonded so with another man."

She raised her chin. She loved her father, but she would never be manipulated by him again. "Nevertheless, he is my Heart-Mate. Will you kill my man?"

Holm choked behind her.

Lark lifted her head. "Will you hurt my HeartMate? Holm Holly is my HeartMate. I declare Holm is my HeartMate, I accept

Holm as my HeartMate. I will HeartBond with my HeartMate, Holm, and my HeartMate Holm and I will marry. That's five times."

Holm made another gurgling sound.

Think! Black Pierre's command to T'Hawthorn was loud enough for everyone to hear. The cat extended the claws of his front paws and pricked them into T'Hawthorn's boot.

T'Hawthorn looked around with an anguished gaze, at the FirstFamily Lords and Ladies who watched him with stony expressions and angry gazes, power and Flair visibly radiating from them. Then at Laev who stared at him with steady, serious eyes in a pale face.

T'Hawthorn's fingers released the blaser and it clattered to the flagstones. He passed a weary hand across his eyes, then his violet gaze pinned Lark and Holm. Through stiff lips T'Hawthorn said, "I have lost my dear and only son. My heir. I will not lose my beloved daughter, too. Chains break!"

Lark pressed back until she was against Holm. His muscles were stiff with tension.

T'Hawthorn inclined his head to Lark and Holm. "Blessings upon you. HollyHeir, tell T'Holly the feud is over. You can take my sword to him."

Lark heard Holm swallow twice before his voice rasped. "I have been disowned. T'Holly is set against me, and even this will not quench his anger."

T'Hawthorn's face twisted. "So I have damaged your Family, too. T'Blackthorn, you are T'Holly's nephew."

Straif jerked a nod.

"You can take my sword. This feud was foolhardy. My valley can be weathershielded to produce prime cinnamon. I wanted the riches and the status that it would give me, perhaps consideration as the next Captain of the FirstFamilies Council. But the feud has cost me my son and others of my Family. It has tainted the Hollys." He turned a haggard face to Lark. "But I had sense enough not to let it cost me my daughter."

Lark flung herself into his arms, and he held her close, closer than he had since she was a young child.

With great dignity he nodded to the other Nobles. "You are my guests and welcome. The amenities of my Residence are yours."

He stretched out his hand to Laev. The boy ran to him, ignoring his hand, and flung himself upon his FatherSire. T'Hawthorn hugged Laev.

Love passed among Lark and T'Hawthorn and Laev. She sensed T'Hawthorn and Laev were closer than they'd ever been. After a moment she withdrew. T'Hawthorn kept an arm around Laev.

Black Pierre mewed and T'Hawthorn stilled. "I accept you as my Fam," he said.

The cat eyed him, then leapt to his shoulder.

T'Hawthorn waved a hand. "Cratag, see to my guests. I'm tired. Laev and I will meditate in T'Hawthorn Grove." Slowly, without looking back, he walked away through an arch.

"Yes, T'Hawthorn," Cratag said. He nodded to Straif Blackthorn. "Come with me. I'll give you the GreatHouse Hawthorn Family Sword."

Straif swept a glance around at everyone in the courtyard, then followed Cratag up the steps and into the keep.

T'Ash, D'Ash, and SupremeJudge D'Elder came forward. Ailim's face was serene, her hands tucked in opposite sleeves. She stopped a pace from them and tilted her head.

"GentleLady Collinson, I advise you that you have acknowledged this man, Holm, as your HeartMate. Legally, you are now bound to him, just as if the HeartBond had been consummated."

"I know. I accept that," Lark said. She reached back for Holm, but he wasn't there. He'd slipped away and stood near the broken doors of the courtyard. He didn't look at her and had angled his body from her.

Holm?

He blocked her telepathy. Panic chilled her. She widened the bond between them until it was the size of a thick golden rope.

He narrowed it to a microfilament. Just as she had done before.

Twenty-eight

❦

*L*ark *swallowed and straightened her spine. So he rejected* her, just as she had done earlier, as she had done so many times before. Well, just as he had persevered in the face of her rejection—he'd known they were HeartMates and that was something they'd need to discuss—so, she would persevere.

She walked to him as he pretended to study the remnants of the courtyard door. "I thought we had an agreement, Holm."

He stiffened but said nothing.

"Either physical or mental-emotional connection," she reminded. She felt his surprise, but before he could recover, she stepped behind him, put her arms around him, and laid her head against his back. He smelled more essentially Holm than ever. His scent made her blood pulse faster.

Holm inhaled sharply. When he spoke, his voice was harsh. "You violated that agreement often enough."

"Maybe I did," she agreed. "But you didn't, until now." His dampened shirt clung to his back. So many ordeals he'd survived today. She pulled all the love she had for him and encased the two of them in a sphere. His breathing turned ragged. Even through the minuscule fiber that connected them, she sensed his confusion and pain. He was torn up inside, doing his best to function in a world gone mad—where he didn't know who he was, how to act.

She hurt for him, and sent her complete acceptance of him through their bond.

He shook his head in denial, as if he didn't understand her, and doubted her feelings. That stung, but she kept the minor pain to herself. She must have hurt him equally over the last eight-days.

Then he stepped away. "No. I can't handle this right now."

And she realized he was close to breaking and that it would wound his pride to be seen as weak.

Lark sighed. "Mental or physical, Holm?"

He turned from her.

She bit her lip but remained close.

After a moment he widened the conduit between them to a small cord. Lark smiled and sent him approval and relief. He didn't look at her, but his neck pinkened, embarrassed because he was glad she was proud of him. She smiled and blinked back tears. Somehow she'd figure out how to win him.

She turned to see the Ashes watching them. Lark inclined her head. T'Ash jerked his in an obvious wish that she join them. She was oddly touched that T'Ash and his lady gave Holm the space he needed to come to terms with the day's events. Obviously T'Ash and Holm's friendship was closer than she'd imagined. She was grateful for that, because she trusted Holm's instincts regarding his Family, and he was sure that his disinheritance was permanent.

Lark shivered a little. Even at her most bitter, she hadn't renounced her Family, and at his most furious T'Hawthorn hadn't disowned her. The irony was incredible.

She joined T'Ash and D'Ash, but kept an eye on her Heart-Mate. *HeartMate!* What a wonderful thing. An idea she'd abandoned. How had it happened? The notion would take time to accept.

"We're going home to prepare a guestsuite for you and Holm. You can stay with us indefinitely. Lord and Lady knows we have plenty of room," said T'Ash. He sent his HeartMate a twinkling glance. "I hope you like animals."

That surprised a smile from Lark. Holm's shoulders relaxed a bit, his shirt had dried, a good sign.

She sobered. "We haven't talked at all. Holm's aware I've been offered the position of Head of Gael City HealingHall." She shrugged. "I wanted that job very much, once. But I want Holm more. He will make the decision whether we stay in Druida or go to Gael City. A Healer is welcome anywhere."

"As is a fighter," T'Ash said dryly.

Lark winced. She knew Holm listened. "I would rather he didn't hire on as a household guard. Another thing we must discuss."

T'Ash glanced at Holm, also aware of his interest. "I don't think that Gael City has a fencing salon. One run by Holm would draw plenty of youngbloods."

"You're right," Lark said.

The door from the keep opened. Cratag Maytree and Straif Blackthorn stepped out. Straif carried a long sword in an intricately figured golden sheath.

Lark said, "I want to say goodbye to Cratag and let him know I'll be moving to your Residence and staying there. I'll bring my things as soon as I gather them."

"T'Furze could transport the contents of your apartment."

Lark smiled and shook her head. "True, but I'm used to counting cost. His charges are outrageous." She looked at Holm and sighed again. The mental-emotional cord still cycled between them, but he didn't want her near. He'd braced himself to go to T'Holly Residence and confront his father and get his belongings.

"I'll see you later," she said and ran to Cratag.

Holm and *Straif walked several city squares in silence.* Straif was used to wandering Celta looking for a cure to his flawed physical heritage. He'd have spent plenty of time alone. The chill in Holm settled a little deeper. T'Ash and Straif had lost their entire families. Now he'd lost his Family, too.

"Nice to be able to walk and not worry about an ambush," Straif said.

It brought back the earlier fight in vivid detail. "Neither you nor T'Ash looked like you were hurt."

"Not a scratch," Straif said cheerfully. "They were after you and Tinne."

"Huathe fell. The other Hawthorns?"

"They were Healed here or at Primary HealingHall. No other casualties. Tinne is resting in his suite—with his wife." Straif winked.

Holm grunted and got his mouth around the words he wanted to say. "T'Holly is not going to forgive me and take me back into the Family."

Straif tensed and sent Holm a slanting gaze. "You sure?"

"Yes," Holm said. Bleakness surged, then subsided. Those emotions were getting easier to bear. A pulse of caring came from Lark through their tie. Holm held on to the feeling until it dispersed into his system.

"The problem," Holm said carefully, "is that a couple of eightdays ago both T'Holly and D'Holly vowed upon their Words of Honor to welcome my HeartMate into the Family."

Straif's stride checked. He stared at Holm and whistled. "Violated Words of Honor are not a good thing. Slowly but surely they cause malaise in the individual."

"True. That's why I'm asking you to stay here in Druida and keep an eye on them. Tinne will have a very busy life. I'd like you to look out for my Mamá and father, too. And, dear cuz, it's time you accepted your own responsibilities. Have you visited T'Blackthorn Residence lately? It's *moldering*." Holm thought he got the lightness of his old tone right, almost as if he was the same man he'd been in the morning.

"Moldering!" Straif grimaced.

"That's right. Once *the* showplace of all FirstFamily Residences. It's now in poor shape. At least from the outside. I'm sorry, but you had to know."

They walked through a square in silence. Straif sighed. "Right. I'll stay and take care of it. What of you and your Heart-Mate?"

A little spurt of joy whipped through Holm at the word *HeartMate*. Despite all the horrible things that had gone wrong today, one thing was better. Everyone knew he had a HeartMate now. It wasn't a silent secret to be guarded. A HeartMate. He was legally HeartBonded. He stopped in his tracks. Legally HeartBonded. No. He wasn't ready. He might have thought he was, but that was when he was Holm Holly.

Probing a little deeper into his own emotions, he realized he

still hurt outrageously at Lark's earlier rejection. There was
something more. His stomach knotted as he realized what else
bothered him. He'd failed today. Failed to protect Tinne. Failed
to evade capture. Failed to even save himself—again.

If it had been left to him, he'd have died. Lark had saved him.

Irrational, but the guilt was all too real. Something that bur-
dened him and hurt. He was ashamed of the irrational feeling.
He set his jaw and stopped thinking about himself. If he continued on this way, he'd be a sniveling, self-pitying coward. A de-
pressed sniveling, self-pitying coward. Just tuck those damned
stupid emotions away.

On to the next topic. "I'm going to Gael City and will establish a salon there," he said.

"A good idea."

Holm said, "I could stay here and fight—fight T'Holly and
try and make him recognize me. But that would only entrench
him in his position. The more I battered against that wall, the
thicker and higher it would get."

Straif tilted his head, nodded. "Right." He glanced at Holm,
then straight ahead. "You know," he said softly, "I don't recall
T'Holly ever admitting to a mistake in his life."

A bark of ironic laughter tore from Holm. "No."

Shaking his head, Straif said, "It's odd how the Family thing
worked out. Lark and T'Hawthorn. You and T'Holly."

Holm's throat closed and he could only nod.

They lapsed again into quiet.

When he looked up, he faced the greeniron gates of the
T'Holly estate, behind which was the glider drive, then the moat
and iron gates of the outer wall. Sweat gilded his muscles.
"You'd better say the spellword, Straif. I doubt it will let me in."
He hoped he sounded matter-of-fact even though his voice was
rough. At least it hadn't trembled.

Straif shot him a glance, then opened the gates.

*H*olm waited until Straif delivered the sword before con-
fronting T'Holly. Holm stood at attention in front of his father's
desk. He refused to sit in the damned wingchair ever again. He
wasn't HollyHeir now; he was a nameless man. His father had
renounced the loyalty tie between them.

To his shock, the Hawthorn sword on T'Holly's desk was broken in two. With the connection between a Lord and his sword, that must have hurt T'Hawthorn. It was one more thing indicating his father's state of mind. Holm could only pray that with D'Holly on the mend and *home,* T'Holly would find some balance.

His Mamá was nowhere in sight. This entire discussion was T'Holly's idea, though D'Holly would never contradict him.

Holm was glad he'd murmured a cooling spell before he'd entered the ResidenceDen; at least T'Holly wouldn't see how Holm sweat. He kept his face expressionless.

"We do not accept your choice of wife," T'Holly stated gutturally.

Going on the attack.

Holm was weary of being wretched. He may have been nameless and houseless, but he would be treated with respect. He'd answer rudeness with rudeness. "She's my HeartMate."

His father didn't meet Holm's eyes. "We don't accept her. She's not a suitable bride. We won't allow the marriage."

"We? Meaning you and Mamá? Or is it just *you*? Did you talk with her?"

T'Holly's mouth set. "I affirm that you are disowned."

"I accept that." It was just as hard to hear this time as it had been the last. "I will remind you that you and D'Holly promised upon your Words of Honor that you would accept my HeartMate. I regret that you and Mamá will have to deal with the spiritual and physical consequences of breaking your Words."

His father looked stunned, as if he'd received an unexpected blow. He rose from his chair, nostrils widening. "You fliggering young whelp!"

Holm flinched.

"You *knew*."

"Perhaps. At the time I believed that our Family was flexible and loving enough to accept the daughter of a feuding Family. A daughter who was estranged from her Family. A woman who is greatly Flaired. A Healer."

His own eyes were probably the same cold pewter hue as T'Holly's. "I would never have believed that my Family would be so ungenerous as to deny me my HeartMate." He unbuckled his main gauche, sword, and blaser and placed them on T'Holly's desk. They all had Holly symbols.

His father stared wildly at the weapons, as if trying to gather his wits.

Holm summoned the ceremonial HollyHeir sword from his suite. The intricate hand guard and central ruby gleamed. "I see you are collecting swords today," Holm said.

He looked down at his clothes. With a Word he retinted his trous from dark green to black. The coloring wasn't altogether successful. It looked as if he had a scabrous disease. He shrugged. He had failed in *everything* and was past caring about appearance.

He shucked his vest and dropped it on the desk, then turned and left.

"You can't go out into the streets defenseless!" T'Holly shouted.

Holm didn't stop.

He closed the door behind him and nearly ran into his G'Uncle Tab. Something seemed wrong with Holm's vision.

"Here, boy." Tab steadied him. The weapons he carried clanged. "Damn' stupid Lord, stubborn, thick-headed . . ." he muttered as he strapped a plain broadsword and blaser on Holm.

Holm adjusted the weapons. He recognized them as those he'd practiced with for years, and was grateful they were familiar.

"T'Holly ain't thinkin' straight. We talked. He thought I'd agree." Tab's eyes blazed silver. "I don't. A person gotta Heart-Mate"—he slashed the air—"that's it. They're two inta one." For an instant Holm saw deep loneliness in his G'Uncle's eyes—loneliness that he'd begun to know himself. "The Family that can't welcome a HeartMate has deep problems. An' everyone knows your gal's a Healer and more Heather than Hawthorn. Pure deep fear, your father's feeling." Tab shook his head. "I wouldn't have expected it of him."

Pure deep fear. Just like Bélla's had. Just like he had now.

"Ya want anything from your rooms, just send me word, I'll get it to ya. Talked to T'Apple. He's shocked. He don't disown ya. Call yourself Holm Apple."

Holm winced. He loved his cuzes, but the Apples were artists, painters, wimps—not fighters. "Apple" sounded sissy.

"I'll call myself Blackthorn."

Tab buffeted him on the shoulder and Holm staggered. "Call

yourself Apple or ya'll irritate your MotherSire. Need all the allies you can get, boy. Glad ya are bein' staunch, though. Good thing."

Apple. Sissy. Holm recalled the lips pendant. He reached for it. Tab smacked his hand away. "You just leave that be."

"It was paid for by Holly gilt."

"Paid for in the *past*. It's also a gift from a good friend. By the way, I'm havin' Clam moved into a smaller tank. He's yours, he'll go with you. No one else wants the ugly son-of-a-mollusk. We'll 'port him nice and gentle to T'Ash's."

"I'll send a scry to Mamá and Tinne."

"T'Ash scried with the coordinates to 'port your stuff, and Clam. T'Ash and D'Ash can use help in makin' T'Ash Residence a home."

Holm inhaled his first deep breath since entering T'Holly Residence. The tightness in his chest loosened. "Lark and I will be moving to Gael City. I'll open a fighting and fencing salon. Think I'll call it The Green Man." He twitched the corners of his lips up in a semblance of a smile.

"You'll do." Tab nodded. "Go and don't look back."

"I won't. I can't." He'd failed. He didn't know how he could bear it, except that he already was, and Tab had lifted his spirits. There was nothing to do but go on.

Plop. Slide. Clink. Plop. Slide. Clink. Plop.

Holm turned to see Meserv dragging a large satchel.

Our stuff. The bag was full to bursting and about ten times the size of the young cat. *We all have fine fate.*

Holm wanted to believe that was true.

T'*Ash, D*'*Ash, and Lark sat in a small, comfortable sit*-ting room with pre-dinner drinks, accompanied by the cats— Phyll, Princess, and Zanth. Their conversation was desultory, as they all waited for Holm.

"It's a lovely room." Lark sipped her wine.

Danith smiled with genuine delight. "Thank you. We're slowly but surely furnishing the Residence. My friend, Mitchella Clover, is an excellent interior designer and a great help."

Lark closed her eyes a moment. "Good friends are precious. One of my best is Mitchella's cuz, Trif."

Danith beamed.

"I'll miss Trif if Holm and I go to Gael City."

"True, but I think that would be best," T'Ash said.

Make sure little Cats go, too, Zanth said. He sprawled on a big, tattered-carpeted platform that streamed hunks of unraveled rug. *Kits cramp my style. They want to hunt with Me. Too puny.*

Phyll huffed from Lark's lap. He lifted his nose. *I no longer hunt. I am HealerCat. First HealerCat of Celta. Sounds good.*

Zanth snorted.

Tinkling chime-notes whispered elegantly through the room. "Holm Apple and Meserv Fam come," said T'Ash Residence.

T'Ash looked startled. "Holm Apple."

"The former Holm Holly's MotherSire, T'Apple, sent adoption papers to the FirstFamilies Council," said the Residence sternly.

"Apple." T'Ash snickered.

"What's wrong with the name Apple?" asked Lark. Danith stared at T'Ash, too.

"They're artists." T'Ash leaned back on his sofa and hooted.

"As you are, T'Ash, with your jewelry," Lark pointed out.

Princess mewed and stretched her neck to show her collar of earthsuns that matched her eyes.

T'Ash scowled. "I'm a blacksmith, *Mayblossom.* Though it's true that Holm has a good hand at calligraphy." He looked at her slyly. "Have you seen it?"

"I have some pieces," Lark replied.

T'Ash's lips twitched. "Anything special?" he asked casually. Lark wondered what he hinted at.

Zanth hopped down and cocked an eye at Phyll. *They in entry hall now, Me will show them to our beau-ti-ful new room.* Zanth trotted out the door.

A moment later Holm stood on the threshold, Meserv curled around his neck. Nothing about his clothing proclaimed him a Holly. Lark's heart sank. Despite the angry and ravaged emotions she'd experienced through their link, she'd hoped beyond hope that all would turn out well and he would return triumphant as HollyHeir once more.

But his face was stark and pale, his eyes dark with hurt and an edge of what might possibly be fear.

She rose and Phyll hopped from her lap. She ran to Holm and his arms closed around her tightly. She knew then. When she was with him, she was home.

Twenty-nine

❦

$\mathcal{L}$ark watched Holm all evening. She tried to appear as a newly HeartBonded woman who couldn't keep her eyes off her lover, but in fact, her Healer instincts were roused.

Now and again Holm would automatically lapse into his old manner, then a lost look would enter his eyes and he'd falter. They all felt the strain.

After dinner they retired again to the sitting room.

Zanth strolled to Danith and gave her a sickeningly sweet smile before flopping down on his side on her feet. *Time to Heal My ear*, he projected smugly.

Lark watched with professional curiosity as Danith stooped and set the cat on his platform, then placed her hands on Zanth's head and cupped the broken ear between her fingers and thumb. Lark could only imagine trying to match energy and vibrations with another species. She shivered. And Danith did it with so many other species. How odd. And how wonderful Flair was.

Zanth stretched his neck for more of Danith's touch, and Lark saw a collar of emeralds. It was fashioned in the tradition of the formal jewelry for a GreatHouse Heir. A very expensive bauble for a cat that spoke Downwind short-speech and looked like a tough brawler, a cat no one could call pretty.

Holm's hand rested on her shoulder, and tendrils of her hair tickled her ear as he whispered. "Don't comment on the jewels. I've convinced Meserv that jewelry is something a cat only receives upon maturity."

She let out a slow breath. "Good thinking," she murmured.

"There. Done." Danith took her hands from Zanth's head, shook them as if ridding them of cat-energy and clapped hard. "You look gorgeous, Zanth."

Zanth smirked and pranced over to T'Ash. *Look at Me. Me perrrfect. Life is good.*

Lark stared. The skin before his ears showed under thin fur and was ridged with scars. Both upright ears held nicks. Old scratches crisscrossed his muzzle.

Me will have earrings now. Two. Maybe four.

Holm laughed and Lark blessed the cat. She reached up, took Holm's hand and smiled brilliantly at the Ashes. "Time for bed," she said. Holm stiffened beside her, but she ignored it.

I'll be gentle, she sent to him.

He cracked a smile and said polite good-nights to his friends, but he acted as if she dragged him to his doom.

When they reached their suite, the sitting room wasn't quite as Lark had left it and she received a little shock. Holm had been in their rooms. After years she was now sharing her space again with a man, a permanent partner. Lark was glad she'd had Phyll to practice on first.

She took a sleepy Meserv from Holm's shoulders and patted the kitten. He opened cloudy blue eyes. She set him on his feet and tweaked the tip of his tail. "Phyll has claimed a closet for himself and you. It's all your own. It has some very soft pillows and"—she bent down to whisper—"some dirty shoe and boot liners of mine and Holm's."

He rumbled purring gratitude as he trotted to the closet.

Lark looked up at Holm, but found him frowning at a striking piece of framed calligraphy standing on the largest table, as if he'd forgotten he'd placed the piece.

She started toward it and he stopped her. He looked at his work, then her, then scowled as if it wasn't good enough.

At least he wasn't chanting his mantra.

He waved to the twoseat, which looked brand-new like all the elegant yet homey furnishings. Lark wondered if Grand-Lord Furze had transferred a suite from Mitchella Clover's shop, the Four Leaf Clover. She wouldn't have been surprised.

She dropped into the twoseat and watched Holm, keeping their link as wide as he allowed—slightly larger than the cord. Incrementally he was letting her open their bond.

"You once said you loathed and despised fighters," he said.

She wondered if he was deliberately trying to keep them apart. Wetting her lips, she folded her hands and said, "You're my HeartMate."

"So the issue really doesn't matter?" There was a hint of mockery in his tone that she hated. She wanted to go to him, but his manner deterred her.

"Much has happened since I said that, and I've thought about everything a great deal. It isn't fighting that I loathe and despise, it's violence—the wish to deliberately wound and hurt another. And you are not a violent man," she ended softly.

He half turned, his fine profile evident in the dim light. "I am under certain circumstances."

"As I could be. I realized it this morning when I saw my father tormenting you. I don't know what I might have done to him, if—" She couldn't go on.

His breath escaped in a sigh. "I like fighting, practicing my skill, training. And I'll be doing that for the rest of our lives, most especially in Gael City."

"But you don't like violence, injuring or taking lives."

"At one time—"

"Not now."

"No, not now."

"You are not a violent man," she repeated.

Holm didn't know how he felt about her change of heart, so he turned back to stand in front of his calligraphy. The papyrus and ink were the finest. The frame was sparkling new, made by T'Ash with true artistry. It had been Holly green, but now was gold with Heather lavender-rose highlights.

He touched the lower right-hand corner of the glass and his mouth twisted. His signature—his former self. Everywhere he went, everything he did was a reminder that he was no longer Holm Holly, even this gift that he'd made the night his Mamá had been taken to the Ship and he'd yearned for Lark.

Taking the piece to the twoseat, he offered it to her. It symbolized all he had been, all that was the past. But the symbols also flowed with all he'd wanted then, and wanted now with her, the future.

Her breath caught. "It's a HeartGift, isn't it?"

He'd hoped she wouldn't ask, because then he wouldn't have had to tell her. His mouth tightened. "Yes. It doesn't have the power of the usual HeartGift, because I just made it." He looked at it, and saw its inadequacy. The parchment he had taken so long to prepare and colorwash with subtle blends, the bold strokes of ink he had practiced again and again, interminably, losing himself in the crafting so his other problems ceased to exist, the ink itself—nothing about it pleased him now.

Holm set his shoulders. He'd done his best. It hadn't been enough. Throughout this whole situation, he'd felt he was trying to catch up with her—her exquisitely civilized philosophy of life, her gentleness and innate goodness.

"I'll send it away," he said. And destroy it in private.

"No." Her hands curled around his wrists and her unexpected touch rocked him. He'd been so withdrawn that he hadn't been observing her, anticipating her moves so he could brace himself. Waves of hot desire and ferocious longing rolled through him.

She scanned his face, and she blushed as she felt the spike in his pulse, the tightening of his body. She took the gift from him, and through their bond he felt *her* arousal—the deepening ache between her legs as her body quickened for his. Her face flushed even more, and she met his eyes squarely and laughed. "Not the effect of a HeartGift made during Passage? How would either of us know? Sufficient enough to stir *my* blood, Holm. I want your HeartGift badly. Very badly. I want you badly."

She closed her eyes and shared the strong impact of his gift upon her senses. When she opened her eyelids, her gaze was deep purple. She set the calligraphy aside, stood, took his hand and led him to the bedroom.

With a Word she undressed him. "Lie on the bed and let me see you, Holm. Let me find any and all little aches and bruises and scratches and Heal them. It's been a wretched day."

He'd lost his wits. He couldn't put together a thought, let alone a strategy for dealing with his woman. He'd run out of emotions, too. Everything she said made perfect sense and was what he wanted. Very odd. So he went to the bed and lay on his back.

With a wordless crooning, she sifted her fingers through his hair. A thousand nerve endings in his scalp tingled. He could almost see it bathed with the glow of Healing. The cut on his forehead closed and the background throb faded.

Her fingers loosened the tight muscles of his neck with a touch, warmed them with the vitality cycling between them, the energy that blended and merged so perfectly, that increased as it circled from one to another. Her hand curved around his throat, pressed the skin she'd bitten during their last wild lovemaking and that she'd Healed that morning, devastating him. She leaned over him and her sweet breath sighed into his ear. "Later. Later we will make love, but this time is for me to comfort and soothe you, to make all your hurts go away, to pamper you and envelope you in my love—as only a HeartMate can do."

He made a sound and sank into the bliss of being cosseted. Time stretched and became blissful. The warmth of her hands, her soft, loving words, her Healing was a balm poured over him, seeping into him to soothe raw emotional pain like honey.

Even when he rolled over and she used her Healer's touch on his front, he experienced affection, caring, love, but no lusty desire. This is what he needed now, more than anything. How could she have known when he hadn't? He drifted off.

Lark sat on the bedsponge and looked at Holm, her tears falling unchecked. All the new injuries he'd sustained in the fight were gone, never to mark his already too-scarred body. His tender nerve endings and muscle fibers, previously taut, were wrapped in small spell-cushions. He slept, but she'd felt his pain and ached at his confusion at the loss of his world. She admired the effort he made to cope.

While Healing, she'd let the stream of her Flair dissipate her raw feelings and wrenching experiences of the day. The shock of Holm's claim that she was his HeartMate—that had been like a blow to her solar plexus; the sight of the street melée had brought back vivid memories of Ethyn's death, her bitterness, and overlaid them with the horror that she might lose Holm, too; the death of a brother she'd never been able to deeply love, and any potential that they could become close.

She cried for that, for Huathe, using Flair to keep her sobs silent and her nose unstuffed, only letting the tears roll down her face and dampen the bedcover.

Worst of all had been the sight of her father ready to kill Holm. Her stomach clenched at the recollection. She'd never forget that sight for the rest of her life, but she hoped it and the emotions that had ripped through her would dim.

Holm shifted as if her upset disturbed him, and she regulated her breathing and packed away the wretched memories. She examined him. He'd rest until his energy levels reached their normal state, then waken. When he did, she'd finish her work. A smile curved her lips as she went to the waterfall to bathe. The next stage of Holm's Healing would be a passionate encounter, and then her initiation of the HeartBond.

She washed vigorously, trying not to think of her father and Laev grieving over a lost son in an echoing Residence, of T'Holly and D'Holly missing their lost son as the place he'd always filled was empty, and her own inner fear that she'd hurt Holm too much to bond together.

*H*er sleep was fitful. He'd move close and his scent would insinuate itself into her dreams, dreams that wove fear and loss and lust together. He'd roll over and his movement would wake her to groggily look and appreciate the fine lines of his back, or even push the linens down to ogle his butt.

Though they'd only spent an afternoon and one night together, she'd already learned his sleep rhythm. She was wide awake a good septhour before she thought he'd open his eyes.

So she looked at him. Again. She didn't think she would ever tire of looking at the man, of wishing she'd been in his life so she could have prevented many of his scars. Though if his attitude had been the same as Tinne's, he would have honored those scars. She shook her head. HeartMates, and what did she know of him besides his basic character? Nothing of the real details of his life.

She pondered how she'd seduce him since she had no experience. Should she whisper him awake with love words? Should she pet him from collarbone to hip and between, as her hands itched to do? She thought and planned and discarded plans and worried.

Then she decided to relax, and in doing so, let her body follow instinct. She steeped herself in his presence—the strong bond between them that could comfort or arouse. She sent him fizzy sparkles of love and passion and he groaned in his sleep and rolled on his side to face her. She snuggled close and let their bodies brush, her nipples against his springy chest hair, her legs along his muscular ones. Close enough that she could breathe in the essence of him, open her lips and dart out her tongue to taste him.

Daring more, wanting more, she lifted her top leg and hooked it over his, opening her body to him. Just with the action, her arousal kicked up a notch. She twined her arms around him and tasted the hollow of his neck. Her breathing quickened and she nibbled the line of his jaw. His sex stirred and grew and touched her between her legs where she needed him, then he shifted and withdrew. She whimpered in frustrated desire, moved so his manhood nestled close again. She needed him inside her, but needed something else even more.

Lark twisted until her mouth touched the spot she'd bitten and Healed before. Holm tensed and wakened. He angled his head so she could fix her mouth better against his throat. She opened her lips and kissed his neck.

They stayed entwined that way for long moments, her leg around his hip and open to one thrust of his shaft. His head back and arched to her open mouth, waiting the nip of her teeth. Lark said nothing, but sent her passion like hot beads rolling through their link, to increase his desire and have it returned threefold to her. The pleasure of anticipation dizzied her until she only felt his skin under his mouth and the dampness between her legs that ached for him.

She broke. She said, "I love you," and bit him.

With one smooth movement he was over her, on her, in her. One lunge and his full, hot sex filled her until she moaned with delight. And he stopped.

"Bélla," he said in a hoarse voice.

"Yes, Holm. Yes. Anything. Everything. Yes. Love me."

He propped himself on his arms. His face was close to hers, but she could barely see the glint of his eyes.

"Slow," he rasped, "good and deep."

She moaned another "Yes."

He settled into her, widening her legs. She gasped at the feel of him stroking her deep inside. "Holm," she pleaded, fit her emotions with his, felt the pulsing of his shaft, the pulsing of her core, the pulsing of their tie.

Holm lifted, sank. Slow, sweet, deep. His thrusts were steady and even and maddening, until she tilted her hips for the best penetration, locked her legs around him, spurred him on with bolts of passion through their link.

Faster, harder, deeper, rocking into her, sending her soaring to the heights in a twisting, twining dance of pure, luscious sensation.

Close, close. The HeartBond. Oh, she needed him. In her body, in her heart. In her soul.

She plucked a thread of pure shining white and spun it. He stroked her, set his hands under her to squeeze her bottom, angle her so they climbed together. She took the starry-white thread and sent it along the link, deepening the connection between them, tying their emotions together.

He moved fast, plunging, panting until their gasping breaths echoed together. She initiated the HeartBond.

He lunged and she screamed. Arrowed the HeartBond to him.

He slammed his shields down, kept her out, and claimed her body.

She plunged from the peak of ecstasy into despair.

Their breathing was the only sound in the darkness. She didn't know what he felt. After his rejection of the HeartBond, she'd constricted their link to a thread again. She let her legs fall to the bedsponge and he withdrew from her. Hurt, and choking to keep tears from welling, she rolled from him, but scooted back so they touched. She wouldn't ever break their agreement again.

She had told him she loved him. He hadn't responded. They were HeartMates, he *had* to love her, but he hadn't said the words. He'd rejected the HeartBond. Rejected her. She supposed she deserved it, that his own feelings were too raw to let all his shields down and meld with her, that she had kept him at a distance too long and too harshly. But it hurt. But what did she know of HeartMates?

He stroked her arm. She tensed, then let him touch her as he pleased. Despite everything, they were legally bound together.

The sex had been great. The emotional connection, until that last act of his, wonderful. They'd only known each other well for a couple of eightdays and under the worst circumstances. They were HeartMates, surely this awful pain would go away.

But it hurt too much right now. Taking the cowardly way out, she whispered a Word and sent herself to sleep.

He clawed his way up from the nightmare an instant before he would have nightported. Gasping, he was relieved that he hadn't further embarrassed himself before his lover. His limbs trembled from the incipient 'porting, then cooled.

Rising from bed, he walked to the windows. Holm stood in the beautiful room as windows streamed in starlight. Nothing in him could appreciate the room or the view or the essential serenity of the night. He stood naked and thought it appropriate. In the depths of the night his doubts had gathered like thunderclouds. He could not forget his failures. He didn't know who he was.

All his identity was wrapped up in his position as HollyHeir, FirstSon of the Hollys. Without relation to his Family, he had no being. Numbness had worn off. Denial was over. T'Holly, his father, had disowned him.

Pain and anger ravaged him. *Who was he?* He fell to his knees. Lark whimpered in her sleep. He turned to her, saw the spill of her black hair against pale bedlinens. His heart tightened and muscles loosened. His head dropped and he sucked in lungfuls of air. This is what came of not finding his balance, his core. He thought it was something he could live without, but now he was lost. He didn't know who he was.

Another small cry from Lark, and she flung out an arm as if to reach him. She hadn't been able to. He hadn't been able to let her initiate the HeartBond. Too hurt and stunned, all his natural shields had been up. He, in turn, had hurt her. But she had accepted his rejection, as she'd accepted and survived rejections before. She knew how to work through such hurtful events. He didn't. He failed at that, too.

Who was he?

Through slitted eyes he saw the thick golden channel of energy exiting his heart and tied to the small woman on the bed. She sighed and rolled over and silver sparkles frothed from her to him. They reached his chest and warmed his torso.

His sense of self was in shards. He didn't know himself outside the role of HollyHeir. Time to learn.

"I am Holm. I am a trained fighter. I am honorable." He knew that much. He breathed it in and out and steadily.

Who was he? He looked at Lark and bubbles of desire fired from his body to hers along their link. He was a man who had won his HeartMate. He planted one foot on the ground, pushed up, feeling the action of tendon and muscle, the good use of physical effort in the simple act of rising to his feet to stand head high and shoulders back.

Despite all odds, overwhelming odds, tragic choices, he'd triumphed in the most important fight of his life. He was a man who'd won his HeartMate. More, after her previous rejection, she'd formally claimed him aloud and publicly, making her own choice to put him first in her life. She lay there, ready for him to claim, physically, mentally, emotionally. Totally. And he would when he reformed some idea of who Holm was.

The sweat that had chilled his body dried warm. He went to the waterfall and let the feel of liquid pour over him. A luxurious waterfall in a luxurious room in a luxurious suite in a luxurious FirstFamily GreatLord Residence. The Residence built by a strong, honorable man whom Holm had fought beside. A man Holm called his best friend. T'Ash.

Holm was a man who had won his HeartMate and had a powerful GreatLord as his best friend. As he dried he let his view widen. . . . He had another friend, once a brother, called Tinne, and a friend once a cuz, called Straif. He had his MotherSire T'Apple who'd accepted him as a son of the Family. Holm Apple. He winced. It could be worse, he supposed, Holm pick-your-own-name-belonging-to-no-one.

When he placed his wet towel over the dryflow and turned to the door, two orange tabby kittens surveyed him. One with blue eyes, one with green. The blue-eyed one carried a dirty boot-liner of Holm's in his mouth. It seemed Meserv needed a little extra reassurance in a new place, too.

He'd earned a Fam, too. Holm really wasn't too shabby a fellow.

The kittens sniffed in unison, and he knew their thought before he heard it. *We all have fine fate.*

"Yes," he said. He wasn't dead. He was Holm and he was

alive with his HeartMate, housed by his best friend. He could start over. "Yes."

You thought very loud. Meserv yawned and the liner he carried fell to the floor. *You done thinking now?*

"Yes." If he wasn't, he'd think quieter.

Good. We all had BIG day. Today probably BIG, too. Time for bed.

Holm thought that was a great idea. He grinned.

Phyll lifted his nose. *I did very well as First HealerCat.*

Meserv gave a subvocal growl. *I helped Heal my Lady, too.* Holm grimaced. He supposed Meserv still considered D'Holly his Lady in cat terms, even though in human terms Holm was renounced.

I was better, Phyll said, trotting toward their closet. *I may need to Heal more today. I will get plenty of rest.*

"Grrrrr," rumbled Meserv softly, then stopped, cocked his head, and followed his brother, grinning. *We are going to Gael City. Lots of good solar sailing there, I heard. You may be HealerCat, but I will be FLYING CAT, and that is LOTS better.*

Phyll sniffed.

Holm shut the bedroom door behind them.

He smiled and a touch of watery, cold thought tickled his mind. Frowning, he examined the room. In one shadowy corner sat an aquarium. Clam.

Holm crossed to it, probed. Clam was well. He liked his new quarters, the change had stimulated him. Holm sighed in relief.

The oyster glowed with an aura Holm sensed was pride. Slowly Clam opened. Holm stared. Inside the oyster was a tiny pink-colored heart. Even in the dim light, it looked more like a human heart than the stylized puffy valentine shape, but tenderness suffused Holm. The gift, when it was grown, would be perfect for a Healer.

Clam suffered an irritant inside of him to mold into a jewel that Holm requested.

Holm was touched.

Lark whimpered in her sleep.

He sighed. He thought he could open himself, thought he'd welcome the Heartbond. Instead he'd been too afraid to trust her. Everything seemed to have happened too quickly. He couldn't let his shields down.

She was his HeartMate and it was just as terrifying as he'd feared. His love had claws and teeth that could rip him apart— would rip him apart if she perished, even though they weren't HeartBound. Look how the injury of his Mamá had affected his father. Holm shuddered.

Glancing over, he wondered if *he* could establish the Heart-Bond. Loving her physically was easy. If he could just take the last, ultimate risk . . . No, she looked exhausted. The day before was just as emotionally draining for her as it had been for him. She'd lost her brother, but had reconciled with her father. Odd how circumstances had played out.

He crawled back in bed and held her close, savoring her warm softness.

But when he fell asleep, the nightmares invaded.

Thirty

❦

Holm awoke the instant they lay in the sweet grass of the center of the Great Labyrinth. *They.* He'd taken Bélla with him. He swore under his breath. How was he going to explain this?

His irritation must have flowed through their bond, because Lark opened sleepy eyes. "Holm?" she asked.

Her eyelids fluttered, then she focused on the towering Ash tree above them. Her hand went to the ground and tangled in tall grass. Eyes widening, she sat up. She looked at him, then down at herself. Finally she stared across the horizon to the circular rim of the crater that rose around them, then up to a sky full of stars and waxing twinmoons. "Holm?" she squeaked.

He didn't think he'd ever been more mortified in his life. Heat crawled from his feet clear up to his forehead. Since he'd been able to see her flush, he had no doubt she observed his. She opened their connection to the fullest and sorted through his emotions. He gritted his teeth.

"It's obvious you know where we are, and how we got here in such a state," she said.

Inhaling, he tried for his most charming smile, tried *not* to think of guilt or failure or any other negative emotion she might sense.

"Ah," he said, standing to dust off grass bits, leaves, and a petal or two. At least he hadn't 'ported with a weapon.

He licked his lips. "We're in the Great Labyrinth."

Lark stared at him and reexamined their surroundings. "I haven't been here since I was a child, before my first Passage, as is the custom. This place is unique." She looked inquiringly at him.

Holm didn't know what to expect, some outrage or upset or distress, an emotional outburst another woman might have made, the grand dramatics of his Family—of the Hollys, he corrected. But she wasn't a Holly or another woman. She was his lover, his HeartMate, and a woman accustomed to dealing with emergencies. Nor did she radiate the pain and hurt of earlier, as if she'd accepted the hurt, dealt with it, and gone on.

"Holm?" she prompted. "Do you want to tell me why you 'ported us here?" Her eyes lightened suddenly, and she smiled. "Is it a Holly HeartBond night tradition?"

Now he felt a rude lout. As he searched for words, she narrowed her eyes and tested their link again. Understanding showed in her gaze, and her expression took on a hint of the Healer. He was in for it now. Better for him to tell the truth.

"I nightported us."

As she crossed her arms, plumping her breasts, a spurt of desire zipped through him. He wondered if he could distract her.

"No," she said. "You can't distract me." Again she smiled. "Yet."

She scanned the landscape, stretched, and when she spoke it was in the same serene tone. "Nightporting and the Great Labyrinth. I'd say you've withheld a few secrets from me, GentleSir." Lark slanted him a look. "Now, I know that we both are very aware of my shortcomings, they revealed themselves in terrifying starkness during our time together. But you"—she rose and tapped a finger on his chest—"have been hiding things from me." She blew out a breath and stalked around the tree to survey the labyrinth. "Just like a man," she muttered.

When she returned, she angled her head. "I'm your HeartMate. Tell me."

He shifted.

Her lips compressed. "Do you want me to guess, to make up a story, to diagnose?"

"No."

"Ha! You can't even get your tongue around words." She frowned and her gaze roamed over him with a disturbing intensity. She was becoming more the Healer every second.

"I was aware," she said slowly, puzzling it out, "that you had what I perceived as a mass of knotted emotions. An inner wound. But I let all the exigencies of our situation distract me." She stepped close, close enough that he could smell her, feel her body heat. She put her hands on his shoulders and tipped her face up at him.

Her expression was open, unguarded, sincere, and it showed loving concern. He could only flush again.

She sighed and wrapped her arms around his back. Resting against him, she sent affection and caring through their link. When she spoke, her breath tickled his chest hair. "Nightporting is an unconscious method of dealing with personal problems. Nightporting to the Great Labyrinth signals that your subconscious knows you have concerns that must be resolved. The Great Labyrinth is a perfect meditation tool, forcing one to walk out, and just by following the path in a steady walk, the rhythm and the innate pattern is impressed upon the mind and heart, helping you to understand your own needs."

"Huh," Holm said. It sure hadn't helped him, and he'd spent a lot of time walking that damned circular rising path to the rim of the crater.

Lark's lips curved against his chest, and he wanted her to kiss him. In fact, if she moved her head a few centimeters, she could suck his nipple. . . . She sent a twist of cold energy instead, dampening his arousal.

"You aren't going to talk to me. Hmmmm. Let's try questions."

"Can't we just start walking out of here?"

"Your pulse spiked. You don't want to talk about this." She stepped back and he hated the cool air that flowed around him, the loss of her touch. She held her palms up and concentrated. Bright gold glowed in her hands. She brought them together and aimed the tips of her fingers at his heart. He saw the large rope of energy then. The bond between them.

"Holm," she said. "I am your HeartMate. How do you expect to hide anything from me? I knew much of the reason you rejected the HeartBond"—her voice cracked a little—"was that I had so long and consistently rejected you and our connection." Warmth poured from her to him, tingling through his veins with a gentle caress. "But it was something more, too. You were hiding your perceived faults from me."

She tilted her head. "Everyone has faults. Everyone makes mistakes." She laughed. "Lady and Lord knows you've experienced mine. My cowardice. My fear of being hurt again, the ease with which people manipulate me, my old bitterness for Nobles, my—"

Now he stepped forward and placed a hand over her mouth. "Hush. You are wonderful. That's why we didn't know we were HeartMates earlier. Why we didn't sense each other during our Passages. Because I had to grow to match you, my Bélla."

Lark's surprise flickered through their tie. "Hard to believe."

Holm grinned. "You flatter me. But it's true. Until Tinne and I went on that trek across the continent, I wasn't 'mature' enough for you." He avoided thinking of the boghole, what happened, Tinne's explanation the day before.

"Ah-ha! Got it." Lark rubbed her hands. "That wound surfaced and I've got it."

He felt a tug inside. It hurt, like a cramped muscle being massaged.

"Sit down," she said.

Since she continued to draw on the tangled mess of his guilt and failure and it hurt, he folded to the grass. His breath roughened and sweat dotted his forehead as she worked at the gnarled mish-mash of his emotions.

She sweated, too. Her face strained. "I'm hurting you. I'm not a MentalHealer. Perhaps—"

"*Do it!*" he snapped. "You have your fingers in it, just do it and let me suffer in peace."

With raised eyebrows, she turned back to the job. A few moments later the hurt subsided. Her hands seemed to smooth his emotional tangle flat. She stroked the now-straight threads and sent them back for him to absorb. Then she plucked at them, and knew him.

Holm flopped back on the cool ground and closed his eyes. She'd leave him now.

"Don't be a stup," she said, echoing Tinne's words. "We're

HeartMates. Do you think I'd walk away from such a joy? There were times in my apartment that I wanted to scream from the loneliness." Now she echoed Tab's words.

Tinne and Tab. Both better men than he. Both wiser. As she was.

"Oh, Holm!" She sat beside him, pushed the hair from his forehead. "Perfection. The golden boy. The HollyHeir."

He winced.

"You thought you always had to be perfect, to live up to the highest standards. You couldn't make mistakes. You couldn't fail. That was not allowed." She chuckled and he felt offended. "Not such a terrible flaw, lover."

Her endearment zinged through him, arousing him instantly.

"What a beautiful body you have," she said, running her hands across his collarbone, measuring the breadth of his chest. Her index finger traced one scar, another, a blaser starburst, and he trembled under her hands. She ignored the blatant thrusting of his sex, but he wanted nothing more than for her to touch him there.

"What are these scars, Holm?" she asked.

He didn't answer.

She lifted her hands from his body. He groaned.

Tilting her head, she smiled down at him. "What are your scars?" she asked again, like a teacher.

He just panted.

"Are they badges of honor?" Her voice held faint censure.

Yes. "Maybe," he said with a thick tongue.

"Lessons?"

His mind functioned again. He lifted and dropped a hand. "Some, probably."

"Mistakes?"

He winced. He didn't want to talk. Especially not about perfection or problems or nightporting. "Yes, a couple are mistakes." He hunched a shoulder. "You train, you make mistakes, you get scars. Marks. That's all scars are, marks."

"They don't make you less of a fighter? Sometimes you even learn from them?"

He sighed, seeing where the exercise was going. "No and yes."

Lark played with the hair on his head. He'd rather she played with it lower, much lower.

"Just like life, Holm. Everyone makes mistakes and sometimes they leave marks. But that's all they are, marks. Are you terribly afraid of getting more scars on your body?"

Holm stared at her. "Only if it will displease you."

She smiled, one unlike any he'd seen. The black cloud of the feud that had shrouded them had vanished. They'd lost relatives, they'd both changed. Life would never be the same, but it could be good.

"Your body is beautiful, despite the marks. So is your character despite any of your perceived failures. Why should you be afraid of making mistakes?"

Disappointing his father. Not living up to the standard of a Noble FirstFamilies GreatHouse Heir. But those reasons were gone. And they weren't the reasons of a mature man. But they were reasons that had been tied up in his identity.

Lark bent down and licked the lovebite on his neck. His body roused to attention.

"I adore you. Look how you survived the blows of yesterday. Now that you've shown your true inner strength, I admire you more than ever before."

"Yes," he said, "lick me. Feel free to demonstrate your admiration."

She laughed, then pressed her open mouth to his, and their tongues dueled, probing, thrusting, until her skin heated and her breath came ragged and he knew she desired him.

Lark drew back, her eyes dilated with passion. She cupped her hands around his face. "I love you *just as you are.*"

He lifted her over him, and she brought him inside her. They both moaned with delight.

She set the pace, riding him, her mind and emotions open, moving on him to maximize their pleasure. And as they climbed, as their bodies plunged together and she demanded his passion, she demanded something else.

She leaned close until their lips met, her breasts sliding against his chest. *You don't need to be perfect,* she sent the mind-whisper to him. *I want to hear you say and KNOW unto your bones that YOU DON'T NEED TO BE PERFECT!*

His heart thundered.

Her words breathed into him. They infused his blood, settled in his marrow, pulsed at the base of his shaft, tingled in his every nerve, twined around sinew and muscle, then throbbed with every beat of his heart until he believed, truly believed as she did. *I don't have to be perfect.*

He knew when all her thoughts dimmed, when all she focused on was the friction between their bodies, the ecstasy of having him pump into her, caress her on the inside, the length and breadth and strength of his shaft and how he gave her pleasure.

She threw out the lightning-white HeartBond, and he caught it and brought it close. She was his, mind, body, soul, her entire being open to him to her very core. "I love you," she breathed.

He groaned, clutched her, blending the surface of their thoughts and emotions, brushed the HeartBond tenderly aside and before she could understand or protest, brought them to the peak to shatter together.

Holm kept the bond between them wide and open and Lark tucked next to his body. He could not bear to hurt her, and himself, again.

Her sharp intelligence returned faster than any other woman's he'd known, faster than his own, he thought ruefully. Though she was puzzled by his action of refusing the HeartBond, his physical, mental, and emotional intimacy reassured her.

When he could speak, he said, "The guilt and failure problems aren't all. There's more."

She just cuddled closer and the back of his eyes prickled. He cleared his throat. "I had a problem with nightporting when I was a child. I'm close to my cuz, Straif Blackthorn, and was worried about his Family when they caught that virus. They all died except Straif."

Lark shivered a little. "All the Healers know of the Blackthorns and their faulty Earth gene that makes them so susceptible to a common Celtan virus."

"I nightported then first." He adjusted their positions so he could stroke her smooth, elegant back. "When Tinne and I journeyed back to Druida from the 241 Range, we fell in the Great Washington Boghole. We nearly died. I tried to reach him, but couldn't. He ended up saving both of us."

"Hard for a big brother, the golden boy of the Hollys, to accept, eh?"

"Yes." He wondered if her own big brother, Huathe, ever cared for her as much as he'd cared for Tinne. Someday the pain would fade and he could ask. He curved his hands around her butt. He liked the shape. He considered another round of loving but knew he had to do something else first. "So I suppressed the memory as much as I could, and the guilt, and the failure."

"And they worked on you." Her mouth was close to his collarbone. She traced it with her tongue and he lost his train of thought. He ran his fingers through her fine, thick hair.

"I started nightporting to the Great Labyrinth at the end of spring. All summer, irregularly." He grimaced. "Finally, when Mamá was wounded, I wore a DepressFlair armband at night."

"Oh, Holm," she sighed.

"But you've straightened me out. It won't happen again."

She wiggled back and looked up at him; her eyes were deep, serious purple pools. "We're HeartMates. You helped me, too. You gave me so much when we first met. Caring, affection—just your holding me Healed something in me." She stroked his cheekbone with the pad of her thumb. "The night after we'd gone to the beach . . ."

"Yes?"

"The Heathers gave me a mental-emotional test. I wouldn't have passed it without the time I'd spent with you. Then I would have had to live at T'Hawthorn Residence or T'Heather's. Everything would have been different."

He brought the palm of her hand to his lips and kissed it. "We're HeartMates. We would have managed to find each other and a way to stay together. Just as we have."

They lapsed into silence for a minute. Lark traced his eyebrows. "So, tell me of this other huge fault you have. It must be terrible if it is so obvious," she teased.

"I can't tap my inner core."

"What?"

"You know the deep link to your essential self?"

"Yes, of course. I use it when I Heal."

That often, and he couldn't even find his. "I don't have a connection with my true self, the rock-solid balance of knowing my inner core."

She looked thoughtful. "Since you always thought of yourself in terms of HollyHeir, your core could have evaded you. Especially since deep thought, meditation, and self-analysis aren't what a person thinks of as Holly Family traits."

He squeezed her bottom. "Wretch."

"But a truthful wretch. Lover—"

Holm stopped her mouth with a kiss, then reluctantly pulled away. "Don't call me that unless you want me inside you. I knew I had to tell you of my lack. Especially since you would have noticed it when we walked the labyrinth."

"True, but Holm, this is an easy thing to correct."

He scowled at her, thinking of all the time he'd spent here, all the time in T'Holly HouseHeart. "Ha!"

She placed his hand on her breast and his irritation vanished. "It is," she said. "We're HeartMates. I can open myself completely. Through our bond you can follow me as I connect with my inner core, settle into my calm center. With that example you can find your own."

He hated that it sounded so simple and logical. He stood and pulled her up. "Let's do it."

Lark linked her fingers with his. The bond between them was open and clear. As she breathed deeply, he matched her breaths. Soon their hearts beat in time.

Holm led her to the start of the labyrinth path that led up and out of the crater. Lark smiled at him and his heart warmed, but his mind doubted.

"Ready?" she asked.

He braced himself. "Yes."

"Don't."

"Don't what?"

"Don't tense up. Relax, let your mind rest, your thoughts ebb and flow." She used her voice like a Healer, calming.

"Ready," he said.

They began walking. It was magical, treading the path. Especially linked physically and mentally with his HeartMate. Instead of thinking of his problems, or his schedule, or observing the Noble shrines each House had provided to decorate the labyrinth, he strolled. The soft night air caressed him, the bright bond between himself and Lark filled him with joy as he trod the pattern. Soon he sensed her sinking deep into herself, into a meditative trance state. She was completely open to him, so he followed her, and listened to her inner mantra that reflected her essential self.

The pattern of the labyrinth, the curving path and the switchback turns, lulled him. He found himself following mental paths he'd never experienced before. He came to a door he vaguely recognized from infrequent dreams. He'd always dreaded opening that door and had retreated. Now the knob turned in his hand and he flung it open. Light encased him. Grounded him. He stopped. And discovered himself.

Lark wept silently when Holm found his core and merged with it. His amazement at the difference he felt touched her. He staggered a couple of steps and she steadied him. Then he moved with his usual grace.

What a man! A beautiful body, a strong heart, an honorable soul. He was truly extraordinary if he'd survived three Passages without centering and grounding himself.

And he couldn't, or wouldn't, tell her he loved her. They'd spent the night together as HeartMates, loving and touching and engaging in passionate sex, yet had not HeartBonded. What a man.

Soon they reached the end of the labyrinth and the rim of the crater. She drew in a breath of sparkling fresh air laden with the scents of growing plants and summoned a robe, soft and silky, flowing over her body to accent the curves. With a snap of her fingers she 'ported her last weapon in this heart duel to her. Her HeartGift.

Thirty-one

♥

*H*olm turned to her with a dazed smile. "Lady and Lord, what a difference! I feel like a new man." His gaze swept the vista. Now they'd left the crater, they could see ragged peaks to the north, the sea to the west, the glow of Druida to the south.

His shoulders shifted. "I am a new man. Holm Apple," he said with only a slight hesitation. "I know my strengths, and my flaws." As he raised his head, his silver-gilt hair lifted in the night breeze. "I know who I am without any reference to the Hollys."

Then his gaze sharpened as he *saw* her. He frowned. "That's seduction cloth."

Lark smiled. "So it is."

"You're dressed."

"Yes."

"I'm not, except for my amulet."

"I know."

He looked at his aroused body. Took her hand and closed her fingers around his shaft, jerked a little and moaned.

Lark stroked up and down, sensing through their bond which touch pleased him the most and brought the greatest response.

"Enough." He grasped her wrist and this time lifted her fingers to his lips and kissed her hand. "Bélla."

Bélla. Always Bélla. A good name, a special name, but she
wanted more. She wanted love words.

An appreciative gleam entered his eye as he studied her. "Seduction cloth," he said lowly, in a voice that was seduction
itself—if Lark hadn't realized that she wasn't the first woman to
wear such a gown for him—maybe not even the tenth. . . .

He nibbled at her fingertips. "Ah, my Bélla. A little jealousy
sparks red through our bond. A nice appetizer." Holm grinned
wolfishly, and she thought she might have miscalculated.

Once more he scanned the view. "Let's walk back in. We can
concentrate on our love and life ahead while we walk to the center. There we can consummate our union."

"HeartBond?"

"Why not? You don't have an ancestral bedsponge or home.
Neither do I. The only better place would be SacredGrove, and
this spot is familiar and even . . . cherished by me."

She melted and swept a lock of hair back from his face. "Of
course." She wouldn't have to use her HeartGift after all. Maybe
she should hold it in reserve. HeartMates or no, there'd be some
rough times ahead.

He took her hand and they dipped back into the night shadows of the crater and the entrance to the path. "I want you to accept the position in Gael City. It will be good for you not to have
to answer to anyone, and to be in charge of others. Gael City will
be perfect for us. Not many Nobles have estates there, it's pre-
dominantly middle and artisan class, has more casual customs.
I'll miss sailing though. *Sea* sailing."

As they walked, the path and the pace cycled Lark down into
a meditative state that she had to struggle against to match wits
with Holm. Despite the fact he'd finally grounded himself and
found his true balance, it was obvious that meditation would
never be a preferred ritual for him.

"I have some gilt and this." He touched the amulet hanging
from his neck.

Dismay shocked her into alertness. "You're *not* selling the
amulet."

"I want to establish a salon—"

"We can do that. *We.* I have plenty of gilt saved for both of us."

"What's your salary as Head of Gael City HealingHall?"
asked Holm.

Lark flushed. "I don't know." She straightened to her full height, several inches shorter than her HeartMate. "Gilt wasn't the reason I applied for the job."

He siphoned a jumble of her memories through their link and swiftly sorted through them. Lark was astonished at how easily and deftly he accessed her thoughts and feelings—even old thoughts and feelings.

Holm smiled lopsidedly. "You wanted to start anew, away from the machinations of T'Hawthorn and T'Heather. I don't blame you. But now you're closer to them both."

She smiled back at him. "A blessing. We'll visit Druida often, and have visitors from here, too, I have no doubt." She gestured to the Ashes' offering—T'Ash's forebears—a grove of towering Ash trees in a semicircle. The current T'Ash had created a circular pavement set with a mosaic of precious stones depicting the World Tree and the Rainbow Serpent.

"Yes. We'll have visitors. There are plenty of good gem stores in Gael City," Holm said.

When they reached the next turn, Holm swept her into his arms for a long kiss. He arched her to him, setting her sex against his own and rubbing. His calloused hands stroked her through the seduction fabric and were as excitingly sensual to her as to him. Desire weakened her knees, making her clench her fingers into his butt.

"Yes," Holm groaned into her mouth. He opened her lips and vanquished her tongue, plundering her mouth and probing deeply, setting up a thrusting pattern that foreshadowed the claiming of her body with his.

Pure, raw male possessiveness roared through her from him. Her last rational thought was that she wouldn't have to use her HeartGift after all.

Holm caught the comment. He disengaged and took a pace back, then shook his head and ran his fingers through his hair. "I heard that. A HeartGift. For me! Give it to me, Bélla."

She arched her brows. "The giving—and accepting—of a HeartGift should be done unknowingly."

He flicked a hand and smiled charmingly. "Rules. We've done very well without rules, my Bélla."

"I've already given you a gift," she pointed out.

Holm's brows drew together. "So you did, and Meserv rescued

it from my former rooms. But the wreath was one you'd give to a onenight lover, not a HeartMate. I made the blossoms permanent, but I want another, with proper HeartMate flowers, fashioned from your own hands." He eyed her. "You aren't wearing anything under that dress, so my gift isn't a wreath."

A sprite of mischief danced through her, and she sent it to him over their link. She wondered if he'd blush again if she gave him the gift.

He straightened to soldierly attention. "I do not blush."

"No? We'll see." From one of the long sleeves she pulled a box, then opened her fingers to show a blue, softleaf-wrapped gift, tied with a deep rose-colored ribbon.

Love surged through Holm, and when he took the wrapped HeartGift, so did deep, aching desire. His brain went numb; all he could think was that he'd be HeartBound soon. "This has power. When did you make it?" The words were awkward on his tongue.

"As you said about mine, the power isn't as strong as usual for a HeartGift because I didn't make it during my last Passage. But I made it after I knew we were HeartMates, after I acknowledged you yesterday. I dedicated it during a small ritual in my apartment." She smiled and Holm sensed there was a surprise he couldn't anticipate. "I made it on the red sofa."

"We *are* taking that sofa to Gael City, I hope." Any suavity he'd possessed seemed to be leaking out of his feet into the ground.

"Oh, yes. And the bedsponge."

He recalled the bedsponge. It was a great bedsponge. He wished it was here, now. He shot a glance toward the Ash tree that marked the center of the labyrinth and wondered how many more circuits there were. He hadn't kept track of the rounds they'd already covered.

Frowning, he knew he was stuck in his old dilemma. Though the HeartBond would be mental and permanent and incredibly special, he wanted Lark with a physical force that shook him.

Holm gazed down at the gift in his hands, then glanced at Lark. She was staring at his turgid sex. She caught his gaze, then licked her lips. He was lost.

He held out a hand. "Come to me, Bélla."

She swayed to him, hips sliding under the seduction gown that made him think how she looked on top of him. Or under him. When she placed her hand in his, the firestorm of their connection aroused him to near pain. He set his teeth.

"Let's 'port to the center," he said.

Lark looked doubtful.

A side of his mouth kicked up. "I've had great experience with this labyrinth. I know the coordinates. Trust me."

Her serious lavender gaze made his heart pound. "I do, lover."

He was doomed.

They 'ported to the center, and he lowered her to a thick bed of moss that he'd cultivated over the last couple of months for his own use, and lay down beside her.

"My HeartGift. Open it," she said.

He'd forgotten about it. He wished he could blame the stripping of all his control on the power of the piece, but he couldn't. He was sure that just being near his Bélla would always fire passion in his loins.

But the present almost clung to his fingers. His hands trembled and he awkwardly tore the wrapping off in shreds, getting his fingers tangled in the narrow ribbon.

She slid a hand up his chest, and his mind clouded further when she toyed with his amulet, absently brushing his nipples as she fingered the chain. "So these lips match mine, do they?" she murmured.

Finally he got the softleaf mostly off and stared at her gift. He choked. Tremors slid into his muscles.

"I bought it from T'Ash. He gave me instructions on how to set it." She shot him a wicked look from under lowered lashes. "My HeartGift to you, the second pink pearl from Clam." Both her hands dropped to caress his rigid shaft.

He panted.

She set the phallic pearl next to his shaft. "I was right. They match."

He pounced. He rolled her under him and had her whimpering in passion in seconds. Their link expanded, without thought he opened all of himself and sent the HeartBond rocketing through him and into her. She accepted it, accepted him, let him possess her and claim her and moan his need.

And when they climaxed she bit him and he knew he could never live without her.

* * *

Later Bel's light peeped over the rim of the crater and woke Lark. She opened foggy eyes to see Holm smiling down at her. The echo of his thoughts, the completeness of his love washed through her.

Pop! Pop!

Two small bodies hit them. Holm grunted. Phyll balanced on their entwined forms to walk up and lick her face. *D'Ash had to help get us here,* he scolded. Meserv burped, then rolled a lumpish bag to Holm. *Clothes,* he said.

"How did D'Ash—" started Lark.

Holm glanced at the large Ash tree above them. "I'd imagine T'Ash has a link to this tree." Holm shrugged. "Now we're Heart-Bound, let's see what a walk out of the labyrinth will bring." He shook out a wrinkled pair of brown trous and shirt and dressed.

Phyll perked up. *Very in-ter-es-ting place.*

I have been here several times, Meserv boasted. *I will show you the best things.* They bounded off.

Pop!

"Merry meet!" trilled a young male voice.

"Oh, no," Holm said. "Don't look. Perhaps he'll go away."

"I bring a note from your Mamá," T'Vine said.

Holm tensed and held out a hand. "D'Holly."

"She will always be your mother."

"That's true. But she isn't my Mamá anymore."

Lark winced.

Holm read the note aloud. "To my dear Holm and Lark. I give you my blessing. A mother's blessing, a GreatLady's blessing. Go with the Lady and Lord."

"You are blessed even without her," Vinni said. "She sent this, too." Vinni handed a music strip to Holm. Lark crowded near to read the title. "Holm and Lark's Wedding Theme."

She sniffed. Holm's hand trembled as he carefully put the music in the envelope and tucked the letter in a trous pocket.

Vinni stared down at something and turned dark red. Lark followed his gaze. Her HeartGift, the phallic pearl set in silver, lay gleaming coral against deep green moss. Lark scooped it up and handed it to Holm. "My HeartGift." She smiled at Vinni. He shuffled his feet and drifted closer to the labyrinth path. "Holm, put it in the box."

Holm's cheeks reddened, too. The pearl disappeared.

"There's always the best vintage of wine in the T'Vine grape arbor about halfway through the labyrinth," Vinni said.

"A very good idea," Holm said. "Was there something you wanted to talk to us about, Vinni? Some little prophetic bombs you'd like to drop?"

"Yes. No. I don't think you need reassurance." He flushed even more. "You two *glow,* and all turned out as it should have. Taught me a lesson," he muttered under his breath.

With a quick hand, Holm grabbed him by his shirt collar. The young lord stilled.

Holm smiled, with teeth. Vinni opened his eyes wide and seemed to huddle in his shirt as if trying to make himself the image of innocence. Lark pressed her lips together so they wouldn't twitch.

Holm bracketed the boy's neck with one large hand and they all *linked.* Lark gasped, thrown into the maelstrom of the boy's mind—with deep spaces, shifting fog and sparkling lights unknown to her. She narrowed her contact to Holm to a thread.

"Another lesson, young GrandLord," Holm said smoothly, but it echoed in her head. "I will teach you to bow properly."

He instructed on both the physical *and* mental plane, imprinting the physical movement on the boy's mind, then Holm dropped his hand and stepped back. Vinni looked almost as dazed as she felt, and she wondered how Holm could be unaffected. No doubt the strength of his physicality and will.

Vinni blinked in the sunshine.

Holm smiled. "Now, bow to my HeartMate."

With a grace she'd never seen from him, the boy swept her a formal bow. Marking the moment with an inclination of the head, Lark said, "Merry meet."

"And merry part!" Vinni grinned and he was all boy again.

"And merry meet again," Lark and Holm said.

"We will all meet again." Vinni smiled, waved, and walked to the path from the labyrinth, leaving them.

"A moment, Holm," Lark said. Slowly she turned around, absorbing the beauty of the Great Labyrinth, its path and the offerings by the Noble Families. She tilted back her head and inhaled the mixture of scents—Celtan flowers that grew naturally in the bowl of the crater and those that had been cultivated by the Families. She saw hawthorn hedges with dried petals beneath them a few circuits into the labyrinth.

Bel highlighted the circular ridge of the crater in gold and the night breezes picked up warmth to caress her. The ash tree was simply one of the most beautiful trees she'd ever seen and she knew why the ancient Earthans chose it as the World Tree. Here in the middle of the labyrinth, it looked as if it might encompass all the magic of the world.

Holm slipped an arm around her waist, and she delighted in his touch, in their bond that deepened intimately every moment they spent together. Knowing this time was precious to her, he waited.

Glancing up at him, she wondered again at her sheer luck in winning such a man.

He grinned. *Not luck. Destiny. And I won you.*

Always the competitor. But her face shadowed.

She gestured to where they stood, near the beginning of the path out of the labyrinth. A path they'd walk together as they would match all the steps of their lives. "This is the end of our lives as individuals." She pointed to the opening between lichen-covered boulders. "This is the beginning of our lives as Heart-Mates." She waited.

After a moment puzzlement showed on his face. He cleared his throat. "You want something from me."

Lark raised her eyebrows. "I'd always heard you were an accomplished lover. I don't know where that idea came from."

He laughed and at least that sounded genuine. "Since I met you, Bélla, I've bumbled my way through this courtship." He placed her fingers on his lovebite. "So confused and clumsy, it was only when I wore this that I felt sure of your love."

"That's right, love. I've told you I love you." Wetness backed behind her eyes. She couldn't bear to say any more. If love words had to be prompted, they were worthless.

"I'm bumbling now, aren't I? I'm failing you, my HeartMate. I'm doing something wrong. Already." His words were rushed, tinged with a hint of panic. If she hadn't been so hurt and irritated she'd have been amused at Holm, the smooth lover, the fearless fighter looking as if he might panic.

Closing and opening her eyes, she decided to try a different approach. She turned in his arms to face him and lifted her palms against his cheeks. Staring into his eyes, she dropped her shields and let him know all of her, down to her core, her Heart-Mate love of him.

"I love you, Holm," she said gently.

His eyes widened. His mouth dropped open. "I've told you I love you, haven't I?"

She shook her head.

He opened his mouth. Shut it. Swallowed. "I love you, my Bélla," he croaked. "That was harder than I thought." He brought one of her palms to his lips and kissed it, then the other. "Perhaps because I've never said the words to any other woman except D'Holly. I love you, Mayblossom Larkspur Bélla Hawthorn Collinson—Apple."

He grinned. "Of course, I will always stand ready to demonstrate my adoration."

An inner kernel of tightness that Lark hadn't realized she harbored vanished. She took his hand and squeezed. "Let's leave the past for the future." Narrowing her eyes, she scanned the flowers dotting the bowl of the labyrinth. "I think there are enough blossoms that I can make a set of HeartMate Wreaths."

Holm lifted their linked hands and kissed her fingers. "Such talented hands—Healing, wreath weaving."

She slanted him a look. "You have good hands, too."

He laughed aloud. "We're well matched in that, as in so many things. Let's go find that wine Vinni spoke of."

The golden flow of their bond sparked between them.

The kittens tumbled back, covered in dust and leaves and blossoms. *Come on!* they cried. They looked up at their humans and grinned, tiny red tongues darting out and flicking at their whiskers. A matched set.

Life is good, Phyll said.

Let's go play! Meserv said.

We all have fine fate, they said together.

Holm looked at Lark and his love blazed in his eyes.

Her own love rushed back to him through their HeartBond. "Come, let's go expand our horizons," Lark said.

"Yes, love, let's." Holm grinned.

They started on the path out of the labyrinth of their past to the brilliant horizon of their future.

Turn the page for a special preview of the next
futuristic romance from Robin D. Owens

Heart Choice

Coming soon from Berkley Sensation!

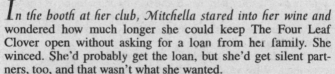

In the booth at her club, Mitchella stared into her wine and wondered how much longer she could keep The Four Leaf Clover open without asking for a loan from her family. She winced. She'd probably get the loan, but she'd get silent partners, too, and that wasn't what she wanted.

Her mouth turned down. She was already lacking because she was sterile—in the huge family of Clovers who prided themselves on being the most fertile family on Celta, Mitchella was the only one in her generation unmarried and without a brood of children. Macha's disease when she was a girl had taken that from her. Sometimes the ache was so soul-deep that she could hardly bear it, even though she loved her ward, Antenn Moss, as if he was her own son. But Antenn was growing quickly and would leave her house for journeyman education soon. Another depressing thought.

So she set her mind back on her interior design shop. To have to admit to her Family that her business was still struggling after four years, when she'd been sure it would be solid and successful by now, was another mark of deficiency.

She took a sip of her wine and grimaced. The Woad Garden was a private club catering to the upper middle-class and lower nobility, but Mitchella's palate had become educated with the fine wines served at T'Ash Residence during her frequent dinners with her friend Danith. Thank the Lady and Lord for Danith D'Ash! Because of Danith and the complete starkness of T'Ash's new Residence, Mitchella had stayed in business this long. She'd even managed an uneasy truce with the GreatLord himself.

She sighed and settled deeper into the smooth furrabeast leather bench. She'd taken a booth in a far room, empty except for her. Everyone was home with their families, their HeartMates, their children this rainy spring night. Only Mitchella was alone. She rolled her eyes at the self-pity, a sure sign she was tired. Usually she had too much energy to indulge in such stupidity. Well, she was human—that meant she had moments of foolishness.

Mitchella pushed her glass aside and leaned back on the firm-but-giving bench back. She nodded. She'd done a good job with The Woad Garden. A smile hovered on her lips. This chamber was a dark hunter green with gleaming oak trim and shutters. With brown leather benches in the booths and a touch of brass in the accessories, it was supposed to appeal more to the masculine patrons, but she'd ensured that a sole woman would feel comfortable, too.

She'd done a good job here, and every place where she'd consulted. Why was it so difficult getting commissions? She tapped her fingers on the table and noticed her nail tint had faded. Feeling like she wanted something a little more elegant than the jade that matched her onesuit, she concentrated. After a moment her nails became a delicate, shimmering pink.

She was still admiring her hands when Weat, the owner's younger son, poked his head into the room. When he saw her, he grinned. It was so good to see someone brighten at the sight of her that Mitchella relaxed and sent him a genuine smile. His eyes fixed on her breasts and his glance glazed a bit, then he hurried to her. "There's a man here to see you about business." Weat darted a glance around the room. "You can use this room for awhile, if you'd like." He grimaced. "We aren't busy tonight."

Mitchella rose and shook off her gloom. A little humming in her bones let her know her future called. She knew it was only a matter of time before The Four Leaf Clover exploded into success. Perhaps this was the moment!

She beamed at Weat. "Thank you very much, GentleSir."

Weat flushed. "I'll send him back."

A moment later a man's large outline filled the shadowy doorway. As he walked into the mellow light, her insides tensed. She studied him, aware of contradictions. He moved with supple grace and carried himself with inherent arrogance—an arrogance that shouted "nobleman." Yet he displayed more than a few rough edges. He should have looked out of place in the elegant club, but he didn't.

His clothes, though once of good quality, looked frayed at the shirt cuffs. And the shirt cuffs showed no embroidery denoting a noble name. She relaxed. Though she cultivated a good, professional manner for Nobles and interacted well with NobleLadies, she didn't like NobleLords.

But this man wore working trous with narrow legs instead of excess, costly fabric caught and cuffed at the ankles. Scuffed and scratched celtaroon boots—and it took heavy duty to scar celtaroon—molded his narrow feet and muscular calves. The celtaroon itself had faded from its original orange and blue pattern to beige and gray, something that took years.

His jaw showed dark stubble, and his body looked far harder than anyone would expect a pampered nobleman's to be. She could only figure that the aura of complete power was due to his competence in the untamed wilds of Celta.

He sizzled her nerve endings. She was a tall woman, built on voluptuous lines, but he was taller still, with shoulders that could block her view. Dark and dangerous, with only a hint of refinement and an undercurrent of sensuality, her senses thrummed to life in pulses that sent a flush under her skin and stirred her insides.

She glanced at his wrists again. He didn't wear marriage cuffs.

Mitchella swept a wisp of tumbled hair behind her ear, glad she was wearing the jade silkeen onesuit that contrasted well with her flame-colored hair. She shifted her shoulders a bit so more tendrils fell over the curves of her breasts, and she smiled, adding a bit of her Flair—charisma—to enhance herself.

The intriguingly sexy man raised his brows as she stepped from behind a wing-backed chair. His eyes widened as they lingered on her body.

Her onesuit was cut less full than fashion demanded, shaping her breasts, waist, and hips. She'd paid an outrageous sum for it, but now it was all worthwhile.

"Can I help you?" She didn't have to lower her voice to huskiness; her attraction to him made it come out that way.

"I'm afraid so." His voice was deeper than she'd imagined, richer, with cultivated tones. "I need some good decorating skill and new furnishings."

She liked the way he said "I need." She could imagine him saying it in more intimate circumstances with the rich, mellow note in his voice turning rough and demanding. Her insides shivered.

Then her mind took over. Good skill and many furnishings, sounded like a nice, expensive job. She refrained from rubbing her hands together, but her smile expanded.

He turned and cocked his head, then again met her eyes. "I'm told you're the best." It rumbled out of him, quietly, and all Mitchella could think of was tangled bedsheets.

She wet her lips. His cobalt eyes fastened their gaze on her mouth.

She hadn't meant to tease him, her throat felt uncomfortably dry, and the effect he was having on her body began to unnerve her. She had to take care, she couldn't afford to lose a lucrative commission.

"I'm grateful for the praise." She struggled to sound calm, his virility kept her off-balance. "May I ask who recommended me?"

He smiled, a curve of well-shaped lips in a strong jaw. Her heart pounded harder. "You may." He took a step forward.

Now she could smell him and the scent of tough masculinity was highlighted by the clean fragrance of sage. Sage conjured up a traveling man, an explorer. And she knew it was true of this man with every beat of her heart. She inhaled and exhaled audibly.

He leaned closer.

"Rrrrowww!" demanded a dainty cat, gliding into view.

"Drina," Mitchella said flatly. Her friend Danith D'Ash had raised Drina.

"My Fam." He shook his head in amazed amusement.

Everything in Mitchella tightened in wariness. Only powerful noblemen had Fams, and she didn't care for noblemen. Danith's husband, T'Ash, had once teleported her across the city with an angry thought. Mitchella had never forgotten the sheer terror of the experience. She and T'Ash still treated each other guardedly.

A Fam, a cat raised by GreatLady Danith D'Ash, and Drina's own sense of complete superiority added up to only one thing: this man was a Noble of the highest class. Mitchella's smile turned merely courteous as she moved behind a large wooden antique buffet partitioning the room, putting a barrier between them. She inclined her head to the cat. "Greetyou, Drina."

Drina sat like a small, elegant white and beige accessory to the room. Her tail curled over dark brown paws. "Prrrp," she mewed politely.

The NobleLord glanced down at Drina. "She had to make an unexpected stop, otherwise she would have arrived with me."

Drina stood, stretched, and with waving tail, began to explore the room.

Mitchella bit her lip. His gaze heated and he strode forward, with masculine grace that almost equaled the Fam's. But now Mitchella's mind was firmly in control of her body. She slammed a door on her desires. Being sterile, there could never be anything more than a brief liaison between her and a nobleman. She cut the small aura of charisma and let her eyes cool.

"And you are?" she asked.

His eyes narrowed and he eyed the buffet between them. His nostrils flared, and he smiled, still attracted.

Too bad.

"Blackthorn," he said in a husky voice. "Straif Blackthorn."

Worse than she'd thought. A FirstFamily GrandLord. Nothing could ever come of a relationship with this man. Never ever.

"I'd heard you were back." All she knew was he'd come and gone from Druida several times in the past years. She didn't pay much attention to noble activities.

She recalled his GrandHouse Residence. Her eyes widened. Oh, how she'd love to get her hands on that house. Passion for her craft surged within her. "Are you going to restore T'Blackthorn Residence?"

The Italianate house of many arches made her fingers itch to return it to its former beauty. She must have the general plans and history of the Residence in her files.

He lifted a brow at her change of attitude from the sensual to the practical, then moved up to the buffet and leaned against it—into her personal space. He didn't stop his own provocative signals of male interest and intent.

Damn! She hoped she hadn't issued a challenge. Straif Blackthorn—she stiffened, remembering old school lessons; the Blackthorns were trackers, explorers, and hunters.

He sent her a hot look from half-closed eyes and she felt the tingle from her toes to her head that sparked small shocks throughout her middle. She refused to react and kept a pleasant smile on her face.

He blinked and the sexual look was gone, replaced by one of measuring consideration.

She could only hope that he'd hire her as a decorator and leave the rest alone, so she kept her expression professional as she reached into a pocket for her business cards that showed room models. Not taking her eyes from him, she withdrew a card and handed it to him.

It was pink. Far too feminine for him. "Wait," she said, "I gave you the wrong business card."

He ignored her and let it sit on his palm. Mitchella suppressed another quiver at the contrast between the pink "marbled" card and his calloused, tanned palm.

He stared at the card, then back at her, a slow smile moving over his face. "It takes a certain kind of woman to carry off pink"—his glance flicked down her again—"and a green silkeen onesuit. I think you're just what I'm looking for."

She tired of playing games. "I'm only interested in restoring your home, GrandLord."

Now he raised sandy brows. "Is that so?"

"Yes."

He watched the rise and fall of her bosom with appreciation. "Drina recommends you," he said.

Drina hummed in her throat. The cat stood at an open shutter, admiring her reflection in the window.

T'Blackthorn looked over his shoulder at his Familiar and smiled with sincere amusement that made Mitchella catch her breath. "Drina says she is a Cat with Excellent Taste."

Mitchella managed a smile. "She certainly thinks so."

His thumb rubbed the indentation on the card, triggering the projection of a model room holo about 1½ by 2 meters. The pink marble walls contained darker streaks for visual interest, and all the furniture was a glossy deep burgundwood. The bedsponge lay on a stand, with diaphanous curtains layered around it and attached to the ceiling. The curtains swirled with the slightest hints of sparkling rainbow-pastel glitter, as if a fairy galaxy had been caught in their folds.

As he gazed at the room model, the sensual tension spinning between them quieted to something deeper and more serious.

T'Blackthorn touched the image and it disappeared. He curled his fingers over the business card, his face taut and his eyes yearning. "I've spent years in the wilds. I've missed the furbelows of very female women, of Ladies, and forgotten how—soft—your sex can be."

"You've stayed with the Hollys." She'd heard that much.

He raised an eyebrow. "My uncle and cuzes, and other relatives, a HouseHold of mostly men. My aunt, D'Holly, is a very dynamic woman."

"And feminine." Mitchella had met D'Holly once.

"T'Holly Residence is decorated with weapons in patterns on the walls—circles and diamonds of knives, spears, swords. All within easy reach. There are paintings of battle, tapestries of hunts," he gestured with the hand holding her pink card, "male stuff." He moved his shoulders impatiently.

"I'll take it," he murmured.

"Take what?"

"The room. I want one just like it in my Residence. You have the job."

Glee blossomed inside her. She could barely keep from dancing around the room. This would make her reputation!

He smiled and she knew she shouldn't be near this man. She should run as fast and as far away as she could from him. But an opportunity to design the interior of one of the twenty-five First-Family Residences would never come again. And T'Blackthorn's! It had been a showplace once, one of the most beautiful houses in Druida. She could make it so again.

She looked into his dark blue eyes.

"I want it." He flicked his thumbnail on the card and the model room spun once again into life. "I'll take it. No expense spared."

Mitchella had always dreamed of hearing those words. Now they tempted her beyond all bounds.

He collapsed the holo and tucked the card in a hidden shirtslit pocket. Then he put an arm on the buffet and leaned forward. "You have more?"

Mitchella backed up. "More?"

"More cards—room models."

She pulled out her cards and offered him the one of mock-furrabeast leather grain. He activated it. A meter-sized image of a masculinely furnished ResidenceDen materialized. T'Blackthorn tilted his head. "Nice. A little conservative for my taste." He shot her a look. "You'll remember that."

"That's my business. Of course."

He nodded.

"We'll meet tomorrow at mid-morning bell, then. I want to start work on the pink room immediately, in the MistrysSuite."

Mitchella stiffened her backbone. "Absolutely not."

T'Blackthorn raised his eyebrows.

She lifted her chin before answering. "Your wife must decorate the suite."

He scowled. "I'm not married." He rubbed the stubble on his jaw. "I think I have a HeartMate. I touched her during my last Passage to free my Flair."

Mitchella should have been relieved. Of course he'd have a HeartMate, someone he'd bond with body, heart, mind, and soul. Most FirstFamily Nobles were that lucky. It came of having great psi powers and breeding for Flair. Bonded HeartMate couples led to more stable Families and increasingly Flaired children.

Inwardly she flinched. He had a HeartMate. It would be complete folly to have an affair with him.

As if he read her mind, he said, "I'm not ready to find or bond with my HeartMate. Everything must be perfect before I do that. T'Blackthorn Residence must be restored and sparkling. Other—problems—must be solved."

So he'd be happy to have an interim affair with a commoner before he sought his HeartMate. Typical man. Typical Noble. The thought bolstered Mitchella's resistance to the electricity between them.

"I'll be glad to make T'Blackthorn Residence as perfect as possible, GrandLord," she said coolly, professionally.

Drina jumped up on the buffet and swiped a paw at one of the pink cards Mitchella still held. The cat impaled it on her claw. She tapped the indentation and the pink model room appeared. Staring at T'Blackthorn, she mewed.

His lips quirked in amusement and he slid a sidelong gaze to Mitchella. "She wants the pink room." Narrowing his eyes, he studied Drina, then glanced back to the model bedroom. Now a small Drina image sat regally on the bed.

T'Blackthorn nodded his head. "She says the room would complement Her, make Her look beautiful. She's right."

They were both right, Mitchella realized. The cat looked perfect in the room.

He gazed at Drina, and when he spoke, his tones were quelling. "Your room is the small dressing room between the MasterSuite and MistrysSuite," he informed the cat. "I'm sure GentleLady Clover can decorate it to your undeniably good taste."

Drina pressed the holo control on the business card again and again, until the pink room, magnified and distorted, over-whelmed the real room they stood in.

"Very well," T'Blackthorn sighed. "I'll indulge you this once. You may have the pink room. We'll decorate the guest room next to the MasterSuite, I'll have a connecting door cut."

Drina flexed her paw and the model room vanished as the card spun to the carpet. It was just a business card again. With a claw-hole in it.

He looked at Mitchella, his gaze lingering on the tumble of her hair, her face, her lips. "I think we will do very well together."

"That's my job."

He offered a hand. Reluctantly, Mitchella gave him her own. Instead of shaking it, he lifted it to his mouth. The soft pressure of his warm lips went directly to her center. She pulled away, pasting on another professional smile.

"Till tomorrow, then," he said.

"Yes." She'd be up all night studying all the information she could on T'Blackthorn Residence. She was sure she recalled it being featured several times in various publications on architecture, furnishings, how the FirstFamilies lived. She needed plans and dimensions. Old holos of how the rooms looked. Perhaps she could even get some sort of idea of the previous owners' tastes.

Then realization struck.

The Blackthorn curse.

She stared at him.

He, just like T'Ash, had lost his entire Family.

But not to a rival Nobleman—to some disease. Her stomach clenched. This man and she had another thing in common. Loss. He had lost all he loved in the past. She had lost the hope of children to love in the future.

T'Blackthorn stilled as if understanding she'd finally remembered the history of his line. She wondered if he read her own heartache.

They shared a moment of silence throbbing with untold griefs. Then, T'Blackthorn inclined his head. "Merry meet."

"And merry part," Mitchella replied through dry lips.

"And merry meet again," he said. "Come, Drina."

Drina brushed against Mitchella, purring loudly, leaving little white hairs clinging to her onesuit, then jumped to T'Blackthorn's shoulder.

"Right," Straif said to his Fam, then looked again at Mitchella. "Drina thanks you for the pink chamber. We'll start with that." Cat attached to his broad shoulder, he strode from the room.

Mitchella let out a breath she hadn't realized she'd been holding. She'd hurry home to research T'Blackthorn Residence. But at least doing the first room would be easy.

It was, after all, her bedroom.

Award-Winning Author
Robin D. Owens

Heart Thief

Get swept away to the planet
Celta—where one's psychic talents
are the key to life...and to love.

"I LOVED *HEART THIEF*!...ROBIN D. OWENS
WRITES THE KIND OF FUTURISTIC ROMANCE
WE'VE ALL BEEN WAITING TO READ."
—JAYNE ANN KRENTZ

0-425-19072-2

Available wherever books are sold or
to order call 1-800-788-6262

BERKLEY SENSATION
COMING IN MAY 2004

Kinsman's Oath
by Susan Krinard
In a future world, two telepaths meet and quickly realize they have nothing in common—except the love they share for each other.

0-425-19655-0

Fade to Red
by Linda Castillo
When Lindsey Metcalf's sister is kidnapped, she enlists the help of Michael Striker, a cop who plays by his own rules. And soon they are both drawn into a seductive and inescapable trap.

0-425-19657-7

A Lady of Distinction
by Deborah Simmons
Lady Juliet Cavendish is an accomplished Egyptian scholar, but when Morgan Beauchamp appears, she finds she'd rather study him.

0-425-19656-9

Charming the Shrew
by Laurin Wittig
A sharp-tongued beauty meets her match in a man who vows to tame her with the power of his love.

0-425-19527-9